Smuggler's Moon

The Raveneaus in Cornwall, Book 1

Cynthia Wright

This is a work of fiction. Names, characters, places, and incidents either are the product of the author's imagination or are used fictitiously, and any resemblance to actual persons, living or dead, business establishments, events or locales is entirely coincidental.

Author Edition published by Boxwood Manor Books

Cover art by The Killion Group, Inc.
Interior formatting by Author E.M.S.
ISBN-13: 978-1495972706
ISBN-10: 1495972704

Printed in the United States of America

Dedication

For my treasured friend, novelist Ciji Ware, with love.

Thank you, Ciji, for inviting me to share an adventure in Cornwall with you 20 years ago. It's because of you that I fell in love with the magical corner of England that is so much a part of Smuggler's Moon*! We've shared many of life's ups and downs over the years and I am very grateful for your friendship.*

Acknowledgments

How lucky I am to have had such a great team to lend a hand during the creation of *Smuggler's Moon*! Heartfelt thanks to my dear friends and fellow authors, Lauren Royal, Ciji Ware, and Danelle Harmon, who read *Smuggler's Moon* and offered invaluable feedback. I'm also very grateful for the expertise of my editor, Jessa Slade, cover artist Kim Killion, and copy editor/formatter Amy Atwell of Author E.M.S.

I'm sending a shout-out to my writing support group, who spurred me on daily, and to the Jewels of Historical Romance, especially our resident Regency scholar, Cheryl Bolen, who guided me out of a few sticky research corners.

I owe a special debt of gratitude to Richard Platt, author of *Smuggling in the British Isles*, who searched for answers to my questions and even helped me with one or two smuggling plot twists!

Gratitude and love to my husband, Alvaro, who followed me into the unknown when we traveled to England in 2013. It was wonderful to watch him fall under Cornwall's enchanted spell!

I'll close with a special hug for every single reader. I write for you, and your encouragement and support mean the world to me. Thank you!

Smuggler's Moon

Bath, England
March, 1798

Julia Faircloth surveyed the charming, sunlit garden and nearly surrendered to an urge to sigh. "I vow, I have never felt so pleased with life as I have been since we left London."

"Indeed," said her sister, Sarah. "I adore Turbans. Even the name of our new home is pleasing." Her delicately lovely features turned pensive. "My only desire is that we might be more conveniently situated."

As their mother clipped a daffodil, she looked southward, down Beacon Hill to the elegant city of golden limestone which lay below, nestled against the winding River Avon. "Whatever do you mean? We have a perfect view of Bath."

"But Mama, it is a rather difficult walk. I would like to be able to stroll to the Pump Room if the mood seizes me, or to Queen Square to meet my friends. As it is, we have only one carriage, and Papa seems to need it most of the time..."

"I shouldn't complain so if I were you, daughter. We've had immensely good fortune this past year." Polly's scolding tone was belied by her fond smile. Turning to her eldest child, she called, "Julia, haven't you an opinion on this matter?"

"You jest, Mama," interjected Sarah. "My outspoken sister never lacks an opinion!"

When Julia turned her head, a gleaming sable-brown curl fell onto her neck, and she smiled. "I do think that we are awfully fortunate Cousin Archibald had no heirs and that he liked Papa well enough to leave the entire estate of Turbans to him." *And an amazing £20,000*, she added silently to herself, wondering how much of that fortune might still be left after Papa's excessive gambling. "This home could not be better suited to us, and I don't miss London in the least. Bath may have its own sorts of social nonsense, but that's so much more tolerable with the countryside at hand."

Their baskets massed with daffodils and primroses, the trio started back toward the house. Overhead, chaffinches trilled from the blossoming pear tree.

As they walked, Polly spoke again. "You are absolutely right. My dear Mr. Faircloth has toiled diligently these many years in our London bookshop, and it is lovely that he can finally rest and enjoy life."

Julia listened to her mother with one eyebrow arched above her crisp dark-blue eyes. Much of what she heard was true. Turbans was ideal for their eccentric family. It had been inspired by Cousin Archibald's journey to Turkey, and the otherwise modest stone manor house featured dashes of Arabian Nights. The wall surrounding the estate was punctuated at intervals by turban-topped columns, and near the gardens stood a crescent-capped minaret with a balcony. The youngest Faircloth, Freddy, had claimed the minaret for his schoolroom, and as the women passed with their baskets, they saw and heard him reciting Coleridge's new poem, "Kubla Khan" from the balcony.

"Mama," Julia murmured thoughtfully, "I agree that Papa has worked very hard and deserves a rest, but do you ever think that he may miss his occupation? In London, he was busy all day long, and he enjoyed chatting with his customers and searching for books."

"Nonsense." Polly stopped, lips thinned, and whispered, "I know what you are hinting, and I beg you to refrain. Your father may have fallen in with a raffish crowd in Bath, and he may have had a lapse at the gaming table, but who can blame him for celebrating a bit after so many years of hard work?" Breathing hard, she added, "There's nothing to worry about, Julia. Mr. Faircloth has given me his *word* that he will never touch another card!"

"Mama is right," Sarah rejoined. "Don't spoil all our pleasure by fussing about nonsensical matters."

"I hardly think that this is nonsensical—" Before Julia could make a proper argument, she saw her father coming toward them from the house. Her cheeks felt hot as she went forward to greet him.

"Bless me, aren't my three ladies a pretty sight?" Graeme Faircloth exclaimed. "Indeed, indeed." He waved to his son on the minaret balcony, calling, "Give us a quote!"

All seriousness, Freddy shouted, "In Xanadu did Kubla Khan a stately pleasure-dome decree!"

"Bravo, bravo!"

"We've missed you, Papa," said Julia. "How are you?" Her eyes sought his, but her father glanced elsewhere. "Won't you come inside and have tea with us? I'll read aloud, just as you have always liked. I came upon the fine, gold-stamped volume of *Robinson Crusoe* that you gave me a full decade ago, for my twelfth birthday! I was thinking that it would be lovely if we read that again, together."

"No, no, much as I'd prefer to accept your invitation, I must decline, my dears." The sight of their three crestfallen faces made him bluster and chuckle even more excessively. "I cannot describe my business in Bath, except to say that it involves a surprise. A certain beauty's birthday doth approach, hmm?" He winked at Sarah, who clapped her hands in delight. "Yes, I must pay a visit to a certain shop in Milsom Street, but of course I'll say no more until the negotiations are settled. Now then, I must be off. I may be rather late returning—"

"Papa," Julia interjected, "have you noticed that you are

wearing a brown coat with gray breeches? I vow, you should find a new manservant to fill the place left by dear old Edwin's death." She set down her basket. "It will only take me a moment to dash inside and fetch the proper coat."

Before he could protest, Julia hurried away up the lawn. Once inside Turbans, she lifted her muslin skirts and ascended the staircase, avoiding the giddy housemaid who had a habit of popping up at odd moments. As she hurried along, she noticed a picture that was slightly askew on the wall and the cobweb fluttering in a corner. Sometimes it seemed that were she not there to supervise, their small staff of servants would run amok.

Her father had his own bedchamber: a vast room with walls of paneled fruitwood, a stupendous Tudor bed, and rugs retrieved from Persia and Turkey by Cousin Archibald. The shadowed dressing room was in a state of disarray that boldly reflected the state of Mr. Faircloth's life. Sadness that Julia didn't fully appreciate caught her in its oppressive embrace.

After opening a curtain to admit a ray of sunlight, she looked through her father's coats until she found the one that matched the old-fashioned gray breeches he wore today. No sooner had she folded it over her arm and started into the bedroom than she heard a rustling sound. Was there a piece of paper in the pocket? Julia's curiosity was piqued. In normal circumstances, she wouldn't have thought of investigating, but her father had been acting so secretive and guilty that she was worried.

Had she not always cleared his pockets of leftover lists and appointment reminders? He could be such a packrat! Her heart began to pound as she reached into the pocket and brought out the piece of fine cream parchment.

Her heartbeat accelerated. Tears filled her throat.

The paper announced, in Graeme Faircloth's own familiar hand, that he owed a debt of £1,000 to a man whose name was completely unfamiliar to Julia.

The note was dated just two days earlier, long after her father's solemn vow that he would never touch another card. *One thousand pounds!* All her life she had counted pennies that her parents were too absentminded to worry about, and the thought that her father could be losing so massive an amount at the gaming table was horrifying. Dizziness swept over her for a moment, but then she straightened her back and took a deep, determined breath.

There was only one solution. Julia would pay a visit to the wicked stranger who had led her father astray. The name was quite clearly inscribed on the note: Lord Sebastian Trevarre of Number Sixteen, Royal Crescent, Bath.

Chapter 2

Lord Sebastian Trevarre sat down on a gilt-wood chair and looked around the magnificent drawing room while Keswick, his manservant, drew off his riding boots.

"Why are you looking at me that way?" Sebastian demanded. "I'd imagine I must have smeared jam on my chin, except I haven't had any jam. Where is our tea? I'm famished! I hope you told the cook to send up an extra plate of scones and clotted cream."

"We are looking at you that way because you should not sit on that chair, my lord. As it looks to be Louis XIV, we suspect you would not care to replace it if it splinters apart under your weight."

"Do you mean to insult me? There's nothing the matter with my weight—"

"Of course not, my lord, but you are exceedingly tall, and strong—"

"For God's sake, don't snivel. I like it better when you're impertinent." Sebastian narrowed his eyes, but a smile hovered at the edges of his chiseled mouth. "In any event, I could have purchased a roomful of these chairs if my brother, the bloody marquess, hadn't gambled away the family fortune!"

"Ah, tea is served, my lord." Keswick concealed his master's boots under the pianoforte and rushed over to help the maid lay out the Caughley porcelain.

Sebastian moved to a sturdier sofa near the fireplace. "Perhaps I ought to have champagne instead of tea," he suggested, casting a hopeful glance toward the maid. She blushed deeply in response, unable to look at him.

"The tea will be quite enough," Keswick assured her. He waited until she had left the drawing room before he turned to his master. "Have you forgotten that you're only borrowing this house from Lord Hampersham? It's only due to his kindness that we are ensconced at this posh address, my lord. We don't really think you ought to abuse the privilege by drinking his champagne at teatime."

"Kindly remember upon whose kindness *you*, and your invisible assistants, depend." Sebastian drank down his tea, then spooned jam and clotted cream onto a warm scone. "I might add that Hampersham himself is not without fault. I suspect that he stood by while my brother gambled his way through Bath, and afterwards he wished he'd tried to stop George before it was too late. Inviting me to borrow his house this month was the least Hampersham could do to cleanse his own conscience."

Keswick's slight, white-wigged figure relaxed slightly. "You do know, my lord, that we actually have only sympathy for you? This is a terrible coil, particularly following on the heels of your parents' deaths..."

"Save your sympathy." Sebastian's tone was harsh.

Just then, Lord Hampersham's butler, Roland, appeared in the doorway. "My lord, you have a visitor. It is Lady Lucinda Barrowminster."

Sebastian's eyes widened. "Show her up, Roland. And, perhaps we should have more tea." When the butler had gone, he glanced over at Keswick. "Do you remember Lucinda?"

"Yes, my lord. We knew her in London, the summer before you took your commission with the Royal Navy. She had just accepted Lord Barrowminster's proposal of marriage, having finally ascertained that you were not in the market for a wife."

Before Sebastian could reply, the lady in question swept into the drawing room, surveying every detail of the décor before focusing on him. "My dear Lord Sebastian! Don't you look devastatingly handsome, in that rather negligent way only you can bring off."

"Thank you. I think." With a wry smile, he bent to kiss her outstretched hand. "I've just returned from a long ride, and I didn't know I was having a guest for tea. If you'd sent word, I would have kept my boots on and my cravat tied."

"And brushed your hair? Please, do not say it. I like you better this way. Look, there are even lines about your eyes. How deliciously rakish." Spying Keswick, she fluttered a hand at him. "Hello. So nice to see that some situations don't change. But, I hear that you two have been fighting the French, and even sailing to North America during these past six years! Do tell me all about it."

Sebastian watched as she settled into a chair and allowed Keswick to pour her a cup of tea. When Lucinda next drew off her bonnet with its fashionable cluster of grapes, he tried not to sigh aloud as he took a chair beside her. "Where have you heard this news about me?"

"My cousin has been playing faro with you. I hear you're the most heartless gambler." She gave him a faint wink. "How did you find New Orleans?"

"Highly exotic. Steamy and hot."

"How cryptic! Rumor has it that you lived in the city rather than on your ship. Were you spying on the French, my lord?"

His tone cooled. "If I were, I couldn't possibly say, could I?"

"I perceive that you are annoyed with me for mentioning your gambling. I hope you haven't lost very much. I heard about your brother George's run of bad luck when he was here in Bath last month."

Sebastian's eyes met Keswick's over the top of her head. "Let's just say that I've been doing what I can to restore, rather than deplete, our fortunes."

"Oh, dear. I've forgotten to tell you how sorry I was to hear about the deaths of your parents. A carriage accident, wasn't it?"

"Yes; on Boxing Day." A shadow crossed his face as he wondered how to hasten her departure.

"And whatever happened to your baby sister? She couldn't have been more than five when you went off with the Royal Navy."

"Isabella is at school in Devon," he said crisply.

"I always thought that you should have been the older son. If you had inherited the title, and you were Marquess of Caverleigh instead of George, you wouldn't have gone off and gambled everything away, would you?" Lucinda leaned forward and ran her fingertip across the back of his brown hand.

"How is Lord Barrowminster? Have you a houseful of children?"

Frowning, she replied, "Only three."

"Your husband is doubtless missing you, and I have an appointment." Sebastian stood up.

"Will you be going to live at Severn Park now? I do hope you haven't lost interest in the horse breeding operation, when you had such a *passion* for it." She drew out the word 'passion' with a flutter of her lashes. "You see, my lord, I remember all the dreams you shared with me that summer in London." Lucinda rose and donned her bonnet, speaking in a rush. "Your lovely mother was wise enough to see that horse breeding would be the perfect way for you to live, since you couldn't inherit. I do hope nothing has changed?"

"You always were a curious chit, Lucinda. That's *one* thing that hasn't changed." With that, he showed her out to the landing above the open staircase. "Do give my regards to Lord Barrowminster."

"But, my dear," she persisted, "you must be quite solvent if you can afford to rent this house."

"I hope you won't mind if I don't see you out. I am in

danger of being late for my appointment with the Marquess of Queensberry."

Turning back from the stairs, she boldly ran a hand over his shirtfront, tracing the muscled surface of his torso. "Age has only improved on your fine qualities, my lord. If you'd like to have a quiet dinner with an old friend, you need only send word…"

"Goodbye, Lucinda." When she had begun to descend, Sebastian stepped back into the drawing room and closed the double doors. He looked around to find Keswick discreetly standing near the window. "Did you hear that last bit?"

The manservant's brows arched high, like a pixie's. "About your lordship's ability to afford the Royal Crescent address?"

"If she only knew, Keswick. She'd tell all of Bath."

"Indeed, my lord. We are grateful indeed that her ladyship does not know."

"Right. Now then, where have you put my fresh neckcloths?"

With eyes wide and pulse racing, Julia Faircloth walked quickly from Brock Street into the cobblestone drive that bordered the Royal Crescent on one side and the lush green Crescent fields on the other. She told herself that there was no reason to be nervous, or to feel inferior among the refined pedestrians who passed on either side of her. After all, most of them didn't live in the Crescent, either. How many could afford these elegant lodgings built of pale golden limestone? People came here to promenade, to see and be seen, from all over Bath. Julia must simply pretend that she belonged among them.

However, when she reached Number Sixteen in the middle of the Crescent, she nearly lost her nerve. At least she had fashionable clothing: a high-waisted gown of ivory muslin, a powder-blue spencer buttoned to her throat, slippers of tan Morocco leather, and a reticule. Her rich curls willfully peeked out amid the confines of a striped silk bandeau. It was a simple and dignified costume, Julia hoped.

She was still staring at the Georgian doorway of Number Sixteen when a richly garbed woman emerged.

"Are you looking for the servant's entrance?" The lady paused to draw on her gloves while a coachman dismounted from the nearby landau and lowered the steps for her. A lady's maid waited inside the equipage.

"No." Julia's mouth felt dry. "I am here to see Lord Sebastian Trevarre."

"Indeed? I am Lady Barrowminster, a longtime friend of his lordship's." Her brows rose expectantly, but she received no response. "Did you know Sebastian before he went away?" This time, she didn't wait for Julia to answer. "I can assure you that he is more *himself* than ever…if you take my meaning. Don't let him intimidate you."

"I shan't." As Julia watched Lady Barrowminster rush off to the waiting landau, she thought how peculiar their meeting had been. What *had* the older woman meant?

On the railing to the right of the entrance was an inverted iron cone: a torch snuffer for the link boys who lit the way for sedan chairs. When Julia peeked inside the door, which was still ajar, she saw a spacious entry hall laid with squares of black and white marble. In one corner stood a leather-covered sedan chair with gilt-trimmed windows. Julia instantly envisioned Lord Sebastian Trevarre as a doddering, gouty curmudgeon who bullied his chairmen and cheated at whist.

"Pardon me." A sardonic voice spoke from the door to the inner hall. "You have mistakenly wandered into a private residence."

Even from a distance, Julia saw that the rude butler was very attractive in that dark, forbidding way she secretly favored. Fortunately, servants didn't frighten her. "You are mistaken, sir, not I. The last caller left the door ajar, and my arrival is not in error. I am here to see Lord Sebastian Trevarre."

"He is engaged."

"I have walked a great distance, down muddy pathways from Beacon Hill, and I won't go back until I have spoken with your master." To her consternation, the butler stopped before a mirror to examine his cravat. He wore boots, buff breeches, and a forest-green frock coat, all of which displayed his lithe, powerful physique to advantage. It really wasn't proper attire for a servant. Julia felt her heart skip at the sight of his black hair curling slightly over the back of his collar.

"Have you an appointment with Lord Sebastian?" the man inquired, not even sparing her a glance. "No, I thought not."

"I will wait right here."

"Impossible. I must lock the door."

"Why are you being so odious to a caller?" she exclaimed. "I shall report your poor manners to his lordship. He will be very displeased!"

"Do you imagine so?" There was a mocking light in his eyes as he consulted his watch.

"I do indeed! You, sir, are insolent, and I mean to tell your master every word you have said."

"Come along, then, and speak your piece."

Completely confused, she followed the servant out the front door, waited while he locked it, and hurried to keep pace as he strode off toward Brock Street. "Where are we going?"

"I am going to the Marquess of Queensberry's home in Russell Street."

"When will I speak to Lord Sebastian?"

"Immediately." He gave her a sidelong glance. "At this very instant."

"I beg your pardon?" Her mind was reeling. When he

didn't reply, she looked up at his cynical, handsome face and perceived the truth. "I—I suppose I didn't expect you to answer your own door, my lord."

"I was on my way out. Will you make yourself known to me now?"

"My name is Julia Faircloth." Her slippered feet barely touched the walkway as she struggled to keep pace with him. "I think you are acquainted with my father, Mr. Graeme Faircloth?"

"Hmm. Yes, of course. I believe we are about to meet again."

"I think not. My father has gone shopping in Milsom Street for my sister's birthday gift." She was annoyed to feel her cheeks getting hot.

"Certainly," Sebastian agreed, clearly unconvinced.

"Perhaps you are unaware of my father's history. Do you know that for three decades he has been a bookseller in London? He labored from dawn until late at night, every day, trying to provide a living for our family. He is truly a dear, fine man. When Cousin Archibald died and left Papa his estate, we came to Bath, and thought that we would never have to worry about material comfort again."

"That's a very touching story, Miss Faircloth." As they turned into the wide circle of Palladian houses known as the King's Circus, Sebastian touched his fingertips to her waist, guiding her clear of an approaching gig. "However, I scarcely know your father. Why are you telling me this?"

"Why—I thought perhaps you didn't realize how fine a person Papa truly is. Only recently, since we came to Bath, has he fallen in with gamesters who spend their waking hours at the tables. Papa isn't like them; I think that he began gambling because he was a bit lonely, and now it's taken him over." Julia began to feel alarmed that he did not show signs of sympathy for their plight. There was nothing left but to offer up the unvarnished truth. "I am telling you in strictest confidence, my lord, that my father is in trouble, and our family has failed in our efforts to help him. It seems that only I am prepared to face facts."

"You're very brave," Sebastian replied, consulting his watch. "We are nearly to my destination. What does this have to do with me?"

They had turned north, uphill on Russell Street, and Julia's throat began to burn as she hurried along beside him. The man might be handsome as sin, but he was either obtuse or shockingly rude. "I know about my father's enormous debt of honor to you. My lord, in these remaining moments, I must ask you, as a gentleman, not to gamble against my father again."

"Miss Faircloth, if you imagine that gamblers are gentlemen, you are in error."

She couldn't fathom the sudden harshness in his voice. "Other players have been kind enough to help, my lord. In recent weeks, two have even forgiven Papa's gambling debts."

Sebastian stopped outside Queensberry's stately home and turned to face her. His voice was deadly calm. "I would say that those men are not Mr. Faircloth's true friends. If they protect him from the consequences of his behavior, how will he ever stop?"

"I will take my leave, sir." Julia thought she might choke on the words. Never before had she encountered anyone so maddeningly difficult to reason with! Turning, she continued up the hill without waiting for him to reply. Her back was straight, betraying none of her inner turmoil, even as she silently berated herself for revealing so many family secrets to the wholly despicable Lord Sebastian Trevarre.

"Miss Faircloth?"

She nearly managed to continue on without a backward glance, but then curiosity won out. Hands balled into fists, she turned halfway, waiting. "My lord?"

"Your father's problem is his own, and only he can solve it."

"Shall I thank you then for your lack of assistance—and compassion?" Julia made a mock curtsy. "Good day, my lord."

Although she gave no outward sign, it was agony for her to walk away from him without attaining any concessions. She had always felt confidence in her ability to persuade others of the best course of action. People usually began to nod in the midst of one of her explanations, and were even grateful for her intercession.

But Lord Sebastian Trevarre was clearly a different sort of animal, one who coolly resisted all her efforts to lead him in the right direction.

Julia couldn't remember the last time she'd felt so frustrated.

Chapter 3

On a low shelf beside Julia's bed at Turbans were her treasures: a song thrush's nest that cupped a speckled eggshell, dried primroses and bluebells from her favorite woodland paths, a piece of blood-red glass excavated from a streambed, a long swan's feather, and a variety of interesting seashells and smooth stones.

Julia knelt in a pool of morning sunlight and examined some of the souvenirs. Each one was beautiful in its own way, but more meaningful were the memories that floated back to her. She remembered exactly where and when she had chosen every blossom, rock, and shell, beginning at the age of three. Many of the treasures she'd discovered while walking with her father, like the thrush's nest that had fallen from a tree in Devon one summer long after the eggs had hatched. Papa might be useless with money, but he had always had a passion for botany, ornithology, and zoology, and had shared all of his considerable knowledge with her.

Just then, Sarah tapped on the bedroom door and peeked inside. "Julia, did you know that Adolphus Lynton is waiting for you downstairs?"

"No." She sighed and stood up. "I did wonder if that was his voice I heard…"

"You shouldn't kneel in your gown, you know. Here, let

me try to smooth out the creases. I do believe you love your rocks and feathers better than suitors!"

"You are harsh. I have a great deal of respect for Mr. Lynton."

"Perhaps, but does your heart beat faster when you see him? Does the touch of his hand make you blush? Do you think that his every utterance is inspired? And, when—"

"You needn't go on and on! I take your point." Julia's brow was furrowed as she started toward the door. Although she couldn't say so, her continuing worry about their father was having an effect on her mood.

Sarah returned to her original topic. "You may be glad that we are in Bath rather than London, but I suspect that you'd be happiest of all if we had a country house, with an assortment of animals, woods to walk in, and a quaint little village nearby. Am I right?"

"Perhaps, but I'm the only member of this family who prefers country life. It would be selfish of me to impose my wishes on the rest of you."

Before Sarah could reply, Polly Faircloth appeared in the doorway. "My dears, what keeps you? Not only is Mr. Lynton waiting patiently downstairs, but Charles Whimple has sent word that he will be arriving after luncheon. He writes that he will bring his latest composition."

"Oh!" cried Sarah, clapping her hands. "Mr. Whimple has finished his sonnet! He has been composing it for nearly a fortnight."

Julia contemplated her sister as they walked from the bedroom together. Had two siblings ever been more different? Although their physical attributes were so similar that they were often mistaken for one another at a distance, Sarah's beauty had a refined quality. From her artfully arranged golden-brown curls to the tips of her delicate slippered feet, Sarah Faircloth was an ideal of femininity. Even her nature was sweet and shy, if a bit spoiled. It simply wouldn't occur to her to want to walk in the rain or converse with the men after dinner or wear breeches to go riding.

"My love," murmured Polly as they descended the stairs, "it appears to me that you pinned up your hair without the aid of a looking glass."

"Oh..." Julia replied absently, "I suppose I forgot. I was looking out the window. Watching the wrens gather nesting material." She stopped then and leaned up to whisper, "Mama, I really don't want to entertain Mr. Lynton today. Won't you help me?"

"My dear, he's come from London to be near you, and he has even taken rooms in Bath. Have a bit of sympathy for the poor man."

"I am fond of Adolphus," she said in an unconvincing tone.

"If that is your notion of fondness, I despair of you ever marrying. What will become of you?"

Before Julia could reply, Adolphus Lynton came out of the sitting room and she descended the stairs to greet him. He was the picture of sobriety, with wavy, sepia-tinted hair above a sallow face that offered dark, deep-set eyes and a heavy jaw. He might have been a passably attractive man if he ever laughed or betrayed a hint of passion, Julia reflected. The only strong feelings she had witnessed from Adolphus were self-righteous speeches about the deplorable condition of Man.

"Good morning, sir." Pasting on a smile, she went forward to greet him. "It is very good of you to visit, but you really should have given me an opportunity to consult with my mother. As it happens, she has all manner of plans for me today, beginning with a basket of mending. Did you know that I am the only Faircloth with perfect vision? I can make exceedingly tiny stitches! It is my secret talent."

Both Sarah and her mother looked away in an apparent effort to avoid eye contact with Julia. Lynton's own dubious expression softened as he replied, "I believe that you are more domestic than you would admit!"

"Do excuse me," said Polly. "I must join my husband in the library."

Sarah exclaimed, "And, as I am expecting a visitor, I must hurry to the garden to gather flowers!"

Lynton put a hand out to bar her way. "But, Miss Faircloth, you have promised to sit with your sister while I play the *cello*!" With that, he stepped aside with a flourish to reveal the large instrument, clearly pleased with his surprise. As he took his chair and positioned the cello between pantalooned knees, he mused, "Is it not fortuitous that I possess the musical talent Julia lacks?"

"Yes," Sarah rejoined with uncustomary mischief, "you have treated us to performances on the flute, the pianoforte, and today the cello. Certainly, sir, you will have very gifted children."

As he launched into a particularly mournful Beethoven étude, Julia reached over, smiling, and pinched her sister. Minutes passed. Several times, Mr. Lynton caused the bow to groan or squeak against the strings, but he valiantly played on. As the performance finally concluded, Julia found herself listening to her parents' voices, rising from the adjoining library.

"Mr. Lynton," she exclaimed amid cheery applause, "do excuse me for a moment. I must see what transpires in the next room."

There, she found her mother sitting with a book while her father paced like a restless spaniel, talking all the while.

"I don't understand why you ask so many questions, Mrs. Faircloth. Can it be that, after twenty-five years of marriage, you do not trust your own husband?"

"I simply wish that you would stay at home, just one day, if only to prove to me that you *can*."

"Do you hear yourself? You're spouting nonsense! Why would you want to make me stay at home for *that* reason?"

Julia's heart beat faster as she listened to them. There was an irritable note in her father's voice that caused her to mistrust him, particularly when she remembered her maddening interview with Lord Sebastian Trevarre. Even then, he'd cast doubt on her father's whereabouts, hinting that he wasn't in Milsom Street, as he had said, but inside the Marquess of Queensberry's house.

"Papa," she said, "where are you going today?"

He spun around, red-faced. "Why, I have been invited to join a group of citizens who are raising funds for the Orchard Street Theatre! Quite an honor, what? And your mother seems to be forbidding me to leave the house!" Nervous laughter sputtered forth. "Can you imagine a bigger piece of audacity than that? Look there, she's primming up her mouth again—"

Julia felt sick at heart. "Now, Papa, you and I both know that there is nothing wrong with Mama that a long, relaxing day with her devoted husband wouldn't cure. Why not send a note to the Theatre and see them the next time they meet?"

"Am I a prisoner in my own home?"

Polly took a deep breath and said softly, "Please, do go into town and enjoy yourself. I don't know what came over me; just a little case of the sulks, but now it has passed and I've a hundred things to do. I've told Mrs. Rittle that I'll give her my recipe for apple pudding, and I'll need to hear Freddy's essay about…"

"Tudor England," supplied Julia.

"Ah, now that's my girls." Mr. Faircloth brightened, as if a dark cloud had lifted. "Ask Freddy to save his essay for me. I'll be off then."

Before the nonplussed Julia could think of what to say next, Adolphus Lynton strode into the library. "Sir, if you are going to the Orchard Street Theatre, I believe I should like to accompany you."

Julia saw her father wink at Lynton and felt a pang of foreboding. She went to her mother's side and held her hand as the men gathered up their hats and coats and made their farewells. Was she simply to stand by and watch her father throw himself to the lions? In her mind, she heard Lord

Sebastian's cynical voice warning, "His problem is his own and only he can solve it!" Yet, it went against her nature to remain silent while someone she loved ruined his own life, and perhaps the lives of his family.

"Mama, I just remembered something I forgot to say to Papa. Will you excuse me?"

A wide stone drive curved past the front of Turbans, and just as Julia stepped onto it, a phaeton emerged from the nearby stables. When she gave an urgent wave, Lynton slowed the horses.

"We're in a bit of a rush!" her father shouted from a distance.

"I won't keep you, Papa." Lifting her skirts, Julia hurried over and reached up to touch his hand. Adolphus Lynton was watching them curiously. "I just wanted to beg you to grant me one promise. Please, tell me that you will avoid that odious Lord Sebastian Trevarre. I—I have heard that he is a very bad man!"

"You're spouting fustian, my dear," he blustered. "I haven't the vaguest notion what you mean. How in the world would I know Lord Tre-whatsit? I'll see you in a bit. Don't worry."

"That's right, my dear Miss Faircloth," Lynton interjected. "I'll be with your father, after all. No cause for concern."

As Julia watched the phaeton roll away and turn onto the Lansdown Road, she reflected that at least her father had had the good grace to flush when he heard her utter Lord Sebastian's name. He wasn't completely without shame…yet.

"I am not certain you ought to bet any more against me, sir," Sebastian said in a low voice.

Staring back across the piquet table, Graeme Faircloth

discarded, then defiantly drew a card, demanding, "Why should *you* decide my course of action? Have I not free will?"

"Of course, but reasonable men have been known to regret their actions while gambling, sir." Sebastian was surprised to find himself remembering the lovely face of Julia Faircloth as she confided that her father was in trouble.

"Speak for yourself, my lord. I have owed you a good deal of money for several days now, and I mean to even the score as clearly as possible before you call upon me to pay you."

The two men were in one of Lansdown Crescent's grandest homes, the entire first floor of which had been given over to gaming-rooms. The elegant saloon boasted a faro-bank, and tables of deep basset and the popular game E.O., but during these daylight hours there weren't many players.

"I suppose I am feeling rather nervous about gambling myself since hearing the sad tale of the Marquess of Caverleigh," Sebastian remarked, while surveying his twelve cards to see if he had any flushes. Keswick, who was playing *vingt-et-un* nearby, glanced over upon hearing his master's words. The two of them never revealed anything about their own connection, or Sebastian's relation to Caverleigh, but they each continued to ask casual questions in an effort to learn what had really happened to George.

"Caverleigh?" Faircloth scratched his head, then looked over at Adolphus Lynton, who was watching the play through his quizzing glass. "Wasn't he the fellow who was here a few weeks ago? Seems to me that he'd just inherited and didn't quite know how to comport himself, what?"

"Quite," Lynton replied in disparaging tones. "He was half in his cups every time I saw him."

"One must learn to indulge oneself responsibly," Faircloth intoned. He returned his attention to his cards.

"Gambling can have an ill effect on the sanest man, don't you think?" murmured Sebastian. "It does pay to take care."

"I am taking care, by winning today so that I won't have

to pay last week's vowels. You see? Now then, let's get on with it."

Sebastian recognized Faircloth's feverish edge. He was ill with the disease of gambling, just as his own brother had been. The only cure was to stay far away from the tables, and it usually took a crushing loss to bring a man to that point. As long as his friends felt sorry for him and forgave his gambling debts, as some had already done that day, Graeme Faircloth would continue to lie to his family and haunt the tables.

As the afternoon unfolded, the two men continued to play piquet and Faircloth's losses mounted.

"Let us part now," Sebastian suggested, throwing his cards on the table after a hand that had been particularly beneficial to him. "You have not evened the score, sir. Just the opposite."

"You cannot turn away from me now, my lord! You owe me the chance to erase this debt! I can feel my luck shifting. The next game will be completely different—"

Sebastian got up to pour himself a glass of wine, and Keswick sidled over.

"We believe that your lordship ought to take the man's money," he whispered. "If he insists on losing, why should you not be the beneficiary? This may be the only chance to win enough to recover your beloved Severn Park. Would you ruin your own future out of pity for a pathetic gamester like that?"

"Aren't you heartless!"

"When we must choose between your lordship and that foolish fellow, it is not a question of heartlessness." Keswick's tone grew more insistent. "We recall that there is more at stake than a simple game."

"I wish that someone had tried to talk sense to George." Sebastian stared into the distance.

"But no one did. Perhaps it was Mr. Faircloth himself who won vast sums of your brother's fortune, forcing him to lease Severn Park to strangers, forcing him to flee to Tuscany in shame! Did any of these righteous Bathonians have sympathy for *his* plight? We think not! Kindly remember, my lord, that we journeyed to Bath to set about restoring your family fortune—which is in the pockets of these very men!"

"Heartless was too mild a word," Sebastian decided with a sardonic glance. "You're nothing short of bloodthirsty." Drinking down the wine, he straightened his wide shoulders and added, "However, you are also correct. And, I may be doing Mr. Faircloth a favor by taking his money. Perhaps, if he loses badly and has to face his family, he'll understand that he cannot gamble again."

Back at the piquet table, he found that Adolphus Lynton had drawn a chair close to Faircloth and seemed to be whispering advice.

"Are you certain that you wish to continue?" Sebastian asked.

Lynton addressed the older man in stern tones. "He hopes that you'll surrender now, so that he may keep the vast sum of money you have already lost. He would like to break down your confidence. Without confidence, a good man is finished."

"That's right. Even my dear daughter Julia has warned me about this rogue. However, I shall persevere, and the forces of good will prevail." Faircloth blotted perspiration from his brow, adding, "I can sense that my luck has shifted!"

The mention of Julia gave Sebastian an uneasy feeling, reminding him that she would be hurt if this continued to go badly. And yet, had he not done everything that he could to persuade Faircloth to stop?

"Right, then," Sebastian said, lifting both brows, "Will you bet, sir?"

"Double or nothing."

A hush fell over the small crowd that had assembled around the piquet table.

"How will you guarantee so large a wager?"

"My home." Graeme Faircloth seemed to struggle for breath. "I'll put up Turbans—but it's only a formality. My luck has shifted. I can feel it!"

Chapter 4

As dusk gathered round the minaret, Julia closed her book of Greek lessons and gave Freddy a smile.

"Don't say that you're setting me free at last?" he cried.

"You shouldn't speak to your tutor in that tone of voice, Master Faircloth." She gave him an indulgent smile. "I must return to the house. Mama has a sick headache and I promised her that I would consult with Cook on her behalf. Don't forget to bring your essay on Tudor England. Papa wants to read it."

Freddy had been shuffling his papers into a pile, but now he paused, brightening. "Do you think he means it?"

"Of course he means it. Papa loves you very much. Why would you ask such a question?"

He stood watching as she wrapped a shawl around her shoulders, protecting herself against the chilly March evening. "You do know what I mean, Jule. Sometimes it seems that he's only pretending to be interested."

"Well…" She felt a telltale flush spread over her cheeks. "Papa has a lot on his mind these days, but it's nothing to do with his love for us. We must be patient and helpful, and trust that he'll work it all out soon."

"Patient? Don't sound a bit like *you*!"

Julia closed the arched door on his laughter and paused for a moment in the fragrant evening air, pondering her brother's uncanny ability to put his finger on the truth. No, she wasn't a bit patient, and if there were truly something else she could think of to do to stop her father from his ruinous pursuits, she would have done it in an instant.

Nearby, an orange-beaked blackbird was pecking in the garden for its supper. Up the hill, some of Turbans's windows were aglow with candlelight, and smoke curled from the chimneys. It was that in-between time of year, when spring beckoned by day and winter crept back by night.

As she started toward the house, Julia made out the figure of her father. He stood beside the wall, his head bent against one of the stone turbans, and something in the set of his shoulders sent her heart plummeting. It almost looked as if his back was broken. She caught the edges of her shawl with one hand and lifted her skirts with the other and hurried up the lawn.

"Papa! Papa—"

As she drew near, he slowly raised his head and looked at her. "Oh…Julia, my dear. Ah, here's another lock of your hair come loose."

She reached for his hands and found them ice-cold. "You're awfully pale, Papa. Come inside and have a cup of tea, or a spot of brandy."

"No. A ride, I think." And with that, he patted her cheek, sighed deeply, and went off toward the stables.

Julia called to him again as he rode away, but this time he didn't seem to hear.

At dawn, Graeme Faircloth's body was discovered by a passing wool merchant. He'd broken his neck in a fall from his horse over a treacherous water jump, and the horse was later found grazing in the meadow adjoining Turbans.

Mrs. Faircloth was inconsolable. She had already spent

the last evening of her husband's life alone in a darkened room, and now she seemed determined never to come out again. Days passed in a fog for the surviving family members. Julia chose the clothing in which her father would be buried, and according to tradition, none of the women attended the interment at the tiny Margaret Chapel, tucked away behind Brock Street. William Bradstreet, the family's solicitor, took young Frederick to the services. When they returned to Turbans, Julia thought that Freddy's pale, stark countenance had never before so resembled their father's.

Mr. Bradstreet had given her a bracing hug, muttering, "Thank God your family has you, my girl. Mr. Faircloth always said you were the strongest one, and I can see that he was right. And, we must all give thanks for Turbans."

Julia brightened slightly. "Yes. At least, for the first time in our lives, we are financially secure. With Turbans, we can soldier on."

Someone had to manage the details of their lives. Julia grasped her duty immediately, but even she felt weak-kneed. There were moments during the day when she would be talking to the housekeeper or picking out a menu and her thoughts would wander off, dismally, to fix on an image of her father's broken body lying alone in a muddy field. Her heart would pound, aching, but she couldn't stop the thoughts. Worst of all, she feared that he had meant to die. Could he have taken his own life in order to escape those horrid gaming debts?

She roused herself, shaking her head, sick with regret and grief and dread. Were more surprises yet to be revealed?

Julia looked around and found herself sitting at her father's desk in the walnut-paneled library. She remembered then that she'd been assembling the notes of condolence to show her mother, though they would doubtless only intensify her weeping.

Looking at the small pile of notes, Julia noticed one she hadn't read herself. The sender's address was inscribed in a bold, striking hand, and the distinctive crested seal had been pressed in haste. She broke it. Inside, she found a few terse sentences:

Please accept my sympathies for your profound loss. Although I was acquainted with Mr. Faircloth only slightly, I don't doubt that he was a fine person. And it was signed, *Yr. Humble etc., Lord Sebastian Trevarre.*

Tears blurred Julia's vision as she stared at his name. So vital was the signature, it seemed that the ink must still be wet. Clearly, she could again hear his voice warning, "Your father's problem is his own, and only he can solve it." And, she could see his gray-green eyes, relentlessly honest, meeting her gaze when she spoke to him. Lord Sebastian had been direct with her, yet she'd felt that he was like smoke. She'd come away completely uncertain about who he was, where he had come from, and whether there was a drop of kindness in him.

Of course there was *not*! His name should be Lord *Satan,* not Sebastian! Angrily, Julia tore his note to pieces. He was a hateful, odious person, and he'd doubtless practiced his verbal fencing on her own poor father! If Lord Satan hadn't been so hard on him, if he'd extended a hand to offer forgiveness, Graeme Faircloth might still be with his family.

The shreds of cream parchment lay before her on the desk, but one fragment of the note was still intact. The signature: *Lord Sebastian Trevarre,* with all its rakish flair, remained in its entirety.

"Miss Faircloth. Miss Faircloth?"

"Hmm?" Julia blinked, realizing that the voice that spoke her name was real. She stood and looked at the housemaid. "What is it, Abby?"

"Mr. Lynton to see you, miss." Bobbing a curtsy, she backed away and Adolphus came forward to stand in her place.

"Ah, Julia, how pale you are." He bowed, looking exceedingly concerned. "As usual, you are taking on far too much, at a time when you should be resting."

Remembering the conspiratorial wink Lynton had received from her father, Julia instinctively felt that he was not really their friend. She came around the desk and gave him a polite smile. "I appreciate your concern, Mr. Lynton, but I am coping. One must carry on, and I have a great deal to occupy me. In fact, although I appreciate your visit, I have a duty to Freddy, who is waiting in the minaret to show me his lessons—"

He caught her hands. "I'll only keep you a moment, my dear. How good it is to hear that my visits are precious to you."

"This truly is not a good time," Julia protested. She found that she was annoyed by the contrast between his severe choice of clothing and the foppish affectation of a quizzing-glass. The simplest aspects of Lynton's person grated on her nerves, now more than ever.

"Ah, I think you'll be singing a different tune when you hear what it is I have to say. Although you have previously been slow to accept my attempts to woo you, if I did not note the change in your current circumstances, I would be a poor excuse for a *man*. That is exactly what you and your family need now: a man with the strength of his convictions. Quite frankly, I have long believed that your household could stand to feel a firm, masculine hand, and I can also offer an impressive array of connections, including certain persons in royal circles!"

"Mr. Lynton—"

"Call me Adolphus. It would please me immensely if you would accept my proposal of marriage."

"Adolphus, please don't say these things!" she exclaimed, horrified.

"Julia, I love you—"

"You must not speak another word." Firmly, she pressed her hand against his bony chest before he could swoop down and kiss her, as she sensed he was about to do. "I do appreciate your concern, but I cannot accept. If you knew me better, you would never speak of love. I am hopelessly flawed. I've decided that I am the sort of woman who should not marry. I—I would only order you about and make you quite miserable."

His sober countenance was set like a statue. "I'm certain you are wrong."

"Well, there you have it. If we can't even agree on whether or not to marry, what chance for success would we have? Now then, I must dash off to the minaret. Do forgive me."

Julia patted his hand, but she could see in his smoldering eyes that he hadn't given up, and the subject was not closed.

Clad all in sober gray on an overcast morning, Julia went alone by carriage to hear the reading of her father's will. Her mother was in no condition to be present, so Sarah stayed by Polly's bedside, and they all agreed that there was no reason for Freddy to go. Everyone knew that, as the only son, he would inherit the entire estate. Julia only went to represent him, and because she felt it was her duty.

Mr. Bradstreet kept a small, stuffy office above his home in Henrietta Street. To find that esteemed address, the Faircloth coachman had to cross the crowded Pulteney Bridge, and by the time they arrived, Julia realized that she was a few minutes late. A pinched looking clerk met her at the door and showed her up a narrow staircase to William Bradstreet's book-lined study.

Through a haze of smoke, Julia discerned Mr. Bradstreet, standing in front of his desk with a clay pipe in his mouth.

"Good morning, sir. I apologize if I have kept you waiting. I fear there was a terrible crush of sedan chairs on the bridge!"

Tall and spare, with wisps of reddish-gray hair, William

Bradstreet extended a hand to her. "Yes, yes, I have a theory that the Baths are more crowded whenever it looks like rain." He smiled at her with his eyes. "You look as if you haven't had a good meal since your father's death. I imagine you must be taking care of the entire household and neglecting yourself."

"Don't worry about me. It helps me to be busy. Speaking of that, we ought to proceed so that I may return home before luncheon. I predict that Mama may venture downstairs today."

"Good for her." He went behind his desk and shuffled paper, clearing his throat nervously. "Suppose I should mention—there is one other person here with us today—"

"Whatever for?" Julia wondered. Turning, she gasped aloud at the sight of Lord Sebastian Trevarre leaning against the mantelpiece with a glass of sherry in his elegantly masculine hand.

He sketched a bow. "We meet again, Miss Faircloth."

Chapter 5

Before Julia could speak, Mr. Bradstreet blessedly intervened.

"Ah, I see that you two have been previously introduced, which of course should not surprise me! Miss Faircloth, I do not need to tell you that Lord Sebastian is a most original man. Perhaps you already know that he has just resigned his commission after several years as an officer in the Royal Navy?"

"Fascinating," Julia murmured. As she untied the gray silk ribbons of her bonnet, she felt a disquieting pang of curiosity. Truly, there was more to his lordship than met the eye. "Is he here to converse with you about his adventures fighting the French?"

Sebastian brought her a small glass of sherry and took the chair beside hers. "No, Miss Faircloth. Do you mind if I listen to the reading of your father's will?"

"Do I have a choice?" Sensing danger from the powerful, sardonic man seated next to her, she flushed.

"Not really," Bradstreet murmured.

"I suppose I must agree, then." She found that she really did not want to know why Sebastian was there. She put her glass of sherry in his dark hand. "I do not care for sherry at this hour of the morning, thank you. You may have both glasses, my lord."

He smiled and set it on the desk. "I would remark upon the subtlety of your humor, but that would be inappropriate, given the circumstances. Rather, allow me to offer my condolences. I was saddened to hear of your father's untimely death."

Something in his voice caused her to look at him closely. She almost believed that he meant it. "Thank you. Mr. Bradstreet, may we proceed?"

"I should take your bonnet and pelisse, shouldn't I." Bradstreet stood by awkwardly while she handed them to him, then returned to the safety of his desk to read Graeme Faircloth's will aloud in a numbing monotone. At the end, he looked up, blinked, and said, "There it is. All goes to young Frederick, of course, but since he is only twelve years of age, the situation will remain as it now exists. You and Mrs. Faircloth will continue to manage Turbans until Freddy attains his majority."

Feeling teary, Julia murmured, "Thank God for Turbans! What would become of us if Papa had not inherited from Cousin Archibald?"

"Doubtless your father would still be laboring happily in his London bookshop," Sebastian suggested.

She stared at him. "My lord, I was trying to say that my family's love for Turbans is the one bright spot in our lives today. We are fortunate to have the comfort of a wonderful home, and a secure income—"

"Well," Mr. Bradstreet interjected, "there isn't quite the sum of money that was in place when Mr. Faircloth's cousin died. There have been some recent—" he cleared his throat and glanced at Sebastian "—financial obligations that have…eroded the total…"

Julia began to feel decidedly embarrassed about revealing even more of their private shame to this virtual stranger. "We needn't delve into all that now. I must go."

When she began to rise, Sebastian put out a hand. "Please, sit down. I am here specifically because of your father's will." He paused, looked away for a long moment, and gave a harsh sigh. "I regret being the bearer of bad tidings, but I have come as a result of actions taken by your father during a recent game of piquet. I made every effort to dissuade him from betting against me; I repeatedly invited him to leave the table while his losses were still manageable, but he insisted."

"Insisted?" Julia repeated icily. "Insisted on doing what, my lord?" Across from them, William Bradstreet had begun to suck on his dead pipe as if he were struggling for breath.

Sebastian reached for the extra glass of sherry she had passed to him, and drank it down. "Your father insisted on making a desperate last bet, in an effort to recoup all that he had already lost. As a result…" From his coat pocket, he withdrew a stack of notes that bore Faircloth's familiar handwriting, and gave them to the solicitor.

Mr. Bradstreet peered at them through smudged spectacles, growing paler by the moment. When he reached the last note, he gasped aloud. "Great God, this cannot be true! Miss Faircloth, I was already aware that your father had lost a large sum of money to Lord Sebastian. But I see here that…Mr. Faircloth lost Turbans, as well!"

Julia felt as if she'd been slapped with such force that the room began to spin. She sat back in her chair, clenching her fists until her bearings returned, then turned on her enemy. "This is outrageous! How—how can you consider collecting such a despicable debt from the grieving family of a dead man? Have you no heart at all, sir?"

"I am not certain I take your point." A muscle moved in his jaw. "Do you mean to imply that I am to blame for your father's debt?"

She struggled to calm herself, to think of a way to outmaneuver this wily fox, this cunning rat, this bunny-snatching stoat in rake's clothing! For her family's sake, she would try to appeal to his protective male instincts. All men had them, didn't they? Even wicked libertines?

"Do I blame you, my lord? Of course not. But, I am befuddled. Do you really mean to come here at this lowest ebb in my family's life, when we have lost our patriarch, and claim Turbans—our *home*?" Julia wanted to squeeze out a tear for effect, but her pride interfered. "Perhaps, in my grief, I have misunderstood your intentions."

His face was impassive. "Not at all. I might add that I am very sorry for your father's actions, and sorry for your family's resulting plight. However, I also strongly suspect that Mr. Faircloth meant to die, hoping that I would forget our card game, forget that I warned him against such stakes, forget that *he* insisted we continue the game and abide by the outcome!" Sebastian paused, eyes blazing. "Miss Faircloth, you are mistaken if you believe that I am responsible for the loss of your home and your income."

Before Julia could obey the impulse to strike him, William Bradstreet came around the desk. He poured a fresh glass of sherry for her, then leveled a cold stare at Sebastian.

"I suggest that you take your leave, my lord. If you insist on pursuing this matter, I will meet with you privately, at a later date."

"As you wish." Sebastian stood, towering over Julia. "I will go, but I must inform Miss Faircloth that she has not seen the last of me. Far from it."

"Of course, my lord," she rejoined tartly. "No doubt you are eager to turn my grieving family out of our home!"

"I am excessively grateful to you for coming with me to the Pump Room so that I can see Charles," Sarah said as she and Julia traversed the enclosed cobbled courtyard known as Abbey Churchyard. "He's written a poem for me about grief, and in his note insisted that he give it to me personally."

"I am glad to do a good deed," Julia assured her. "And I

don't see that it should damage our reputations if we're seen taking the waters so soon after Papa's death. The Pump Room, after all, is hardly a den of sin. Are we to lock ourselves in at Turbans?" She lowered her voice as a passing nobleman glanced toward them. "What would that serve? It won't keep Lord Sebastian Trevarre from snatching it away from us!"

Sarah paled. "I still cannot believe that it's true…that Papa could have lost our home and our livelihood in a silly game of piquet!"

"Papa didn't lose it so much as Lord Satan stole it away from him. What chance did dear Papa have against such a villain?"

"Is his lordship really so wicked?" Sarah shuddered. "There must be some remedy we can employ against him!"

"Believe me," Julia said grimly, "I am wracking my brain to think of one, and I shall."

There were sedan chairs, with and without roofs, lined up outside the Pump Room. Nearby, the burly chairmen dozed in the sunshine, waiting to be hired by invalids who were either drinking the waters or soaking in the King's Baths.

The sisters entered the Pump Room to the strains of music spilling from a balcony in the middle of the grand interior. Julia led the way to the counter, where people were purchasing glasses of water from the pumper.

"I have heard that it tastes like warm old eggs," whispered Sarah. "Can it really be so good for us?"

"I doubt it," Julia allowed. "But at least we are having a bit of diversion from our predicament at Turbans."

Armed with their glasses of hot water, they shared dubious glances before joining the other visitors who were pacing up and down the room, socializing as they drank their potions. Gouty old men in chairs watched from the fringes of the crowd.

Soon, nosy dowagers began to stop the Faircloth sisters and offer their condolences.

"Such a pity about your father," murmured the Countess of Bunthaven. "I suppose he simply wasn't able to cope with the change in his circumstances, hmm?" Peering at Julia through her quizzing-glass, she scolded, "Dear child, you must drink your water! It's best to take it while it's as hot as possible."

"Thank you, my lady." She took hold of Sarah's arm and led her away. "I see Mr. Whimple in the doorway. Why don't you go and have a word with him in private, and then I'll come along to get you in a few minutes."

They set down their glasses, tipped the pumper, and Sarah hurried through the main doorway that opened onto York Street. Her cheeks were pink and her eyes sparkled as she approached a thin young man with haunted eyes. Charles Whimple's entire expression was transformed to one of adoration when he caught sight of his lady-love.

Julia, meanwhile, moved along the fringes of the crowd in an effort to avoid any more elderly acquaintances. She just couldn't bear to hear another piece of well-meaning advice.

Musicians struck up a Haydn concerto in the balcony overhead. Spying another dowager, she ducked behind a conveniently placed column, only to bump against another person who was already standing there.

"Ah, Miss Faircloth. Were you looking for me?"

The familiar masculine voice sent a chill down her spine. "Lord Sebastian!" she exclaimed. "What are you doing lurking about here?"

"Hiding from inquisitive dowagers, the same as you. If you call that 'lurking,' then I'm in good company." He lifted both brows with a knowing smile. "I'm rather surprised to see you out in society so soon."

"I accompanied my sister on an errand of some urgency."

"I see. Is that she with that very earnest-looking dark-eyed fellow?"

Julia nodded, flushing slightly under his interested regard. "Mr. Whimple writes poetry."

"I'm sure he must be very gifted. Miss Faircloth, you must think that I am a villain, and perhaps I am. However, I would like to meet your family and see Turbans for myself. Will you allow me to visit on Thursday next?"

She found herself staring at the angles of his tanned face. He really was a dangerously attractive man, and the instinctive response she felt in his presence made her like him even less. "Since Mr. Bradstreet confirms that Turbans is actually *your* house now, I suppose that we must receive you whenever you choose to visit, my lord."

"Shall we say four o'clock?"

Nodding as he sketched a bow, Julia bade him goodbye and went off to fetch her sister, seething with impotent frustration.

"I'm sorry, Mr. Whimple, but we must take our leave," she told the poet, who was still holding his latest effort in one thin hand.

Sarah looked dreamy as Julia took her arm and they set off, nearly colliding outside with one of the new Bath chairs that were replacing sedan chairs in fine weather. The contraption, invented to cater to the city's large population of gouty old men and dowagers, was propelled along on three wheels.

"Look out, ye foolish lassies!" shouted the elderly occupant. He shook his cane at them as they stood aside to make way for the chair, its wheels rumbling on the cobbles.

"Perhaps Turbans was not so dull after all," said Julia.

"I am ready to go home," her sister agreed.

"Yes. I shall have to round up the house maids and begin dusting." She sighed and tears threatened. "On Thursday next, Lord Satan will arrive to inspect his winnings!"

Chapter 6

"I have it all planned," Freddy announced darkly. "I'm going to smile and offer Lord Satan sugar for his tea, but I'll have soaked his sugar lump in arsenic."

"Frederick Faircloth!" Sarah gasped. "Where do you get such ideas?"

"From my books. And Shakespeare plays. Don't you approve of Shakespeare?"

"Thank heaven Mama can't hear you. This is one time I'm grateful that she's still in her room."

Julia, who was lying on a chaise in the sunlit conservatory, couldn't suppress her laughter any longer. "Don't worry, Freddy, you won't have to poison his lordship. I've been studying that creature and I think I have hit upon a method to make Lord Satan go away and leave us alone."

Sarah, who had been looking very pale, hurried to her sister's side. "Oh, Julia, I knew that you would think of a plan. But, I do wish you hadn't shared your naughty name for Lord Sebastian with Freddy. He's bound to accidentally call him 'Lord Satan' to his face!"

The clock in the entry hall struck four and the trio jumped a little in surprise. Freddy said, "Since Lord Satan's due at this very moment, you'd better be quick with the plan, Jule. Otherwise, I'll be forced to resort to the arsenic!"

"I implore you to stop saying those things!" cried Sarah.

"Calm down, both of you," Julia soothed them. Sitting up, she straightened her shoulders. "His lordship doesn't strike me as a punctual person. Now then, when he does deign to arrive, we must present a united front. Although it's tempting to mount a counter-attack, that would only undermine our cause. There's nothing for it but to arouse his sympathies." Seeing the worried faces of her siblings, Julia didn't add that she doubted whether Lord Satan even possessed sympathies. "We must grieve openly in his presence and allow him to see that we are crushed by Papa's death and our own impending fate."

"I hear a carriage!" shouted Freddy. He went running from the conservatory.

Sarah followed him, pausing only to remark to her sister, "His lordship would seem to be punctual after all."

Before Julia could even draw a breath, Freddy came dashing back through the entry hall, his brown eyes wide and his face flushed. "I saw *him*! I saw him climb down from the finest high-perch phaeton *ever*! There's another fellow, but it's easy enough to tell who's the *lordship*. He's wearing an excellent greatcoat and very tight pantaloons the color of champagne and one notices the intricacy of his cravat even from a distance, and his hair unpowdered, of course, and windblown!"

"What does any of that signify if he is an evil villain?" asked Sarah. "Tell us, what sort of person does he appear to be?"

"His lordship looks positively terrifying! He has the look of Ali Baba himself!"

There was a knock at the door and Abby opened it and immediately the air inside the house changed, as if a storm had silently come in. The little maid crossed to the sitting room, followed by two male figures, and blushed while announcing, "Lord Sebastian Trevarre is here, accompanied by his manservant, Mr. Keswick."

Julia felt a shocking urge to look at herself in a mirror, to fix her hair properly and pinch her cheeks and smooth her muslin gown. Instead, she went to meet Lord Sebastian, smiling with all the humility she could feign. "We are honored to have you in our home…or, should I say *your* home? We hope you will forgive us if we need a bit of time to adjust to this turn of events." She looked at Mr. Keswick, a thin, white-wigged fellow with dark brows that made peaks. "It's very good to meet you, Mr. Keswick. I hope you will feel at ease in your employer's new home."

He had the good grace to look abashed. "We are honored to make the acquaintance of your family, Miss Faircloth. His lordship speaks of you only in tones of admiration."

Although momentarily perplexed by Keswick's use of the plural "we," Julia moved smoothly ahead with her plan and invited Lord Sebastian to accompany her on a tour of Turbans. "After all, that is the real reason for your visit today. We do not delude ourselves that you wanted to see *us*, my lord!" She paused, and her siblings joined in her polite laughter with its undercurrent of sadness.

"Miss Faircloth, are you trying to tell me that you secretly hoped my motive for coming here was of a personal nature?" His eyes were agleam, like those of a cat who has quickly cornered his prey.

She backed away. "You are wicked, my lord."

"Surely not wicked. Charming, I would hope." Sebastian glanced over at Keswick, who was nodding in sober agreement, and flashed a smile. "I am ready for our tour if you are, Miss Faircloth."

Sarah and Freddy excused themselves to go outside, while Keswick picked up a volume of poetry and took a seat near the garden window. "We will be right here, waiting, my lord," he said to Sebastian.

As she showed his lordship around Turbans, Julia pointed out every nook and cranny that might appear unstable, or need repairing. "You'll notice that Turbans has exquisitely decorated ceilings, even if they do show a great deal of peeling paint. No doubt it's nothing to worry about, except after the winter rains. Although you might soon need to replace the roof, and perhaps a few of the intricately plastered walls, there are excellent craftsmen for hire here in Bath."

"How fortunate that the exterior is stone," came his dry rejoinder. "It's an extraordinary house; I think that its charming eccentricities more than make up for the defects you've pointed out so conscientiously."

She felt his eyes on her, but she wouldn't meet them. Instead, Julia squeezed out a sigh. "I suppose you can afford to make all the necessary repairs."

"You might have as well if—" He broke off, as if suddenly remembering that her father was dead, and his character flaws were no longer fit topics for conversation. "I beg your pardon. I nearly misspoke."

She wished he would at least show a little shame or guilt for the situation in which they found themselves. Instead, he was respectful. That alone wouldn't get Turbans back for the Faircloths.

"Does your mother continue to be indisposed?" Sebastian inquired.

"I fear so." Julia seized on this, pointing to Polly's closed door as they approached. "She has been inconsolable. I truly do not know how we shall persuade Mama to leave her room, let alone move away from Turbans. But, you mustn't give that a moment's thought. Perhaps, when the time comes for us to leave, your manservant can cart her into the street. As you have pointed out to me, you are not to blame for our sorry situation."

His dark brows lifted slightly. "It is gratifying to hear you say that you no longer resent me for being the person to whom your father lost Turbans."

"Have you noticed the broken places on the bannister?" she asked through clenched teeth. "And you know we have had terrible problems with voles in the garden. It's useless to try to grow anything."

"If this house is so riddled with flaws, you must be secretly relieved to be moving out."

How maddening he was, like a cat toying with a mouse! Halfway up the stairs, Julia whirled around and found herself staring into his compellingly masculine eyes. She had intended to tell him off, but her wits deserted her. "You—you are—"

"Yes?"

Julia was swept up by an unexpected wave of sensation, the likes of which she'd never felt before. She had an urge, both powerful and puzzling, to touch Sebastian's wide chest and cravat, which was snow-white in contrast to his sun-darkened face. His mouth and nose were suddenly fascinating; as finely chiseled as any Roman statue. His strong, elegant fingers drew her gaze, and his raven hair gleamed in the pale golden sunlight that streamed through the window on the landing.

"Miss Faircloth, are you unwell?"

She blinked, swaying slightly, and he caught her arm. Wondering herself if she were going mad, Julia tried to think of an excuse, and then she looked at him and saw the knowing glint in his eyes. He knew perfectly well what had come over her. It doubtless happened to him regularly. Blood rushed to her face as she contemplated the revolting prospect of becoming one more in a long line of females who swooned over Lord Sebastian Trevarre.

"You'll have to excuse me, my lord. I was daydreaming for a moment, about my suitor, Mr. Lynton." She hoped her flushed cheeks didn't give away the lie. "He's been such a comfort to me during the entire ordeal of Papa's death."

"Ah, of course." An ironic smile touched his mouth. "Adolphus Lynton. We have met."

She'd rather that they were not acquainted. How could he believe that she could be enamored of such a man? And what if Adolphus had told him of her rejections? "Do you know him well?" she inquired softly.

"No—"

"I thought not!" Relief drenched her voice.

"I was about to add that Mr. Lynton and I met on the last day of your father's life. He was there when Mr. Faircloth and I were playing piquet. I am quite certain that, when I encouraged your father to stop play, your ardent suitor urged him to continue."

"That's ludicrous. You have a way of misunderstanding situations and people in the worst ways possible!" Julia swept past him with all the dignity she could muster. "Let us have tea. I am famished!"

He made no reply, but followed her into the sitting room, where refreshments were being laid out on a delicate table. For a moment, as Julia stood consulting with the maid, Sebastian studied her. She closely resembled her sister, but her style was direct and artless. She truly didn't appear to be vain about her appearance, or concerned with the judgments of others. In a society where young ladies spent hours each day, fussing to be certain they had the perfect clothing, accessories, jewelry, hairstyles, and even the right gossip to exchange during conversation at the Pump Room, Julia was quite refreshing.

Yet, would not a woman like that be pure hell to live with? She was stronger-willed than most men he knew, and her disdain for the opinions of others might create endless problems.

"Do join me," she called to him, adding a wide, radiant smile. "Cook makes the best scones in Bath, or so I believe."

Why was she suddenly smiling at him? It occurred to Sebastian, as he walked toward her, that he would need all his wits to deal with Julia. "Does Cook serve her scones with clotted cream?"

She nodded. "And raspberry jam, made from our own berries."

"So you were able to keep the voles out of some bits of the garden? That's encouraging news."

Julia seemed to ignore him as she poured the tea, still smiling. "Shall I invite Mr. Keswick to join us, or have a cup of tea taken to him in the library?"

"Don't give Keswick another thought. He's a servant, after all." He saw her glance toward the door that connected them to the library. "Ah, I see. Let me close this to ensure our privacy."

When Sebastian rose, Julia couldn't help noticing again how splendidly made he was. His shoulders were straight and wide, his legs were long and hard-muscled, and he moved with casual grace. Giving herself a mental shake, she forced her attention back to the tea.

"Do you take milk, my lord?"

"A bit, yes."

When they had both sampled the strong, hot tea, she said, "We really know very little about you, my lord, beyond what was said in Mr. Bradstreet's office about your years in America with the Royal Navy. Won't you tell me what has brought you to Bath?"

"My parents died, and my brother George, the new marquess, visited Bath and began to gamble to excess," he said abruptly. "I came here to look into the matter."

"Why, that means that you do understand how insidious a problem gambling can be, and how deeply it can divide families!"

"I do indeed."

Julia saw that the light had gone from his eyes. This was the moment that she had meant to pretend to be helpless and appeal to his sympathies. However, when she began to speak, she realized that her emotions were real. Memories of her father and his tragic end brought tears welling up from her throat. "I can only hope then, that given your own brother's experience, you will find it in your heart to take pity on us. My papa was better than you think."

"As was George," he replied coolly. "Unfortunately

neither of our relatives had the good sense to walk away from the gaming tables when they realized that they were taking ill-considered risks."

"But if you came to Bath to avenge your brother's losses, why turn on us? My father didn't win his lordship's money!"

"Even if I knew who had beaten George, I would not expect him to reverse the outcome and give me back his losses." His expression turned angry as tears spilled onto her cheeks. "For God's sake, stop looking at me like that! It was your father who behaved like a damned fool and lost Turbans. It was his mistake, not mine!"

"Don't you dare call Papa names!" Sniffling, she covered her face with her hands.

Sebastian stared hard at her for a long moment, seeming to realize why she had clearly tried to soften his mood, and how she had wanted the doors closed. He leaned over to proffer a starched white handkerchief before remarking, "Clearly you haven't had much practice with sympathy tears, Miss Faircloth. This really isn't your style."

She peered at him, bleary-eyed, over the handkerchief. "Do you think that I am pretending?" The fact that she had *planned* to pretend only made her angrier. "What sort of person do you take me for?"

"I think that you are a fighter, which is quite admirable."

"My lord, I can assure you that my pain for my poor papa is very real!" To her chagrin, more tears spilled forth. "And—and my anguished concern for the welfare of my family is also very real."

"Perhaps, but this scene between us was planned, wasn't it?" He gave her a knowing sidelong glance. "You simply aren't the sort of woman who cries on the shoulder of a man, particularly the man whom you perceive to be the cause of all your family's troubles."

"A self-absorbed person like you would not have the smallest ability to judge my character. Why, I have more character in one hair on my head than you possess in your entire heartless being!"

Sebastian began to laugh, then held up an open hand to beg her pardon. "I'm sorry. Only a cad would laugh at a weeping woman, but you do say the most amusing things."

"Do I?" Julia turned frosty. "My lord, you do not know me in the least."

"I think I may know more about you than you'd like."

"You are spouting fustian, as usual."

"I know that you have never been kissed." His tone was offhand, but his gray-green eyes were provocative.

"You are not only rude, but quite wrong!" She could feel the traitorous blood rushing to her face.

"Now you have challenged me to provide proof." In one easy movement, Sebastian had risen, reached down, and lifted Julia into his strong embrace. He bent her backward and kissed her bare throat, then the base of her neck, and she could feel her pulse leaping there. Then, smiling into her stricken eyes, he said, "You're past twenty, aren't you? You shouldn't remain unkissed. If you're going to begin weeping on men's shirtfronts, you ought to know what you're letting yourself in for."

To her horror, Julia discovered that she was shaky and filled with hot excitement. She knew she ought to struggle, and the mischief in his eyes told her he knew it too, but she couldn't bear to deprive herself of this singular experience. When he drew her completely into his arms so that she felt every thrilling inch of his male body pressing against her, she surrendered to the moment. Now that her family had lost everything she would doubtless die a spinster, but at least she would have shared a kiss with this magnificent rogue.

Sebastian's mouth, firm and hot and commanding, covered hers. Shocking waves of bliss flooded Julia so that she could scarcely breathe. His kiss was intoxicating beyond anything she had imagined. The feeling of his strong arms embracing her, his hands caressing her back, her breasts seeming to swell against the hard expanse of his chest, combined to unravel all her defenses. Just as she was about to wrap her arms around his neck and touch the crisp dark hair that curled over his collar, he released her. Touching her shoulders with his fingertips to steady her, he smiled.

Julia pressed a hand to each of her burning cheeks. "I—I—"

"You're about to admit that I was clearly right."

"Right?" Her breasts were tingling and she felt unable to form coherent speech. "What do you mean?"

"You have just received your first kiss."

Julia's wits came rushing back. "Oh the contrary, I was about to say that you are a scoundrel, Lord Sa—" She stopped herself just in time. "That is, Lord Sebastian. How could you make such remarks about my age, then force yourself on me in my own home?"

"Force myself? My dear Miss Faircloth, I waited to hear a word of protest, before our kiss, and you were as docile as a lamb."

"A lamb going to the slaughter!" Gripping the back of her chair, she was relieved to feel her wits returning. "I was in shock, my lord! By the time I found my voice, it was too late!"

Sebastian finished his tea and smiled. "Well, there was no harm done, was there? It was just an amusing duel between two friendly adversaries, and I would say each of us won. I proved my point, and you have crossed one of life's great societal barriers." He folded his napkin. "Perhaps the next time a man kisses you, you won't be paralyzed by rapture."

"Rapture! You jest, my lord!"

"Well, perhaps rapture won't be the issue if it's Adolphus Lynton who kisses you next." Their eyes met as he added, "Why not admit the truth? Now that you know what you've been missing, aren't you the least bit grateful to me?"

"You are *demented*!"

Just then, the door swung open and Sarah and Keswick stood together on the threshold.

"I was worried," Sarah said hesitantly. "So much time had passed…"

"We hope we are not interrupting a serious discussion," Keswick muttered, taking in the situation with a shrewd look.

"You couldn't have come at a better time," Julia assured him. "His lordship was just saying that he must leave now."

"Is there any—good news?" wondered Sarah in tremulous tones. With her porcelain skin, burnished curls, and damp eyes, she resembled the subject of a romantic painting. "I know it is very bold of me to ask…"

"There, there," said Julia, putting an arm around her. "My poor sister has had a terrible time lately. She was so very attached to our father, and to Turbans."

"I cannot believe we are going to lose our home," Sarah rejoined brokenly. "Dear Mama can scarcely get out of bed, so profound is her grief. When Papa inherited Turbans, we believed that at long last we had a home for life." Nervously, she addressed Sebastian. "It was security we had always dreamed of."

"Miss Faircloth, I regret that your father wagered and lost this estate, and I shall do everything possible to ease the situation for your family."

Keswick took a step forward and cleared his throat. "Miss Faircloth has confided her worries about locating a suitable house to rent, and then moving from Turbans. Given her mother's current state, tasks such as sorting and packing a lifetime's worth of possessions may be especially difficult."

"I do not desire to contribute to further tears being shed by Miss Faircloth," Sebastian said. As if sensing Julia's outrage, he added, "Of course, I am referring to *both* Misses Faircloth! You ladies must look after your mother, and take as much time as you need to resettle your family."

Sarah smiled at him through her tears. "You are kinder than I expected you to be, my lord."

"That is the nicest thing anyone has said to me today." Gently clasping her hand, he made his farewells.

Julia felt blindsided. When he reached next for her hand, she said, "We'll keep you apprised of our progress, my lord."

"Oh, Miss Faircloth, I am certain that we'll be in close touch over the coming weeks. Thank you for showing me around Turbans, and thank you for sharing your teatime with me. It was most enlightening. Don't you agree?"

She snatched her hand back and saw the laughter in his eyes. "Good afternoon, my lord."

Minutes later, Sebastian and his manservant were back outside in the spring air, climbing up to the phaeton's high perch.

"Keswick, when we are back in the Crescent, I'd like you to send a note round to Lady Barrowminster. I believe I might like to see her again after all. An intimate supper, perhaps?"

"Yes, my lord." Keswick pressed his lips together in disapproval.

Sebastian surveyed the lush lawns and gardens as he took the reins. "Do you see any sign of voles?"

"Pardon?"

"*Voles*. The enchanting elder Miss Faircloth insists that the grounds are infested with them."

"We don't see any, my lord."

A moment passed as they picked up speed, then Sebastian remarked, "Do you not find Miss Sarah Faircloth to be lovely in the purest sense of the word? One would never tire of gazing upon her."

"Just so, my lord. We have additionally observed that she and her older sister have very similar looks."

"Have you indeed? I suppose there is a superficial resemblance." He didn't wait for a reply. "I must tell you that I feel the younger Miss Faircloth's beauty is more remarkable because she is so agreeably docile. Not at all opinionated and argumentative like her sister."

"We surmise that your lordship and the elder Miss Faircloth don't get on very well?"

Urging his horses to an even greater speed, Sebastian laughed. "That's putting it kindly, Keswick. I'd sooner have tea with a hedgehog. It couldn't be any pricklier than Miss Julia Faircloth!"

Chapter 7

All three Faircloth women were sipping morning chocolate in the Turbans garden when a liveried footman arrived with a letter for Sarah.

"My dear Charles is so romantic," she murmured, watching the gilt-edged footman depart. "He's pretending that we are nobility!"

Julia spread honey on her puffy Sally Lunn roll and smiled. On such a fragrant and glorious morning, she could imagine that all was well. For three days, since returning into the fold of the family, Polly had been pretending that very thing. She didn't mention her husband's tragic end; she behaved as if he were off in Bath as usual. The subject of losing Turbans never was broached. Julia and Sarah had taken to reading rental listings while their mother was resting in the afternoon.

"It's such a shame that Mr. Whimple isn't wealthy," said Julia, watching as Sarah broke the seal on the letter. "He could rescue us from our predicament."

"I wish you would not use such unpleasant words," Polly exclaimed. "I can't bear gloomy conversation."

"What does he say?" Julia asked her sister. "Is it a poem?"

Sarah's face had gone white. "No. No, it's not a poem. In fact, it's not from Charles at all!" She pressed a hand to her heart. “This letter is from Lord Sebastian Trevarre!”

“It must be a mistake.” Julia felt very dizzy. “The footman delivered it to the wrong Miss Faircloth!”

“You appear awfully emotional for someone who dislikes the man so vehemently,” Sarah said, giving her a thoughtful look.

“I don’t trust him, that’s all. I’ll wager he’s playing a trick on you.” She leaned forward. “What does it *say*?”

“He expresses several very civil sentiments, then asks if he may visit me here at Turbans, at our earliest convenience.” Paling, she looked up. “He wonders if tomorrow would be too soon!”

“You must refuse,” Julia said quickly. “He has no business with you, my dear, and you owe him nothing.”

“But, he was so kind when I told him of my worries about leaving Turbans! How can I snub him?”

“Very easily. I’ll even write the note for you. I know exactly what to say to him.”

Polly interrupted in strident tones. “You will do nothing of the sort, Julia Faircloth! His lordship has too much power over our lives to be trifled with; I won’t allow it. We must invite him to luncheon tomorrow and discover what it is that he wants.”

“Luncheon! Mama, you go too far! It’s power that he wants. He’s already bested Papa and won Turbans, and now we are all pawns in a game of his devising.”

Sarah sniffed. “Sometimes I think that you are the one playing games.” She looked back down at the creamy parchment and sighed. “I’ll take your advice, Mama. Perhaps his lordship will surprise us and do something shockingly nice!”

It was nearly noon and Julia couldn’t keep her mind on her brother’s European History lesson. At any moment, the clock would chime and she could hurry back to the house to see for herself exactly what Lord Sebastian Trevarre was up to.

"You're not listening to a word I've said," complained Freddy.

Before she could reply, her mother slipped in through the minaret door and stood with both arms outstretched across the portal.

"I was just about to start back," said Julia. "As it happens, I am very hungry, and quite relieved that his lordship's visit means we shall have a hearty lunch."

"I'm sorry to say, I don't believe a word of that. I think you only want to join us for lunch so that you can interfere." Polly's plump face was blotchy, betraying her nervousness. "You stay here with your brother and share his lunch. We'll let you know when his lordship has gone."

Julia was on her feet and quickly beside her mother at the door. "Mama," she coaxed, "you cannot mean it! You don't know him the way I do. He can't be trusted!"

"No. I won't allow you to disrupt this luncheon. I mean to discover exactly what it is that Lord Sebastian wants." With that, she turned her back, went out the door, and locked it with a key.

Julia's heart was thundering with outrage. She tried the door. Then she lifted her skirts and ran up the narrow, twisting steps to the minaret's balcony, built into the curve of its crescent-shaped cap.

"Freddy," she called down the stairway, "don't you know a secret escape route?"

"Why don't you forget about them, Jule, and let's have a game of backgammon?" His freckled face appeared near the bottom step. "If you're forever bursting in on Lord Sebastian, he'll begin to suspect you're in love with him."

"Frederick Faircloth! That is a vile thing to say."

"I know." His voice drifted off as he went to get out his backgammon board.

Frustration tied knots inside her. Of course, Freddy was right. The last thing she really wanted was to see Lord Sebastian again. Whenever she remembered the way he had treated her during his last visit to Turbans, her face grew hot and her breasts felt very odd. Her reaction was, she'd decided, the strongest sort of outrage.

Still, it seemed imperative that she oversee today's meeting with Lord Sebastian.

Since she had been old enough to realize that her parents were not responsible adults, Julia had felt that it was up to her to lead her inept family through the challenges of life. The thought of what might happen if she were not there today filled her with panic. What was he plotting? Sarah and Polly were both very naïve when it came to men of his ilk, but Julia clearly recognized that he was an unprincipled libertine.

"Come on, Jule!" came Freddy's strident voice from below. "I've set up the board and put away the lessons!"

"Just a moment—" Biting her lip, she peered out over the grounds and spied Lord Sebastian and Sarah strolling into view. They passed under blossoming dogwood trees, and then Julia watched them emerge into the open sunlight, close enough to give her a clear view. She gasped. The villain had tucked Sarah's tiny hand into the crook of his arm, and she was smiling up at him, looking ridiculously innocent.

"Oh, look!" exclaimed Sarah. She turned and pointed up at the minaret balcony. "It's my sister! Halloo, Julia!"

She went crimson. To her horror, his lordship merely raised his hand to her. Then, he steered Sarah off in a new direction, but not before Julia perceived the wicked glint in his eyes.

There was an awkward silence at the luncheon table. Sebastian looked at Sarah Faircloth and her mother and discovered that both of them had finished their goblets of trifle. He folded his linen napkin.

"That was a delicious meal. I appreciate your invitation, particularly in view of your recent tragedy."

"You are very thoughtful, my lord," Polly replied. "Shall we have coffee in the sitting room?"

Sebastian agreed, but as soon as the three of them were seated close together by the garden window, he said, "I fear that I'm in danger of overstaying my welcome. Allow me to explain the reason I asked to visit." He turned slightly to look into Sarah's lovely, thick-lashed eyes. "Miss Faircloth, I have come to ask if you would do me the honor of becoming my wife. This doubtless seems sudden, but I realized when I was here last that you are exactly the sort of lady I ought to wed."

Sarah had gone white as a ghost. Polly blinked, then tittered. "My lord!" she exclaimed. "You do my daughter a great honor! I am certain that she must be conscious of this!"

He smiled ruefully. "I can see that Miss Faircloth is shocked. That is natural. I should add that I have been considering marriage for some time, and since the death of my parents and my brother's exile—"

Little wrinkles appeared in Polly's brow. "I beg your pardon, my lord?"

"My older brother George, now the marquess, began to gamble after he received his inheritance. He lost a good deal right here in Bath, and eventually was forced to leave England. He now resides in Tuscany." Sebastian added, "You may surmise that I have added responsibilities, including one to carry on the Trevarre line since I am not certain what will become of my brother."

"You have our sincere sympathy, my lord," Polly assured him.

He winced. "I don't want sympathy. I'd prefer that we reach an agreement that will benefit all concerned. If Miss Faircloth agrees to marry me, you would then be part of my family, and you and your son and daughter may remain at

Turbans. In addition, Mrs. Faircloth, I would provide you and my wife's siblings with an allowance…"

"That is a very generous offer, my lord." Polly stared hard at her younger daughter.

"Are you quite certain you didn't mean to ask Julia?" Sarah wondered meekly. "We are so similar-looking that people often confuse us. She seems to be much better acquainted with you than I have been."

"Absolutely *not*." There was a hard edge of irony in his voice. He couldn't say it aloud, but in truth he desired a marriage with as little emotional involvement as possible, and he was well aware that the very air was charged whenever he and Julia were together. "You, not your sister, are precisely the sort of woman I envision as my wife. You appear to possess every quality I find pleasing. Of course, I am also glad to think that uniting our two families would solve the problems that were upsetting you so much when last we met."

She nodded slowly, looking as if she might faint at any moment. "I see."

"My daughter is honored by your proposal," Polly prompted her.

"Yes. Yes, of course. And I realize…" Sarah paused for a deep breath. "I realize that there is only one answer I can give, my lord. I accept. Yes, I will marry you."

By the time Julia was released from the minaret, dusk had gathered and dinner was being served. In near silence, the family ate lamb with mint sauce and squash with rice. Julia asked for wine, then watched in surprise as her sister drank two glasses. Although still determined not to converse with her horrid mother, curiosity forced Julia to break down and inquire of Sarah whether or not Lord Sebastian's visit had caused this uncustomary intake of spirits.

Sarah stared vacantly at her. "Hmm?"

"You are drinking wine for the first time in my memory…and you haven't touched your meal. Did his lordship upset you?"

"Upset me?"

Julia cast a suspicious look toward her mother. "Clearly, something important transpired during Lord Sebastian's visit. Who will tell me?"

"Why, it is exceptionally good news!" cried Polly. "Your sister is going to be Lady Sebastian Trevarre!"

"Do not make so cruel a jest, Mama." Her heart seemed to have stopped. "Tell me the truth."

"Why would I jest? His lordship proposed marriage to Sarah and she wisely accepted. It means, of course, that we shall stay here at Turbans, and Lord Sebastian will provide us with an allowance. It's good news for all of us!" She fussed with the silverware flanking her plate. "Your sister has rescued us, and in the bargain she's made herself a *splendid* match! Are you aware of Lord Sebastian's ancestry, Julia? His late parents were Marquess and Marchioness of Caverleigh, as well as Earl and Countess of Trevarre. *Impeccable* lineage. The Trevarre title dates back to Tudor times, and I wager there have been Trevarres in Cornwall since King Arthur!" Polly patted Sarah's hand. "My darling child, what a coup you have achieved!"

Freddy's face was a study in confusion. "Sarah's going to marry Lord Satan? But, what about Charles?"

Next to him, Julia felt terribly cold. She looked at Sarah, who had gone white, and wanted to put her arms around her.

"Mr. Whimple was merely a pleasant diversion," Polly said. "A perfectly nice young man, but hardly in a class with Lord Sebastian Trevarre!"

"This is an outrage, Mama!" cried Julia. "What you have done is—" Something made her stop, before she poured out all her fears about his lordship's carnal appetites. What if Sarah went forward with the wedding? Perhaps there was more to it than Julia realized. Perhaps Sarah secretly cared for Lord Sebastian. She ought to learn more before voicing any more of her strong opinions. "I have lost my appetite. I am going to bed."

Julia stayed up, reading by candlelight as long as she could, waiting for Sarah to come to her. Since they'd been children, Sarah had taken her troubles to her sister, who was three years older, rather than either parent. In London, it had been easier, for they had shared a bedchamber. At Turbans, Sarah had to say that she was borrowing a book or a bit or ribbon if their mother happened to appear in the corridor when she was stealing into Julia's room.

Tonight, hours passed, and Julia began to feel sleepy. It had been an enormously trying day, after all. Deciding that the night air was turning a trifle chilly, she pushed the tall windows closed, then padded across the threadbare Persian rug and climbed into the big bed. It had been one of Cousin Archibald's great finds: a dark, heavy, Moorish piece that Julia had tried to soften with plain white bed-hangings and an embroidered coverlet.

She was leaning over to blow out the last candle when the door opened a few inches and a nightgown-clad Sarah scampered in.

"Shh!" she warned. "Mama is still walking the halls. I've been waiting for her to retire for hours! Oh, Julia, what in the world am I going to do?"

A smile broke over Julia's face. "I was afraid I'd offended you. Or, worse yet, that you actually wanted to marry Lord Satan!" Throwing back the covers, she made room for her sister to join her.

Sarah's chin was trembling and her eyes brimmed with tears as she climbed into bed and they embraced. "All I can think of is poor Charles," she confessed, gulping back tears.

"Although, in fairness, I must say that his lordship is not as terrible as you maintain. He's quite the most dangerously handsome man I've ever come near." Her eyes were like saucers. "I'd faint if he touched me, I think."

"Well, I would not!"

"Of course you wouldn't."

She felt her face turning pink. "What I mean to say is that I would never allow a wicked man like Lord Sebastian to frighten me or make me faint."

"I know that's what you meant to say."

Their eyes met and they began giggling, covering their mouths so that the sound wouldn't travel to their mother's ears. "That's better," Julia gasped at length, and patted Sarah's back.

"I wish I could stay right here forever. I feel very safe in this bed." They were both silent for a moment, then Sarah murmured, "I remember when we were children and I first began to realize that you were the one who was holding this family together. It was a very cold winter day. I think Mama and Papa had quarreled, as they so often did, and Papa didn't come home from the bookshop in the evening."

Julia nodded. "He would lose himself in books when he couldn't cope with life. Remember how he used to keep a stack at his desk in the shop and very often he would read rather than balancing the accounts or organizing the shelves? And then he would just keep reading and lose track of time."

"Yes," her sister whispered. "He didn't mean to hurt anyone, though."

"Of course not. And neither did Mama. I felt so sorry for her that day when it snowed and she stayed in bed with a sick headache, even after dinner time."

"Yes…But you just took charge. I don't think you were more than eight or nine; Freddy wasn't even born yet. You built up the fire, lit the lamps, and wrapped me in a blanket, and then you cooked for us. Cheese and some vegetable soup with a dumpling. It wasn't very good, but I thought you were simply brilliant!"

Tears burned Julia's eyes as she remembered that night and the immediate relief she'd felt when she took control. She had gone to her mother's bedside that long ago evening and called to her, but Polly had only moaned helplessly. *It's all up to me*, she'd thought, and set about doing the simple things her own parents so often neglected. In the times when they could afford servants, Julia could plainly see that their housekeeper was better at seeing to the daily essentials than either Mama or Papa, neither of whom seemed to be very well suited to coping and raising children in the real world. There were even moments when Julia felt *she* was the parent…the only thing standing between the three young children and complete chaos in their household.

"I'm still here to help you, darling," she said now to Sarah. "How can our own mother sacrifice you to that man? It's unthinkable."

"But Julia, she is trying to do the right thing for everyone concerned. She doesn't understand me, or take me seriously, the way you do. She thinks that my love for Charles is merely a girlish fancy. And of course she thinks that I ought to be honored by his lordship's attentions…"

"Our dear mama can be rather a toad-eater."

Sarah giggled and wept at the same time, pressing the pillow to her face. "What can I do? There's no way out. And of course, I know that it's worth any sacrifice to keep Turbans in our family." She peeked at her sister. "Perhaps he isn't as bad as I fear. Mama tells me that my life will be like a fairytale."

"Beauty and the Beast," Julia agreed.

"Can I tell you a secret? I'm quite terrified of marrying him…if you take my meaning. He's so strong, and cynical. What on earth does he want with me?"

"I can guess," Julia replied dryly.

"What will Charles do when he hears? Have you already guessed that we are deeply, secretly in love? He may go mad. He's terribly sensitive, you know!" Sarah sighed, then added,

"A few weeks ago, I took an evening walk in the garden and made a vow before God that I would only ever engage in the…*sacred union* with Charles."

"Sarah, for heaven's sake, please stop crying. You're getting my nightgown wet."

"What am I going to do?"

"You are going to stay right here at Turbans with Freddy and Mama, and carry on your romance with Mr. Whimple, and your life in Bath that you enjoy so much."

"How?" Sarah drew back in shock. The fluttering candle flame made magical patterns over her face. "How?"

Julia had never felt more determined. "It's quite simple, actually. I intend to marry him in your place!"

Chapter 8

The morning had been lovely, but now the puffy white clouds had assumed a threatening look, the cerulean sky had gone ash-gray, and cold raindrops spat at Sebastian's face as he strode across the Pulteney Bridge toward the Sydney Gardens.

"Why does everything in Bath have to be so—so decorous?" he muttered to Keswick, who was trotting a few steps behind. "I find it a dead bore."

"We perceive that you are referring to the carefully planned arrangements of classical buildings and gardens?"

Sebastian didn't reply because he had caught sight of a young lady beyond the bridge, who was alighting from a modest carriage. "Ah good, there's Miss Faircloth."

"Miss Sarah Faircloth?"

He stopped abruptly and turned to stare at his manservant. "Of course. Why would you imagine that I should be meeting Miss Julia Faircloth?"

"Perhaps because my lord has spent far more time with the elder Miss Faircloth than with her sister."

"You are insolent. And stop calling me that."

"My lord?"

"Exactly. When you overuse it in that fashion, I am immediately on alert." Looking around, Sebastian saw a bookshop among the shops near the end of the bridge. "Go in there and choose a book while I speak to Miss Faircloth."

Keswick blinked. "Yes, my lord."

Sebastian went on alone, emerging from the shop-lined bridge that spanned the River Avon. Just ahead was the elegant Sydney Hotel, the centerpiece of the Sydney Gardens. In front of the hotel, which resembled a country manor house, stood Miss Faircloth. Her coachman was conversing with her as Sebastian approached, allowing him to study her unobserved.

The brim of a pretty feather-trimmed blue bonnet concealed all but the delicate edges of her profile. When a sudden breeze caught the hem of her soft pale gray morning dress, it fluttered out to reveal graceful ankles and slippers of peacock-blue leather, and clung to the curve of her hip.

Sebastian was caught off-guard by a shock of arousal. He stopped, wondering at himself for being so stirred by so simple a sight. Perhaps, he reflected with an arch of one eyebrow, he was more deeply attracted to his new fiancée than he had realized.

Just then, as if feeling the heat of his gaze, she turned to face him. "Ah, good morrow, my lord."

He blinked, realizing that it was not Sarah who addressed him, but her vexing sister, Julia. The two females might look remarkably similar, but there was no mistaking Julia's crisp gaze or the very direct tone of her voice, and now he could see the sleek sable curls that peeked out under the brim of her bonnet.

"Miss Faircloth, good day. Where have you hidden your sister?"

"Sarah wasn't feeling quite the thing today, so I have come in her stead."

"To walk with me in Sydney Gardens?" he inquired coolly, fooled not at all by the radiant smile she turned up at him.

"I came because you were expecting her, and because you wrote her that you needed to know her precise Christian name before the banns can be posted for your wedding."

Noticing that the coachman appeared to be eavesdropping, Sebastian lightly grasped her elbow and led her away toward the gardens. "All right then, let us walk together, since it appears that we have matters of business to discuss." He gave the man a short nod. "You may wait for Miss Faircloth. I shall return her to your care shortly."

Julia looked up while hurrying along at his side. "My lord, once again, your manners are sorely lacking. Are you certain that you are of noble birth?"

He wanted to tighten his grip on her arm, but forced his fingers to relax. "I shall overlook your impertinence. Have you seen the labyrinth, Miss Faircloth?"

"No, although I have heard that it is twice the size of the one at Hampton Court. Would it be prudent for us to wander in a maze if we mean to have a serious conversation?"

"Prudent?" Sebastian gave a short laugh. "That is one of my least favorite words."

She surprised him by laughing herself, in a refreshingly spontaneous fashion. "I am forced to admit that I agree with you, my lord. "

"Do you indeed?" He arched a brow. They had come into a sylvan glade carpeted by butter-yellow daffodils that nodded under the darkening sky. "A shocking development!"

Julia let him guide her onward, past the bowling green. Her senses were thrumming with something that she realized was more than just the antipathy she liked to tell herself stemmed from Lord Sebastian's treatment of her father, and now her entire family. When he drew a branch back to allow her to pass, she found herself noticing the breadth of his shoulders. And again, she was struck by the strong male beauty of his ungloved hands, remembering for a tingling instant the sensation of those hands touching her the day he had kissed her at Turbans.

"Shall we sit on this bench to converse about the license?"

Julia blinked. "I beg your pardon?"

His knowing gaze was maddening in the extreme. "Are you well, Miss Faircloth?"

She looked around at the shady little grotto that was overarched by budding trees and evergreen shrubs. In the center was a whimsical stone bench. It really wasn't a bit proper for them to be alone together in such a setting, but this was a business matter, after all. "Yes, thank you, I am fine." She tilted her nose up at him and perched on the bench. "This is much better than that maze. Even with the map, we could easily become lost there, and rain threatens."

"I defer to your greater wisdom, Miss Faircloth."

There was a faintly mocking smile that played over his fine mouth, making her heart beat faster with an array of vexing feelings. Drawing off her gloves, she opened her reticule and extracted a folded sheet of parchment. "I have brought the information that you requested."

"I hardly think that you needed to write it down. How many names can your sister have besides Sarah?"

"Well, it's a bit more complicated than that, my lord." To her consternation, Julia felt hot blood rushing to her cheeks, and prayed he wouldn't notice.

"I am in suspense."

"You see, my mother is very fond of the letter *J*. So fond, in fact, that she gave all three of her children names that began with that letter." As her words poured out, she stole a glance at Sebastian and saw that one of his eyebrows had begun to arch. Sitting up straighter, she continued firmly, "It's preposterous, I know, but that is the nature of our mother. She named me 'Jillian Julia' and Sarah was christened 'Julianne Sarah.' My brother's given name is 'Julian Frederick.'"

"Fascinating."

"So you see, to avoid confusion, our relatives quickly began to refer to us by our second names." She gave a bold laugh so that he would not suspect that she was trembling inside as her lies mounted. "Julia, Sarah, and Frederick...rather than Jillian, Julianne, and Julian."

"Ah. I see." His expression was wary. "And which of these names does your sister plan to use during our wedding?"

"Why, of course, the license should read 'Julianne Faircloth,'" she replied briskly. "And the vicar would address her as 'Julianne' during the ceremony."

Sebastian stared at her. His head had begun to hurt. He watched as Julia held up a paper with the name she had just spoken written out in clear letters. "A most bizarre situation."

"Quite fitting, my lord, since you have had a hand in creating it." She looked directly at him, her gaze compelling under the blue brim of her bonnet. "I would like to ask you a question."

The pounding at his temples increased. "Proceed."

"Why do you want to marry Sarah when you barely know her, and certainly do not love her?"

"Gad, Miss Faircloth, you are brash. I will tell you only that I know that love is the least important ingredient in a marriage. In fact, it is to be avoided, for *love* only leads to misunderstandings and disillusionment." He actually had come to believe that love in any human relationship was a conduit for pain, but it was too intimate an opinion to share with Julia Faircloth. Instead, he continued coolly, "You females, I perceive, have grand notions about romance, but that is all they are: notions. Romance between two people is fine as an amusing interlude, but far too ephemeral to last a lifetime."

"You have not answered my question, my lord. Why do you insist upon marrying my sister if you have no tender feelings toward her?"

"I am in need of a wife, and I like her. She is lovely and soft and docile, which suits me. She will not fight me at every turn."

Julia looked as if she would like to strangle him. "You are shocking!"

"Have I shocked *you*, Miss Faircloth?" He laughed softly. "Perhaps I may acquit myself by adding that I have chosen Sarah because I saw that it would save your family from losing Turbans as well as your income. And she will be content as my wife, I can assure you. No doubt Sarah will come to enjoy all that London society has to offer, and will scarcely notice if her husband is not following her about like a puppy."

"Do you assume that my sister is lacking emotional depth?"

"This conversation grows tiresome and I am hungry. I should return you to your carriage."

Bright spots of color stained her pretty cheeks. "Take this, then, my lord."

When Julia thrust the paper at him, their bare fingers brushed for an instant, and Sebastian felt an unwelcome stirring in his loins. He stared at her, nostrils flaring slightly. There was a palpable heat radiating from her body, and he wanted to take her in his arms and kiss her, to open her prim gown and reveal her breasts, to hear her moan aloud…but of course, that wouldn't do, particularly now that he was betrothed to her sister.

In one smooth, powerful movement, he stood and coolly extended a hand to her. "Your servant, Miss Faircloth. And, may I add that there will be no banns posted. I shall procure a special license and the wedding will take place one week hence."

The kitchen building at Turbans was fortunately located a few steps behind the house itself, so that if Cook, who was elderly and forgetful, set something on fire, the entire estate wouldn't go up in flames. Nearby, there was a pretty kitchen garden, complete with a variety of herbs planted by Julia.

On the day before her wedding, Julia went to visit Cook. Passing through the garden, she glanced at her herbs, which were just pushing out of the ground again in the spring sunlight. What would become of all the projects she'd overseen at Turbans? What if her mother took to bed again? And who would see to it that the wild birds were fed each day?

"Ah, Miss Julia, it's a treat to have a visit from you," Cook called out. Her plump cheeks were red with the exertion of mixing the cake batter, but the results looked promising. "Leave it to you to see that everything is being done properly. What would your family do without you?"

Julia's heart sank. She made her way to the stout wooden table where Cook was pounding almonds mixed with a bit of orange flower water. Nearby, the new roasting range gleamed in the morning light, and the baking oven was heating in anticipation of the cake pans.

"You're just trying to make a plain spinster feel useful," she said lightly.

"What a lot of nonsense. You know better." Cook began grating a bit of nutmeg.

Julia sighed. It was the most difficult decision she'd ever made, choosing between her life at Turbans and a new life as Lord Sebastian's bride. She told herself that sweet Sarah might not survive the trauma of a wedding night to a man she did not love, but that she could, and then go on to make something useful of the match. It was the only logical plan. Her family would remain at Turbans, and she had the backbone to deal with a loveless marriage.

Still, whenever she thought of becoming Sebastian's wife, a pleasant sort of gooseflesh broke out all over her body. The future might be daunting, yet it was also thrilling beyond her understanding.

First there was the wedding to get through. Her plans could easily come apart. If Sebastian saw through her flimsy scheme, poor Sarah might find herself in his marriage bed after all, and there would be nothing Julia could do to save her.

"Highly unusual, having a wedding in the evening," muttered Parson Cumberstone, squinting through the shadows that filled the Turbans library.

Julia smiled. "The hour was requested by my sister, the bride," she explained. "Sarah wanted a family wedding, away from prying eyes, and we decided that she was right, given the recent passing of my father. Will you have more wine, vicar?"

"Awfully dark in here, though, don't you think?" He extended his glass. "Yes, thank you."

The library was lit by a few flickering wall sconces, a fitful blaze in the fireplace, and a branch of tapers near the window where the ceremony would take place. Outside, thick rainclouds choked the rising moon, further darkening the walnut-paneled room. "I hope you will be able to make out the marriage service, vicar."

He gave a snuffling chuckle. "I don't need to see it. I've performed so many weddings, I could recite the service in my sleep." Just then, there was a loud knock at the front door and Parson Cumberstone jumped. "I say, was that thunder?"

"No, I believe it is the groom, announcing his arrival. Will you excuse me? Do help yourself to more wine." As she hurried out into the entry hall, Julia thought that Lord Sebastian couldn't have found a better vicar to perform the ceremony. Parson Cumberstone hadn't previously met the Faircloth family and, handicapped by the dim light and too much wine, he would be aware of the vows and little else.

Flinging open the front door, she was positively beaming. "Welcome, my lord!" Spying Keswick standing behind the bridegroom's imposing figure, she added a second greeting.

"Do come in out of the wind, gentlemen. Rain is threatening, I believe."

Sebastian glanced around. "Where are your servants, Miss Faircloth?"

"They had to attend some family festivities of their own, and we rather liked the idea of keeping this gathering small and cozy. Don't you agree? My sister is very shy, I fear, and like all of us she is missing Papa. It will be easier for her if there are only a few of us present tonight." Julia had been staring at him, quite struck by the rakish picture he made in his caped greatcoat. His dark hair was windblown, and his eyes were as stormy as the rain clouds. "You seem a trifle tense, my lord..."

"Not at all!" he snapped.

"Would you care for a whiskey?"

"Perhaps. There is a bit of a chill in the air." Sebastian found a mirror and straightened his snow-white cravat. "Nothing for Keswick. He does not imbibe."

Behind his back Julia smiled at Keswick then rushed into the sitting room to pour drinks. Returning, she put the whiskey in his lordship's exceptionally attractive hand. "I think you'll be more comfortable in the library, where a fire is burning quite merrily. You and Mr. Keswick may join the vicar there. Meanwhile, I'll hurry upstairs to see if your bride-to-be is ready..."

Sebastian drank down the liquor. "I know the way, Miss Faircloth, and I'll get myself another whiskey en route. Tell your sister that she must not rush on my account."

Keswick watched him and sighed. When Julia had disappeared up the stairway, he muttered, "We wonder if we are napping and having a very bizarre dream, my lord! Whatever possessed you to propose marriage to Miss Sarah Faircloth?"

Walking off in search of the whiskey, Sebastian replied cynically, "I don't remember. It must have been divine inspiration."

"Thank heavens you've come, Julia," Polly Faircloth cried as she met her in the upstairs corridor. "Your sister won't put on her wedding dress, and she won't come out of *your* bedroom!"

"Let me have a word with her."

"I've talked myself blue in the face, but she won't listen!"

"Mama, please!" Julia's nerves were worn to a frazzle as she hurried into the room where Sarah was sitting in a corner, reading from a stack of Charles Whimple's love poems. "I thought I asked you to pretend to Mama that you were going along with this charade."

"I can't. I've never been able to deceive her the way you can."

"Those are hardly the words I would have chosen, but I won't waste time arguing semantics. What if Mama tells Lord Satan?"

Suddenly the door burst open and Polly entered, her face drained of blood. "What is it? What mustn't I tell Lord Sebastian?" Her expression was anguished as she pointed at her elder daughter. "Julia Faircloth, why must you always put your fingers into everything and spoil it? Why couldn't you simply let your sister do this one thing for me in peace?"

With that, Sarah burst into copious tears. "Oh, Mama, how can you say it? If I'm forced to marry anyone but my beloved Charles, I shall wither away and *die*!"

Julia tucked her sister into the big four-poster bed, bade her rest, and led her mother to the window. One side was cracked to admit a storm-scented breeze. "We haven't time to discuss this situation, Mama. You must do as I tell you—"

"I will not!"

"Kindly listen! The wedding will proceed, and you will keep Turbans. Does that cheer you?"

"Why…yes! But, my dear, how can it be?"

"Simply enough. I shall take Sarah's place."

"Madness!" Polly wailed.

"Sit down. It's simple enough, Mama. She is in love with Mr. Whimple, and I could not allow her to be sacrificed when there is a much more reasonable solution. I'm strong enough to bear this match, don't you see?" She lowered her voice to a whisper. "The fine points of marriage, at the hands of Lord Satan, would be devastating to Sarah, but I shall endure."

Polly was staring at her through narrowed eyes. "He's quite splendid, or hadn't you noticed? The two of you talk as if Lord Sebastian were some sort of wild boar!"

"I take your point, Mama, but you must concede that he is fearsome. Hardly Sarah's cup of tea."

"On my honor, I cannot take part in so great a deception!"

"Don't be nonsensical. Why should we suffer pangs of conscience about tricking his lordship when it was he who tricked poor Papa and caused him to wager Turbans? It is Lord Satan's fault that we have lost everything, including dear Papa, and now he means to steal Sarah's virtue as well!" Warming to her speech, Julia paced to and fro, wagging her forefinger. "Why shouldn't we thwart him?"

From under the covers on the bed, Sarah called weakly, "I believe that Julia has feelings for Lord Sebastian, Mama."

"So does a murderess before she raises her dagger, child!"

"Oh, for heaven's sake!" Julia cried. "Can we please get on with it? Mama, do go downstairs and inform the vicar and his lordship that I have suffered an attack of dyspepsia. Then, say that Sarah will come down to the library for the wedding in just a few minutes." She grinned as a new plan occurred to her. "Have Freddy come for me. I'll enter on his arm."

"And just how will we make his lordship believe you are Sarah? You two may resemble each other, but not enough to fool him!"

Julia laughed. "Oh, I have my ways, and I'm aware that you have it in you to spin a tale or two yourself if the need arises." She gave her wide-eyed mother an encouraging little shake. "Fortunately, Lord Sebastian believes that his bride is very timid, especially tonight. Now then, do go downstairs, Mama, and give everyone another drink. Perhaps by the time I glide into the library, they won't care what I look like!"

Chapter 9

"This is the oddest damned wedding I've ever encountered," Sebastian whispered, brows lowering.

"We strongly agree, my lord," said Keswick. "And we find ourselves thinking of your departed parents. One can only imagine what Lord Caverleigh would have to say."

The thought of his father, who had never had anything good to say to him, gave him a cold pain in the region of his heart. "You may keep those thoughts to yourself. I don't give a damn what his lordship would have thought, and you know bloody well that my mother would have been crushed, so why mention her?"

"Yes, my lord," Keswick replied. "We regret having spoken so hastily."

Sebastian tossed back his whiskey and felt a bit better. He surveyed the shadowy library. The rain had started outside in earnest, and the wind sent budding branches rattling against the windowpanes. "Devil take it, I can scarcely locate the rim of my glass in this gloom!"

Suddenly, Polly Faircloth was beside him. "Did I hear you remark that your glass is empty, my lord? May I fill it for you?"

"Ah, Mrs. Faircloth, I fear that if I have another whiskey, I might embarrass my bride. And, speaking of the beauteous Miss Faircloth…where is she?"

She went white as a ghost and her eyes flicked all around the room. "Your bride will be here at any moment, my lord! She is terribly—"

"*Shy,*" he put in, with a decided edge to his voice. "Yes, so I have been told. But, I am as gentle as a lamb. Will you not tell her so, and encourage her to make haste?"

"Gentle? As a lamb?" Polly began to titter nervously just as a figure wearing a dove gray round gown and a large bonnet appeared in the doorway. "Oh, my, there is my dear—Sarah!" She clapped her hands. "Places, everyone!"

Latecomer William Bradstreet, Esq. rose from a corner chair and went to offer the bride his arm. Parson Cumberstone regretfully left his fourth goblet of wine and stood in front of the guttering candles. Gathering nearby were Keswick, Polly, and young Freddy.

Sebastian narrowed his eyes. "For God's sake," he muttered under his breath. Sarah's rose-tinted bonnet featured bows, feathers, ruffles, and a deep piece of netting across the huge brim that partially obscured her face. And where was Julia? Leaning toward Polly, he whispered, "Should we not wait for your elder daughter?"

Her cheeks flamed. "She has suffered an attack of dyspepsia."

"Indeed?" This news gave him pause, but just then the vicar sent him a bleary yet stern glance. Sebastian sighed deeply, resigning himself to the entire dreamlike scene. After all, it was his own doing.

"Dearly beloved..." the vicar intoned, his prayer book upside-down. "We are gathered here this morn—that is, *evening*...."

Sebastian felt oddly peaceful as he held Sarah's gloved hand. There was something about the sensation of her slim fingers in his that was comforting, even familiar, to him, and he was just foxed enough to take it as a favorable sign. The service passed in a haze. When it ended, and he attempted to lift the netting on his bride's bonnet, she dipped her head and shied away into the protective arms of William Bradstreet.

"Please, my lord," came her meek whisper. "Not yet."

Polly was beside him, weepy and overwrought. "Such an honor, if only my dear husband could be with us! To think that one of our own girls is now nobility, never have I dared dream!"

"The honor is mine," he muttered. "But will you not speak to your daughter and implore her to remove that bonnet? There really is no reason for her to conceal herself from me. Confound it, one might imagine she's afraid of me!"

"My dear Lord Sebastian, my *son*, I must beg that you be patient and gentle with my little girl." Then, with a conspiratorial wink, Polly drew him off to one side. "I must confide that she is hiding her face for an additional reason, other than her aforementioned shy nature."

His temper flaring, Sebastian took the whiskey that someone put into his hand and ground out, "Confide away, then."

"My daughter has…a *spot*." Her own face was beet-red as she pointed to her nose. "Right there on the very tip, I must confess. Now, to a man of the world like your lordship, that may seem a trifling matter, but to a timid girl like Sarah, whose only confidence is her great beauty and perfect skin, such a flaw is shattering! She nearly cried off completely. 'Twas Julia who convinced her to wear the bonnet, with the netting, and to trust your lordship to be gentle and considerate…"

He held up a hand, unable to bear another word. "What does she expect to do, keep that thing on all night?"

"How bold you are, my lord!" Polly pretended to swoon. "No, of course not. However, Julia did mention, just before falling ill, that perhaps we might persuade you not to light the candles in your marriage chamber, so that when Sarah faces you for the first time with her spot revealed, she may imagine that you don't notice…"

"Are you certain this is not someone's notion of a jest? Your highly creative daughter, Julia's, perhaps?"

She went from red to scarlet. "Why, certainly not!"

Sebastian wanted to glare accusingly at Keswick, but remembered then that the manservant hadn't agreed with any part of this wedding plan. Instead, he walked back to his new bride and offered his arm. "The hour is late, my lady, and I understand that you are in no humor for a celebration. Shall we be on our way?"

"To—where?" she peeped.

"Any place." Sebastian's mood was darker than the sky. "Any cursed place at all. Are you brave enough to take your husband's arm?"

It was nearly midnight, and sinister-looking clouds still blanketed the moon, when Lord Sebastian's fine traveling coach rumbled into the yard of the Goat in Boots Inn. Rains had been chasing the small party from the moment they'd left Bath, and the two men on horseback were now being pelted regularly by stinging droplets. Out of patience, the bridegroom had selected the Goat in Boots the moment he glimpsed its swaying sign.

"I like this hostelry's name," he told Keswick as the two of them dismounted and turned the reins of their horses over to a water boy. Then, pointing toward the wooden sign, Sebastian laughed at the rendering of a goat walking on his hind legs, clad in a Cavalier's ruffled costume and great bucket-topped boots. "Does he resemble me?"

Keswick shook his head. "We do not understand how you may jest recklessly, when your entire life may be ruined. And what of that meek little flower in the coach? What will become of her?"

"Oh, for God's sake. People regularly marry for logical, rather than romantic reasons. I certainly didn't extract her vows at pistol-point." He scowled. "It's late, and I am getting wet. I'll hire our rooms and you may escort my bride to her marriage chamber and bid her await me."

"My lord—"

"Can you not simply obey me, without argument?"

With a loud sigh, the manservant bowed and scurried off toward the coach.

Julia noticed, even in the dim light, that Keswick was looking at her oddly. Surely the reason was the hideous bonnet she wore, rather than suspicion of her true identity. Who in his right mind would suspect such an outrageous plot?

It was even beginning to seem mad to her. Now, standing in this low-ceilinged room, while rain and wind lashed at the ancient windowpanes, Julia wondered what had possessed her.

"My lady," Keswick said, bowing, "we suggest that you rest until the servants arrive with food, and other…comforts. If there is anything at all that you require, you need only ask a kitchen maid."

And then he was gone. No sooner had she collapsed on the lumpy bed and pulled off the large, ugly bonnet, than a knock came at the door. Her heart raced, though of course she would have to face Sebastian eventually. The thought of how he might react was suddenly terrifying.

"Who is it?"

"'Tis only us wit' yer supper, yer ladyship."

She stood behind the door while two maids bustled in and out with trays of wine, fresh bread, kidney pie, raisin pudding, and other assorted delicacies. They left amid promises to return momentarily with a bath for her.

A half hour later, Julia was sweetly scented and rosy from her bath and the two glasses of wine she'd consumed. While drying off, she looked at the thin batiste nightgown that had been laid across the bed. Where, she wondered, had it come from? Had her mother put it in her trunk?

Lulled by exhaustion and the wine, Julia sat on the edge of the bed and combed her long, curls. Perhaps he'd fallen asleep in his own rooms. That notion lifted her spirits. Perhaps he had no intention of ravishing her! After all, she was supposed to be Sarah, pitifully shy—

A sudden rapping at the door nearly sent her through the beamed ceiling. "Wh—who is it?"

She heard deep male laughter, then, "Your husband, of course. I wish to come in."

Julia feared that she might expire right then, from terror. Fumbling, she blew out the lamps and candles, then tugged the bed-hangings closed as if to hide from him. "Wait—" she gasped. When she had tucked the covers up to her chin and turned away from his side of the bed, she called, "You may enter."

In the corridor, Sebastian was surprised to find the door unlatched, and even more surprised to discover that his marriage chamber was completely drenched in darkness except for an intermittent flicker from the fireplace.

"Sarah, my dear, are you in there?"

"Mm-hmm," came her faint reply.

"Asleep so soon?"

"Mm-hmm."

"Did I not see the maids returning with your empty bath mere minutes ago?" This time, she made no response. Frowning, he pulled off his riding clothes, poured water into a basin, and washed by the light of a very weak moonbeam. His head hurt. Too much whiskey at Turbans, and too much strong wine in the taproom downstairs. It was the oddest night in his memory. "Are you well, my dear?"

"Quite…sleepy," she whispered.

"We'll share a glass of wine, then. That should revive you."

Sebastian knew that he should make this experience a

slow, exquisite awakening for his timid bride, but it had been a trying day and he was ready for it to end. If he had feelings for Sarah Faircloth, it would be easier, but after all that was the very reason he'd chosen her. He didn't want to feel anything, particularly for his *wife*!

His eyes were adjusting to the dim light, and he found the bed without crashing into any heavy furniture. Drawing back the rather musty draperies, Sebastian climbed into bed, naked. His bride was huddled far away, her face hidden.

"My sweet, will you not show yourself to me? Have a sip of wine; it will ease your mind." She didn't stir, and his patience waned. "I know that you imagine you aren't perfect, but I am your husband, and you must trust me to look beyond such trivial matters. You're a beautiful woman, Sarah. The tiny flaws that come and go in daily life matter not to me."

Julia curled into a ball and was utterly still. Her heart, however, had begun to pound again, louder to her own ears than the thunder outside. She understood how a fox felt when cornered at last by a pack of ravening hounds.

His hand closed around her shoulder; his voice hardened. "You must face me. Taste the wine, my dear. Talk to me." He paused, then added, "This is our wedding night, you know."

She pressed her lips together, stubbornly, but her palms were moist and her heart pounded furiously. The moment of truth had arrived.

"All right," she managed, "have it your way. Here I am." And, with one lithe movement, she turned and sat up to look into his stunned eyes.

"I—I knew I'd drunk too much—"

She watched as he blinked, while the glass he held sloshed wine onto the coverlet. "Sebastian—"

"Don't speak until I get a candle. My eyes are playing tricks on me, or perhaps it's the wine our innkeeper served to poor fools like me." He yanked on breeches and took a candle to the fireplace, where only a sputtering flame survived. Returning to the bed, Sebastian climbed in with candlestick in hand. He held it close to Julia's face, and this time she did not shrink away, but met his horrified gaze with frank audacity. "Devil take it," he cursed.

"It's too late for that."

"What the bloody hell are you doing here? Where is your sister?" His expression revealed a range of strong emotions. "You've hidden her, haven't you? I expect you think Sarah couldn't survive the trauma of my marriage bed, and so you've decided to sacrifice yourself in her place." Leaning closer, he grasped her soft upper arm and brought her face close to his. "Confess, Miss Faircloth, and show me your sister's hiding place."

"Sarah is at Turbans, of course, where she belongs. No doubt she is enjoying a visit from Charles Whimple, her true love, and he is reciting the latest poem he's written in her honor." Julia discovered that she was shockingly stirred by the candlelit nearness of her new husband. He exuded a raw energy that was exciting, and his wide, lean-muscled chest aroused her curiosity. Even his breath, smelling faintly of tobacco and wine, appealed to her.

"What the devil are you saying?" he demanded. "Miss Faircloth, I am in no mood for this foolishness. Bring me my wife, and leave us."

"I am your wife, Sebastian." The sight of his darkening countenance propelled her onward. "You see, I'll warrant, that it's just as you have said. I knew Sarah couldn't bear it; not only this night, but the entire marriage. You simply wouldn't have suited, and then there is Mr. Whimple."

"Stop saying that. I will not be bested by a cursed, sallow-faced poet named *Whimple*!" he shouted.

"In any event, Sarah wanted to do the right thing. We all did, and of course we wanted to keep Turbans—"

"You can't be saying that it was *you* wearing that deuced bonnet!"

"Yes, that's right," she said softly. "It was never anyone's intention to make you appear foolish. There just didn't seem to be any other way."

Setting the candlestick back on the washstand, Sebastian raked both hands through his thick black hair. "I shouldn't have drunk so much whiskey. My wits were dulled."

"If you'd been happier about the wedding, you wouldn't have needed the whiskey. You didn't really want it any more than Sarah did."

"Why'd she accept then?"

"Obligation, to the family."

"As if I'm some sort of deformed misfit? That's hardly the impression I've gotten from countless other women—"

"You're simply not Sarah's cup of tea. For heaven's sake, my lord, don't take offense. You know as well as she that the two of you didn't suit. And we both know that's precisely why you chose her." Julia stared hard at him in the dim golden light. "You didn't want a wife you might fall in love with, or who might love you. That would have been far too messy and unpredictable."

He couldn't look at her. In an instant, Sebastian was out of bed again, pacing. "I was perfectly kind to her. What was it about me that repelled her so?"

"I wouldn't choose that word. Let us say that Sarah was frightened of you."

"That's the most ludicrous thing you've said yet. I always behaved as a gentleman toward your sister."

"Perhaps she saw past that, to the glitter in your eyes."

That brought him back, hands braced on the mattress as he glared at Julia. "If you're trying to make me angry, it won't work."

"Why would I want to do that?"

"Why indeed?" His hand shot out and caught her wrist. "So, you took Sarah's place to save her from marrying a terrifying beast—"

"And because I felt that the entire scheme was ethically wrong."

"You're a fine one to talk of ethics!" Sebastian blazed. "I surmise that *you* are not frightened of me—are you? No, of course not. You've shouted and shaken your fist at me more times than I can count." A wicked smile touched his mouth. "Not quite the sort of woman I had in mind for my wife, but you do have other more agreeable qualities."

Her face burned as his bold gaze surveyed her thinly clad body. "I—I—"

In an instant, he was kneeling before her, and his muscular brown arms were drawing her into his embrace. "You're not frightened of me," he repeated, his breath warm against her ear. "I'll wager that, while you were plotting to hoax me on my wedding day, you were also dreaming about this moment. Hmm?"

She could scarcely breathe, but couldn't let him know that. Instead, somehow, she made her voice as determined as his. "My lord and husband, I can assure you that I have had more immediate concerns than this moment. And, I can further assure you that I will not be forced, if that is your intention."

"Don't say that you will play me false a second time in one day, Julia. There are remedies for that, and don't think I'm not pondering them even now."

She knew what he meant: the marriage might still be annulled, and her family turned out of Turbans without a shilling. "Kindly let me finish. I was going to add that, while I won't be taken by force, neither shall I cower from you in the corner. If you will behave decently, I will keep my part of this bargain."

"Decently?" His low laughter echoed in the dark room. "My lady wife, how little you know of me."

And as he shifted so that they were lying down and began to kiss her with slow, hot lips, Julia felt a hard part of him pressing intimately against her inner thigh. There was no turning back, she realized. To her further shock, he lifted her nightgown and fit his big hand to the curve of her bare leg.

"My lord—" she gasped.

Sebastian laughed softly. His hand slid along the length of her leg, then caressed her hip and boldly cupped her buttock. "Lovely," he whispered.

"I believe," Julia managed to utter, "that you ought not take such unthinkable liberties with my person."

"You are in jest, madam!" Drawing back, he stared at her in the candlelight, both brows arched in frank amusement. "No, I see that you are not. But, what can you mean by 'unthinkable liberties?' From what, did you imagine, were you saving your sister?"

"But surely—what you are doing—touching me in that manner, is beyond the bounds of common decency."

"We're married, Julia. Decency is not an issue."

"But, respectable people could not possibly—"

"I can assure you, they do. And if they do not, they wish that they were!" He was laughing again, and realized that he felt a twinge of delighted affection for her.

Julia couldn't breathe as he moved over her, restraining her head with a palm on either cheek. It came to her that he was exerting his dominance over her, and on a primitive level, she was thrilled. He kissed her deeply until she surrendered, then his lips trailed over her throat and shoulders until she heard her own moans. Finally he opened her nightgown to claim her swelling breasts.

"Oh!" she cried. "I do not think—"

"Shh," he commanded.

Julia let him touch her with feather-light fingertips and felt a tingling heat spread from her breasts directly to the place between her legs. When she began to tremble, he took one of her puckered nipples into his warm mouth and suckled until her hips moved involuntarily against the waiting heel of his hand.

"Please," she begged, "you're frightening me."

"I don't believe you." When she glanced up at him, Sebastian gave her a roguish grin and she blushed. "You'll learn to like the marriage bed, or there'll be no marriage, my lady."

Secretly, Julia adored the sensation of his hard male chest on top of her, and his tongue exploring inside her mouth, and his hands searching out places on her body she'd never understood before. When his fingers deftly stole between her legs, caressing until he'd drawn out the most maddeningly pleasurable sensations, she opened her thighs to him, helpless to stop herself from growing wetter by the moment.

"Touch me, Julia."

She obeyed, her heart racing ever faster. His manhood was big and unyielding in her delicate hand, not at all the way she imagined it would be. And it was warm, seeming to pulse with his blood. Her mother and her friends had spoken of unpleasant obligation. Was this what they meant? No doubt Sebastian was wickeder than other men, and yet she was hungry for more.

He made a laughing-groaning sound, then quirked his mouth in a way that made him look sinfully appealing. "You're ready then…to proceed?"

"Quite, my lord."

"How brave you sound. This shouldn't be quite as terrible as the rack."

When he slowly entered her, Julia felt a burning mixture of pain and pleasure, and she closed her eyes so that he would not see the tears. His hands fit themselves to her bare bottom, and he pushed past her maidenhood. She bit her bottom lip, determined not to let him see her discomfort.

"Julia…are you all right?"

"Yes."

"Liar."

When Sebastian began to kiss her, slowly, she melted into him, lifting her hips to accept his thrusts. At length, he pushed in to the hilt and made a low animal sound. Julia clung to his back as his breathing slowly returned to normal, feeling as if she had gained entrance to a secret, rather forbidden world.

"Mmm." He withdrew from her and lay back against the pillows with a sigh.

Within a few moments, his changed breathing told her that he was asleep. She lay in the hard-muscled curve of his arm until she was certain that he would not awaken, and then she crept out of bed to wash the blood from between her thighs. She would have liked to put her nightgown back on, but saw that he was lying on top of it.

Returning to the bed, Julia stared at her slumbering husband. Sebastian was the rugged, black-haired, rakish hero of her dreams; better, in fact, than her simple maiden's imagination could conjure. The sight of him, sprawled magnificently naked amidst bedclothes faintly streaked with her virgin blood, stirred the deepest corners of her soul.

Yet, this was no dream, and he was no hero. Sebastian had not meant to marry her, nor did he love her, and he was a hard, combative man. These circumstances were hardly the makings of a fairytale.

With a sigh, Julia extinguished the candle flame and climbed back into the big bed. Rain was rattling the leaded windowpanes, and Sebastian's breathing was a low growling sound. How fiercely beautiful he was in the silver-blue shadows! She felt a stab of longing to be cradled in her husband's arms, to share intimate words of affection with him.

To her surprise, he reached out for her, caught her by the waist, and drew her against him. Julia knew that he was asleep, and doubtless had no idea who he held, but the warmth of his strong body was reassuring all the same. She fit her hand around his forearm and surrendered to sleep.

Chapter 10

Julia dreamed that her mother had taken to her bed again, and Sarah was delivering the news over a breakfast of porridge. Near tears, Sarah worried aloud about the future, and whether she would ever be able to marry the impoverished Charles Whimple. Freddy was waiting to show Julia his Greek lessons, and Cook was marching up from the kitchen building with a new market list in her reddened hand. Julia couldn't decide whose needs should be seen to first. Even before she opened her eyes to the morning light, she felt pressured.

A moment passed as she lay on her side, taking in her surroundings. By daylight, the bedchamber at the Goat in Boots was shabbier than it had seemed last night. A thin layer of dust covered the worn pieces of furniture, and the floor sloped northward. Her thin pillow held a trace of Sebastian's scent, and that realization brought her fully awake.

Sebastian! Dear God, they were truly married, and the ache between her thighs reminded her of the rest. A hot flush spread up Julia's face. Looking over, she found that the only reminder of his presence in their marriage bed was a dent in his pillow.

Julia's thoughts bumped against one another as she considered her new married status while wondering suddenly if her family at Turbans could cope without her. Already, she could imagine a range of situations that would require her attention that very morning, for she imagined her family to be quite helpless without her.

And where was her new husband? How did he feel by the light of day?

She was about to climb out of bed and dress when the door swung open and Sebastian strode in carrying a breakfast tray.

"Oh!" exclaimed Julia. "How kind of you!"

"Not at all," came his sardonic reply. Lines etched his face, his cravat was half-knotted, and his hair was wind-tossed. "Keswick is finishing our travel preparations, and I am out of patience. I brought your breakfast to speed you along."

Realizing that she was still without a nightgown, Julia tried to fasten the sheet under her arms as she sat up to accept the tray. When one pink nipple peeked out for an instant, she blushed.

"Think nothing of it," he advised. "After last night, I imagine that I am more intimately acquainted with your breasts than you are."

Julia sipped her chocolate. "I was brought up to believe that there are subjects one does not discuss."

"Indeed? I have been under the distinct impression that you are quite fearless, my lady. It's a relief to hear otherwise." He paused, waiting until she finally looked up to meet his bloodshot gaze. "I have something to say, and since I feel like the devil himself, I should like to dispense with this banter."

"I am listening, my lord."

"As I explained to you in Sydney Gardens, I chose your sister to be my bride because I wanted an attractive, obedient wife who would not make demands on me. Sarah Faircloth seemed an ideal candidate, and I was pleased to be able to help your family—"

"Control us, you should say!"

"Let me finish," he ground out, his jaw hardening. "Do you have any idea how angry I am to be tricked into marrying you instead of Sarah? Who are you to accuse *me* of trying to control this situation?"

"I have already explained that I was thinking of my sister's needs, not yours, my lord!"

"How noble you are." Sarcasm dripped from his voice as he sat down facing her on the edge of the bed and helped himself to one of her raisin buns. "Now then, about the future. It seems that I shall have to make the best of this coil you've fashioned for me, since I lost my head last night. The marriage is consummated, so even if I were to argue that I'd meant to marry the *other* Miss Faircloth, it's too late."

Julia's eyes burned as she watched him rise and restlessly pace across the room, the muscles of his thighs flexing under his snug doeskin riding breeches. Why should his rudeness make her heart ache so?

"I hadn't bargained on a wife as thorny as you are," Sebastian said.

"Do you mean to insult me, or is it happening completely by chance?"

He whirled around and pointed at her. "I am angry, and I have every right to be! I am *married* to you, madam. Your scheming has altered the entire course of my life!"

She swallowed, realizing that he had a point. "Perhaps you have a right to feel angry, but you needn't behave as if marriage to me is a fate worse than death."

"I want to be clear that I do not intend to spend my future days sparring with you, or getting you out of scrapes, and I certainly will not be transformed into a romantic husband. If you've been harboring any secret hopes of *that*—"

"Say no more. I take your meaning, my lord." She drew a deep breath, and felt herself trembling. "In fact, we are in agreement. I do not hunger for your attentions. I am an independent woman, and as I have explained, I married you to save Sarah from—"

"Don't go on. We have already suffered together through the horrors from which you saved Sarah. I'll leave you now to dress." His demeanor was cool and remote. "May we expect you downstairs in half an hour?"

Julia managed a stiff nod, staring into her cup of chocolate until she heard the door close.

No sooner had the coach route brought them to the outskirts of London, than all of Julia's old feelings about the city came bubbling back to the surface. She'd spent most of her life in London, yet remained ambivalent. There was too much rudeness, filth, and vice. If one's eyes were opened to it, degradation was everywhere. The rich needn't look further than their downtrodden staffs of servants, many of whom trudged miles each day to work along roads that were dust-choked in summer and knotted with mud and ice in winter.

Spring was relatively pleasant, and as the coach rolled down fashionable Park Lane under a veil of plum-hued twilight, Julia thought it might be possible to enjoy living in London as a married noblewoman. Accompanied by her husband or a female companion, she could amuse herself with forays to dressmakers and milliners, pleasure gardens, the theatre, print sellers, and all manner of assemblies and drawing room soirées.

Could such a life possibly make her happy?

As the coach turned into Grosvenor Square, Julia watched a nearby lamplighter climb his ladder to illuminate a street lamp. They drew up outside a four-story, colonnaded townhouse built of mellow stone and Sebastian brought his horse alongside the coach and dismounted. He bade her wait with Keswick, then approached the entrance.

Standing before the door, Sebastian wondered if it was really a good idea to bring Julia to Caverleigh House. Granted, George had fled to Italy and Isabella was away at school, but still, it made him uncomfortable to think of her seeing all his parents' possessions, the family portraits, the servants who had known him since he was christened…

He lifted the massive lion's mask knocker and waited. A familiar, labored step sounded in the entrance hall before the door swung open to reveal Roderick, the butler.

"Lord Sebastian!" The tiny man seemed to have been old all his life, and he rarely betrayed even a trace of emotion, but the sight of Sebastian seemed to have a rousing effect. "I am surprised to see you."

"Are you? Someone had to take matters in hand, Roderick, and I've come to do just that. I know that my brother is not in residence, but I'll need rooms for a few days. I regret that I couldn't give you and Mrs. Butter more notice."

Blood rushed to the wizened butler's face. "You have not heard, then, my lord?"

Sebastian suddenly felt a chill. "Heard? I have heard a great many unpleasant reports since the death of my parents, but none that would affect my request to stay in our family home. Kindly enlighten me."

Roderick began to perspire. "Before traveling to Italy, his lordship, um…sold Caverleigh House. The new owners were kind enough to keep us on."

"Sold? New—*owners?*" It was almost more than he could take in. "God's death, how can this be?"

Just then a tall, dark man came out of the study and walked toward them. His clothing was impeccably tailored, his top boots were burnished, and his skillfully tied cravat was white as snow. As he drew closer, Sebastian realized that he was older than he had first appeared to be, for there were silver strands in his black hair, and rakish lines around his gleaming gray eyes.

"*Bon soir*, Lord Sebastian," the stranger greeted him.

Glimpsing the thin white scar that traced the man's jaw, and hearing his slight French accent, Sebastian knew a flash of recognition. "Ah, it's Captain Raveneau, is it not? I haven't seen you for years, sir."

André Raveneau nodded and extended his hand. "I believe the last time we met, you were still in school. Won't you come in? Can I get you a drink?"

"Do you mean to tell me that *you* are the new owner of Caverleigh House?"

"I am. I felt it was better that I, as a friend of your family, help your brother out of his predicament than some stranger who would have no regard for your home."

Dazed, Sebastian took a step backward. "Clearly, I shall have to accept your offer of a drink so that we may converse at greater length. However, a more pressing matter is finding lodgings for the night. I am newly married and my wife waits in the coach."

Before Raveneau could reply, a petite and lovely woman with an upswept cloud of red-gold curls appeared in the entry hall. She immediately hurried toward Sebastian and reached for his hand.

"Do you remember me, my lord? I am Devon Raveneau. My husband is about to declare that you must stay here, with us. This is still your home. Bring your new wife to me and I shall see that she is settled comfortably."

Julia perched on the edge of a chair in a gracefully appointed sitting room, near a tall window overlooking Grosvenor Square. As darkness settled outside, Devon Raveneau lit lamps and directed the servants who brought fine linens and a fresh water-jug for the washstand.

"You must be very tired," she said, her accent American. "What can we get you? Dinner will be served in two hours, but in the meantime, you must have sustenance!" Before Julia could reply, Devon turned to one of the housemaids. "Francis, will you please bring some refreshments up for her ladyship? And, let's give her a choice between tea and wine, shall we?"

Julia thought she must be dreaming. No sooner had Sebastian brought her indoors and offered a rather confusing explanation about his brother selling Caverleigh House to some friends, than Devon had appeared and whisked her away. She had no idea what had become of her husband.

"Are you wondering about Lord Sebastian? I believe he went off with my husband. I've given you this lovely suite; the bedroom is on the other side of that dressing room." She pointed to an arched doorway. "Would you care to lie down and rest?"

Julia met her hostess's candid blue eyes. "I am quite fatigued, but I don't think I want to be alone."

Just then, a servant appeared with a tray laid out for two, and set it on a pretty Pembroke table near Julia. Devon drew another chair over and sat down, nodding. "Will you have tea or wine?"

"Perhaps a small glass of wine…"

"And I will join you!" Beaming, she proffered a delicate goblet. "My husband is French, you know, and we have excellent wine. Let's share a toast to our new friendship."

Julia gratefully raised her glass and sipped. Quickly, the wine and the warm manner of her hostess put her at ease. "Have you known Sebastian for a long time?"

"Yes, a dozen years, at least. We first met when he was at Eton, when Andre and I were newly married and we came to London after America's War for Independence. Even now, we live in Connecticut most of the year and are only in England for a few weeks at a time. As a consequence, I have only ever known Lord Sebastian in passing. Our former home was across the square, and we occasionally encountered Lady Caverleigh and her children." Devon paused, sipped her wine and gazed out the window for a moment. "My husband told me that he and the marchioness had known each other in France, when they were much younger."

"How interesting. Was she French?"

"No, I don't believe so. As I understood it, Charlotte came from Cornwall, which of course is just across the Channel from Brittany. She visited with her family, and I believe that is how she came to know André. She was a lovely woman; such a tragic death."

"It was a carriage accident?"

"Yes. Lord and Lady Caverleigh were in Devon, visiting Isabella, and I believe that his lordship was driving too near a seaside cliff. He was a notorious whip and, I fear, rather bad-tempered. Thank God the child was not with them."

Julia wondered if the wine had fuddled her memory. "Isabella? I'm afraid I don't know who that is."

"Really?" After a moment of clear surprise, Devon smiled. "I suppose Sebastian must have swept you off your feet. He seems just the type to be mysterious." She patted the new bride's hand. "Isabella is his *sister.* So sad for her, losing her parents, but of course she didn't spend much time at home."

"But—why not? How old is she?"

"About fourteen, as I recall. It seems that Charlotte had her late in life, when Sebastian was at Eton, and she wasn't prepared to raise another child. Isabella attends an academy for girls in Devon."

"Away from family? That's very sad, I think."

"I agree with you," Devon said, nodding. "All my children are here with us, but as you know, such arrangements are quite common in England." She paused. "She was having rather an awkward time of it when we saw her last. Perhaps, now that her brother has married, her situation will be a bit less lonely."

Julia took a bite of plain cake with lemon curd so that she might think for a moment. Sebastian had a younger sister, who was now an orphan! She did sums backward and forward, realizing that he must be about thirty years old, which was younger than she'd guessed from the lines on his rakish face.

Just then, there was a timid knock at the door. "Mama?"

Laughing, Devon called, "Come in, sweetheart!"

Slowly, the latch turned and a toddler appeared, clad in a miniature muslin round gown with a pink sash that matched her cheeks. Strawberry-gold curls covered her head, bouncing as she hurried across the room.

Devon lifted her onto her lap and kissed her. "Lindsay, this is our guest, Lady—"

"Julia. Please call me Julia."

Lindsay Raveneau regarded the stranger with somber gray eyes. "H'lo."

"This is our baby," Devon explained. "We also have a daughter, Mouette, who is sixteen years old, and believes that she is a woman. Our handsome son, Nathan, is eleven. You'll meet them when we dine tonight."

"I *free*," Lindsay announced, holding up three fingers.

"A little lady, indeed!" Julia exclaimed.

"I think I hear the men," said Devon. "I'll leave you now to rest and prepare for dinner. We'll have more time to talk tomorrow. Perhaps we can go shopping while Lord Sebastian sees his solicitor." Standing, she lifted her daughter in her arms and tossed Julia a mischievous smile. "I want to hear more about the woman who brought this notorious bachelor to heel!"

Sebastian noticed that, after Keswick had taken his coat, the manservant continued to stand a bit too close. Clearly, something was on his mind.

"What are you looking at?" Sebastian asked as he tugged at the crisp folds of his cravat. He didn't care for the cross note he heard in his own voice, but seemed powerless to repress it.

"We are wondering if we might assist you with your boots."

"The devil you are. There's something you are itching to say to me."

Just then, there was a tap at the dressing room door and Julia entered. He wasn't sure why the sight of his new wife annoyed him so, but it seemed to have something to do with the growing sense that he had lost all control of his life.

"Ah, hello. You must be very tired. Perhaps you'd like to rest until dinner." He gestured toward the massive four-poster, wondering again why Devon Raveneau had seen fit to push them together into one bedroom when he knew perfectly well that Caverleigh House was filled with larger suites of rooms. Turning to Keswick, he said, "You may leave us. I am quite capable of managing my own boots."

"As you wish, my lord, but first I must organize your belongings." Keswick glanced sympathetically toward Julia. "My lady, I understand that a lady's maid is being assigned to assist you. She should be here shortly."

"Thank you, Keswick. You are kind to think of me."

Sebastian wondered if this was some sort of backhanded set-down aimed in his direction. He looked directly at her and she calmly returned his gaze, her back straight and her chin slightly raised. He wished she would lie down on the bed and take a long nap so that he could continue with his normal life—not that anything about this situation was the least bit normal!

Following Keswick into the candlelit dressing room, Sebastian discovered that his trunk was open next to Julia's portmanteau. It was a disquieting sight, symbolizing both the loss of his personal space and enforced intimacy with a woman he scarcely knew.

"My lord," came Keswick's weighted whisper, "we observe that, once again, you are scowling."

"Can you blame me?"

"She is your wife, my lord. No amount of your ill humor can alter that fact." With that, the little man turned away and began to unpack the trunk.

Sebastian stood alone for a moment and took a few deep breaths before returning to the bedroom. There he discovered Julia, standing at one end, looking at a small, oval-framed portrait of his mother that hung above a pair of chairs. His strong sense of discomfort commenced again.

"Is this Lady Caverleigh?" asked Julia. "I can see something of you in her face, though her coloring is very different."

"Yes, that is my mother." He looked at the woman in the portrait, whose light, unpowdered hair, was arranged in elegant, upswept curls. Her eyes, the color of new spring leaves, gazed calmly back at him. "It's bizarre to be in this house, filled with her things, but to know that all of it now belongs to Raveneau and I am but a guest."

Julia was nodding. He watched as she stepped closer and put a hand on his arm. "It must feel as if your world is upside-down, and everything that you once knew has changed."

"Exactly!"

"I am acquainted with that feeling," she said softly.

Sebastian's heart stung as he looked down at her. "Yes, I suppose you are." He felt an urge to put his own hand over hers, but couldn't quite bring himself to do it.

"We've both seen our worlds irretrievably damaged through the actions of people we loved…who seemed to care more for gambling than for their own families."

Longing to put an end to this prickly conversation, he contemplated kissing her. There was something appealing about the physical conquest of a self-possessed, intelligent woman like Julia. That moment of capitulation, when the flare of arousal caused her to come unmoored from her intellect, was intoxicating. Reaching out, he fit his hand to her waist and stepped closer. Through the thin stuff of her gown, he could feel the lovely curve above her hipbone and his own body began to warm in response.

"I understand," Julia said, "that there are many things I don't know about you. Devon Raveneau tells me that you have a young sister."

Sebastian instantly withdrew his hand and stepped backward. "You may be the most provoking woman I have ever met."

"I am your wife, not a stranger who is prying into your affairs."

"All right then, yes, I have a sister. It's hardly a secret. Isabella is away at school and you needn't concern yourself with her." Just then a knock sounded at the door and he looked vastly relieved. "Ah, your maid arrives. Not a moment too soon."

Chapter 11

"Good afternoon," said Sebastian.

Miles Bartholomew, Esq. looked up from his cluttered desk. "Ah, greetings, my boy! I'm delighted to see you. It's been far too long, but of course I'd rather the circumstances were different."

"So would I." Sebastian's tone was heavy with irony. He brushed dust off a chair and drew it up to the desk.

"I was surprised to hear that you had resigned your commission in the Royal Navy, with its secure income. It was a very sensible career for a second son like you."

"Miles, you know bloody well I've never been the sensible sort. I'd had enough of that regimented life and living with a lot of men on a ship year in and year out. I served the Crown for six long years, I survived a serious wound, and I was ready to come home to the horses and Severn Hall."

"I see. I assume that you made those plans before you learned of George's...disgrace?" Miles paused, sniffing the air. "I say! Have you been drinking?

"What a question! I've been to White's, that's all, and perhaps to Boodles for a bit." Sebastian frowned. "I may have had a drink or two in the process of socializing."

"You'll pardon me for worrying, given George's multitude of *problems*..."

"I'm nothing like George!"

"You're brothers."

"For God's sake, don't be an ass." Sebastian stared at the man he'd known since birth, who had overseen his father's estates and often joined the family for meals when they were in London. It was tempting to share his deeper feelings with Miles, but as usual he waited and the urge passed. Instead, he rose and walked to the window. Through the panes, with their filmy coatings of dust, Sebastian could observe the activity at the East India Company, located just across Threadneedle Street.

Miles put on a smile that caused an extra chin to emerge above his collar. "My dear boy, I have not congratulated you on your marriage! I am eager to meet your bride. No doubt she is a worthy match for you."

"If you mean that she won't back down from an argument, you're right, but that can be tiresome. As you know, my own parents seldom conversed at all, so I was hoping for a more docile bride." He deftly steered the conversation away from himself. "But, I'm not here to discuss the merits of marriage with you, Miles. I am waiting to see a written account of my brother's financial damage."

Blinking as Sebastian turned back and pinned him with a razor-sharp stare, Miles shuffled the stacks of papers on his desk. "Of course. Of course. I have it all here..."

Although Sebastian presented a cool exterior, inside he felt sick with dread. "I hope it's not worse than I've already been informed."

"I wish I could assure you otherwise," he replied with feeling. "I wish I could have intervened somehow, but George was as slippery as a pudding. Whenever he thought I was coming to talk to him, he sneaked out into the garden and—"

"That's enough," Sebastian interrupted, pained.

"You may as well hear, now that I've begun. It's wretched news. I can't give you the keys to Caverleigh House because it's no longer in your family. George sold it without telling me, to raise money for his life in exile. I didn't even know he'd done it until the papers arrived after he had fled to Italy!"

"I know that he sold it. And I know the new owner, André Raveneau. He was a family friend, after a fashion. When I—we—arrived last night, he and his wife were kind enough to insist that we lodge with them, but it's a horrible situation. Paintings of my family are still on the walls, the house is still filled with our furniture—"

"You *knew*? Why didn't you say so?"

Sebastian ignored the question. "Is there more?"

Squeezing his eyes closed, Miles shook his head with disgust. "Truly, I have no idea how desperate the situation really is. Many of your brother's creditors have visited me, but I informed them that George was in exile, and you were serving the Crown in France, cut off from communication from me. I made it clear that you were the second son, and your own source of income was your Royal Navy commission. Now that you're back in London, and married, I can't help worrying that those creditors will begin to pursue *you*."

Sebastian went to the musty cellaret and poured himself a brandy, drank it down, then brought two half-filled goblets back to the desk. "Here's to poverty, old friend."

"You look like Satan himself when you arch that eyebrow," Miles observed. "Are you implying that your bride hasn't brought a fortune to your marriage? Why else would a libertine like you take a wife?"

"Stop. I'll be ill if you ram one more unpleasantry down my throat." He drank the second brandy. "I went to Bath in an attempt to win enough at the tables to reclaim Severn Park. I'd planned my whole life, for God's sake, to breed horses, and when I returned from France to the news that George had sold my horses, and then lost Severn Park, all I could think of was winning enough to reclaim them."

"Don't tell me that you also had ill luck in Bath?"

"No. Yes." He grimaced. "Actually, I won a fine estate,

called Turbans, and nearly £20,000…but all I have to show for it is Julia." Burying his head in his hands, he muttered, "It's a Byzantine tale. I don't want to bore you."

"Bore away."

Every word was painful as he told the story of Graeme Faircloth's deadly addiction to gambling. "Unfortunately, I was the recipient of his promissory notes. When he died, apparently by suicide, his wife and children behaved as if I were a villain for trying to claim my winnings. Julia was the worst, calling me every vile name she could conjure."

"Then…how? Why?" He spread his pudgy hands, palms up, in confusion.

Although Sebastian knew he could trust Miles to be discreet, he strove to keep his own feelings out of the messy story. "Summing up, I took pity on them. Sarah, the younger daughter, is lovely and docile, so I proposed marriage to her with the condition that the family could continue to live at Turbans. Then, Julia decided that she couldn't send her sister to a marriage bed with a savage beast like me, so she donned a disguise and sacrificed herself in Sarah's stead."

"I'm not certain I understand."

Sebastian offered details about the dark, stormy night, the heavily be-ribboned bonnet, and his own state of intoxication.

"That's quite a tale, my lord, but I remain confused. Why not sell Turbans to raise capital for your own needs? It's not your fault after all that this Faircloth fellow had a weakness for piquet! You could still provide the family with a modest allowance, out of charity." As he spoke, Miles watched the shadows dart across Sebastian's face. "I can't help wondering if there's more to this saga. Perhaps you're not really disappointed that your Julia took her sister's place? Perhaps you have feelings for your bride after all? Why else would you go soft when you need the money so badly?"

"You're as nonsensical as ever, Miles. I'll sort things out with the Faircloths. I just need time, particularly in light of their patriarch's recent death. Have a heart, old man! As for Julia, I haven't time to think of her at all." He scowled for emphasis. "No. I have too many matters of real importance on my mind! Furthermore, if she is unhappy, it's her own doing. She should be grateful that I didn't leave her behind at the Goat in Boots Inn!"

The solicitor squirmed with discomfort before changing the subject. "You'll be pleased to hear, I do have some cheery news to end on!" With that, he rummaged around in his desk and withdrew a pouch made of sapphire-blue velvet, tied with a golden cord. "Your mother left something for you. Of course, it wasn't in the will, but she had given it to me privately, asking that I keep it for you in the event of her demise."

"And you call that *cheery*?"

"My dear fellow, must you be so unrelentingly cynical?" He handed the pouch across to Sebastian and waited. "Aren't you going to open it?"

"In front of you? God, no."

"Well then, I have one more piece of business to discuss." Breaking the seal on a folded sheet of parchment paper, he peered through his steel-rimmed spectacles. "My lord, I have here a document, signed in my presence by your brother, the Marquess of Caverleigh. He writes that he begs your pardon for leasing Severn Park to a stranger. He adds that, even though it was entailed to him, he realizes that it was always understood that you would live there and oversee the horse-breeding operation."

"Meaningless, at this point," Sebastian said through his teeth.

"His lordship goes on to write that he invites you to make yourself at home at the other family estate, Trevarre Hall, in Cornwall. Gad, sir, I had almost forgotten about that old pile of rock!" Miles began to chuckle, but stopped abruptly at the sight of Sebastian's stormy expression. "Ah yes, as I recall, you never cared much for Cornwall."

"I detest Trevarre Hall."

"Ahem! Well then, your brother writes—right here," he stabbed a finger at the paper, "'If it were in my power to give you this last ancestral estate, I would do so. Failing that, I beg you, Brother, to think of it as your own home. Perhaps this gesture will win me a measure of forgiveness.'"

It seemed to Sebastian that his blood had turned to molten lava. "Trevarre Hall is the one place in all of England that I don't want to occupy, and George damned well knows that! I may not have sold Turbans to raise funds, but I'd have no qualms about selling that ruin in the Cornish hinterlands."

"You know that's impossible. Trevarre Hall is your mother's ancestral estate, as I recall, and Lady Caverleigh brought it to her marriage with your father. It was in the Wentworth family for three centuries or more!"

"Right. Didn't it used to be called Wentworth Hall before my father decided to put his own family name on it? The real Trevarre estates, on godforsaken Bodmin moor, were so desolate that they fell into ruin a century ago." Sebastian shook his head in disgust. "What a bastard he was."

Miles blanched. "Oh now, my lord, it was his right. Your mother's property became his own once they were married. And fitting, perhaps, that he would call it Trevarre Hall since the first Earl of Trevarre emerged from Cornwall centuries ago!" Miles came around the desk and patted Sebastian's broad shoulder. "At least you and your bride will have a roof over your heads. Perhaps Trevarre Hall will be in better condition than you remember it. Perhaps you can farm? Or, what about that handsome lime kiln on your land? That may be the answer!"

"Of course. Perhaps I can keep bees and raise berries," Sebastian parried in acid tones. "The estate used to turn a profit with wool, but no more. George has sold all the sheep." Raising a hand, he waved Miles off. The wheels of his mind had begun to whirl and he was suddenly anxious to take his leave. "Never mind those dull plans. There *are* ways to raise money in Cornwall, but I can't speak of them…not even to you." He cocked his head. "To Keswick, perhaps, but not to you."

In the walled garden behind Caverleigh House, Julia sat on a stone bench beside Devon Raveneau and sipped tea. Old roses clambered up and over the stone walls, the tree branches needed pruning, and wild violets nodded rebelliously throughout the garden. Nathan Raveneau, a handsome boy on the brink of adolescence, was leading baby Lindsay in search of a fluttering butterfly, while their elder sister, Mouette, had perched on a second bench near the women.

"Mama, what shall we plant here?" the girl asked, assessing her surroundings with a faint air of distaste. "Wouldn't it be lovely to have a *proper* rose garden?"

Julia looked over at the sixteen-year-old beauty who had inherited her father's striking coloring, and raised her own teacup to hide a smile.

"I rather like it just as it is," Devon replied. "True, it needs a bit of loving care, but I have always preferred my gardens to be a trifle untamed."

"What about the name of the house?" Mouette persisted. "We can't continue to call it Caverleigh House. It's nothing to do with them now."

"What a thing to say. What puts such thoughts in your head?"

"But, Mama, don't you think 'Raveneau House' has a lovely ring to it?"

Devon laughed and shook her head just as Miss Dowling, the children's governess, emerged from the house, calling, "Mouette and Nathan, there are unfinished lessons waiting for both of you. Time to return inside."

"I think I would rather go to a proper academy, with other young ladies my own age," Mouette complained as she stood and smoothed her muslin gown. "How tiresome it is to do lessons with Nathan in the same room. He thinks of nothing except making mischief!"

When the two children had followed their governess back into the house, Devon sent Lindsay off with a tiny basket to pick wild violets before turning her attention to Julia.

"Would you care to go shopping?" she asked.

"Oh, well, I don't think so. Truthfully, I…I'm uncertain of my financial situation."

"How tactless of me." Although Devon's eyes were bright with curiosity, she took a breath. "Actually, I had been hoping to choose a wedding gift for you, my dear. For both of you, of course, but especially for you."

Julia wavered. "I just don't think we should. I have a perfectly acceptable wardrobe, after all, and I don't believe that my husband and I will be engaging in a lot of social activities."

"Is everything all right?" Devon reached out to clasp Julia's hand, and her warm gaze was penetrating. "I can assure you that any confidence that you share with me shall be closely guarded."

To her horror, Julia felt tears prick her eyes. "You wouldn't tell Captain Raveneau?"

"Normally, yes, but not in this case. You and I are women, and a friendship between women demands a special kind of loyalty."

"I have *longed* to confide in someone." Something seemed to give way inside Julia. "You see, this marriage is based on a lie."

"Indeed?" Devon blinked, clearly uncertain of how to proceed. "Can you tell me what you mean by that?"

"Sebastian doesn't love me. In fact, he despises me. I have made a terrible mistake, but I had no choice! My sister could never have withstood marriage to a man like Sebastian—"

"I must tell you that I am completely confused." Producing a gauzy handkerchief from her reticule, Devon reached over to blot the tears from Julia's pink cheeks. "Let me pour you another cup of tea and then you can tell me everything. From the beginning."

Fortified by the tea and a piece of seed cake, Julia began to tell her new friend everything that had happened, beginning with her family's acquisition of Turbans, continuing through the day she first confronted Sebastian after discovering his name on the I.O.U. in her father's pocket, and finishing with the moment in the bed at the Goat in Boots, when her new husband had discovered that he had married the wrong sister.

"It didn't stop him," she revealed with a rueful smile. "He was angry, but…"

"Oh, you don't have to tell me this part. I can imagine perfectly! Your Sebastian is very much like my André, and we had our own share of tempestuous scenes in the early months of our romance." Devon laughed. "If you could call it a romance!"

"Were you married? Is that why you stayed?"

"No, we weren't married. Far from it! André was very slow to surrender his heart, but once he did, he gave it completely. I stayed with him…partly because there was a war on and I'd been forced to flee my town during a battle. But, to be quite honest, I stayed because I loved him madly, in spite of his bad behavior. My heart trusted in something I couldn't understand."

"And you've been happy, that's quite clear." Julia studied her friend, whose expression had softened with emotions that caused her beauty to glow. "I have so many doubts, though, about a future for us. We really don't know each other very well, and I tricked him into marrying me and he's not a bit ready to forget that."

Devon's smile was warm and a bit mischievous. "You have done something desperate and foolish and admittedly wrong. But, although Sebastian would rather die than admit it, I'll wager he is charmed by your ingenuity and courage. He may say that he wanted a docile miss for a wife, but his heart knows better."

"Sometimes I am not sure he has a heart."

"Utter nonsense!"

"My siblings and I used to call him Lord Satan. It was very fitting!" Julia paused until Devon's laughter had subsided, then she said, "Of course, I would be a poor excuse for a woman if all I cared about was whether or not he has a heart, or if it might warm to me. In fact, I have always been the strong one in my family, the one who has guided all the others, even my parents. I will tell you that I have a good mind and I have many interests of my own. The thought of being powerless in an ill-conceived marriage with a hard man who doesn't want me is discouraging, to say the least."

Devon leaned closer to her, blue eyes twinkling, and touched her cheek. "But what about that night at the inn. Was it terrible?"

Julia blushed. "No…but—"

"I thought not! There is something between you two, or you wouldn't be here. If Sebastian were really so cross about this marriage, he wouldn't have had his way with you on your wedding night. If, as you said earlier, he *despised* you, he would have taken you back to Bath and left you at Turbans with the rest of your family. No matter what he *says*, you must remember that it is his actions that count. And, my dear," now she tapped Julia's cheek lightly, "the same is true for you. You chose this path, and perhaps you shall have to wait and see where it leads."

"Oh my, that is not in my nature. I like to be the one drawing the map and organizing the expedition."

Just then, André Raveneau's voice reached them. "Is there a little girl in this garden?"

Lindsay's face came up and she went running on her sturdy little legs to meet him, dropping the basket of violets on its side midway across the stone terrace. "Papa, Papa, I am here!"

Scooping her up as if she were a feather, he buried his dark face in her baby curls. "How pretty you are today, *ma fleur*!"

The child nodded in sober agreement and they all laughed. Julia watched as Raveneau approached them, clearly focused on Devon. His immaculate riding clothes accentuated the hard lines of his physique and the breeze ruffled his dark hair, its liberal strands of silver glinting in the sunlight.

"How nice to have you home," said Devon, rising to meet the embrace of his free arm. Her eyes were gleaming. "I've just been telling Julia what a cruel pirate you were long ago, before Mouette was born."

He glanced toward Julia with one brow arched in a way that reminded her of Sebastian. "But of course, you didn't believe her, did you?"

"You must confess, darling," Devon scolded him, cuffing his chest. "It will give her hope for that scoundrel she's married."

"In that case, whatever my wife has told you is true. And no doubt she has only scratched the surface of my villainy."

"That is terribly encouraging," Julia replied with a laugh. "Thank you so much for your candor, sir."

"My lady, I can assure you that if I could reform, there is hope, even for a devil like Lord Sebastian Trevarre."

Chapter 12

Roderick the butler admitted Sebastian to Caverleigh House when he returned from his appointment with Miles Bartholomew. No sooner had he greeted the tiny old man than a voice called to him from the direction of Raveneau's library.

"Won't you come in, my lord, and join me for a brandy?"

Looking around the wide doorway, Sebastian beheld his host sitting at the large, carved desk that had once belonged to his own father. "I don't want to disturb you, sir."

"Please do." Raveneau had been writing on a sheet of vellum paper, but immediately set down his quill. "I've been endeavoring to compose a response to a letter I've had from President Adams. It seems that the United States Congress is quite upset by the latest dealings with France. Negotiations to resolve matters have broken down and some are calling for an all-out war. The president seems to be hinting that I might travel to Paris and speak to Talleyrand, then send him a report."

"I *am* disturbing you.'

"On the contrary, I was just about to stop for some refreshment. Please, join me."

"All right, but I'd better have tea instead, since I've probably already drunk too much brandy today," Sebastian replied, taking a chair on the other side of the desk. "I visited

Watier's after my rather torturous appointment with our solicitor. Beau Brummell was there, having just resigned his commission and returned to London. Do you know him?"

"Slightly. I believe he's about to come into a considerable inheritance."

Sebastian gave a sardonic laugh. "It will be very welcome, I'm sure, given his expensive tastes."

A footman entered with tea and poured for both men. When they were alone again, Raveneau said, "I imagine it can't be easy for you, being in this house filled with your family's things but seeing my family in residence."

"Rather bizarre, I must admit."

"I want you to know that I would be happy to pack up the entire contents of Caverleigh House and ship it off to—wherever it is that you will be living."

"That's very kind of you, but where I'm going, all of this would be starkly out of place." Pausing, Sebastian loosened his cravat and ran a hand through his thick hair. "I might accept one or two small paintings of my mother." The sight of Raveneau's arched brow caused him to add, "Also, there is a watercolor Mother made of the Cornwall coast. It was one of her favorites."

"I know the one you mean," his host replied. "It's hanging above her writing desk, in the morning room. Charlotte was more talented than she knew."

"I'm surprised you're familiar with that painting."

"I wasn't—but when I saw it, I knew it must be one of hers. She was already painting when I knew her in France." Suddenly, Raveneau's thoughts seemed to wander as he gazed out the window facing Grosvenor Square. "*Mon Dieu*, that was a long time ago."

Although momentarily taken aback, Sebastian quickly moved on to other matters. "I should express my appreciation to you for purchasing this house when my brother decided to sell. It could have been some villain who wouldn't have given a damn about my family."

"I'm very pleased I could do it. And I want you to know that Devon and I would return it to your family if you should have a change in fortunes."

Sebastian shook his head. "I won't want it back, and George doesn't deserve it, so you must forget about the past and make this house your own. My own desires lie in Hampshire, where my brother has leased Severn Park to a stranger. When I was serving in the Royal Navy, I looked toward a future there, overseeing the horse breeding operation that my mother and I began."

"Right. I had assumed that you and your new wife were going to Severn Park. What do you mean to do about this?"

"Thank God, the estate was entailed, so George couldn't gamble it away, but he did sell off all the horses. It's sickening to me. Fortunately, there are records for all the sales, and once I can afford it, I intend to begin tracking them down and buying them back."

Raveneau leaned forward. "Where will you live in the meantime?"

"At the end of the earth, in bloody Cornwall," Sebastian replied grimly. "Trevarre Hall is the only place that George didn't manage to dispose of. It's entailed as well, but I surmise that he couldn't find anyone to pay him rent for it."

"But what will you do there to raise the capital to purchase those horses? Did your solicitor advise you today?"

"Is that meant to be a jest? The only thing Miles advised me of today was my state of penury." Sebastian let a bitter smile play about his mouth. "He did suggest that I might restore the estate's old lime kiln. May I ask you, Captain Raveneau, if that would be an attractive solution if you were in my place?"

Their eyes met in unspoken understanding. "No. Not a bit."

"I thought not. I do, however, have a solution in mind, but I won't speak of it here."

"A wise course, no doubt." The scar on Raveneau's jaw

seemed to tighten. "Were you aware, my lord, that I was a privateer captain during America's War for Independence? It was a very dangerous game—so much so that I feel entitled to advise you against pursuing similarly risky ventures."

"Indeed?" Sebastian's gaze was flinty as he pushed away his cup and saucer and prepared to rise. "I shall remember that."

"Did nothing good come of your meeting with Miles Bartholomew?"

"There was one thing." He was curious to see what was in the pouch Miles had given him and this seemed as good a time as any to find out. Taking the small sapphire-blue bag from his waistcoat pocket, Sebastian loosened the golden cord. "It seems that my mother privately entrusted this to Miles, with instructions to give it to me if she died."

"Very interesting," Raveneau said, his gaze intent. "If she hadn't, it would be part of your brother's inheritance and he might have gambled it away by now."

As Sebastian gingerly shook the pouch, two delicate rings dropped onto the leather desk blotter. "Hmm." He held one up and saw that it featured a small sapphire and a diamond mounted side-by-side. "It's odd; I don't remember ever seeing her wear this ring. I can't imagine why she made a point of leaving it to me."

"I—" Raveneau broke off. "That is, perhaps you weren't paying attention to what she wore. I certainly couldn't tell you a thing about my own mother's jewelry."

"I suppose it must have had some special significance to her. A memory that included me, perhaps?" He held the ring in between his thumb and fingertip, staring for a long moment before he returned it to the blotter and picked up the other circlet of gold which featured a round piece of painted ivory trimmed in tiny sapphires. "How very unusual. It must be one of those eye miniatures I've heard about."

Together they stared at the tiny painting of a compelling

slate-gray eye set off by black lashes and a slightly arched male eyebrow. A clock ticked to mark the long moment of silence.

"I've never seen this before," Sebastian said at last. "I can't imagine what the devil it means."

Exhaling harshly, Raveneau said, "It looks like your own eye, my lord. Perhaps she had it made for herself, as a remembrance when you went off with the Royal Navy."

"Perhaps. But then, why would she give it to Miles to keep?"

The older man shook his head and moved away. "I haven't a clue. What I do know is that I must finish writing this letter before dinner is served." He sat down again and picked up the quill again. "Would it be rude if I asked you to leave me now?"

"Of course not, sir." Feeling strangely unsettled, Sebastian dropped the rings back into the pouch, returned it to his pocket, and took his leave, pausing in the doorway just long enough to glance back and see André Raveneau staring out the window, his thoughts clearly far away, the quill and parchment seemingly forgotten.

After a light evening meal that featured Florentine rabbit, fresh peas, and a delightful summer pudding, Sebastian declined to have port with his host, explaining that he must consult with Keswick in advance of their departure on the morrow.

Julia looked at him from across the table and raised her chin. "May I inquire as to our destination, my lord?"

Feeling the eyes of the entire Raveneau family on him, Sebastian colored slightly under his tan. "Of course, my dear. As soon as I am finished with Keswick, I shall see you in our rooms and tell you our plans."

He excused himself then and went off in search of his

manservant. It was one of those moments when he thought he would choke if he didn't get out of this house, with all its memories of his dead parents, and better yet, out of London. He longed to mount his favorite stallion, Lucifer, who it now appeared he would never see again, and ride all the way to the coast without stopping.

Unfortunately, that was not an option. Instead, he searched everywhere for Keswick, who he finally discovered in his dressing room.

"I've looked for you everywhere," Sebastian complained.

"Indeed? But, where else should we be on such a night but here, organizing your lordship's belongings for the journey?"

"Sometimes I think that you believe that you are the master and you are just pretending to be my servant."

The little man ignored this, continuing to carefully fold an array of starched white neckcloths.

Sebastian closed both doors leading out of the candlelit dressing room. "Are you not curious about our destination?"

"Trevarre Hall, my lord?"

"How do you know that?"

"Did you not tell me?"

Sebastian scowled. "You of all people know how much I despise that ruin."

"You do Cornwall an injustice, my lord."

Suddenly, Sebastian was flooded with memories of his boyhood summers in Cornwall, when his parents had often left him behind with a sour governess while they traveled to the seashore or sailed across the English Channel to France. George had been older, Isabella had not been born yet, and only he was at an age too awkward to be included in their summer plans. His mother had been sympathetic, but his father was strict to the point of cruelty. Eventually Sebastian had learned to hide his feelings so that no one could guess he was sad or lonely. He didn't want to cause his mother distress, or give his father the satisfaction of seeing his weakness.

"You were the only person who made it bearable, Keswick."

The manservant looked up at that and their eyes met in unspoken communication. For a moment, he seemed to forget his habit of referring to himself in the plural. "I was only the stable master at Trevarre Hall. I had no official role in your life, not then."

"You took an interest in me when no one else did." Sebastian paused. "You saved my life. That's why you've been with me ever since I was old enough to choose for myself."

Clearly uncomfortable, Keswick fussed with a fine pair of doeskin gloves. "We shall be with you in Cornwall again, sir. We know Trevarre Hall very well; we'll assist you and her ladyship in making it livable."

"That's not what I want to talk about. I have no patience for raising sheep or restoring the lime kiln," Sebastian said dismissively, even as his jaw hardened. "I must accumulate real wealth, Keswick, so that I can get the bloody hell out of Cornwall and return to Hampshire. I intend to track down my horses and buy them back, no matter the price, and then I will choose an estate of my own where I can do as I please. Perhaps I can even lease Severn Park from my brother. You can see that's the only solution, can't you?"

"Perhaps, my lord, but at what cost?"

"Don't pretend you don't know what I'm talking about. I know you were more than a stable master at Trevarre Hall. I've heard about your secret, lawless past, and I am counting on your help."

Keswick shook his head. "We have grave doubts that a nobleman such as yourself should engage in so a dangerous venture."

"Of course you do!" snapped Sebastian. "But this decision is not yours."

Just then, the door to the bedchamber swung open, sending a spill of light over the two men. Julia stood there, still clad in her slim muslin gown, a soft blue cashmere shawl draped around her shoulders. The curls secured atop her head had begun to come loose, softening her look of surprised discomfort. It was an expression that immediately set Sebastian's nerves on edge.

"Pardon me," she said. "I thought I heard voices."

Resisting the appeal of her soft voice, he opened his mouth to remark that apparently there was no privacy left to him now that he was married, but Keswick spoke first.

"There is nothing left for us to do." The manservant smiled at Julia. "Your own maid came to pack your things while you were dining, my lady. Everything is in order for our morning departure."

"How lovely," Julia murmured. "Thank you so much for telling me, Keswick."

"I will be on my way, then." Bowing to his new mistress, he backed out the other dressing room door and closed it.

"How can one person be at once sniveling and overbearing?" Sebastian mused as he stared darkly at the door.

"Surely you don't mean Keswick? I find him quite charming, and certainly reasonable."

"Of course you do." He walked past her, back into the bedroom, and poured water into a gold-rimmed bowl he remembered from his childhood. "Was there something you needed? I am at your disposal."

Yet he didn't look at her.

Julia watched him, wondering how to proceed.

"I hoped that we might talk for a bit."

"Talk? Haven't you been talking to Devon Raveneau all day?"

She felt herself bristle. Who would not bristle at such treatment? "You are my husband, sir, and we are about to embark on a journey together—into a future of which I am wholly ignorant."

"Madam, have you forgotten the rules we discussed for this

marriage? Be glad that I am pretending to go through the motions. Most men, in my place, would have taken you back to Turbans and never laid eyes on you or your family again."

Julia watched as he reached for a linen towel to dry his face. Even though what he said might be true, it still hurt. "Your rudeness is unpardonable, my lord."

"Yes, yes. First you hint that you would like me to play the romantic, considerate husband and now you attempt to trade insults with me again. I thought I made it quite clear at the inn that I will have neither." Sebastian began to unfasten his snug pantaloons. "I am going to bed. You may find this difficult to imagine, but I have countless other problems to occupy my mind other than this hoax you call a marriage."

Julia turned away while he stripped naked and climbed into bed with a sigh of exhaustion. Every word he'd said had stung her to the core, but she swallowed the angry words. Instead, she looped her shawl over the back of a chair and walked over to present her back to him.

"I do not have a maid tonight, sir, so I would ask that you kindly assist me. No doubt you have unfastened a lady's gown before?"

His hand reached out to catch the crook of her elbow with long, taut fingers, drawing her down until she was sitting close to him on the bed. Julia, who knew so little of men and their passions, nevertheless felt something in his touch that made the baby hairs on the nape of her neck prickle. Moments later, his fingertips flicked open the tiny buttons on the back of her gown, occasionally brushing her sensitive skin, while delicious shivers coursed down her spine and clustered unexpectedly between her legs. When all the buttons were open, he parted the thin layers of muslin.

"No stays," Sebastian said, his voice husky. "I like that."

Julia did not reply. She despised stays, which her mother had always urged her to wear to push her bosom ever higher and to make certain that curves of her body could not be discerned through the gauzy fabric. For her own part, she preferred an extra layer of muslin and her own natural shape.

"Thank you…for your assistance." Slowly, she turned to look into his wary eyes. "Do you think that now you might talk to me? I realize that you are still angry, but it would be so much nicer if, going forward, you could at least be civil to me."

He gave a tired sigh. "You already know that George sold Caverleigh House to finance his exile in Tuscany. Everything is gone, it seems, except our desolate ancestral estate in Cornwall."

Julia held her breath for a moment and looked back at Sebastian's hard, chiseled face. "Do you mean—that we are going to Cornwall? That we'll live there?"

"Exactly. You and I are going to embark upon our spurious marriage in the place I detest most in all the world. Do you begin to understand why my mood only grows blacker?"

"Yes…" She longed to ask why he hated it so, but his expression warned her away. It was a relief to hurry across the room and change into her nightgown in the shadows. Glancing back at the bed, she saw that Sebastian had lain back on his pillow, one bare, hard-muscled arm bent across his eyes. The little flurry of sensations commenced again in her nether regions and she was grateful he couldn't see her telltale blush. By the time she had washed her face and cleaned her teeth with a new boar-bristle brush and her husband's fine tooth powder, it seemed that he must be asleep.

Tip-toeing back across the room, Julia blew out the candle and climbed up onto the bed. She lay down beside Sebastian and stared at him in the dim bluish light. A surprisingly powerful wave of tenderness washed over her. It came to her that they had more in common than she had realized, for both of them had been rendered powerless by the betrayals of loved ones. Perhaps, in time, they might bind up each other's wounds and draw strength from one another.

"Julia," he rasped, reaching out to draw her firmly into his arms. "For God's sake, close your eyes."

Her face flamed as she nodded against his cheek. How had he known she was watching him? Could he feel the power of her emotions?

Sebastian took a deep, exhausted breath and whispered against her curls, "I am aware that I've been a beast these past two days."

Her heart skipped. "Well, looking back, I can see that I have given you cause to feel vexed toward me."

When he made no reply, Julia realized that the cadence of his breathing had changed. Sebastian was asleep, still holding her fast. Lying with her cheek against the warm strength of his chest, she felt a momentary glimmer of hope shine through a crack in her heart.

At the other end of the corridor, in the grand suite of rooms that had recently belonged to the Marquess and Marchioness of Caverleigh, Devon Raveneau slept beside her husband in a towering carved bed hung with embroidered blue silk draperies.

Her eyes flew open for the fifth time that night, just as a clock on the landing softly chimed two o'clock. Devon turned from her back to her side, wondering if the bed was to blame for her restlessness. Not only was the style far too opulent for her taste, but there was something about it that just didn't feel right.

And where was André? Usually he held her, even in his sleep, or at least kept a hand on her waist. They'd never needed a very big bed because he stayed so close to her.

Turning the other way, Devon opened her eyes and tried to focus in the faint moon glow. To her surprise she saw her husband, lying a distance away on his back, staring at the canopy above them. His expression was so serious that she hesitated to intrude on his thoughts.

At length, Devon reached out and touched him, her hand pale against his brown arm. When André didn't immediately respond, she murmured, "Darling, is something wrong?"

He took a deep breath, clearly pulling himself into the present moment with an effort. "*Petite chatte*, what could be wrong when you are near?"

"I have very good instincts, you know."

"Oh, I do know." Turning, he brought her into his embrace and stroked her back. "I love you."

It was a reminder to Devon that no matter how well she might know her husband, and no matter how deep his devotion to her and their family, there were private places deep inside him that he would always guard.

"I love you, too," she whispered, and closed her eyes, relaxing against him.

"You remind me of all the blessings in my life." He pressed a kiss to her brow and soon they were both asleep.

Chapter 13

As the sun broke through the clouds, birds began to sing in the elegant garden that was the centerpiece of Grosvenor Square. Sebastian's coach had just been brought around from the mews behind Caverleigh House and he went forward to check the luggage. Everything seemed to be securely in place, including the paintings he'd chosen, now carefully wrapped and stowed safely atop the other items.

"Do you have everything you need?" asked André Raveneau as he approached.

"Yes. I can't thank you enough, sir. Your hospitality has been a godsend."

"We've enjoyed having you and Julia here more than you can imagine," Raveneau said. He looked into Sebastian's eyes for a long moment before he added, "You'll be in my thoughts. In fact, if I am called on to travel to France after all, we may visit you in Cornwall."

"Although we should be happy to see you, I must warn you that Trevarre Hall may not be fit for guests. In fact, I have grave doubts about taking Julia there."

Before Raveneau could reply, the front door opened and the women emerged with Lindsay, Nathan, and Mouette trailing in their wake.

Sebastian gave his wife a pointed glance. "What's that crate with your name on it?" he asked. "I didn't notice it before."

"Those are my books," she informed him calmly. "Books…and some small keepsakes. They are all extremely valuable to me."

"No doubt," he replied with a sigh. She looked so crisp and fresh, as if she hadn't a care in the world. A breeze caused her muslin gown to dance around her ankles, and her dark curls gleamed in the sunlight. Yet, it was that face that he found most arresting. Lovely Julia might be, but she always had the look of someone who could do anything she put her mind to, no matter how daunting. The memory of her demeanor the first time they met came to him, unbidden. She had told him off, in firm yet polite terms, in her determination to protect her father.

Sebastian wanted to ask if, in that present moment, she felt even a quiver of uncertainty or even fear when she gazed into their decidedly murky future. Did Julia imagine that she could bend it to her will, no matter what?

"Is there something you wish to say, my lord?" she inquired.

He blinked. "Only that we must make our goodbyes and be on our way. Cornwall is a long way off, you know…nearly at the end of the world."

Traveling southward, Julia was grateful for Keswick when it came time to break their journey at midday. Standing in the yard at the Rose and Crown, Julia conversed with the amiable manservant while they watched the horses drink. Sebastian made no protest when she insisted that Keswick join their table inside the inn, seeming relieved to have another person between them.

The afternoon brought them into the gently rolling countryside of Hampshire. Spring had colored the trees and meadows a fresh vivid green, and leaves were replacing the blossoms in the orchards of fruit trees. Everywhere Julia looked, there were creamy yellow primrose blossoms, growing in wild profusion along every roadside and around every tree.

Julia tried to look at the scenery and not think about Sebastian. She asked herself, what could be gained by dwelling on the unpleasant episodes that had spoiled the first days of their marriage? Her own mother had always said that men possessed a fierce quantity of pride, and she'd never understood what that meant until now. Pride had caused her father to take his own life, and pride fueled Sebastian's harsh feelings toward her. When she considered the full import of what she'd done, tricking him at the altar, she had a glimpse from his perspective. She had to be patient, as Devon had advised.

What other choice was there?

And, studying her husband through the coach window as he rode just ahead on horseback, Julia realized that there were more reasons to wait and see. She was intrigued by the adventure that lay ahead. The thought of living in the wilds of Cornwall appealed much more to her than London had. And, in her heart, she could admit that most appealing of all was Sebastian himself.

With so much to see, and so much to ponder, Julia remained occupied as the day slipped by. At length, she began to doze, and when the coach stopped suddenly, she was startled back to wakefulness.

"Where are we?" she called to Keswick when she caught a glimpse of his white wig through the window shade. "Where is my husband?"

"We are still in Hampshire, my lady," he replied. "His lordship will return shortly, and bids you rest within the coach until then."

Julia instantly sensed a mystery. "Keswick, please let me come out. I'll go mad if I have to spend another moment in this box."

He did as she asked, but was clearly uneasy.

Looking around, Julia saw that they were stopped midway along a drive lined with chestnut trees. Clipped, verdant parkland spread out on either side. Farther ahead of them, the drive turned a corner, and she thought that she could still see a bit of dust lingering in the sunlit air there.

She straightened her Prussian-blue spencer and gave the manservant a confident smile. "How lovely the air smells! It's bliss to be outside after those hours of confinement. Do you know what I should love better than anything, Keswick?"

"We do not, my lady."

"I should adore a short promenade. Won't you grant me that small request? I promise to return shortly, and my mood will be greatly improved by the exercise."

"My lady, is it not enough that you are here in the fresh air? His lordship has given us explicit instructions!"

This comment grated at her. Did Sebastian imagine that she was his prisoner? "Keswick, I wish to walk a bit after sitting for so long. Is there any good reason why I should not do so?"

"My lady, we beg you to be brief," he said, capitulating to her persuasive smile.

Julia started off up the drive, but turned back to add, "You really mustn't let him frighten you, dear Keswick. He's just a man, you know."

This piece of advice caused the little man to raise a hand to his brow and groan aloud.

Walking quickly, Julia soon reached the place where the drive turned, but when a magnificent manor house came into view, she came to an abrupt stop. Built of red brick, in the classical Georgian style favored in recent decades, it featured beautifully manicured boxwood hedges, rows of white-trimmed windows and grounds that swept gracefully into the distant woods. To the east stood empty stables and pasturelands.

The sight of Sebastian dismounting from his horse on the other side of tall hedges sent Julia hurrying off the drive to take shelter behind a chestnut tree. No sooner did he approach the manor house than the front door flew open and two elderly servants, appearing to be the butler and the housekeeper, rushed out.

"Lord Sebastian!" the woman cried. "I saw you riding up the drive from the upstairs window and I knew it was you from the first moment, when you and the horse had just turned the corner."

"Ah, Mrs. Blodgett, how good it is to see you! And you too, Hartly." Genuine affection softened Sebastian's expression.

Julia, overhearing, tried to make herself smaller behind the tree. She could only pray that he didn't see her as she trespassed on this secret and clearly cherished world from his past.

"My lord," Hartly said, "tell us that you have undone your brother's lease of Severn Park. The new occupant is due to take up residence within the next fortnight! Tell us that you have come home for good, to reclaim your life here."

"I wish that I could say those things, but I cannot. As it happens, I am en route to Trevarre Hall, in Cornwall, and I had to come up to see you, to see the house one more time." Patting Mrs. Blodgett's shoulder, he added, "It sickens me to consider the damage my brother has done to so many lives."

She began to weep. "Your beloved horses are all gone. Of course, you must know that. Oh, your lordship, it breaks my heart to imagine what your mother would have thought about this tragedy. She always said that you should live here where you belong, to continue the work you and she began, breeding horses and—"

He broke in. "I mean to recover the horses, as soon as I am able. Hartly, have you kept records of their buyers? I am especially determined to find my Lucifer."

"I believe we do have those documents, my lord," said the butler. "I will make inquiries and send word to Trevarre Hall when I know more. As for Lucifer, I recall that he was purchased by a Cornish gentleman with an estate near Lerryn."

"Indeed?" Sebastian's shoulders straightened and he cocked his head. "That's very interesting. I'm grateful for your good memory, Hartly."

"Lord Sebastian, we'll go on praying for your return." The housekeeper reached out to clasp his hand. "I wanted to tell you that I personally looked after your mother after the carriage accident. His lordship was killed outright, but your mother was brought back here, and lingered for two days, though she never awoke. She had the best of care, from the physician and from all of us. And, when your brother, the new marquess, came and began sorting through the valuables, I hid some of the things I knew she would have wanted you to have."

When Julia saw Sebastian swipe fingertips across his eyes, she wished that she hadn't come. There was no possibility of escape without detection, and the chance that he would see her was very real. Could he ever soften his heart toward her if he discovered that she'd spied on him?

"My lord," Hartley was saying, "may I be so bold as to request that you come inside to speak to the staff? It will reassure them to see you again."

"Of course, though I must be brief." He followed the butler and housekeeper up the steps to the main entrance.

No sooner had the doors closed behind them than Julia came out from behind the tree and hurried off down the drive, back to the safety of the waiting coach. Her heart was thundering as she considered how close she'd come to being discovered, and she promised herself that she would never take such a chance again.

The nuggets of understanding that Julia had gleaned at Severn Park carried her through the remaining three days of their journey, during which Sebastian kept more to himself than ever. When she could study his brooding profile from a safe distance, she felt her heart ease a little toward him. The memory of him talking with Mrs. Blodgett and Hartley, and the trio's very real expression of anguish for what Sebastian's brother had so carelessly discarded, haunted her.

Meanwhile, Julia struggled to regain some control over her own fate. She reasoned that, since her husband did not mean to look after her future happiness, she would look after it herself. Immediately, her inner turmoil eased. Taking back control of her own destiny gave her a sense of freedom that was thrilling, like standing bareheaded in a rainstorm.

That feeling settled over her in earnest after they crossed the River Tamar that divided Devon from Cornwall. Julia soon wondered if there was magic in the misty breeze that blew in from the English Channel, for each time she breathed deeply, she felt exhilarated. They kept to the south coast, where fishing villages clambered down the sides of rocky cliffs, and the blue sea shimmered in the distance. Everything was unexpected, from the clusters of whitewashed cottages to the narrow, twisting roads hemmed in by wildflower-studded hedgerows.

How little I knew of the world, Julia thought, enraptured. Although she had loved Turbans and the refined beauty of Bath, Cornwall stirred her senses as dramatically as Sebastian did. It seemed that part of her had been waiting, slumbering, until this place of liberation and light could be discovered.

She had always believed that people shaped their own fates, but now she reconsidered. It seemed that everything in her life had been leading up to this moment, when she gazed out at the enchanted place Sebastian had called "the end of the earth."

It felt to Julia as if fate had delivered her to Cornwall.

It was a glorious May afternoon when the coach rounded a wide bend in the road and came rumbling to a stop on a cliff high above the River Fowey. Even Sebastian was startled by the sudden view, and when he glanced back and saw Julia's radiant face at the coach window, he swung down from his horse. Before he could fetch her, she had come to meet him, her face alight with enthusiasm.

"I have never seen a more picturesque spot!" she exclaimed. "Are we near Trevarre Hall?"

"Very near." Something prompted him to put an arm around her waist as a cool breeze swirled about them, and he lifted his other hand to point southward. "Do you see, there are three villages. There, on this bank of the river, where the harbor mouth meets the open sea, is Polruan. It's known for its staggeringly steep lanes and pilchard fishermen."

"Ah. I see," she replied, smiling broadly.

"And, across the river, that attractive town that resembles a French harbor is Fowey." He pronounced it 'Foy,' and indeed, it was a handsome place. Terraced streets of slate-roofed dwellings formed a sloping maze down to the river's edge, where tall-masted sailing ships rested at anchor. "Finally, at the bottom of this very cliff lies the tiny hamlet of Bodinnick, which isn't much more than one narrow lane with a few cottages plunging down to the ferry."

Julia looked, and saw the ferryman pushing off with his pole toward Fowey at that very moment. Shielding her eyes against the sunlight, she thoughtfully retraced her surroundings. From their vantage point, she could see that most of the verdant, rolling landscape was taken up with woods, meadows, and plowed fields. On the cliff across from Polruan, a small round castle stood guard against the sea. Sebastian pointed southward to a wide gap in the riverbank, saying, "That's the mouth of Pont Pill, a tidal creek that meanders through some of our land."

"What an odd name for a creek."

"In fact, 'pill' is Cornish for 'creek.' There's a little, ancient footbridge by our old lime kiln, so that's the 'pont.'"

"I can hardly wait to explore," she murmured dreamily. "I should love to have a tiny boat of my own!"

Sebastian looked at her in surprise, the wind tossing his black hair. "Would you, indeed? Perhaps that can be arranged."

At that, she quite forgot herself. "Oh, Sebastian, how can you not love this place?"

Drawing back, he grasped her arm and led her back to the coach. "You have no notion at all of my life, or of my family, or of the godforsaken place that is Trevarre Hall. If you believe that you can will me to feel differently, you are sadly mistaken."

Stung, Julia fell silent as he put her inside and closed the door.

With that, the tiny band of travelers continued north to a hidden lane high above Bodinnick. Passing between stone gateposts, Sebastian rode ahead of the coach down a muddy, weed-choked drive that, nonetheless, provided Julia with a panoramic view of the River Fowey and its pastoral environs. In the golden light of late afternoon, the effect was one of pure enchantment.

However, alighting from the coach, she saw that Trevarre Hall was not enchanting in the least. The barns, stables, and other outbuildings were tumbling down and the farmyard was filled with ill-tended chickens, goats, pigs, and sheep that roamed at will right up to the ancient manor house. The sprawling Hall itself, though soundly built of stone and slate, was in a state of disrepair. A scruffy orange cat peered out at Julia through a broken window.

"My goodness," she said softly.

"It's even bloody worse than I remembered." Scowling, Sebastian caught her before she stepped in a large pile of horse excrement. "Now do you understand? I can send you home to Turbans. I should have sent you back the moment I learned where we were being forced to live."

"Absolutely not!" Julia looked back toward the view of the beguiling world spread out along the river, and lifted her chin. "I feel as if I'm coming home."

"Madam, kindly spare me any further glad sentiments this day, or I may choke." With that, Sebastian swung her out of the mud, up into his arms, and started toward the forbidding manor house..

Chapter 14

The remaining servants at Trevarre Hall were clearly not expecting visitors. When Sebastian knocked on the old carved door, there was no response. He found the rusted knocker and let it fall with a loud thud, and eventually the portal creaked open to reveal a tall woman of perhaps three score years. Her ill-fitting gray gown was pinned closed, and the bodice was crisscrossed by a fichu.

"What d'ye want?" the woman demanded. A scent of strong spirits clung to her words.

"Is that you, Mrs. Snuggs?" Sebastian could hardly believe his eyes. The housekeeper he remembered was younger, cleaner, and definitely more respectful.

"It be me," she snapped, peering at him. After a moment, she blinked and straightened her mobcap. "Lord Sebastian Trevarre? Can it be true?"

"It is heartening to know that you recognize a member of my family." His voice was heavy with irony. Looking past her, he glimpsed the sitting room off the front hall, cluttered and dirty. There were two big dogs slumbering in the middle of the tapestry rug, and a chicken scratched at the wide floorboards. "It would appear that you had forgotten us."

Just then a bent, unshaven old man came through from the back of the house. "Mrs. Snuggs!" he shouted. "Where be my cider? D'ye drink it all again, woman?"

"Mr. Snuggs," she replied, "can ye not see that there be visitors? 'Tis our own Lord Sebastian and his—his—"

"Wife," supplied Sebastian.

"It be his lordship an' her ladyship, come to see us." Her tone had turned reverential. "Come and greet them!"

Mr. Snuggs, sporting a soiled red waistcoat that did little to camouflage his large belly, looked as if he wished he could disappear. Bowing to the visitors, he added a toothless smile and inquired hopefully, "Do ye be passing on yer way to Truro?"

"No, Snuggs, we are here to stay." Sebastian arched a dark eyebrow. "My wife and I will be *living* at Trevarre Hall."

For a long moment, the old couple stared at each other in horrified disbelief, but before they could speak, a third servant came clattering down the stairway. The chubby young woman with brown hair, freckles, and a snub nose was carrying the same orange striped cat Julia had seen looking out the window when they arrived.

"Look who I found, skulkin' about! Sly Dick never stops tryin' to court our Miss Clover," the girl exclaimed. The sight of the visitors caused her to stop short and nearly drop the scraggly cat. "My stars! Who's this?"

Mrs. Snuggs dug an elbow into the girl's side. "Primmie, meet Lord Sebastian Trevarre an' his new bride. They do be plannin' to *live* here now." Turning to Sebastian, she said, "This here's Primula Prim, yer lordship. She did come to the Hall backalong I be ill with the ague and needin' help with my duties."

He cast a dubious eye at his surroundings. "Perhaps you ought to hire a few *more* serving girls," he commented.

Primmie tossed Dick the cat unceremoniously out into the yard, then returned to spread her aproned skirts, curtsying. "I be honored to meet your lordship and ladyship!" She glanced over at Mrs. Snuggs again and whispered, "Where'll they sleep? Did you not boast that your own chamber do once be that of Lord and Lady Caverleigh?"

Mrs. Snuggs had the good grace to turn red. "Foolish girl, come with me. There be work to do!

As the two women hurried away, Sebastian glanced at Julia and muttered, "Amen."

Moonlight streamed between the embroidered hangings to illuminate the bed where Julia lay wide awake next to a slumbering Sebastian. He resembled a Greek god to her, stretched out on his back, one brown hand splayed across his hard-muscled belly while his other arm was flung upward, above his tousled hair.

His male beauty was almost enough to make her forget the room's pervasive mustiness that mingled with the acrid scent of candle smoke. There was so much to do! Every surface was covered with dust, and when Julia had opened the big wardrobe that stood against the far wall, she'd discovered mouse droppings. When the sun rose, she intended to lead her rag-tag new staff in a thorough cleaning of Trevarre Hall.

An owl hooted from the broken-down barn outside. The melancholy sound sent a fresh wave of uncertainty over Julia as she reflected on the life with her own family that now seemed so distant. Remembering the evenings that she and Sarah and Freddy had laughed together over games of casino or efforts at making profile portraits of one another, she blinked back tears. She longed even for the hand wringing of her mother and lessons with Freddy in the minaret.

Most of all, she longed for her father, who had been flawed yet so constant in his love for her. Grief was an ache in her heart that never quite left her, no matter how distracted she might be by the unfolding drama of her new life.

"Papa," Julia whispered softly, "I miss you."

"Come here."

She looked toward her husband in surprise, wondering if she were hearing things. His eyes were open, watching her with a smoldering intensity that made her skin prickle. "I am sorry if I woke you, Sebastian. I didn't mean to speak out loud."

"Come here," he repeated, and gathered her into his arms.

The comforting strength of his embrace almost caused her to whimper with relief. He slowly began to stroke her back with one deft hand, up and down, while he murmured sleepily against her ear. She closed her eyes, thinking that he smelled wonderful.

"Julia, I'm sorry…sorry for your grief, and my part in it."

Knowing how hard this must be for him, she nodded, blinking back tears. "I am sorry, too…for tricking you."

He held her closer and soon her searching mouth found his. They found one another in a tangle of moonlit bedclothes, suddenly exchanging hot kisses with wordless urgency. Sebastian's caresses roughened in response to Julia's muffled cries. She couldn't get close enough, tugging at her own nightgown to fit herself against him, her fingers searching the hard contours of his buttocks, his hipbones, and then finding the firm pulsing length of his maleness.

Sebastian quickly drew off her nightclothes. Her breasts were pale and rounded above the narrow span of her waist and the curves of her hips. Since she wouldn't stop touching him, he pressed her back into the lumpy mattress and held her arms down by her wrists. His mouth went straight to one swollen nipple, bathing it with hot strokes, then fastening on it and suckling rhythmically until he heard her moan deep in her throat and she struggled to open her thighs to him.

Julia was throbbing and wet with a need that was incomprehensible to her. She couldn't get close enough to him and somehow he seemed to understand, doing magical things with his mouth until she was shaking. Soon he was burning his way up to her neck and then kissing her mouth more deeply than ever before. She could feel his powerful heartbeat when he lay on top of her, dominating her in a way that she suddenly found utterly thrilling. Her hands were in his hair, his fingers probed so gently between her legs and she made low animal sounds in her throat. She felt him nod, his crisp dark hair moving against her sensitive breasts, and her fingers were tracing the contours of his face, as if he was a warm, living work of art.

"Wait, wait," Sebastian urged her. His kisses burned the satiny hollow of her belly, and then he was hovering above the damp tangle of curls between her legs. Softly, he let out a warm breath.

Julia couldn't think, only need, and it went far beyond her urgent physical longing for him. Her thighs were trembling. His fingertips deftly teased the swollen, sensitized bud as she emitted low broken cries.

"Christ, you are so hot and wet," he muttered.

She sank her fingers into his hair and urged him closer, not even sure what she wanted, knowing only that her world was centered there and it seemed she would die without fulfillment. When his tongue found that most sensitive spot, Julia began to pant, unable to stop herself from pushing against his mouth. He suckled so gently, pausing and then beginning again, that at last sensations exploded outward from that swollen bud, shaking her to the core.

He held her hips as she shuddered against him, and then he shifted upward and entered her, groaning with pleasure as he pushed inside until their bodies were joined. She met each of his thrusts with a fervor that surprised them both until Sebastian couldn't hold back any longer and his own release came in burning waves of bliss.

When dawn came and Julia opened her eyes and discovered that she was alone, she wondered at first if it had all been a dream. Then she saw that she was still naked beneath the sheets and she felt the tenderness of her breasts, and the soreness between her legs, and she knew the truth.

And when she turned her face into the pillow, she inhaled Sebastian's subtle, intoxicating scent and felt a new sort of ache, this time in her heart. A memory returned from the middle of the night when she had awakened to find his arms around her, brown against the paleness of her torso, as if it were the most natural thing in the world.

Just then the door swung open and Primmie appeared with a tray. "You be awake, my lady? I have your breakfast. Tea and porridge."

Julia sat up, holding the blankets close to her breasts. "Thank you, Primmie. Set it on the table, please."

"Yes, my lady." When she glanced at the bed, a blush stained her chubby face.

Unable to help herself, Julia asked, "Is his lordship here?"

"No, my lady. He went off on horseback at dawn, with his manservant. My lord bid me tell you that he would bring food back later today."

"I see. All right. Well, then, I shall dress and join you downstairs shortly. Tell Mrs. Snuggs that we all have a lot of work to do to put this house in order."

"Yes, my lady," Primmie replied doubtfully.

It was a discouraging day for Julia as she tried to establish some authority over her new and unwilling staff. She quickly realized that they were trying to test her. Mrs. Snuggs did a bit of cleaning up in the rustic, whitewashed kitchen, and then when Julia went to look for her to begin dusting and scrubbing the floors, she found the old woman asleep in a chair in the sitting room, a plush smoky-gray cat curled on her lap.

"Mrs. Snuggs!" She shook her bony shoulder. "Wake up. We have a great deal of work to do and there is no time for resting."

"My lady, I do not be *well.* If you don't leave me be, I'll be of no use to you at all."

Julia soon realized that the methods and habits of these servants were shoddy compared to the domestic staff at Turbans. No one had trained them properly and they strongly resisted taking orders from her. So, she tied a kerchief around her own hair, found a patched apron to tie on over her plainest frock, and took Primmie in hand.

As they dusted and scrubbed every piece of furniture in the Hall, Julia asked the girl, "Did you know Lady Caverleigh, Primmie?"

"I do only meet her one time after I come here to work. She be a lovely lady, talking about a lot of plans to restore the house, but she and Lord Caverleigh never did linger with us. His lordship do have business in Fowey and once it were finished, they sailed off to France."

"Were they alone?"

"No, my lady. Young Lady Isabella be with them."

Julia longed to ask more questions, but just then the plump gray cat wandered over and rubbed against her skirts, purring. "Hello, puss."

"That be Clover," Primmie said. "She fancies herself the queen of the manor."

"And is Dick the king?" Julia asked, remembering the scrawny cat that had been evicted from the house upon their arrival.

"Ha! He'd like to be! But Clover do want no part of that scoundrel. He won't give up, though, and sneaks into the Hall at every opportunity. Determined to have his way with her, Dick is, if it's the last thing he does!"

The cat looked up with her great golden eyes and exclaimed, "Me-oww!"

Laughing, Julia reached down to pet her. "You're a wise

kitty, Clover. I suspect you know that loving a rogue will only lead to heartbreak."

Sebastian and Keswick returned at dusk, bringing sacks of spring vegetables, flour and barley, spices, honey and sweet butter, a tin of black tea, a round loaf of brown bread, and two large chickens, already cleaned and plucked. Julia was overjoyed. She roasted the birds on the spit in the kitchen fireplace and taught Primmie how to make a vegetable stew that was thick with tiny red potatoes.

When Sebastian joined her at the dark trestle table set with just two places, Julia saw that he had washed and shaved and was wearing fresh clothing. She, too, had managed to find a hipbath that afternoon and persuaded Primmie to heat water so that she could wash properly.

"You look very nice," she told him as they sat together in the candlelight.

"Thank you," he replied with a jaunty grin. "So do you. I like the way you've styled your hair."

Julia smiled as she touched the soft curls that she'd pinned up while still damp. "Sebastian, shall we invite Keswick to join us? He is perfectly welcome."

"God, no. He's eating in the kitchen with Primmie and the others, and I can assure you that that is exactly where he wants to be." Casually, Sebastian added, "He used to live here, you know. He was the stable master when I was a boy."

"Really! I had no idea."

He had focused on his meal, tasting a bite of chicken with a look of wonder. "I know Mrs. Snuggs didn't cook this. Was it you?"

She nodded, suddenly feeling shy. "Yes. I'm trying to teach Primmie to cook—and to clean, for that matter, but I must tell you that it is a struggle to get any of them to do any real work. In fact, I suspect that Mr. and Mrs. Snuggs are into the port and cider most of the time."

Sebastian finished swallowing a spoonful of stew and began to laugh. "I'm sorry, but the thought of you trying to herd this band of recalcitrant servants is an amusing image. I know their faults all too well."

"You could help, you know," she told him with a frown.

His laughter subsided and he put on a serious expression. "Perhaps I could. I'll speak to them in the morning."

"Can I ask another immense favor?"

"Mmm. After that meal, how can I say no?"

She looked into his eyes which were usually so cool and detached, but now gazed at her with new warmth. "You told me I could have a little boat. I am longing desperately to explore the woods and creeks that we saw from the hilltops while approaching Trevarre Hall."

"Ah, Julia, I am not sure that's a good idea at all, and I certainly didn't agree to get you a boat."

"It doesn't feel fair that I should be left behind here, day after day, while you go off and do whatever it is that you and Keswick are doing."

"You certainly can't come with me, if that's what you are implying." He set down his fork and pushed back from the table.

"I don't want to come with you, but I must admit that I wonder what is so mysterious that I must remain ignorant of it."

"You try my patience, Julia." Running a hand through his hair, he lowered his voice and added, "It's only a business venture that I hope will restore our fortunes, much more quickly and successfully than a lot of bloody sheep or a lime kiln. Tedious but necessary."

She held up a hand to silence him. "All right, but I won't be a prisoner here. I simply want some freedom of my own, freedom to explore the villages, meet the people, but most of all, to enjoy the abundant nature that Cornwall clearly offers." Her expression softened as she added, "Primmie tells me that there is a swan sitting on a nest at the head of Pont Pill."

"Swans can be vicious," Sebastian grumbled. "I was bitten by one as a child."

"Kindly refrain from changing the subject."

"All right." He looked across the table at her, surprised anew by the degree of pleasure he took in her direct cobalt-blue eyes and her equally direct manner. "I yield, my lady. I think there may be a rowboat in the old boathouse, very near your swan's nest. I'll explore the matter further when I have an opportunity."

"Splendid!"

Although Julia was smiling at him, Sebastian thought that he perceived a reckless gleam in her eyes…

Chapter 15

At first light, when Sebastian came into the stables to find Keswick saddling his horse, he remarked, "I have been told that my beloved Lucifer was purchased by a landowner from Lerryn. My recollection is that is very near here."

"Aye, near enough to walk there, my lord," he confirmed with a nod. "Could it be the Penrose family? Their estate is very fine."

"I was wondering the same thing. I remember Tristan Penrose. He used to follow me about when I spent summers here. He was a child then, several years younger than I, but he must be a man by now. Perhaps his father bought my horse."

"Do you have it in mind to get Lucifer back, my lord?"

Sebastian slanted a half-smile at the manservant. "Perhaps. But I'll need a persuasive amount of money before I can approach him with an offer. Lucifer is a rare steed."

Before Keswick could reply, a slight figure appeared in the stable doorway. Both men turned in surprise to see Julia silhouetted against the soft flush of dawn. She was wearing a pair of breeches and a jacket.

"Keswick," she exclaimed with a radiant smile, "I almost didn't know you without your powdered wig!"

"Good morning, my lady," he replied with a little bow, revealing a full view of his thinning crop of curly gray hair.

"This is no place for a wig, we fear. It's a long way from Bath and London."

She turned to Sebastian. "Are you ready to take me in search of my little boat?"

"Julia, I don't have time for this today." His voice held a trace of annoyance. "I said that I would look into it and then we shall see."

"'Look into it?' 'We shall see'?" she echoed sweetly. "That sounds alarmingly vague. I have learned, my lord, that if I want something to happen, I cannot wait for others to accommodate me. If you will simply tell me where this boat is located, I shall be perfectly content to go in search of it myself."

"You are *not* to do that!"

"Then you intend to accompany me—this morning?"

"No, I have other business to attend to. "

"No doubt Primmie can direct me, since she has mentioned the swan's nest and you said the boathouse is near that nest." Turning, Julia nodded to both men and turned to start back to the Hall.

Sebastian gave Keswick a look of white-hot frustration and, pursuing his wife with long strides, soon caught her by the elbow. "You are vexing," he accused. "I have important business to attend to this morning!"

"Yes, I perceive so. I won't keep you from it." She tried to twist free of his grasp, to no avail. "Loose me, sir!"

"Devil take it," he ground out, still holding fast to her arm. "I'll take you to see that cursed boat! Kindly make haste, madam."

Following Sebastian as he strode toward the old apple orchard that spread between Trevarre Hall and the River Fowey, Julia succumbed again to the spell of enchantment that she had felt at the moment of their arrival two days earlier.

As they entered the orchard, she noticed a stone roof top peeking above the trees a few dozen yards to the east. "What is that?"

"Oh, it's the old chapel. An ancestor of my mother's built it here in the mid-1300's as a private oratory for the family and their servants and guests."

When they came closer, Julia saw that there was a narrow lane leading up a slope that afforded a better look at the chapel. It was still quite lovely, built of local slate with a pitched roof, an arched doorway, and a bell tower at one end. However, closer inspection revealed a gaping hole in the roof, vines climbing up every stone surface, and windows completely open to the elements.

Peeking inside, Julia gasped. The chapel was filled with old farm equipment and broken furniture. A large birdcage teetered atop some splintered wooden chairs. Above them, birds flew about in the beautiful oak cradle ceiling, and the old upper gallery was filled with straw.

"How could this happen?" she exclaimed.

Sebastian shrugged. "After the Reformation, private chapels like this went out of use. My mother dreamed of restoring it, but Father naturally thought that was a ludicrous idea." He glanced up at the ceiling with its curved, intersecting beams. "It is rather amazing."

"It's a terrible shame to see it become a ruin! Can't we do something about it? It's like falling back into the past, especially when one imagines what it was once like."

"Julia, I have neither the funds nor the time. The whole farm is crumbling, in case you've forgotten, which is one more reason why I don't want to live here." He took her arm. "Come. We can't linger if we're going to find you a boat."

Her sadness for the decaying chapel diminished as they set off again through the old orchard. Soon they climbed over a stile and came into a wood laced with meandering paths lavishly bordered with bluebells and pale yellow primroses. Birds were flitting and chirping among the tree branches and Julia quickly recognized goldfinches, wren-like robins, and wood warblers.

"I can scarcely wait to come back and collect some specimens," she murmured.

"Specimens?" Sebastian repeated in surprise. "Do you mean to kill something and dissect it?"

"What a terrible thing to say! No!" She realized then that he knew nothing of her collection of pressed flowers and leaves, abandoned birds' nests, shells, and feathers, nor was he aware that, since childhood she had kept records of every bird and animal she had seen. "I was talking to myself. I like to collect bits of nature, like fallen leaves or interesting rocks. I don't want to kill anything."

Glancing down at her as they walked, Sebastian gave her what appeared to be a grudging smile. "You are a highly original female, Julia. Where did you get those clothes?"

"They were my brother Freddy's. A pair of breeches can be invaluable, particularly when exploring nature."

They continued on, emerging intermittently from the woods to look down from high above the river and enjoy a sweeping view of the picturesque town of Fowey on the opposite bank.

"This wide path has existed for three centuries, when my mother's ancestors, the Wentworths, laid it out as an ornamental promenade. Legend has it that the first King Charles walked here and was shot at during the Civil War. Unfortunately for England, a fisherman was struck and killed instead." He pointed to a long bench that backed up to a stone wall and was sheltered by a shallow roof of slate angling out above. "That was constructed during the sixteenth century, I'm told. Doubtless King Charles sat there to catch his breath after nearly being shot dead."

Julia stopped for a moment, imagining the ill-fated king and how history had nearly been altered on this very spot. Then, Sebastian took her hand and started off again. They walked through more woodland pathways, turning eventually to skirt hilltops that sloped down to a wide stream opening off of the River Fowey.

"That's Pont Pill," he told her. "It's a tidal creek that flows off the river, and this is all Trevarre land."

Between tree branches hung with trailing vines of traveler's joy, Julia viewed the pastoral sweep of the creek. It gradually widened until it merged with the river, where quaint boats rested an anchor, their sails furled. "Sebastian, it's simply magical!"

To her dismay, he only shrugged.

"How can you *not* adore it?" she cried.

"Perhaps the circumstances weren't happy," came his cryptic reply.

Julia longed to know more, but she sensed the invisible barrier he'd erected. He started forward again, no longer holding her hand. Soon they were clambering down from the steep hillside along a wooded path. In the distance, she saw a cluster of stone and slate buildings where the creek narrowed as it traveled inland.

"This is Pont," Sebastian explained. "When I was a child, this tiny settlement was very active. There are quays, a warehouse, and a malt house on the north bank, and a lime kiln and a couple of cottages and farm buildings on the far side. Vessels sailed up the creek to unload cargoes like timber and limestone, but since the Trevarre family declined to live at the Hall except for occasional visits, it has all fallen into disrepair." Looking around, he shook his head. "Even the sheep we once raised are gone, sold by my brother to finance his Italian exile."

Near the vine-covered lime kiln on the creek's south bank stood a whitewashed farm house.

"How sad that no one lives here," Julia said, peeking in one of the windows. "It could be charming."

Just then, a swan glided under the footbridge, heading upstream, while a flash of turquoise alerted Julia to a kingfisher swooping down from the wooded hillside in search of fish for its breakfast. She could hardly wait to have her boat and begin exploring this magical world.

As if reading her mind, Sebastian pried open the doors to a rubble-slate boathouse that stood at the water's edge. "Ah-ha."

She rushed over to see for herself and gave a little cry of delight. The rowboat was small and plain, but it appeared to be undamaged and that was all that mattered to her.

"Will it do?" Sebastian asked. His tone suggested that he expected her to change her mind.

"Do?" Julia repeated in wonderment before throwing her arms around his neck. "It's absolutely perfect! Thank you, Sebastian."

His arms slipped around her slender back. She looked up into his dark face with all its secrets and yearned for him to let her in. Standing on tiptoe, Julia turned her face up and felt a frisson of arousal when she realized that he was going to kiss her.

Just then came the sound of hoof beats on the narrow lane that traced the progress of the creek inland. They broke apart and turned to see a ginger-haired young man riding toward them on the most magnificent black horse Julia had ever seen.

"Lord Sebastian!" shouted the stranger. "Can it be you?"

As he drew up beside the lime kiln and swung to the ground, Sebastian guided Julia forward with one hand and reached out to the young man with the other.

"Tristan? Good God, you are a grown man!" he exclaimed, and together they began to laugh. "I was just speaking of you to Keswick this very morning. How did you find me?"

Filled with curiosity, Julia watched as they embraced. The fellow called Tristan was perhaps a decade younger than her husband, but lean-hipped, strong, and very handsome. He had russet hair that clearly rebelled against a comb, sea-blue eyes, and a sculpted face with an infectiously roguish smile. He wore proper riding attire, from his expensive boots to a finely tailored coat and knotted white stock.

Sebastian turned back to Julia then and drew her forward. "You must meet the Honorable Tristan Penrose," he told her. "This handsome young fellow is heir to Lanwyllow, one of the finest estates in the Fowey River Valley. Tristan, allow me to present my wife, Julia."

The laughter went out of Penrose's eyes, replaced by frank surprise. "Indeed! My lady, it is an honor to meet the woman who has brought this stallion into the barn." Clasping her hand and bowing to kiss it lightly, he added, "Welcome to our magical corner of Cornwall."

"Thank you, sir! I confess I am already under its spell." Laughing, she added, "How polite you are to make no sign that you are shocked by my breeches."

"I am charmed rather than shocked."

"Tristan, you haven't answered my question," Sebastian persisted. "How did you know I was here?"

"I heard that you and Keswick had been sighted near Bodinnick, but I didn't know that I'd find you at Pont." He pointed a thumb backward, over his shoulder. "It was my horse who brought me. I think he must have heard his master's voice."

For the first time, Sebastian focused on the black stallion. "I was so distracted by the sight of you, Tristan, that I didn't realize…"

"Yes, it's your Lucifer! We were bound for Polruan, but as we passed the turning for Pont, I think he may have heard your voice. I was powerless to stop him."

"My God. I can't believe it." Sebastian went forward and held the horse's big head in his hands. Lucifer closed his eyes for a moment, pressed his face closer, and seemed to let out a sigh. "What a great day."

Julia was moved by the sight of her husband's eyes agleam with tears, and she longed to embrace him and share in the tender scene. Instead, she turned to Penrose and smiled. "How lovely to meet you, sir."

"You must call me Tristan, my lady." He glanced over at his old friend. "It is a great day indeed. Are you truly here to stay?"

"For the foreseeable future," Sebastian allowed.

"I was so sorry to hear about Lord and Lady Caverleigh."

"Thank you. Unfortunately, since my parents' deaths, my dear brother has gambled away virtually every family possession except the Hall. That is why we have come here to live." He arched a brow at the younger man and grinned. "And what of you, my friend? The last time we met, I had just left Oxford and your voice was deepening."

Tristan laughed. "Yes, quite a few things have changed since then."

"How are your parents?"

"My mother is well, but I am sorry to say my father died last year. I am now Viscount Senwyck of Lanwyllow."

After more condolences were exchanged, Tristan came to stand beside Lucifer. "Sebastian, I heard about your brother's difficulties, and so I purchased Lucifer when the opportunity arose and I have been keeping him against the day that you would return from the Royal Navy. I know how much you have meant to each other."

"Don't spout fustian. He is your horse now, Tristan."

"You know that if I didn't bring him to you, he would find a way on his own." He laid a hand on his friend's shoulder. "Truly, this has been my plan all along. Indulge me."

A rare, joyous smile transformed Sebastian's face. "You have persuaded me, my friend. I'm very grateful." Looking toward Julia, he added, "Perhaps I should thank you, as well, for bringing me here today despite my resistance."

"Are you saying that you've enjoyed our morning, my lord?" She was suffused by a wave of contentment as she leaned against him for a long moment, drinking in the warm strength of his arm under her cheek.

"Perhaps I am," Sebastian admitted with a short laugh. His eyes met Tristan's then and he said, "Let's all go back to the Hall and celebrate with a toast, shall we?"

Chapter 16

Tucked into the sunlit courtyard behind Trevarre Hall was a little brick-bordered kitchen garden that had long ago fallen into disuse.

"How could you have let this happen, Primmie?" Julia demanded. As she pushed new seeds into the dark earth, Clover wound her way between them, purring all the while. "If you and Mrs. Snuggs had taken care of this plot, you could have had all the herbs and vegetables you needed right outside the back door."

"Mrs. Snuggs be a good deal more worried about having enough port, not vegetables! And, it weren't up to *me* to oversee the care of this estate. There ought to be a factor to do that job, don't you suppose?"

"Yes, there should. I wonder who it used to be?"

"Jasper Polarven, I hear, but his sons be free-traders and they drowned in a wreck last year. The Revenue men was chasing them at sea, during a storm. He's not been the same since." Primmie wrinkled her nose in the direction of the kitchen. "Mr. an' Mrs. Snuggs couldn't be depended on to feed the cat here, let alone look after the gardens, the stables, the animals…"

"Clearly not," Julia agreed drily. They continued to work for several minutes before she spoke again. "That's a very sad story about Mr. Polarven's sons. Are there many local boys who have turned to smuggling?"

Primmie grew animated. "Oh, my lady, practically every man I do know is involved somehow, and the rest of Cornish folk just look t'other way." Leaning closer, she whispered conspiratorially, "Plenty of cottages and even churches do have hidey holes for concealing contraband liquor, lace, an' tobacco. The taxes the king demands be impossible, you know, so folk do find other ways to make ends meet." She paused, then added, "The very best smugglers do get quite wealthy, and they be generous with the village folk."

"What kind of taxes are you referring to?"

"Well, Cornish fishermen do need salt, an' lots of it, to cure the pilchard and pig meat that we must eat over the winter. But my brother says that the King wants revenue to pay for the war with France, and now the salt *taxes* be higher than the cost of the salt itself!"

"I had no idea."

"Fishermen've already lost markets overseas because of that horrible war. And now, because they can't afford the tax on salt, the pilchards we do need to salt down for winter rot instead and be spread on the fields as manure. Mayhap the King don't care if us starve. What choice do Cornishmen have but to turn to smuggling if they want t' feed their families?"

"But still, Primmie, there are so many risks! The Revenue men are in pursuit, the weather is treacherous, and perhaps most important of all, smuggling is unlawful. As I recall, it's punishable by transportation…or even hanging!"

The girl stared as if she couldn't credit that she'd heard correctly. Pursing her lips with disapproval, she went back to planting seeds and mumbled, "As you say, my lady."

After Julia completed her own early morning tasks and gave Primmie and Mrs. Snuggs a list of chores for the day, she hurried through the enchanted wood to Pont, as was now her habit. The swan's nest that nestled upstream against the scrubby creek bed, was always her first stop. It was a work of art, fashioned of countless long, bent twigs and large enough to comfortably hold the regal female swan while her mate glided up and down the creek all day, guarding his family.

Julia exchanged calls with the birds, and set off in her little rowboat on a new water adventure. Today, she wore a simple cocoa-colored gown, carrying a bundle with the breeches she preferred, because she intended to visit the town of Fowey, on the opposite bank of the river.

The tide was in and Pont Pill was calm as Julia rowed, passing coppiced creek-side woods where yellow wagtails danced among the branches. Out on the river, the currents were more vigorous and the wind tossed her little boat upon the water. As the ferry from Polruan came alongside, one of the two strong men who rowed it called to her.

"Can you manage, mistress?"

"I think so," she replied with a nervous laugh. "Thank you!" Again, Julia wished that females could wear breeches in public without being censured. If her little boat should turn over, swimming would be nearly impossible in the confines of her gown.

To the south, a pair of blockhouses guarded the harbor mouth, beyond which stretched the English Channel. Julia put her head down, curls blowing in her eyes, and pulled at the oars until she saw the stone quay in Fowey's town center loom up before her. The burly Polruan ferryman who had spoken to her on the river now came to her aid. After tying up the rowboat, he handed Julia onto the quay and swept her with a long, curious look.

"Mistress, I do not believe we have met before. Might you be a new resident at Trevarre Hall? Word spreads that Lord Sebastian Trevarre be in residence."

"Yes, I am his wife," she replied.

"Indeed? Welcome. My name is Robert Mixstowe and I be honored to know you, my lady." Then, as if unable to help himself, he added, "I confess to surprise that his lordship does approve of you setting out alone in that rowboat. Such adventures could be perilous."

"I thank you for your words of concern, Mr. Mixstowe, and I assure you that my husband would agree with you. I am doubtless too adventurous for my own good."

Carrying the bundle that contained Freddy's breeches and jacket, Julia started up the stone steps. At the top, she turned and waved to the ferryman, calling, "Sir, may I ask the name of your friend who told you that my husband had returned to Trevarre Hall? Was it Viscount Senwyck?"

Mixstowe laughed, his face ruddy in the sunlight. "No, my lady, 'twas Ezra Keswick, stable master at the Hall backalong I were but a boy! We do drink a pint together at the Ferry Inn in Bodinnick last midday."

Waving goodbye to the ferryman, Julia set off to explore the twisting lanes of Fowey, many of which were too narrow to accommodate a carriage. As she walked, she pondered everything that Mixstowe had told her. It was still a challenge for her to think of Keswick, the perfectly proper, white-wigged manservant she was used to, as a Cornish stable master who fraternized with a plain-spoken working fellow like Robert Mixstowe. Clearly, Keswick had deeper roots here than Sebastian, who appeared to be relying on his manservant to guide him in his new endeavors.

Villagers nodded to Julia as she walked past the handsome old church of St. Fimbarrus and its grand neighbor, the Treffry family's castle home, called simply "Place". She sensed their curious glances, and knew that soon enough her identity would be revealed, but for now she cherished her anonymity. The hills above Fowey, which she knew would lead to the sea, called to her. She was walking up a steep lane when she spied a young man entering a half-timbered house. Something about him was familiar, even from behind, but when he turned his head for an instant to reveal an austere profile, Julia blinked in disbelief.

Could it possibly be Adolphus Lynton? By the time he had disappeared into the low doorway, she had chuckled aloud at her own imagination. What in the world would Adolphus Lynton be doing in the wilds of Cornwall? It was a ridiculous notion.

Soon, Julia had reached the crest of the hill above the village. Continuing in a westerly direction, she came upon a sheltered grove of trees and happily changed into her breeches and jacket. After concealing the bundle containing her gown between some tree branches, she started down a path that followed a wooded valley toward the sea. The soft breeze was cooler here, with a tang of salt, and she quickened her step.

The cliffs, rising on either side of the little valley that led down to the sea, were decorated with ox-eye daisies and sea campion. When, at length, Julia emerged from the tree-canopied path, she saw a small stone cottage snuggled against a pebbled beach. It appeared to be an abandoned fisherman's dwelling.

Charmed, she circled around, saw that the door was slightly ajar, and dared to peek inside, where she was surprised to find signs that the cottage might have been recently inhabited. Overcome by curiosity, Julia stepped inside for a closer look. There was a rustic bench against one whitewashed wall, a rough table with a jug of cider and an empty mug on it, a hard chair, and a few books propped on a deep windowsill.

Julia wrinkled her nose. Was it possible that she detected the faintest suggestion of tobacco lingering in the cottage? Or perhaps it was just the damp of the stones. Looking around a doorway, she discovered that there was another room that held a bed and a chamber pot. And, in the wooden floor between the two rooms, one wide board was slightly askew. Primmie's voice came back to her, with her tales of smugglers and their hidey-holes.

She shouldn't be there, she realized. Turning, she took barely a step back toward the door before the sound of hoof beats reached her ears.

Julia stood frozen near the narrow bed, her heart thundering. She could hear the horses snorting as they were reined in beside the cottage, then the sound of boots hitting the ground as riders dismounted.

Moments later, the outside door creaked loudly and a deep male voice demanded, "Who trespasses here?"

Looking around helplessly for a weapon, Julia grabbed the heavy ironstone chamber pot and managed to lift it overhead. As the first man took a step through the doorway, she tried to bring the pot down, but he was too tall to hit over the head, and before she could react, he had wrested the foul thing from her grasp.

"Julia!" he shouted, holding her fast with his free arm. "What the devil are you doing—*here*?"

"Sebastian?" She focused in disbelief, first on her husband, and then on Keswick and Tristan, who were right behind him in the doorway. "What in the world are *you* doing here?"

"I can't believe my eyes! Don't you realize, I could have done you serious harm, thinking that you were a—a—"

"Why should you be suspicious of a person in this little cottage?" she interjected. "It has nothing to do with you."

For an instant, he glanced back at his companions before replying, "That's not the point. Come out here and sit down for a moment." Without waiting for her response, Sebastian pulled her along into the main room of the cottage. He drew Julia down next to him on the bench, while his companions looked on with expressions of expectant curiosity. "Stop gawking, you two, and sit down!"

When Keswick and Tristan had obeyed, Sebastian turned to his wife. "This is not about me."

"But why are you here?"

He ignored her question. "You must not roam around these parts alone. It's dangerous, especially for a female. Do you think that you can behave as a man just because you are wearing breeches? I swear, I will lock up that rowboat if you do not obey me."

"Have you gone mad? You are not my master!"

Keswick cleared his throat. "Perhaps we should wait for you outside, my lord."

"No. Her ladyship and I are not going to quarrel. I only intend to explain to her that she must stay away from Coombe Cottage for the simple reason that it is haunted."

Julia's eyes widened and she gave a little gasp of laughter. "Are you joking? Surely you do not believe in such nonsense."

Across from them, Keswick's brows pricked upward. "My lady, this is Cornwall."

"And what is that supposed to mean?" she cried.

"I would suggest that you calm down and heed those of us who *may,* just this once, know more than you do," Sebastian instructed sardonically. Then, schooling himself to look stern, he continued, "A century past, during a terrible storm, a ship was dashed on the rocks of Coombe Hawne—"

"Hawne? What is that?"

Keswick offered, "It's an old Cornish word for a harbor, my lady, or a haven."

"Will you kindly cease interrupting and give me your attention?" Firmly, Sebastian continued, "After the ship was wrecked there came a pounding on the door of this tiny cottage. It was a dower house then, I suspect, because a very old woman lived here, and she was very frightened. When she peeked out the door, she saw a half-drowned man, his clothing torn, his eyes wild. He clung to her, dripping water, begging to come in. Terrified, the old woman pushed him backward into the storm and slammed the door. At dawn, when the gale had ceased, she looked outside and found the man lying face-down on her door-step—dead!" He pointed through the low, crooked entrance for dramatic effect. "I can almost see his body on that very spot, can't you?"

"Why, that's a horrible tale!" cried Julia.

"Indeed. Yet very true. This cottage has been haunted ever since. That's why the Pryces, who own the farm at the head of the valley, don't come here any more, and why you must vow to stay away as well!"

"But clearly, someone does come here!" She gestured toward the items on the table, and the books on the windowsill. "Perhaps the ghost is gone now."

Suddenly, he was facing her, his hands lifting her off the bench, his eyes blazing into hers. "Julia, this is not a matter for discussion. I am *ordering* you to stay away from Coombe Cottage. Do you understand?"

She opened her mouth to protest, but was swept up by the heat of his gaze and the strength of his fingers. The notion that Sebastian could truly believe in a ghost was ludicrous, but the emotion behind his order was very real.

"All right," she said reluctantly, "I despise that word 'order,' but because you are so insistent, I will agree."

Chapter 17

Pont Pill was not the only tidal stream flowing out from the picturesque Fowey estuary. Farther upriver the even wider Lerryn Creek curled eastward, hugged by dense, ancient woodlands that hid the estate of Lanwyllow from the view of sailing vessels trading with the village of Lerryn.

Built in the mid-1700's of gray stone, the handsome manor house was set back from the water, and on this night it was quiet, with only a few windows aglow. Formal gardens ringed the house like jeweled bracelets. Closer to the creek, through a tunnel of magnolias, a charming thatched cottage snuggled against a grove of beech trees. In contrast to the grand manor, the cottage was ablaze with light and the muted sounds of male voices.

When Sebastian and Keswick rode up the darkened path, a stable boy came to meet them, holding a lantern aloft.

"Lord Senwyck bids ye join him an' the others, my lord."

Through a mullioned window, Sebastian could see the cluster of men sitting together at a table, smoking their clay pipes and drinking ale. They were the roughened Cornishmen he'd known all his life, weather-beaten, plain-spoken, and struggling to feed their families.

"Ah, you're here!" It was Tristan, opening the door to let mellow candlelight spill into the garden. "I can imagine it wasn't easy to leave your house tonight."

"Julia wasn't happy," Sebastian confirmed wryly. "She can smell a secret and it is driving her mad."

"After that ghost tale you spun for her yesterday, I'm not a bit surprised if she's suspicious!" Laughing, Tristan brought the two men into the room and closed the door. There was a footman, looking out of place, who served them mugs of ale before he returned to the house.

A hush fell over the group as they realized that it was Lord Sebastian Trevarre who had arrived, although he was looking more like a libertine than an aristocrat on that cool spring night. After removing his midnight-blue coat, he was clad only in buff breeches, riding boots, and a fine broadcloth shirt with a simply tied cravat.

"Thank you all for coming," Tristan was telling the group, "and for keeping this meeting place a secret. Tonight you'll learn more about our plans, but first, allow me to present Lord Sebastian Trevarre."

Sebastian looked around the table at the expectant yet wary faces, bathed in flickering candlelight. Some of the men, like Jasper Polarven, he'd known since childhood. "It's good to see you all. Jasper, I was very sorry to hear about your sons."

"They be only doin' what they must do," the wizened middle-aged man replied dolefully. "Bringin' salt from France to cure the pilchard when that King's boat do run 'em down during a storm an' sank their lugger. What man can prosper as a fisherman if the King do tax more for salt than the fish will bring? What bleddy choice did my boys have but to be free-traders?"

"The salt taxes be wrong," chimed in a sallow-faced young man to his left. "Everyone do know it."

"I agree," said Sebastian. "And I intend to organize this free-trading enterprise so that the risks will be minimized for everyone. That's why we are meeting here tonight." He turned to his erstwhile manservant, who put on a jaunty smile. "Do all of you remember Keswick? He was the stable master at the Hall for many years before kindly agreeing to look after me."

Robert Mixstowe, the Polruan ferryman, grinned at Keswick. "I do recall you be a free-trader, too, backalong you was a stuggy young man, Ezra Keswick!" He reached across to clasp the smaller man's hand. "My mum yet prizes the fine French lace that you did bring her late one night."

"Your mum was always kind to me," Keswick replied with a grin. "It pleased me to find a way to repay her."

Sebastian raised a hand to quiet the men. "I trust Keswick more than any man, so he will speak for me if I cannot be present myself. Is that understood?" He waited for everyone to nod before he continued, "If we're to be successful, we'll need to carefully address all the aspects of free-trading, for as you all know, it's much more than just sailing across the Channel and then returning with a lot of goods from France that would be highly taxed by the Crown."

"Aye, proper organization be what we want," Jasper agreed. "If every man be loyal, in his assigned role, we can succeed and be safer, too."

"Yes. All right then, let's get down to it." As Sebastian spoke, Tristan passed the jug of ale around and the men refilled their cups. "I am your leader. This is my undertaking, and I shall be responsible for planning and executing our runs. Keswick will be at my right hand when we're at sea, and he'll be responsible for hiring and overseeing the crew, consulting with me at all times. As for Lord Senwyck—"

"I am honored to play the role of venturer," Tristan interjected. His tousled hair shown in the candlelight as he grinned at Sebastian. "I'll supply not only the capital we need to operate, but also my own fast two-masted lugger, the *Peregrine*. Additionally, there are hiding places for contraband here on these grounds, and a tunnel that a free-trading ancestor was farsighted enough to dig from the woods to the house."

"How thoughtful of him," Sebastian said with a short laugh. "You must show it to me."

"I mean to be useful in other ways, though," Tristan persisted, looking into the faces of the other men. "I'm certainly not some fusty old squire who needs a cane to ambulate; I want to be part of the crew, if Lord Sebastian will have me."

Mixstowe shifted impatiently in his chair. "D'ye suppose we might dispense with the Lord this and Lord that when we be together as free-traders? It do hardly be an occupation that lends itself to such airs!"

"Just so," Sebastian agreed with a nod. "Among us, I shall be Trevarre, and Lord Senwyck is Penrose. I suspect we are both more comfortable with those names."

"But, my lord," Keswick protested with a frown, "we really do not think—"

"I haven't asked you." Waving him off, Sebastian continued, "Jasper, as the factor at Trevarre Hall for many years, you have proven yourself to be a skilled administrator. Are you up to the task of organizing matters once the cargo reaches land? We'll need someone to arrange the landing and transport of goods. And we must hire tub-carriers, as well as batmen to protect them from the Revenue men."

"I should like that, sir," Polarven murmured gruffly. "I should like it very much."

"Excellent. And I'll find a place for you, Keswick, and me to meet, perhaps in Bodinnick, which is just a short distance from Trevarre Hall."

"Sir, that be the village where I do live! The barman at the Old Ferry Inn be my nephew, and the inn do have a storeroom, tucked away in back."

"Indeed? How convenient." A knowing smile touched Sebastian's mouth as he turned to Robert Mixstowe. "I understand that, as the Polruan ferryman, you know everyone in the river valley. Is that true?"

The burly man puffed out his chest. "Indeed, sir. And I

do share the joys and cares of all of 'em."

"We shall need a man to handle the distribution of goods once we have brought them ashore. As I see it, there are many avenues you can pursue. If you want to hire another trustworthy fellow to join us who can arrange for a variety of locations where we can safely stow our goods until they can be distributed, I will gladly pay him. It might be better for someone else to make the arrangements for hiding contraband under farmhouse floors, in unused carriages, and churchyards. If you attempt all of those connections on your own, people would surely notice and become suspicious, and as you are all aware, there are more Riding Officers in town and on the cliff tops than ever before."

"I do know someone, sir, my own brother, Preston," Mixstowe replied. His voice dropped to a whisper as he added, "Preston be a farmer, so he do often travel the roads. I know I can speak for him and say we should both be honored to be entrusted with such important duties. Duties that will ensure the success of our…enterprise."

"I can see that you mean to be careful, as well," Sebastian said as he lit a thin cheroot with the guttering candle flame. "We all must exercise absolute caution at all times. One misplaced word or idle boast in a tavern could spell arrest and even death for all of us." After watching them all nod, wide-eyed, he continued, "So then, Robert, after your brother has overseen the concealment of all our cargo, your job will be to organize its distribution, not only to those who will buy the quantities of brandy, lace, tea, and tobacco we bring, but also to give away the salt I intend to import, to those poor fishermen who cannot afford to pay a ninety percent tax."

"Sir?" exclaimed the boy who sat beside Jasper Polarven. "You be plannin' to *buy* salt in France and then *give it away* in Cornwall?"

"What's your name, young man?" Sebastian asked.

"Colvithick, sir. Drew Colvithick. I be here tonight with my Uncle Jasper."

Every pair of eyes at the table was trained on Sebastian as he replied coolly, "I can assure you, Colvithick, that I intend to make room for the salt only when we have acquired a principal cargo of luxury goods that will bring us a tidy profit. But what sort of person would I be if I did not address the injustice of local fishermen being taxed at ninety percent to finance the King's wars? I have seen—and smelled—the pilchard, rotting because the fishermen run out of money to buy the salt to cure them. If local Cornishmen like you will sign on with me, the least I can do is pledge to help your families and friends put food on their tables."

Polarven was blinking in wonderment. "My God, sir, you'll make us proud."

"Just do your jobs, all of you, and give me your solemn word that you'll not breathe a word to anyone, not your wives or your parents or your closest friends. The Revenue men are out in force, and they must not get wind of us."

Robert Mixstowe wore a bemused smile as he said, "Ye do have a challenge, sir, if you mean to keep her ladyship in the dark. I did make her acquaintance when my ferry came upon her, rowing madly across the River Fowey! She are a lively one all right!"

"Truer words were never spoken," Sebastian rejoined with a wry smile, "but my wife must not know what we are doing, for her own safety as well as ours. Don't worry; I shall deal with her."

"We wish you good fortune in that endeavor, my lord!" One of Keswick's pixie brows flew up as he spoke. "Her ladyship may be more formidable than the Revenue Men."

After the clock on the cottage mantel had struck eleven and everyone had gone, Sebastian stood with Tristan and Keswick at the edge of the moon-silvered gardens.

"Goodnight," he told their host. "I'll be in touch very soon."

"Wait. Don't go," Tristan said in hushed tones. "I want to show you something,"

Sebastian watched his friend look around as if suspecting that someone might be lurking in the shadowed trees. "It's late—"

"You must see this," Tristan whispered urgently. "It's not far, perhaps halfway to the creek."

And so they set out into the darkest depths of the ancient woods, Tristan holding a lantern up before them to light the way down the steep, forgotten path. Owls hooted and there were rustling noises in the undergrowth as animals scurried into their burrows.

After perhaps a quarter-mile, he turned off the path and led them through the leaf-carpeted underbrush before stopping at what appeared to be a giant rock. "We're here."

Tired and annoyed, Sebastian glanced around in the darkness. Even the moon was blocked by the dense canopy of leaves overhead. "And where the bloody hell might 'here' be?"

Tristan took a few steps toward a raised ivy-covered earthen bank and gestured to the other two men. "Come closer." He raised the lantern to faintly illuminate what appeared to be a cave, carved into the hillside. The opening was framed with slabs of granite.

"Ah…" Sebastian exhaled with a sound of wonder. "I begin to understand."

"I remember this place now," came Keswick's excited whisper. "I heard that there might even be a tunnel inside, but old Lord Senwyck wouldn't let anyone come close enough to discover the truth."

"That's because my father was financing smugglers himself," Tristan confirmed. "There's a tunnel leading from the cave to the thatched cottage where we met tonight, but it's full of rubble. At the moment, that passage is unusable."

"What a fantastic discovery!" Sebastian's grin flashed in the darkness as he patted the younger man on the back. "We'll have a better look by daylight, but you've given me plenty to dream about in the meantime."

Keswick arched a brow. "Considering her ladyship's suspicions, we hope you do not talk in your sleep!"

Chapter 18

Julia sat on the high-backed wooden settle near the parlor fireplace, sipping a small glass of port as she contemplated the paintings that Primmie had haphazardly propped against the raised hearth.

"You should go to bed," she told the girl. "I've kept you up far too long."

"I don't like to leave you alone when his lordship be away." Primmie gave the ticking clock a meaningful glance just as it began to chime eleven-thirty.

"Shall we think about the best places to hang these paintings? Since my husband is apparently too busy to make these decisions, he shouldn't mind if I do."

The glowing fire, banked for the night, combined with the light from numerous candles to illuminate the newly-unpacked paintings.

"Her ladyship be fair artistic," Primmie observed.

"I think so, too," said Julia. "I saw some of her paintings when we were at Caverleigh House in London. The new owners, André and Devon Raveneau, sent these with us. I believe that my husband chose them."

"This one be lovely. I do know this spot on the cliffs," the girl said, pointing to the watercolor that had hung above Lady Caverleigh's writing table in London. "You can make out the shape of the Brittany coast there, on a day with sun."

Julia lifted the framed canvas and stared at the painting. Sebastian's mother had chosen her colors so carefully; the blues of the water and sky were unique and evocative, and there were bright dots of wildflowers adorning the cliffs on either side of a beckoning path. In the distance, partially shrouded by soft drifts of clouds, Julia perceived the faint, almost dreamlike shape of the French coast.

"It's clear that she had special feelings for this scene," she whispered. "I would love to find this spot one day myself."

Primmie had perched on the edge of the hearth and, although she nodded in reply, her eyelids were drooping. "Mmm-hmm."

"We should go to bed." But even as Julia spoke, she felt someone watching her. At first it seemed to be the stern Lord Caverleigh, who glared from his portrait as if he were angry with the artist. Julia leaned forward slightly, gazing back at him, suddenly curious about the unfriendly looking man who would have been her father-in-law.

"What the devil are you doing?" came a male voice from the darkened kitchen.

"Sebastian?"

"Who else would it be?" he demanded as he strode into the parlor, drawing off his riding gloves. In the dimly lit, low-ceilinged room, he seemed taller than usual. "Primmie, you ought to retire if you're going to be of any use to Mrs. Snuggs in the morning. Go on, then."

Blushing deeply, she clambered to her feet and rushed toward the door. "As you say, my lord! Goodnight, my lady."

Sebastian watched the girl leave before stopping at the cellaret to splash some brandy into a glass. "I would have thought you'd be asleep long ago, Julia."

"Primmie and I decided to unwrap the paintings the Raveneaus sent with us from London. Since you appear to be so occupied with other matters, I thought I would make myself useful. You don't mind, do you?"

He narrowed his eyes at his wife, bracing himself to resist the appeal of her lovely yet faintly defiant profile. There was too much at stake to let himself soften toward her now. "You are an impossible minx."

"Truly?" came her tart reply. "No one has ever called me anything so appealing before."

"That's not exactly what I had in mind."

"I can assure you, I know that," Julia laughed. "But don't be cross with me. Which reminds me, I've been sitting here looking at this portrait of your father and thinking that *he* appears to have been a very cross man. Is that so?"

"Father?" His voice flattened, but he came to sit next to her on the wooden settle. He wanted to tell her that Lord Caverleigh had been a heartless bastard, but that would carry them into a conversation he couldn't bear to have. "Perhaps he was suffering with dyspepsia while posing for that portrait."

"Did your mother paint it?"

"Julia, you are too curious for your own good."

"You know my family and all their faults. Can I not know yours, even from a distance?"

"My parents are dead," he said harshly. "And if no one has killed my brother yet, he might as well be dead. There is no point in talking about them."

"But you have a sister—"

"Don't think that I've forgotten Isabella. She's the victim in all of this, the one who deserved a normal, happy life and yet cannot have it now."

"But, we may be able to remedy that, don't you think so? I would welcome your sister into our home."

"You make our *home* sound so cozy and domestic!" It seemed that the walls were closing in on him as he swallowed the rest of the brandy. "Of course, our marriage is not what it appears to be. And furthermore, I won't bring my sister to Trevarre Hall. Perhaps once I have regained Severn Park, I'll send for her to visit."

"Do you really mean for us to leave Cornwall?"

He gave a derisive laugh. "Have I not made that clear?"

A long silence stretched between them. Although he was uncomfortable in the situation, he had no desire to leave Julia's side, and even less desire to examine the reason why.

"Sebastian?" She touched him and the muscles of his forearm hardened under her hand. "Won't you tell me why you despise Cornwall so? The longer I am here, the more I love it and the more I wonder at your cold feelings."

Sebastian stared into the dying fire, feeling as if his parents were watching him from their separate portraits propped against the hearth. At length, he sighed and offered up a few fragments of the truth. "It's a long story, too long for this hour. I will say that, during my childhood, I was often left here on my own, with only a sour, selfish governess and a few servants who couldn't wait to misbehave once my parents were gone. My memories of this estate are mostly miserable."

"Did something particular happen?"

Sebastian sat up straight and glanced over at Julia, touched somehow by the gentle tone of her voice. Her steady, compassionate gaze made him long to share more with her, yet he wasn't sure he could bear the pain if he released the armor forged over so many years.

"The past is dead; there is nothing to be gained by dredging it up. It's enough for you to know that when you and I arrived here, I had a completely different point of view, my dear." Rising, he gathered up the paintings. "It's been a long evening and I am very tired. Please don't ask any more questions."

With that, he headed toward the stairway, steeling himself not to look back at his wife.

In the soft, lavender light of dawn, Julia lay next to

Sebastian in their bed and watched him sleep. These were the moments she secretly cherished, for there was no sign of the hard man who held her so relentlessly at arm's length, and he couldn't avert his face from her gaze.

As long as he slept, she could imagine that things were different between them.

Secretly, Julia found her husband unutterably appealing. Just looking at his proud nose, the sooty spikes of his eyelashes, and especially the firm yet sensual contours of his mouth made her long for him in a way that could only be described as carnal.

"Mmm." Still apparently asleep, Sebastian turned partly on his side, toward her.

Holding her breath, Julia waited. His arm moved under the covers and his strong hand settled over the mound of her breast. Instantly, she was suffused with longing for him. Her nipple puckered against the warmth of his palm and she felt the wetness between her legs.

Sebastian's eyes were still closed, his breathing regular. Julia lifted the sheet by inches to peek at his hand, loving the sight of his masculine fingers against the pale swell of her flesh. Oh, if only they could openly share such moments with tenderness and love!

She was still holding the sheet up, sighing inside, when she heard a throat-clearing sound. Blood rushed to her cheeks as she turned to find Sebastian regarding her with drowsy gray-green eyes, one brow arched. Quickly, Julia lowered the sheet.

"Good morning," she whispered.

"You've been watching me again." His voice was scratchy with sleep.

"It's the only time I can study you in peace, you know. If I look at you when you're awake, you avert your face or simply walk away."

His hand hadn't left her breast. Very slowly, gently, his fingers flexed and Julia nearly gasped aloud with arousal.

"You will say anything." His eyes darkened with desire.

"Would you care to look at another part of me if I promise not to walk away?"

She could scarcely breathe as he turned her toward him and levered the sheet with his elbow. The sight of his male arousal sent so fiery a tremor through her that she instinctively closed her eyes.

"Now who is avoiding whom?" Sebastian taunted softly.

"Touché, my lord. It's just that…that is a very impressive display."

"Ah, thank you." His fingertips lightly pinched her nipple, then blazed a trail over the curve of her hip, across her belly, before gently probing into the curls between her legs. Of course, she was slick and swollen, and a knowing smile touched Sebastian's mouth. "You are quite impressive yourself, my lady."

Their eyes locked, smoldering. When his glance drifted toward her breast, Julia trembled with the realization that he meant to take her nipple into his warm and skillful mouth, to—

Just then, a loud thumping came at the front door of the Hall, followed by a strident male voice demanding, "Open! I demand that you open to me, in the name of the King!"

The spell was rudely broken.

Clearly annoyed and, Julia thought, perhaps even a bit alarmed, Sebastian looked toward the window. "Who the devil is that?"

Julia had known at once, but couldn't bring herself to tell him.

It was Adolphus Lynton.

From below them came the sounds of Mr. Snuggs throwing open the door and shouting back at the intruder, "Are ye cakey, man? What ails ye?"

Sebastian was already out of the bed. In seconds, he

pulled on his clothes and left her behind without a backward glance. Lying there alone, Julia felt the warm, tingling desire seep out of her body, replaced by anxiety. What on earth could Adolphus Lynton want, and why was he here, behaving like a constable with a warrant? Part of her wanted to avoid him, to stay put until he'd gone, but curiosity won out. Soon she had buttoned herself into a simple day dress, draped a pale rose shawl around her exposed arms, and started down the steps. She lifted her hands to her tousled hair as she went, twisting it into a rich dark-brown coil that she pinned up atop her head.

There were voices rising just outside the door, and she recognized one of them all too well. The memory returned of her walk through Fowey, when she had seen a man who so resembled Lynton that she nearly called out to him. It had seemed impossible that he could be in Cornwall, but clearly he was, right outside her home.

"My good man," she heard him exclaim, "I must inform you that you are speaking to the Searcher of Salt! I am here in the service of His Majesty the King, to ferret out the criminals who are smuggling salt into Cornwall."

"You are a ridiculous buffoon," came Sebastian's curt reply. "I ought to toss you into the river for trespassing upon our peace at this hour."

"Your rudeness is shocking, sir. Furthermore, this is an hour at which all *honest* folk are about, tending to their work. Only those who labor in secret, under the indecent cover of darkness, would still be asleep at this time!"

Just then, Julia emerged through the arched doorway, into the sun-dappled garden. "Hello, Mr. Lynton," she said calmly. "We meet again. It is indeed a small world we live in!"

Adolphus looked as if he were on his way to the Pump Room instead of a rustic estate in the wilds of Cornwall. Wavy hair lay across his brow, he was fashionably pale and thin, and he wore pale yellow pantaloons and a gray striped frock coat. The sight of Julia made his eyes bulge.

"M—Miss Faircloth! Can it be you? Yes, yes, I see that it *must* be you, but I cannot understand what brings you to..." Then, a slowly dawning awareness of the situation made him close his mouth, frowning.

She went to Sebastian and slipped her hand through the crook of his arm. "Did you not know of my marriage, Mr. Lynton?"

"Yes. Yes, I did hear that you married, but nothing about Cornwall." He glanced suspiciously toward Sebastian. "I had understood that you wed a stranger to save your family from poor Mr. Faircloth's unfortunate debts. That seemed to be the only plausible explanation, since I have been well aware that you were adverse to matrimonial ties for yourself."

"How cryptic you are, Mr. Lynton," Sebastian said. "Is it possible that she might prefer me to you?"

"I would request that both of you speak of something else," Julia exclaimed.

"Yes, tell us why you have charged onto my property at dawn, Lynton. Do you suspect me of stealing salt from the local fishermen?"

Adolphus pursed his lips until they began to turn white. "My good man—Trevarre?"

"My husband is Lord Sebastian Trevarre," Julia corrected him.

"By all means then, my *lord*, I will tell you again that my goal, as Searcher of Salt, is to root out the blackguards who are illegally bringing salt into England. As you are doubtless aware, that salt is used to cure the locally caught pilchards, and is often *smuggled* in from France, thereby depriving the Crown of necessary tax revenue. 'Twould seem that Cornish folk believe they are beyond the law."

"More likely," Sebastian replied in acid tones, "they can barely purchase the salt to cure their fish, let alone pay His Majesty's exorbitant taxes!"

Julia looked up at him in surprise. She hadn't seen her

husband so angry since he learned that he'd been tricked into marrying the wrong sister.

"It is the King's law," Adolphus persisted, "and must be obeyed."

"And if the taxes mean that the fishermen cannot feed their families?"

"We must each tend to our own matters. Perhaps you would like to feed the local people yourself, my lord? For myself, I have criminals to apprehend and I must be *vigilant*!"

Julia could feel the tension in Sebastian's body and knew he was very close to picking Adolphus up by his intricately tied cravat and tossing him into the woods.

"Good morning!" came a call from the corner of the manor house. It was Tristan, striding toward them, looking carefree, his ruffled hair agleam in the sunlight. When he reached the trio, he turned to Julia with a look of mischief and bent low over her hand. "Your servant, my lady."

Sebastian looked annoyed by this latest distraction. "What brings you here, Senwyck?"

"I have been seeking Adolphus Lynton, Searcher of Salt. A fellow in Bodinnick told me he saw him come this way."

"I am the Searcher of Salt," cried Lynton, puffing out his chest. "And you may also address me by another title, recently earned: Lieutenant Lynton, Supervisor of His Majesty's Riding Officers!"

"Indeed? What good fortune to discover you here, sir!" Tristan bowed before continuing, "Allow me to present myself. I am Tristan Penrose, Viscount Senwyck, and my home is Lanwyllow." He glanced toward Sebastian, adding, "His lordship and I have been acquainted for many years and I am particularly pleased that he and his bride have settled in our charming corner of the world."

Adolphus began to relax. "How good it is to become acquainted with a Person of Quality such as yourself, my lord. May I ask what brings you in search of me?"

"It is not long since my father passed on and I became

Viscount Senwyck, a title which brings with it a certain burden of responsibility. I have become concerned of late about some illegal activity in the area—"

"You must mean the nefarious practice of *smuggling*!" Lynton exulted.

"Indeed, sir," came Tristan's grave response.

Standing across from them, Julia felt as if something wasn't right. She looked up at Sebastian and saw that his face had been wiped clean of expression. Whatever he was thinking or feeling as he watched his friend ingratiate himself to Adolphus Lynton, was a secret.

"And how might I assist with your concerns?" Lynton inquired.

"I want to be of service to my King, and to my people, sir. If you will have me, I would like to join you as a Riding Officer for the Crown, in pursuit of those who would twist the law to suit their own purposes."

Adolphus Lynton gave Sebastian a triumphant look before bowing to Tristan and replying, "I welcome you, Lord Senwyck, to the service of the King!"

Chapter 19

"Kindly enlighten me," Sebastian said to Tristan as they sat on a bench in the garden and drank mugs of hot tea. "What the devil were you on about with that pompous fool?"

The younger man laughed. "Is it safe to speak openly?"

"Yes. Julia is directing breakfast preparations in the kitchen, so she won't overhear. But be quick. She'll be bringing the food before we know it."

"I was in Bodinnick this morning when I saw Lynton turn his horse into the lane leading to Trevarre Hall. After a villager told me he was not only a Searcher of Salt, but also the newly appointed supervisor of the local band of Riding Officers, I rather feared that our 'enterprise' was ended before it had truly begun. When I arrived here, I heard you insulting him and defending smugglers, which seemed imprudent, to say the least."

"One minute in the company of that puffed-up halfwit destroys any patience I possess. I found it impossible to hold my tongue—"

"Until I arrived," Tristan reminded him.

"When you started fawning over him, I was stunned into silence."

"You've got to admit that it distracted him from your behavior, which was damning, to say the least. I half-expected you to loudly announce that *you* were a smuggler, then challenge him to a duel!"

This brought a grim smile to Sebastian's face. "And what about your brilliant solution? I thought you'd lost your mind when I heard you declare that you aspired to become a Revenue Officer!"

"An inspired plan, if I do say it myself. Since there seems nothing for me to do on the ship, I shall be a double agent by spying on Lynton and keeping him distracted. Additionally, I can cover your tracks when he becomes suspicious, as he most certainly was today!"

Sebastian stared at his young friend. "Yes, it might work." Glancing at the house, he saw Julia carrying a tray through the open door and rose as she drew near. "You can also keep an eye on my wife while I'm at sea."

"That would be my pleasure," Tristan said with a boyish grin as he assisted them in laying out breakfast on the garden table.

"What's that, my lord?" asked Julia.

Sebastian looked at his lovely wife who was still a bit disheveled from their bed, her sable locks pinned up so that tendrils curled haphazardly around her face. His gaze drifted to the fashionably low neckline of her gown and lingered on the first curves of her breasts. The heat that had been building between them earlier returned in a wave, and suddenly not only was he hard again, but he longed for that sense of playful closeness between them.

From a distance, he heard Tristan speaking: "My lady, I was just telling Sebastian that I should be delighted to look in on you if he is called away on business. It would be my pleasure!"

"You needn't keep saying that," Sebastian said. "It sounds as if you're trying to woo my wife."

They both looked at him in surprise. "I advise you to sit down and eat something," said Julia. "Clearly that visit from Mr.—that is *Lieutenant* Lynton has put you out of temper."

"Perhaps because that fool was leering at you as well! Everyone, it seems, lusts after my bride."

"My past with Adolphus is not a secret."

He nearly choked on his bite of warm biscuit topped with honeycomb. "Your—*past*?"

Tristan was grinning at them from across the little table. "I must say, you two are vastly entertaining!"

"My lord," Julia said to Sebastian with maddening calm, "do you imagine that you are the only person in this marriage who has enjoyed the attentions of persons of the opposite sex?"

"Exactly what sort of *attentions* are you referring to?" Sebastian demanded, annoyed that he was unable to remain as unruffled as she. Then it came to him: a long-ago moment at Turbans, when Julia had referred to Lynton as her suitor. It had been the same afternoon that Sebastian had given her what he would still swear with a blood oath, had been her first kiss.

"When we were in Bath, Mr. Lynton begged for my hand in marriage."

"Did he indeed?" His confidence restored, he gave her a lazy smile. "I presume that you refused him because you were occupied with planning *our* exceedingly romantic wedding?"

Their eyes met above the pots of jam and honey, sparks flying. Julia, ever candid, replied, "If you think to bait me, I must disappoint you, sir. I did not mean to imply that I ever had feelings for Mr. Lynton, only that other men have wanted me."

"Before I courted you and proposed marriage?"

"Would you kindly help me bring out a fresh pot of tea, my lord?"

Sebastian watched as she walked away toward the house before he rose as well. "I would counsel you to pay attention, my friend," he told Tristan. "Marriage is a challenge at every turn."

No sooner he had come through the small door into the back of the house, than Julia grasped his arm and pulled him around the corner into a tiny room where ancient-looking jars of preserved fruits were stored.

Her eyes flashed up at him. "I do not enjoy being toyed with, as if I were a mouse and you the cat!"

"What the devil are you talking about?"

"You, sir, referencing not only our 'courtship' and your 'proposal' of marriage to me, but also our 'exceedingly romantic wedding,' when both of us know that it wasn't that way at all. You taunt me in front of Lord Senwyck because you know that it embarrasses me and I cannot respond as I would like."

"Gad, Julia, must you always speak so plainly? Can you tolerate no subtlety in conversation?"

"Subtlety—at my own expense! Isn't that what you mean?"

He inclined his head slightly and bit back a smile. "Perhaps."

"Oooh!" She raised her small fist as if toying with the notion of striking him. "You make me furious."

Sebastian caught her wrists and backed her into the rickety shelves of jam jars until his strong body was fully in contact with hers. He could feel the quickening beat of her heart through his linen shirt. Her soft lips were parted in outrage, and he wanted so much to kiss her that he did it.

"Mmmph!" cried Julia. She struggled for a moment and then, as he pinned her wrists against the shelves, he felt her succumb to the wave of arousal that surged through both of them at once.

For a long minute, they kissed hungrily. Julia's breathing quickened and her nipples made tight peaks against the thin stuff of her gown. Sebastian was just about to throw caution to the wind and press his erection against what he knew was by now a swollen, aching need between her legs. Where could he have her? Would she allow him to carry her away up the stairs while Tristan waited in the garden?

"Mmph!" Julia cried again, and this time the sound conveyed a different meaning.

Panting, Sebastian let her end the kiss. Looking into her heavy-lidded eyes, he was absolutely certain that she was in the grip of just as much passion as he, but now she had brought her hands up to his shoulders and was pushing at him with all her might.

"Are you mad?" he demanded.

"Certainly not, but I think you must be! I brought you in here to tell you that I will not suffer your outrageous behavior a moment longer, that you must treat me with respect rather than thinly veiled mockery! And how do you respond? By ravishing me in the storeroom as if I were some sort of—*trollop*!"

For the second time that morning, he was left with an aching need that was destined to go unsatisfied. Watching Julia whirl around and flee back into the kitchen, Sebastian decided that it was just as well. This was no time to make love to his wife. On the contrary, he was a newly minted smuggler and ought to cut every tie that was not related to that treacherous enterprise.

Back in the courtyard garden, Sebastian discovered Tristan drinking cold tea and chatting with Keswick. He joined them at the table, but felt annoyed by the trill of birdsong and the sight of butterflies gliding to and fro among the flowers that Julia had been tending in the garden.

Tristan reached into his fashionably cut coat, drew out two letters, and presented them to Sebastian. "I nearly forgot, there was another reason I visited here today. When I was in Bodinnick, the mail coach stopped at the Ferry Inn, and these were left for Trevarre Hall."

"I can't imagine who knows that we live here."

"One is from Bath, the other from London. I saw the name 'Raveneau' above the seal."

"My lord," Keswick said, "can you have forgotten that you now have close *relations* in Bath? They must know her ladyship's whereabouts."

He gave the little man a dark look. "You have a talent for saying precisely the thing that will provoke me."

Tristan shifted on his chair and surveyed the cheerful bees and butterflies. "I was just telling Keswick, Trevarre Hall has been transformed, inside and out, since you brought her ladyship to live here. Thank God she agreed to marry you."

"I will thank you to keep your observations to yourself."

Tristan and Keswick exchanged glances, then lifted their teacups and drank in silence.

"And you two can stop looking at each other that way. I'm not blind, you know."

Keswick cleared his throat. "We surmise that his lordship is out of sorts, particularly regarding her ladyship, because of the new undertaking we three are engaged in. It must be very difficult to not be able to share something so weighty with one's own wife, especially when that wife is still a new bride." His peaked brows rose higher. "If you take our meaning."

Nodding vigorously, Tristan exclaimed, "Just so! Sebastian, why not tell her ladyship? She is such a levelheaded female. No doubt she would be happy to be enlightened, and you would be in a much better temper once that great secret is out in the open."

"But, then it wouldn't be a secret anymore. And in case you have forgotten, lives are at stake, and that Searcher of Salt would doubtless be very happy to not only entrap a band of smugglers, but also to put them in prison so that he might have Julia all to himself!"

"Do you mean to imply that she might divulge the secret?" Tristan exclaimed. "Perhaps to Lynton himself? Oh no, I think you are wrong, my lord. Quite wrong. She's not that sort at all."

"It's true," Keswick chimed in. "Her ladyship is made of much sterner stuff than that."

Sebastian wanted to crack both their heads with his mother's favorite Spode teapot. "Sterner stuff or not, my wife is still human—and Adolphus Lynton is much cannier than he appears to be. I can't take the chance that he might trick her into accidentally divulging something to him." His expression was stormy, and his eyes held something deeper. "I'm concerned not only about the lives of all the men who are part of our enterprise, but also about my wife. Can't you see—her safety must come above any reservations we may have about excluding her from our plans."

"Of course, you are right," Keswick murmured. He rubbed his jaw. "The question is, how do you mean to do it? Her ladyship is not some meek, submissive bride who accepts what is told to her without question."

"I can assure you," Sebastian ground out, "that I will find a way. Her protection must come before the pleasures of marriage."

Tristan stood up. "Clearly, you know best. And now I am off to Polruan to fetch the *Peregrine* and sail her back to Lanwyllow. Our friend at the boatyard has finished making the special alterations you requested, in preparation for our impending journey."

"Excellent. I'll come with you. It will do me good to stand on the deck of a ship." Sebastian rose, draining his teacup, and looked at his manservant. "I'd like you to stay here and keep an eye on her ladyship."

"We shall try, my lord, but you of all people should know that that is easier said than done…"

Julia was relieved when Sebastian and Tristan left together. She stood in the upstairs window overlooking the courtyard with Clover cuddled in her arms and watched them ride off up the rutted track that passed for Trevarre Hall's entrance lane.

Not for the first time, she wondered why she worked so hard to make their home more inviting when her husband couldn't be bothered to do his part. Keswick seemed to care more than his master. Since their arrival in Cornwall, he had given up most of his valet duties, trading them for the more physically demanding tasks of getting the stables back in order and organizing much of the work that needed to be done to maintain the hedges, fix the gates, and repair the countless broken bits of the old manor house.

Although Clover was fast asleep in her arms, Julia set her down on her favorite chair in the extra bedchamber. Dick had been lurking around the corridors that morning, so she closed the big door on her way out and latched it.

The woods and the creek were calling to her. Julia hurried down the narrow steps and came into the kitchen, only to find Keswick sitting at the gate-leg table, chatting amiably with Primmie. The girl stopped in the midst of stirring the pot of vegetable soup that simmered over the fire. Lifting her apron, she wiped her brow.

"'Twill be a warm day," she told Julia.

"I think it already is. Perhaps you should put a lid on that and let the fire die back." Smiling at Keswick, Julia added, "Since the ill-tempered Lord Sebastian isn't here to scold me, I have decided to treat myself to a stroll along the Hall Walk and a visit to Pont Pill to check on our mother swan."

"An excellent plan, my lady. And we've brought you something to read when you pause to rest." Smiling, he extended a letter. "The mail coach brought it from Bath."

Her heart leaped at the sight of her sister's familiar handwriting. "How lovely. Oh, thank you so much, Keswick. You're a dear!"

Before she could leave, Keswick added, "And, we would encourage you to be forgiving of his lordship. He isn't as black-hearted as he might seem."

"I shall try to remember your advice," Julia sighed, her heart aching. "It isn't easy, though, Keswick. He is a hard man, and he will not let me forget that it was not his choice to marry me."

"We believe that 'stubborn' might be the word to describe his lordship."

With a rueful smile, Julia waved goodbye and set off past the old chapel and the apple orchard, then over the meadow toward Pont. The Hall Walk, which overlooked the river, was a far prettier route, but this was quicker.

Julia had put the letter into a pocket tied to the waist of her gown, and it swung two and fro as she scrambled over the stile that kept the cows and sheep out of the woods above Pont. Down the path she went, her footing sure after countless walks like this one. The tide was in, the creek shimmered dreamily in the mid-day sun, and a turquoise kingfisher swooped down over the water.

Her first stop was always the swan's nest. Trees lined the bank of the creek, and golden light spilled between the leafy branches, dappling the moss and rocks under Julia's slippers. After many visits, the mother swan had grown accustomed to her, so she didn't pause before rounding the last old oak tree.

The nest, big enough for her to crouch inside herself if she had cared to try, was right where it had been for weeks. It took a few moments for Julia to realize that the mother swan was not in it. Peeking inside, she saw the big shards of eggshell. Her heart began to pound.

She turned and went back, skirting the edge of the widening creek. Before the little stone footbridge at Pont came into view, Julia saw them. There was the mother, gliding regally in a beam of sunlight, with a quartet of gawky, tan-and-gray cygnets paddling close behind her.

"Oh, you did it!" she cried. "Bravo!" Tears stung her eyes as the swan slowed and seemed to look her way in greeting. Julia took one of two biscuits out of her pocket and threw pieces of it onto the water. The cygnets followed their mother's lead and dipped their black beaks down to gobble the food.

By the time Julia reached the footbridge, she could see the father swan swimming toward her up the creek, proud and strong. It looked as if a knife was parting the water in his wake, and she was reminded of Sebastian's male assertiveness.

She returned to the little rubble-slate boathouse and perched on a flat rock before slipping the letter from her pocket and breaking the wax seal. For a moment, Julia just looked at the words written by her sister. It was strange to see Sarah's familiar hand in the midst of this new world she had come to love so much, a world that seemed a lifetime away from Bath.

On the banks where the tide had begun to recede, a pair of curlews stepped delicately over the mud. She watched them for a moment before turning her attention to the letter. Sarah wrote of how much they missed her, and how curious they all were about her new life, especially since receiving Julia's hastily composed note explaining that she and Sebastian were living in Cornwall, not London. Sarah wrote: *We beg you to write to us and enlighten us further!*

Sarah went on to say that their mother was *much the same*, still retreating to her bed whenever a challenge presented itself. Freddy was spending more time than ever in the minaret, studying, and they had found *a new, young tutor for him who is doing a splendid job!* They all continued to grieve the loss of their father, *but at least we remain in our beloved Turbans, and for that we must thank you, dearest Julia. I can assure you that I understand all too well that you sacrificed yourself for the good of your family!*

Julia set the letter in her lap and considered her sister's words. How could she ever explain to Sarah that she had—always!—secretly thrilled to each moment in Sebastian's presence, and that it was sheer bliss to lie in his arms in the intimacy of their marriage bed. In other dealings, he was difficult, even impossible at times, but she had come to relish the to-and-fro of their relationship.

Pondering these feelings, Julia felt her heart begin to race and her cheeks grow warm. It was true that she loved this enchanted world in Cornwall, but her new roots went deeper than that. Even if she could turn back the clock and return to Turbans, she would not.

How I miss our whispered late-night chats in your bed, wrote Sarah. *Life is not the same for me without my bright and resourceful older sister. Will Lord Satan allow you to visit Bath and reunite with your family again?*

Although she smiled at her sister's reference to "Lord Satan," Julia realized that she had no desire to leave Trevarre Hall—or Sebastian—and go to Bath. Perhaps her family could visit Cornwall?

Sarah's parting words were, *You are ever in my thoughts, darling sister. Will you be shocked if I confess that I long to know what…*it *was like? Was it a sacred union, or something much more carnal? I hope that Lord Satan was, at least, respectful of you.*

I send affectionate regards from all of your family,

Your devoted sister, Sarah.

Julia re-read the final sentences with a bemused smile. *Respectful!* She gave a soft laugh. Her husband was not respectful, especially when they had engaged in the intimacies of wedded life, but she preferred him that way. It was certainly not respect that she had searched for when she embarked on the masquerade that began their marriage.

With that, Julia folded Sarah's letter, returned it to her pocket, and started back to the Hall. This time, after climbing back up the wooded path, she continued to follow the creek as it flowed out into the River Fowey.

Then, just before Julia turned into the leafy tunnel of the Hall Walk, she glimpsed a splendid boat sailing upriver. Something about it made her stop, stare, and sigh. The small ship was so graceful, her sails snow-white against the blue sky and the sparkle of the water. The figurehead that extended high above the bow was a bird, Julia decided; a hawk, perhaps. She wished she had Freddy's telescope to get a clearer look at the men on deck. One of them, who had broad shoulders and dark hair, reminded her of Sebastian, but of course it couldn't be him…

Her reverie was broken by a soft whimpering sound. It seemed to come from the wooded bank that sloped down toward the far-away river, and the sound held a sense of urgency, as if an animal was in distress.

Julia acted immediately. She left the path and clambered down through the leaves and branches, following the soft cry of distress. When she saw the young badger, lying in a hole filled with dried leaves, her heart sank. Its back foot was caught in a crudely made snare, its eyes were closed, and its cries were growing softer by the moment.

Without a thought to propriety, Julia found a piece of sharp rock to make a tear in the muslin of her gown. She ripped away the front of the skirt until she'd separated a piece large enough to hold the badger. The snare, cobbled together with bits of wood, leather, and wire, was broken easily enough, but she couldn't free the animal's bloody leg without help. It was a risk, she knew, to touch a wild badger, for their teeth could be fierce. But she was unafraid. Something in the small animal's helpless expression tore at her heart, and she knew that it was near death.

"Now, you must not fear me," she murmured, spreading out her torn skirt over the cub. "I know you are hurt, and I am going to help you. Will you trust me? There's a sweet girl."

Julia continued to whisper soothingly to the badger as she gathered it into the fabric until all its face and body, as well as the deadly snare, were snugly enclosed. Fortunately, it was young and light enough for her to lift. The badger gave a cry of pain when she held it against her midsection and got to her feet, but then the injured animal grew quiet.

Scrambling up the hillside with her burden, Julia reached the Hall Walk and set off toward home.

"It's all right," she murmured. "You're safe with me. I don't imagine that your mother gave you a name, so I'm going to call you Daisy."

Chapter 20

Nearly a half hour later, Julia pushed through the gate behind Trevarre Hall's farmyard. There was blood on her hands, her lungs burned, and her slippered feet were bruised. All the farm workers were off working in the fields, but as she passed the cattle barn and the piggery, she saw Keswick walking a lame horse.

"Oh, Keswick! I've never been so glad to see someone in my life." The expression on his face when he looked up and focused her torn gown and her ankles showing beneath the hem of her thin chemise was nearly enough to make her smile.

"What's happened, my lady? Have you been attacked?"

"No, I'm fine—just a bit tired." She leaned back against the stone wall of the cattle barn and pulled aside the edges of the cloth surrounding the badger cub. "Look, Keswick. She's been hurt. I had to bring her home."

His eyes widened and his white brows flew up. "A badger! God's blood, give the thing to us. You could be badly bitten!"

"Little Daisy won't bite me. She's nearly dead, I fear, but I am determined to help her."

He didn't question the fact that she had already given a name to this wild creature. Instead, he took the bundle from her and led the way into the stables where he had a room he shared with the blacksmith. Soon, Julia had made a little bed for the unconscious badger out of some old horse blankets, but she kept the torn gown as the top layer, agreeing with Keswick that the animal would remember her scent.

She held the badger while he cut away the wire that bound the cub's leg. Together, they cleaned and dressed the wound.

When they were finished and Julia remained kneeling beside the little animal, Keswick shook his head with a sigh. "It doesn't look good, my lady."

"We shall do our best. At least she is a bit older and won't have to be bottle-fed. Do we have any earthworms? I seem to recall that that's what they like to eat."

He gave a snort of laughter. "My lady—"

"Yes, I know, you think I'm ridiculous, but I don't care. I have a special relationship with animals like Daisy. I always have."

"We have no doubt of that."

"I will ask you to sit with her while I go inside and change my gown. Then I shall return and stay with Daisy. I think that she knows that I'm here." She folded one side of the torn gown over the badger cub, like a blanket, and touched its black-and-white striped head. "She's a lovely little thing, don't you think so?"

"My lady," he replied, "we will sit with this badger if that is your wish, but we refuse to call it lovely."

Throughout the afternoon spent sailing the *Peregrine* upriver, Sebastian kept the unopened letter from Raveneau in his coat pocket. Once the boat had been tied up at the Lanwyllow quay, tucked into a secret location off Lerryn Creek, he bade Tristan goodbye and headed home.

Riding up the overgrown drive to his own estate, Sebastian slowed to a stop near the stone gateposts and dismounted. He then led Lucifer down a little-used path that brought them to the 14th century chapel perched on a hill behind the farm.

No one ever came here anymore. Sebastian's mother had often bemoaned the fate of the chapel, which had been built by her Wentworth ancestors. She had once proudly told her son that King Charles I had worshipped here during a visit to what was then Wentworth Hall, but today the chapel was a virtual ruin

Sebastian sat on the steps leading to the arched north entrance and remembered the morning he and Julia had stopped here. Although he'd known the chapel all his life and had never given it much thought, he now took another look, seeing it through her fresh eyes. Perhaps she was right; it was a shame to see something so special continue to decay

Remembering the letter, he broke the seal and spread out the page. The sight of Raveneau's strong handwriting made his heart catch, for something about it was arrestingly familiar.

Lord Sebastian,

I bring you greetings from all of my family, especially Devon, who I fear has fallen under your spell. She urges me daily to make contact with you and your bride, to inquire after your well being, and to invite you to visit us.

I confess that I find myself thinking of you as well. Perhaps it is my past connection with your mother that causes me to feel close to you, and of course your recent visit with us has strengthened that bond. Allow me to tell you again that you may call on me, for friendship or assistance, at any time.

By the time you receive this letter, Devon and I will have traveled to France. In Paris, I shall meet with Talleyrand at President Adams's request, then we will go on to Roscoff, on the Brittany coast, for some shipping business. When the clouds lift and we are able to see Cornwall across the Channel, I shall think of you, my friend.

Yrs., etc., Raveneau.

Sebastian felt a strange twinge of emotion, and his eyes misted slightly as he stared at the scrawled signature. This was the sort of affectionate letter he had always hoped to receive from his own father, but it had never come.

"Ah, there you are, my lord."

He looked up to see Keswick walking up the little hill behind the stone cattle barn. Lucifer went to meet him and accept a piece of carrot.

"I thought to steal a few moments of solitude," Sebastian said.

"From us? Surely you jest, my lord. Besides, there is too much of importance on your schedule for us to leave you alone."

"I can assure you, old scold, that I am fully aware of my own schedule." He got to his feet and brushed bits of straw from his breeches. "You'll be pleased to know that I just read Raveneau's letter."

"We are pleased indeed. Do you mean to ask him for help?"

"Help?" One of Sebastian's brows slanted upward. "I don't bloody need *help*, and even if I did, I shouldn't ask Raveneau. I'm a grown man, Keswick. Surely you haven't forgotten that?"

"Of course not, my lord, but we happen to know that he is in a position to offer you the best kind of assistance. Not only is Captain Raveneau the owner of several extremely fine ships, some of which are anchored at Falmouth, but he has wisdom and experience—"

"I suggest that you stop talking before you insult me outright." Taking Lucifer's reins from the manservant, he walked down the hill toward the stables. "I shall expect an apology from you after this first expedition has reached an immensely satisfactory conclusion!"

While Sebastian was having a bath, and the household servants were occupied with keeping it hot enough for his comfort, Julia sneaked Daisy upstairs. Trevarre Hall was a maze of small chambers, and she had converted one into her dressing room. It was much more than a place to keep her clothing, though; it held the trunk she had brought from Turbans, filled with cherished books and all the keepsakes she had gathered in nature.

Now, after quickly changing her torn gown, Julia brought the badger cub to the bed she had made inside an empty drawer. It was filled with rags and handfuls of meadow grass, which she hoped would smell like home. Daisy, however, continued to sleep and her snout was warm and dry.

"Look what I've brought you, little girl," Julia whispered. From her dressing chest, she fetched a small wooden bowl containing a handful of walnuts and some freshly excavated earthworms. As a child, she had read in one of the books from her father's shop that badgers liked to eat small rodents, insects, berries, and nuts, but their favorite food was earthworms. She'd never forgotten it.

Now, to her delight, Daisy began to sniff. Carefully, Julia crouched beside the little cub, took one of the earthworms, and put it on her black mouth. A few moments later, Daisy's tongue came out and half the worm was gone. Julia was flooded with relief and elation. She wanted to hold Daisy in her arms and pet her, but for now she knew she must keep her distance.

"I don't believe my eyes."

The sound of Sebastian's voice was so unexpected that Julia gasped out loud. As she looked up to find him towering over her, frowning, her first thought was for Daisy.

"You might have knocked!"

"The door was ajar." He was wearing a slate gray dressing gown, his hair was damp, and he held a glass of brandy in one exceedingly attractive hand. "For God's sake, Julia, what the devil are you doing with a badger in my house? It's a wild animal and you could be hurt!"

She scrambled up from the floor to face him, determined to protect Daisy. "I'll have you know that this is my house, too, whether you like it or not."

"See here, I didn't mean to imply—"

"And *she* is not a 'thing.' Her name is Daisy."

"You are outrageous."

She faced him unblinkingly. "Would you care to sit and discuss this as two adults?"

He sat on a hard bench by the chamber's single mullioned window. "I am listening."

Surprised, she joined him, but kept a little space between them. "Thank you."

Julia quickly became aware of his potent magnetism. Sebastian's sage-gray eyes were hooded and the candlelight threw shadows under his cheekbones and over his hard, sensual mouth. As she glimpsed the damp surface of his chest through the loose front of the dressing gown that he dared to wear without a stitch underneath, Julia knew exactly how he would smell if she pressed her face there.

Instinctively, she shifted farther away and started to tip off the edge of the bench. Sebastian reached out with one hand and pulled her back just before she lost her balance and toppled to the floor. Now their legs were touching.

"Perhaps you'd like a sip of brandy to calm your nerves," he offered.

Julia sighed. "All right." She welcomed the burn of it on her throat, and the warmth that spread over her.

"You can drink it all if you'd like. I have another bottle." A faint smile touched his mouth. "Are you ready to tell me why there is a badger in your dressing room?"

She stared at Daisy's still form, nestled in the drawer that was now her bed. "I came upon her while walking home today from Pont. Her back leg was caught in a snare, and although at first I thought she might be dead, she was not. I brought her home and Keswick helped me remove the rest of the snare and clean the wound." After another sip of brandy, she handed the glass back to him. "I brought her upstairs for the night because I know that she might need me. She may not survive until morning."

"You just carried an injured badger through the woods all by yourself? Are you aware that they bite, especially when hurt and afraid?"

"Daisy is only a cub. She wasn't very heavy, and I made a covering for her out of part of my gown. I wrapped it completely around her, so she felt snug and safe, and she couldn't see me if she did awaken."

"Sometimes it seems impossible that you are gently born and bred, and that I met you in the elegant town of Bath." Sebastian shook his head. "You are like a wild creature yourself. You won't be tamed, no matter what anyone says."

"It's quite true that I will not be tamed, especially by you." She wrinkled her nose and looked away from him.

"Is the concept of a wife's deference to her husband so impossible to accept?"

She pretended not to hear him. "Part of the reason I love Cornwall, and don't miss Bath in the least, is that I can be myself here. Being in nature, especially in this place, allows me a sense of freedom that I have yearned for all my life."

Sebastian's gaze moved around the crowded chamber until it fell on the open trunk that overflowed with her treasures. "Do I see a bird's nest there? Are there more animals in this room that I don't know about?"

"No. That's the trunk you asked about when it was strapped atop the coach at the Raveneaus' house in London."

"You said it held books…and keepsakes, as I recall."

"It does." Julia went to kneel beside the chest. "The books are packed on the bottom, and the top is filled with treasures that I have collected since I was a tiny girl—not gems or gold, but treasures of nature." She held up two long, white swans' feathers. "I still remember finding this one when I was just four years old, and the other belongs to our swan at Pont. Do you know that her cygnets have hatched? I saw them swimming today!" She turned to the nest he'd mentioned. "This belonged to a song thrush. Can you see the speckled eggshell that remains inside? And these are shells that I gathered during a family holiday in Devon."

As Julia lifted the keepsakes one by one and described them, Sebastian rose and crossed over to sit on the floor beside her, leaning against the wall and stretching out his legs so that his bare calves were exposed against the oaken floor.

"My favorite times, growing up, were when we left London for the countryside," she said, growing animated as the memories cascaded back. "Sometimes we visited Cousin Archibald at Turbans, and I would wander over the grounds and gardens for hours. My mother's sister lived in Moreton-in-Marsh, in the Cotswolds, and I found some of my best treasures there: flowers and leaves to press, and many of the prettiest stones. My father often walked with me, just the two of us, and it was he who taught me about the birds and animals we saw."

Sebastian leaned forward and wiped a tear from her cheek, watching her intently.

"When we would return to London, Papa would take me to his bookshop and give me beautiful books about the wildlife we had seen, many with hand-painted illustrations. He always inscribed the date and a little message inside." She looked into the trunk and gave a deep sigh. "I have them all, still."

"We must make a proper case for them," he said quietly. "For all of your things. One with glass doors, to protect them from our clumsy servants—and Dick the cat, who we know can't be trusted. Would you like that?"

Julia closed her eyes and allowed herself the luxury of leaning against his shoulder. "I would, very much. Thank you."

Sebastian gathered her onto his lap and held her close. Something in the air seemed to dissolve the armor he usually wore so relentlessly. "I am sorry that you lost your father, Julia, but at least you have good memories of your years together. At least he was a loving father to you."

"Yes, that's true, and a comfort," she whispered. "Sebastian, won't you tell me more about your father?"

He fought the instinct to lift her away and get to his feet. "Ah, well…there's nothing to say that you would enjoy hearing, I'm afraid. It's really a subject that's best discarded."

"Please."

His eyes stung. He wanted to ask her what she was doing to him, and how, but instead he turned his rough cheek against her soft curls and surrendered, just a bit. "There isn't much to tell. My father couldn't be bothered with me, nor really with any of us, though he did give George some attention because he was the heir. I'm not even certain if he ever cared for my mother. He wore her on his arm like an expensive jewel, and whenever she was in his presence, there seemed to be a shadow over her."

"How sad."

"I warned you—"

"I want to hear it. You know all the nasty bits about my family, after all."

They shared a grim smile before he continued, "My father often had business in France and he insisted that Mother be at his side, always. It was almost as if he was afraid that she might run away if he left her behind. So, we came quite frequently to Cornwall, especially in the summer, and they would sail on to France. Even as a young boy, I pleaded to stay at Severn Park with the horses, but as soon as Father discerned my true wishes, he always did the opposite."

"And then something bad happened…?"

"Yes, at the time, it seemed impossibly bad." The only person Sebastian had ever spoken to about that day was

Keswick. All his instincts urged him to stop this conversation with Julia, and yet when she turned toward him with a gaze that was at once direct and compassionate, he felt an invisible barrier give way deep inside. "I never liked Cornwall or Trevarre Hall. The people seemed odd to me, and many still spoke Cornish, which I couldn't understand. The Hall was gloomy. My mother wanted to make improvements, but Father was always impatient to leave. I sometimes felt that we only came so that they could leave me behind here…"

"What about your brother? Was he not with you?"

"No. George was either away at school, or with my parents." In a tone that dripped acid, he added, "My father was obsessed with instructing him in the endless duties of the aristocracy."

Julia wrinkled her nose, but made no reply, and Sebastian continued, "One summer when I was fourteen, Mother took pity on me and persuaded my father to let me bring Apollo, my favorite horse, with us from Severn Park. He wasn't used to the twisting tracks or the hedgerows, though, and one day, as we descended that steep path that drops down to Pont, a heron took flight and spooked him. Apollo reared up, then lost his footing, fell, and broke his leg. I heard it snap. I had no choice but to leave him alone, writhing, and go for help."

Julia continued to listen quietly, her eyes soft with emotion. When Sebastian's voice caught, she reached for his strong hand and squeezed it. "Truly, I cannot imagine."

He took a painful breath as the past returned in a flood. "God, I hate talking about this! I ran full out back to the Hall and brought Keswick, who was our stable master, back with me. Of course he told me that nothing could be done." Tears clouded his vision. "I held Apollo while Keswick shot him. It was the most horrible moment of my life. I knew that it could never have happened in Hampshire, only in a wild, terrible place like Cornwall, and I hated it here more than ever. Later, when my father learned of Apollo's fate, he blamed my horsemanship, my judgment, and he said—"

After a long moment, Julia whispered, "Yes?"

"He said, 'Be a man! If you can't hold onto the things you want, you don't deserve to have them.' I despised him."

"I am so very sorry. What a tragic experience for a boy to suffer!"

Abruptly, Sebastian felt that the walls of the tiny room were closing in on him and he had to get away. As he disengaged from Julia and rose to his feet, he muttered, "Yes, well, it happened, and it's best left in the past where it belongs."

She scrambled to her feet, too, and touched his arm. "Your father was an appalling person!"

"Exactly so," he replied. "He was just as unpleasant as he looked in that portrait downstairs. And now you know why I didn't want to discuss him with you."

"You mustn't let him poison your life, Sebastian."

"On the contrary, I never think of him." His composure restored, he crossed the cluttered chamber to look into the drawer that served as a warm, snug bed for the badger cub. "If it lives, you can't keep it, you know."

"Of course I know that, but what a thing to say—"

"It's a wild animal. If it survives the night, you must release it."

"Stop calling Daisy *it*, as if she didn't really matter."

"All right then, you must release her as soon as possible. She'll be needing to return to her sett, to her family, to the pleasures of her life searching the hedgerows for worms and wasp nests. Hopefully, her family will welcome her back."

"It's hard to believe, looking at her so small and helpless, that she is a wild creature."

"Indeed? Have you taken a close look at her claws?" Sebastian found his glass of brandy and took a long drink. "I need some air. Will you excuse me?"

"Of course." Julia's voice had gone flat.

Ducking to exit through the low door to the little dressing room, he resisted a strong urge to look back at her.

Chapter 21

Peaceful Lerryn Creek, tucked away off the River Fowey, was so wide that many called it a river. Just before the quaint village of Lerryn, there was an inlet that branched north, but few vessels sailed in that direction unless they were visiting the Penrose estate of Lanwyllow.

The manor house that stood a good distance away on the top of the densely wooded hill, had its own boathouse, and farther up the inlet an old stone quay nestled against the hull of the light, two-masted lugger Tristan called the *Peregrine*. Leafy green branches bent all around the craft, providing effective camouflage.

"This is one of the most beautiful places in Cornwall, I believe," Sebastian said to Tristan as they stood on the scrubbed deck. "Julia would be enchanted."

The younger man glanced over, brows raised. "Perhaps I'll bring her here while you are at sea. Would you mind?"

Sebastian felt unaccountably annoyed. "Why would I mind? But I wouldn't recommend it. She might get into mischief here. She's much too clever for her own good, and who knows what she might notice."

"I see. All right then." But Tristan's expression suggested that he didn't see at all.

"She'll lead you on a merry chase as it is. Did I tell you

that I came home yesterday to discover that she'd rescued an injured badger and brought it into our house? By tonight, she may have dressed it in a lace gown and be rocking it in a cradle."

"Her ladyship has a very tender heart," Tristan said, smiling. "If she sees fit to lead me on a merry chase, I will be happy to follow."

Sebastian knew an urge to toss his friend overboard. Instead, he changed the subject before his temper got the better of him. "Your friend at the Polruan boatyard has done well with these sails he has added to *Peregrine*. But, there is a great deal yet to do if we are to sail with the tide. Why don't you show me the other alterations he made before we meet with Jasper and Keswick?"

Tristan led the way past the crewmembers who were laboring to make certain that everything was in working order for tomorrow's voyage. Although Keswick was on hand to oversee preparations, the crew had been well prepared and needed little supervision.

Below decks, space was severely limited. There were a couple of dark, tiny cabins for crew members, outfitted only with bunks and buckets. Between the cabins, Tristan paused to touch a panel on the bulkhead. It gave to the pressure of his fingers, revealing a generous length of hollow space.

"*Voila*," he murmured with a roguish grin. "Perfectly sized for casks of brandy."

"Well done."

"There are several more false bulkheads like that, all expertly concealed, and a secret cargo hold that will be perfect for the rather bulky salt you intend to transport."

"Very ingenious." Sebastian surveyed the surroundings and rubbed his jaw. "I'm impressed, though I must confess that this lugger is a far cry from the ship I served on with the Royal Navy. I wasn't really prepared for how small it would be."

"A bigger vessel couldn't maneuver these tidal creeks,

with their fluctuating water levels. And since most smuggling ships are even smaller and more spartan than this, I think you'll approve of your own quarters. If you will follow me…" Tristan crooked his finger and led him to the captain's cabin. It was the only one that allowed any light to come in, through a modest transom that spanned the *Peregrine*'s stern. Although the space was restricted, there was a comfortable-looking bunk. A compact desk was built in nearby, and there was extra storage and a wooden binnacle to hold the captain's extra navigational equipment.

Sebastian gave a dry smile. "It will do nicely. I'll let Keswick organize my things, since he hasn't given up on being my manservant." Pausing, he took a good look around. "There isn't a hidden compartment in here, is there? I can't see any sign of one."

"Excellent!" Laughing, Tristan approached the bunk. There was already a latched door that opened to a storage area, large enough to hold the captain's trunk, but the expanse of varnished wood next to it was completely smooth. Tristan pressed there and an opening appeared, swinging back on concealed hinges. Behind this secret panel was a cavity that extended beyond the bunk and spanned the width of the ship.

"Good God," said Sebastian with a laugh. "We can put a massive quantity of tea in there, and who would suspect that it would be in so obvious a place as under the captain's bunk?"

"Right. And all the while, we'll have normal things in the ship's cargo hold, just in case anyone is suspicious. I'm happy to pay the exorbitant duty on a few items, just to throw them off our scent." As they emerged back onto the sun-dappled deck, Tristan continued, "I think our entire arrangement is flawless, right down to you, Captain. So many smugglers have been disreputable, immoral thugs. The last person the King's Men would imagine to be a free-trader is Lord Sebastian Trevarre, a nobleman!"

"If we weren't dealing with Adolphus Lynton, the bloody Searcher of Salt, I might agree with your assessment, but I think he is longing to find me guilty of something so that he can clap me in irons and have his way with Julia."

"I am getting the feeling that you think every man in Cornwall wants to have his way with Julia."

Sebastian narrowed his eyes. "Do you mean to be flippant? I am deadly serious when I tell you that I expect you to keep my wife from harm while I am away. If you accomplish nothing else, that alone will be sufficient."

Before Tristan could reply, Keswick came toward them with a pipe-smoking Jasper Polarven. The four men moved to the far end of the deck, overlooking the lazy green waters of the creek, to discuss plans for the coming days.

After assessing that Jasper and Keswick had no concerns to report, Sebastian told them, "All right then, we'll sail at dawn, with the wind and the morning tide. The crew should stay in place here tonight. Keswick and I will ride over before first light." Turning to Tristan, he added, "I'll leave Lucifer in your care."

"Everything be ready for the landing, Cap'n," confirmed Jasper as he sucked on his pipe. "Trustworthy tub-carriers and batmen be signed on, as well as ponies to carry the goods inland to Mixstowe's distribution points. They just be waitin' to hear when and where you want 'em."

"Good work, Jasper. And I know that Robert and his cousin Preston have their plans well laid for dispersing the goods." As he spoke, Sebastian could feel the electricity charging the air around the four men. "If all goes well, we will sail first to France, where I will meet with our contact in Roscoff to confirm arrangements for a cargo of brandy, tea, lace...and salt." It pleased him to utter this last word, for that very morning he'd smelled the rotten pilchards as he'd ridden past a farm near Bodinnick, discarded as fertilizer because fishermen couldn't afford the salt to preserve the fish for winter. There would be plenty of profit in the luxury goods they smuggled to allow him to make a gift of the salt to needy fishermen.

"If we yet had saints in Cornwall, you'd be among 'em, sir," Jasper told him with feeling.

"I am no saint, for I mean to benefit from this enterprise as well." He leaned against the railing and the trio gathered closer. "From Roscoff, we will sail to Guernsey, to meet with a merchant ship from the West Indies that pledges to share its cargo with us, and the *Peregrine* will then return to our bases, here and at Coombe Haven, to off-load those goods."

"And after that—back to France for the main cargo?" asked Jasper.

Sebastian nodded. "That's right."

"When should I assemble the tub carriers and ponies?"

"If all goes according to plan, in ten days. It could be sooner, but the full moon is just passed and we must wait for moonless nights. We'll hope to land here on the evening of June twenty-fifth. Jasper, don't forget that, if you need him, Penrose will be here in his role as a Riding Officer."

"Yes, a smuggler disguised in the King's colors!" exclaimed Tristan, and the others joined in his laughter. "You may depend on me to assist Jasper with the tub-carriers and batmen if that need arises. And, when the time comes, I shall give the signal from the cliff above the beach at Coombe Hawne that it is safe for *Peregrine* to land."

"We are bound to remind your lordship that this plan, while daring, is fraught with risks," murmured Keswick.

"Of course you are, but kindly refrain from elaborating," Sebastian said. "And stop calling me that."

Tristan had brought out a bottle of port and poured cups for all four men. "Here's to these first expeditions. May we all keep our wits about us and find good fortune in the days to come!"

"Here, here!" shouted Jasper as their glasses clinked.

The quartet were too caught up in the spirit of celebration to notice that young Drew Colvithick had stopped coiling lines and had moved near enough to overhear their conversation.

Riding home across the folds of lush, green hills that separated Lerryn Creek from Trevarre Hall, Sebastian was alive with the thrill of impending adventure. It was a feeling he hadn't experienced since the best days of his naval career.

"My lord," Keswick remarked in mild tones, "we discern that a once-familiar flash has returned to your smile. We have not seen it since our return to England and the news that your brother had gambled away the family fortune."

"How astonishingly observant you are," came Sebastian's mocking reply. However, as his old friend nattered on, he found his own thoughts pulled inexorably toward Julia.

He was surprised to feel a longing to hasten their progress home so that he might share the events of the day with her, down to the smallest details of the *Peregrine* and his first sight of the ingeniously designed hiding places for their smuggled goods.

He wanted to tell her how he had felt as the deck swayed under his feet and he inhaled the scent of the damp sails with their promise of a salt breeze, the open sea, and unimagined adventure.

But of course he could not say any of this to Julia. Because she absolutely must not suspect his connection with smuggling, he must hold her at arm's length so that she wouldn't look into his eyes and glean some nugget of truth that might eventually put her in danger.

For if she were to ask him, straight out, he might be able to lie to her with words, but he feared that his eyes could never fool her.

"What's that fellow Lynton doing in Bodinnick?" muttered Keswick as they crowned the hill atop the tiny village.

Sebastian's head swiveled toward him. "What?"

"Just as we suspected, my lord; you were not listening to a word of the advice we were imparting," he scolded. "If you risk being so preoccupied while at sea, we fear for the outcome of this enterprise."

"You said something about Lynton."

"He is there, my lord, walking his horse off the ferry and looking almost heroic in his new uniform."

"Don't bait me, Keswick. I haven't the patience for it today." Shading his eyes against the afternoon sun, Sebastian watched the Searcher of Salt mount his horse and come slowly up the steep hill. "I suppose we had better wait. It wouldn't do for him to think we were avoiding him, would it."

"Well, Lord Sebastian, we meet again. What a coincidence!" crowed Adolphus Lynton as he drew near and doffed his plumed bicorne hat. Then, after focusing on Keswick for an instant, he blinked and pointedly ignored him.

"What brings you to Bodinnick, sir?" Sebastian asked, forcing himself to be polite.

"Were you not aware that my territory stretches to Polperro? I must ferret the criminals from their very nests."

Sebastian's face was impassive as he bit back a smile. "I pity the unsuspecting smuggler whose nest you mean to invade this afternoon."

Just then, the sound of hoof beats reached their ears and they all turned to see Tristan, now resplendently in uniform, cantering toward them on his dark-red roan. When he had reached the three men, he extended his gloved hand to Adolphus Lynton.

"Good day, sir. I am not tardy for our appointment, I hope." He smiled politely at Sebastian and Keswick as if he had not just been drinking port with them on the *Peregrine*. "Hello, my lord. You are well?"

"Quite. That uniform becomes you. Are you rejoining your regiment in France?"

"No, as you may recall, I have begun service as a Customs Riding Officer." Tristan straightened his shoulders and added gravely, "I am assisting honest Revenue men like Lieutenant Lynton in capturing the criminals who would steal from the Crown."

Sebastian wanted to laugh and congratulate his friend on his acting abilities, but instead he only gave a sober nod. "I see. I have no doubt that, with the aid of good men like you, right will triumph in the end."

"Thank you. And how do you fare, my lord? Has Cornwall become more agreeable to you?"

Grateful for the opportunity to account for his whereabouts over the coming week, Sebastian sighed. "Sadly, no. In fact, I continue to search for the means to restore Severn Park to my family. I depart for Hampshire on the morrow. As you may recall, my passion is breeding horses, and Severn Park has an established operation for that."

Adolphus Lynton looked bored. "I'm afraid I haven't time for this fascinating conversation. Lord Senwyck and I have a previous engagement and must bid you adieu." This time he only touched the brim of his hat. "Lord Sebastian, I must charge you to pass my sincere regards to your lovely wife. I confess, I find it impossible to imagine her ever being happy in this rustic outpost."

Through clenched teeth, Sebastian bade them both farewell and wheeled Lucifer around to start toward the road that led to Trevarre Hall. When they were out of earshot, he glanced at Keswick and muttered, "I despise that little stoat. It will give me immense pleasure to watch him squirm with frustration in the coming weeks, as he wildly attempts to catch the smugglers!"

Chapter 22

Julia stood between Mrs. Snuggs and Primmie at the long, scrubbed pine table in the center of the kitchen, chopping freshly picked parsley and then turning to sprinkle it into the pot of fragrant soup that simmered over the fire.

When the last bits of parsley had been added to the soup, Julia paused for a moment to survey the whitewashed room with its centuries-old stone floor and polished copper pots "How inviting the kitchen looks," she said approvingly. "I know that both of you have worked very hard, and I appreciate that. Trevarre Hall is becoming a proper home that we can all be proud of."

"Thank'e, mistress." Mrs. Snuggs peered out from under her mobcap as if expecting the compliment to be followed by a new list of tasks to further improve the manor.

Julia laughed. "Even your apron is clean. I am so pleased."

The old woman looked uncomfortable. "Yer ladyship be a good mistress." Then she glanced at Primmie and waggled her eyebrows.

"My lady," Primmie chimed in, "we are wondering where the badger has got to? When we went in to clean your dressing room today, it weren't there."

"I do never hear o' such a thing as a badger in the house!" interjected Mrs. Snuggs.

Julia used a towel to remove a fragrant golden-brown loaf of bread from the baking oven. Setting it on an iron trivet, she looked at the two women. "Daisy is in the stable. I decided that it would be better for her, since she is so much improved, to be with the other animals."

Before they could reply, the sounds of the back door opening and boots being scraped reached their ears.

"His lordship!" Mrs. Snuggs exclaimed.

Julia's heart began to thump. Ever since the interlude she and Sebastian had shared in her dressing room, she had sensed that a barrier between them had been breached. In spite of the way it had ended, with his harsh words about Daisy, she felt that there had been a fundamental shift in their relationship.

Sebastian had unlocked an inner door to her and Julia knew very well how much that meant.

She was in the midst of untying her apron strings with one hand and reaching up to smooth back her wayward curls with the other when he appeared, ducking slightly under the low, beamed kitchen doorway. Tall, wide-shouldered, and lean-hipped, his raven hair tousled by the wind and his cheekbones darkened by the sun, Sebastian perfectly fit Julia's image of an irresistible male—tonight, more than ever.

"I'm not used to such enticing smells coming from my kitchen," he said with a smile.

Julia felt warm blood staining her cheeks. "While you are off doing God knows what, we are cooking."

He came closer, tantalizingly handsome in supple leather topboots and riding clothes, his white cravat loosened. "What is in that pot?" Reaching for a long spoon, Sebastian dipped it into the soup and tasted. "Ah, you've added barley. Delicious."

"The barley were my idea, my lord," boasted the housekeeper.

He flashed a grin. "Why, Mrs. Snuggs, I believe that you

have become respectable! Not only are you masterminding my dinner, but you've also put on a clean apron and cap."

She gave him a reproving glance. "Ye do make an old woman blush! Now, leave my kitchen, yer lordship, afore ye cause a spill."

Julia cut a thick slice of bread, spread it with yellow butter, and followed her husband into the parlor. "Are you hungry?"

"You're an angel." He eyed the bread longingly.

"You didn't think so last night, when you were scolding me about Daisy." Feeling bold, she lifted the warm bread to his mouth, waiting.

Sebastian stared into her eyes and took a bite. After savoring it for a long moment, he arched a brow. "I didn't 'scold.' I was merely pointing out to you that a badger is not a pet."

When he paused to lick a bit of butter from his thumb, Julia felt a tingling sensation between her legs and her cheeks warmed. "I realize that you haven't asked, but I shall tell you all the same that Daisy not only lived through the night, but she was so improved this morning that I took her to the stables."

"I didn't ask because I already saw her there when Keswick and I returned tonight. And, you did the right thing."

Julia put a hand on his arm and looked up at him. "Sebastian, I—I realized that you are right. As much as I may love her, Daisy is a wild creature and it would be wrong for me to keep her here one moment longer than necessary."

"I'm proud of you."

"Well, it's a lesson I am only beginning to understand. " She felt tears threaten and blinked them back. "I can't dictate to others, not even a badger cub like Daisy. You would think I would have learned that after what happened to Papa."

"You couldn't have changed that outcome, no matter

what you did or didn't do." His hand covered hers for a long moment and his gaze grew tender. "Julia, I…"

"Yes?" Her heart skipped.

Sebastian blinked as if he'd caught himself on the verge of a fall. "I should find some soap and water before we dine. You've prepared too fine a meal to serve it to someone as travel-stained as I am."

As her husband backed away, then turned the corner and started up the stairs, Julia wondered if he could possibly be running away from her.

Throughout the delicious meal of soup crowded with fresh vegetables and herbs, roasted chicken, and more warm bread with butter, Sebastian tried to talk to Julia in a congenial yet slightly remote manner.

Although he found her more appealing than ever, something inside him instinctively remained at a distance. Perhaps it was the part of him that sensed it would be too hard to continue to hide his secrets about the smuggling expedition if he let himself get closer.

And Julia was amazingly perceptive, Sebastian reminded himself. If the sparks of intimacy that had sprung up between them last night caught fire, it would be impossible to hide the truth from her…and God only knew what dangers could result from that.

"Did you see Tristan today?" she asked.

"Briefly. He was going off with your Lieutenant Lynton to hunt for free-traders."

"Free-traders? Why give them such a romantic-sounding name when they are really just villainous, murdering, unwashed smugglers?" Her eyes sparkled as she added, "And, incidentally, Adolphus Lynton is not *my* anything."

"Why are you so ill-disposed toward smugglers? You have been told, have you not, that most of Cornwall is involved somehow in running goods? And that the taxes levied by the Crown to pay for the war with France are so high that ordinary folk like fishermen would starve if there was no other course of action?"

"It is a crime, punishable by transportation or hanging." Julia shook her head. "And I've read some horrifying accounts of atrocities committed by smugglers."

"What sorts of atrocities?" He really wasn't certain he wanted to know.

"There was a book in Papa's shop with engravings of Sussex smugglers who whipped men, cut off one's nose, forced another poor fellow to dig his own grave and then buried him alive."

Sebastian raised a dismissive hand. "That was many years ago. Those men were certainly brutal criminals, but that doesn't mean that anything like that is happening in Cornwall today."

"What about the wreckers? And the shocking stories of smugglers who board vessels with legitimate business and then proceed to kill the crew, steal the cargo, and sink the ship?" She paused for a moment to sip her wine before adding, "I must say that I find your views very surprising. Your friend Lord Senwyck certainly feels otherwise!"

Sebastian made a rude noise. "Tristan is very young. He's been away at university and in the Navy. What does he know about the real world, and the struggles of Cornish families?"

"For a man who despises Cornwall and longs to live elsewhere, you are awfully sympathetic to the people here."

With studied nonchalance, he cut a bite of chicken, grateful for the flickering candlelight and its attendant shadows. Again, he fought the urge to lean forward and share the truth with Julia, but every word died before it could leave his lips. Instead, he must deceive her.

"Since you mention my intention to reside elsewhere, I ought to tell you that…in the morning, I am going away, to Severn Park, for a short while."

"I don't understand." She set down her fork and waited.

"I'm taking Keswick and our intention is to…try to discover a way to live there again, perhaps by renting it in place of the current inhabitants. As you know, my goal, my dream, has always been to breed horses at Severn Park." To his own ears, he sounded false and forced, but her expression reflected more confusion than disbelief.

"How can it be anything but a dream? We are nearly penniless, are we not?"

He pushed back his chair and stood up. "Perhaps we are, but I am going nevertheless."

"And Keswick is going with you? What are we to do while you are away—rely on Mr. Snuggs?"

"Tristan will look in on you." Although Sebastian sensed there was much more Julia wished to say on the subject, he continued, "I've already spoken to him about it."

"It was very kind of you to spare a few moments to consider my wellbeing." She folded her arms across her chest.

"Clearly, you are not interested in continuing this conversation."

Julia rose and summoned Primmie to clear the table. "I'm going to check on little Daisy."

"And I am going to pack."

"Of course you are!"

They both turned away at the same moment and exited through opposite doors.

In the middle of the night, Julia awoke, her heart aching.

Beside her, Sebastian lay in a pool of moonlight, the soft summer breeze whispering over his hard-muscled body that was only half-covered by a sheet. Through the open window came the muted, churring call of a nightjar.

Julia thought of Daisy, as she had been a few hours before

when she'd visited her in the barn. It was almost impossible to believe that the badger cub had been near death just two days before, for now she was wriggling around in the straw-lined wooden box they'd fashioned for her, eating all the earthworms and nuts and berries they brought her. She even rolled over on her back so that Julia could rub her tummy. The cub's injured leg was much better, and Julia knew that Sebastian would not be the only one to leave her tomorrow.

She would have to take Daisy back to the vast underground sett herself, in the evening, when the other badgers would emerge to begin foraging for food.

It felt as if there was a little storm inside her as she thought of losing both Daisy and Sebastian in the same day. What if Daisy was not accepted back into the sett? What if her leg became worse again?

And all manner of things could happen to Sebastian that might delay his return to Trevarre Hall. Perhaps he would meet an old love in Hampshire, or quickly achieve his goal to recover Severn Park and—

"Julia," came a husky warning from the shadows, "for God's sake, go to sleep."

To her horror, she felt her eyes brim with tears. She came nearer to him and dared to rest her cheek against his broad chest, which was at once hard yet warm and infinitely appealing. Unbidden came a memory of the first time she saw him, when she had thought he was Lord Sebastian Trevarre's butler. The corners of her mouth twitched.

"What amuses you?" he murmured.

"I was only smiling. I certainly didn't mean to interrupt your sleep." But then she couldn't help adding, "I was thinking of the first time we met. Do you remember?"

"Of course."

But how could he, when he had seemed so bored by her that day? "I came to find you, to ask you to forgive Papa's gambling debts, and I thought you were the butler—"

"Julia, I can assure you, I remember it very well."

She rose up on her elbows then, laughing into his eyes as the starlight streamed over them. "I couldn't see the humor in it then, but now—"

"You were the most confounding female I had ever encountered. So sure of yourself—"

"Oh, but not really. It was just that someone in my family had to take charge, and since no one else ever seemed capable of doing so effectively, I had grown used to stepping into the fray." She gave a little sigh. "I came to feel that it was all up to me."

His eyes softened as he regarded her for a long moment before replying, "What a burden for a child to have to carry. Or perhaps your father was better able to cope when you were younger?"

"No, not really. Papa was a very kind man, but not a practical one. He spent a lot of time in his book shop, escaping into the tales that he was supposed to be selling."

She expected Sebastian to yawn and suggest sleep again, but instead he reached out and traced her delicate jawline with one long, tanned finger. A delicious shiver ran down her back.

"You doubtless didn't have many dreams for yourself," he remarked.

"No, but that's because I was too busy managing the lives of my family members. I imagined that they couldn't cope without me." She could hear the note of irony in her own voice and gave him a bemused smile. "Apparently they are carrying on perfectly well since I left Turbans. Such conceit!"

"And did you never harbor secret dreams of romance for yourself?"

Suddenly, she had to look away from his smoldering gaze. "I—I don't remember."

"I was wrong, I think, to rob you of the sort of romantic first kiss you deserved. I rather made a mockery of it for you."

"No!" Oh, how wrong he was, but how could she tell him

there was no one else she would have rather kissed? Even the scene itself had been perfectly suited to her tastes. "I've never been a female who aspired to sweet romance. If a man had come to me on one knee, with a posy of violets, and recited a poem to preface our first kiss, I fear I should have despised him."

"You preferred someone wicked and arrogant like me?"

She felt herself blushing in the shadows, nearly overcome with desire for him. "Perhaps."

He started to turn toward her and gather her near, and Julia burned to feel his hard maleness pressing between her legs. Already she was wet, yearning, and when the aroused length of him brushed her hip, she knew that he wanted her, too.

"Sebastian." Boldly, she reached up and slipped her fingers into his black hair, drawing his head closer to hers, waiting for his arms to tighten around her, aligning their bodies, and for his mouth to claim hers. It had been too long!

"It's late. I have a long journey tomorrow and I need rest." He was disengaging from her. "Please, go to sleep."

His words were like a slap.

The sharp sting of humiliation caused her to roll away from him and turn toward the wall. Covering herself with the sheet, she murmured, "Of course. Good night."

She heard him sigh, and thought for a moment that there was something deeper in the sound, but then he fell silent, and eventually she closed her eyes as well.

The bedchamber was still cloaked in darkness when Sebastian rose, feeling as if he hadn't slept at all. He washed with the aid of a pitcher and bowl, dressed, and sat down carefully on the side of the bed to pull on his boots.

Of all the nights for Julia to bewitch him so completely! God, what agony to want her so much and yet be unable to make love to her. It just couldn't be, though, not yet. A little voice in the back of his mind taunted, *what harm could it have done to show your wife that you want her?*

"Is it morning?"

Running both hands through his damp hair, he turned to see Julia sitting up with the sheet tucked over her lovely breasts. "Not quite, but I must go now." He couldn't tell her that the tides ordained that he and his men must sail at dawn. "Julia, I apologize if I was abrupt with you during the night. I have a great deal on my mind."

Her long, rich hair was appealingly tousled and she blinked at him sleepily. "If you say so, my lord."

Sebastian wanted to strip off his clothes and climb back into bed with her, but that was impossible. "I have something for you. A gesture of good faith for the time we are apart."

Her expression softened. "What do you mean?"

Rising, he went to the armoire and found the blue velvet pouch that Miles Bartholomew had given him in London. After plucking one item from it, he returned to the bed. "This belonged to my mother. I'd like you to have it."

As he gave her the ring with its unique miniature of a man's eye, she looked at it in surprise. "I've heard of eye rings, but I've never seen anything like this. Is that your—father's eye?"

"I suppose so, though it doesn't look a bit like him. I showed it to Andre Raveneau when we were in London and he suggested that it looks like *my* eye and that perhaps my mother had it made to remind her of me?"

"It's very striking, and I am glad to have it, but I can't help wondering why are you giving it to me now?"

"Must you probe beneath the surface of every moment we share?" Sebastian stared at her violet-shadowed face for a long moment, then abruptly reached across to lift her by the waist and bring her, sheet and all, onto his lap. "Devil take it, Julia, just accept it for what it is."

Then, unable to stop himself this time, he slid one hand inside the sheet to find her warm, firm breast, and immediately the nipple puckered against his rough palm. Deftly, he turned her upper body and bent her back. He gazed into her startled eyes for a moment, then he was kissing her, his tongue invading the sweetness of her mouth, telling her what he could not say with words. Julia began to moan, arching against him, and he was on fire for her. One more moment and it would be too late.

"I must go." It was wrenching to lift his mouth from hers and set her away from him, especially when he heard her soft whimper of protest.

Sebastian quickly began to gather the rest of his gear. Standing, he looked down at her. "I won't try to prevent you from seeking adventure because I know you are far too headstrong to obey me, but please, have a care. And Julia, give me one promise."

"Wh—what is that?"

"For God's sake, stay away from Coombe Hawne."

Chapter 23

"I forgot to ask him how long he would be gone," Julia said to Tristan as they tramped across the meadow path, headed toward the woods below the Hall Walk.

Tristan was carrying Daisy in a thick sack, tucked under one strong arm. "I suppose it is hard to know how long such an errand might take."

"I still don't understand why he and Keswick had to go to Severn Park. I am quite certain that we haven't the money to rent or lease it back from his brother George, and of course the entail prevents any further measures. Severn Park must remain in the possession of the Marquess of Caverleigh, correct?"

The young man looked uncomfortable. "It would seem so. Of course, I know very little of your husband's affairs."

"You're awfully quiet today. Is everything all right? Are you enjoying your new occupation?" She gestured toward his uniform as she spoke.

"I suppose so. I can't say I enjoy spending time with that windbag Lieutenant Lynton, but I do enjoy the adventure. I had rather missed the Navy."

"Is that why you became a Riding Officer? I must confess, it didn't quite sound plausible when you explained it in our garden, in front of Mr. Lynton. Or perhaps I was just perplexed because your opinions about smuggling were so different from Sebastian's."

"Yes, I am attracted to the adventure of being a Riding Officer," he replied with a distracted expression. "But it's also true that I don't share your husband's views on smuggling. Cornish people have a history of looking the other way when it comes to free trading, especially when the Crown sets taxes at exorbitant levels, but the fact remains that it is a crime."

"That's what I tried to tell Sebastian last night. I don't understand why he gets so angry about it."

Arriving at the wide promenade of the Hall Walk, the pair crossed over the pathway and descended into the steep, wooded stretch of land that continued to the banks of the River Fowey. Following an old hedgerow, Julia stopped so suddenly that Tristan almost bumped into her.

"Here we are," she whispered, pointing into the underbrush where there was a mounded hole with a little pile of leaves and twigs near its entrance. "That's Daisy's sett, I believe. I found her snared beside the hedgerow."

"Good enough. Let's release her here, then." He smiled and added, "I have loved watching badgers near Lerryn Creek since I was a child. The setts, which can be hundreds of years old, are fascinating, and I admire the way they clean house and leave the piles of debris, like old bedding material, outside the entrance. They're wonderful animals."

"I hope so much that Daisy will be welcomed back into her home."

"I suppose we must trust in nature. You've done all you could within the bounds of logic and decency and now you must leave it up to fate."

"Yes," she replied, considering his words. "It's a good challenge for me."

"Here you go then, my lady."

Julia accepted the bag that Tristan put into her arms and sat down next to the hedge of red currant and blackthorn, heedless of her skirts of floral-patterned muslin. "Come on then, darling, are you ready to go home to your family?"

Peering inside, she smiled at the sight of two small eyes, bright as stars in the shadowed sack. Her throat was thick with tears as she gently lifted the badger cub out into the gathering twilight. "I shall miss you, dear Daisy."

For a moment, the cub seemed to nuzzle its black nose against her cheek.

"Is that safe?" Tristan wondered aloud. "Badgers can have ferocious teeth, you know."

"She trusts me. She was nearly dead when I found her, you know. Her leg is still healing, but Sebastian convinced me that it's best for her to be back in the sett now that she is out of danger."

"Your husband is a wise man."

"Do you really think so? He can be quite wicked. And arrogant." A smile teased the corners of her mouth.

"Well—yes, perhaps."

"Sometimes I dream that I might change him, but I don't suppose that's possible."

"My lady, it's more likely that you could train Daisy to live in your house and eat at the dinner table than change Sebastian."

Julia blushed. "I know."

Tristan paused for a moment, watching her cuddle the badger. "Besides, would you really wish to alter him? What did you have in mind—a civilized gentleman, content to sit by the fire and read? Or perhaps one who quaffs ale and hunts regularly with a pack of hounds?"

Laughing, she shook her head. "Point taken. It's just that I sometimes wish he were more…"

"Yes?"

"Oh…he can be quite harsh, you know. And, it's so frustrating to know that he would rather be in Hampshire than here. It seems that Sebastian would rather chase a dream that he may somehow recover Severn Hall than work to make Trevarre Hall a thriving estate again."

"I perceive that you're angry with him." Though

Tristan's tone was casual, his sea-blue eyes watched her carefully. "Do you really like Cornwall so much?"

"I adore it," she exclaimed passionately. "The moment we crossed the River Tamar, I was bewitched, and when I first saw Trevarre Hall, I knew I had come home."

"Trevarre Hall?" Tristan repeated, laughing. "With its broken windows and holes in the roof?"

"Exactly," Julia replied with a touch of defiance. Then, as the little badger began to squirm in her lap, she looked down. "I fear I may have lingered over this conversation to delay my parting from Daisy. Are you certain it's dark enough?"

"Yes, the others are coming out. I heard a badger foraging on the other side of the hedge. In fact, you and I should be on our way. Rub her off with the inside of the sack to diminish the scent of your hands."

Her eyes misted as she obeyed him and set the young animal on the ground, expecting her to huddle against her leg as she was wont to do at home. However, Daisy started forward, limping slightly. She had only advanced a few feet when she threw Julia a last parting glance and waddled off to find the currants that had fallen under the hedgerow. There was something in her manner as she sniffed and looked about that proclaimed her joy that she was back in her true element.

Julia ached inside, but the feeling was not unpleasant. "Goodbye, Daisy," she whispered. "I'm glad I could help you. Enjoy your freedom!"

"Well done, my lady," Tristan said warmly.

"Thank you for coming with me," she replied. "Let's return to the house and have dinner, shall we? There is some fine soup and bread, left over from last night."

As the days passed, Julia found plenty of tasks to keep

herself busy. The garden was producing more and more, and she rose early, eager to discover what new vegetables were ready to be picked and how many eggs the hens had laid. When she had her hands in the earth, she was happy. Clover often followed her mistress into the courtyard and rubbed her plush gray face against Julia as she worked.

Later, after breakfast, Julia and Primmie washed windows, aired out the maze of rooms that hadn't seen daylight in years, and even painted the parlor a shade of palest gold that caught the afternoon sun. And in the afternoons, Julia went off on her own, sometimes walking in the woods, sometimes rowing her little boat in Pont Pill or across the river to Fowey to walk up and down the steep, winding lanes.

She enjoyed looking in the shop windows, and dreamed of buying a new bonnet, gown, or reticule, but such extravagances were out of the question. Instead, she cherished the eye ring Sebastian had given her. She wore it on a thin gold chain around her neck, tucked into the bodice of her gown, and sometimes before Julia went to sleep alone in the big bed, she held the ring close to the candle flame and studied the tiny, detailed eye, painted by an unknown miniaturist long ago. André Raveneau might be right, she finally decided. It did look like Sebastian's eye.

One day, Mr. Platt, the butcher, called out to Julia when he saw her outside his shop and invited her to take a leg of lamb home. When she protested that she had no money to pay him, he insisted, chuckling that he would get it from her husband another day. He made a little package that she could carry in the rowboat, and when she arrived home and opened it, she discovered that he'd included a slab of bacon, a dried cod, and packets of both salt and sugar.

"How kind the Cornish people are!" Julia exclaimed to Tristan two days later as they walked through the sun-dappled woods, down to Pont to feed the swans. "Mr. Platt's generosity was followed by a gift from Mistress Thomas, the milliner. She made me take a new bonnet I'd admired, and when I was walking by the Higgins Farm, their son ran out with a bucket of carrots and blackberries."

"No doubt they are aware that his lordship is away and they feel protective of you."

"Indeed? I've never known anything like it before; certainly not in Bath." She glanced over to see Tristan looking decidedly uncomfortable. "What's wrong? You look as if you're holding something back that you need to tell me. Is it bad news?"

Quickly, he laughed and shook his head. "No! Nothing's wrong. I was just—just wondering about the time."

"It must be midday because I'm feeling rather peckish." She watched him as he went ahead to hold back a tree branch that blocked their way. Tristan was certainly a splendid young man with his wayward ginger hair, sandy brows over blue eyes that crinkled at the corners when he laughed, and square jaw. His tall, broad-shouldered frame lent itself perfectly to the dashing naval uniform he wore, and she couldn't help wondering who might be a worthy match for him. "Do you ask the time because you have another appointment? With a young lady perhaps?"

Color stained his cheekbones. "What a thing to say!"

"It wouldn't surprise me, my lord! No doubt every female in the parish swoons when you pass."

"The only appointment I have is with Lieutenant Lynton. He wishes to ride along the cliffs near Lansallos this afternoon."

"Ah yes, I heard from Primmie that a smuggling ship has been sighted in recent days, somewhere to the west. They say its captain is dangerously attractive!" As she spoke, they emerged out of the trees, into the sunlit meadow above the little bridge at Pont. The tide was in and the swan and her gawky cygnets were swimming near the slate boathouse, as if waiting for them. "Of course, Primmie is nonsensical. No one on shore could possibly view the captain clearly enough to see what he really looks like. Furthermore, smugglers are repellant villains, and it is foolish for anyone to romanticize them, don't you agree?"

He looked stunned. "Of course!"

"I told Primmie that she must not dream of this pirate captain climbing into her bedroom window, for if it were to come true, he would doubtless be fat, toothless, and foul-smelling!"

Tristan gave a nervous cough of laughter. "My lady—"

"Do I shock you? Yes, I can see that I do." With a playful smile, she reached into the pocket tied round her waist and took out a chunk of stale black bread. "Look how quickly the cygnets are growing! Won't you help me feed them?"

As they tossed bits of bread to the swans, Tristan surveyed the lime kiln. No longer in use, one side of the tall, rectangular tower was now covered with vines, and birds had built nests in its nooks and crevices.

"I remember when there were lots of ships sailing up Pont to bring lime here," he said. "I was just a boy, but the memories are quite vivid. It's a shame that it's stopped being used in recent years. Lord and Lady Caverleigh came here less and less before the accident, and the farm just crumbled away..."

"Oh, I dearly wish that Sebastian would turn his attention from Severn Park to Trevarre Hall. There is so much here that we could use to make the estate profitable again, but he scoffs at the notion of managing a lime kiln and raising sheep."

"Yes, I can imagine him doing so."

"I am trying to accept the fact that I cannot manage him, and I shouldn't try, but perhaps if *you* were to speak to him...? I know exactly what you could say."

Tristan had begun to laugh, shaking his head. "You are incorrigible, do you know that? What makes you imagine that it's any different if you enlist me to make your arguments to Sebastian than it would be if you did it yourself?"

"Oh. I see your point." Julia flushed. "I can't seem to help myself, after a lifetime spent arranging the lives of my family members. They were much more accepting of my directions than my husband is."

"I know one thing about Sebastian. He has a mind of his own, and he must reach his own decisions. If I tried to persuade him, it might make matters worse."

Julia cocked her head and gave Tristan a rueful smile. "You are right, of course. It's a perverse trick of destiny that I find myself married to a man like Sebastian who is harder to govern than a wild stallion."

"No doubt there are lessons for you in this twist of fate."

"I am beginning to realize that." Tossing the rest of the bread onto the rippling waters of the creek, she took his arm. "Shall we go back? I wouldn't want you to be late for your appointment with Adolphus Lynton. Perhaps you'll capture the smugglers and can regale me with stories when next we meet!"

"My lady, I just come from my cousin's house by Gribbin Head, where I hear tell that the smuggling ship be seen again. They do say it's near Polridmouth Bay, a perfect place for a landing!" Primmie had been nearly shouting in her excitement, but now she lowered her voice. "Cousin Martha whispers that the captain and his men be having their way with women all along the coast!"

"Fairytales, I'll wager, concocted by a lot of silly girls." Julia finished the last of her oatmeal, which she'd eaten standing up at the kitchen worktable. On her stool was a box containing a tiny hedgehog, snuggled into a bed of grass and soft rags.

"Martha do say that they call him Captain Rogue. Roguing be a nicer word than smugglin' don't you think so?"

"What I think is that this conversation is ridiculous. Now

fetch your apron so that you can help me clean the carpets. We'll start with the big one from the parlor. I thought we might hang it over a low branch on the beech tree in the garden."

"Without a man to help us? What about Snuggs?"

They both looked out the window toward the farmyard, where Mr. Snuggs was hobbling along in his red waistcoat, taking his time scattering feed for the chickens.

"I don't think he would be much use. His gout is flaring up, and as you know, Mrs. Snuggs has had an attack of dyspepsia." She moved the box with the newborn, abandoned hedgehog, christened Henry, to a shelf near the hearth. "Be good and sleep now, Henry. You're almost ready to go out on your own!"

Primmie frowned, but followed her mistress into the parlor. Together, they began moving the furniture off the Turkey carpet. "'Tisn't right that we be here without a man. Why'd his lordship have to leave, and take Keswick? What's he want with Hampshire? It don't make sense to me."

Julia wanted to reply that it made no sense to her either. With each passing day, she missed Sebastian more, yet also felt more resentful toward him. How could he leave her so soon after their marriage, and with so little notice? Did he ever ache for her as she did for him, and if he did, why wasn't he there beside her?

"Perhaps your Captain Rogue will climb through the window and come to our aid, Primmie," Julia remarked with a light laugh. "Do you think he would object to carrying a large carpet into the garden for us?"

"Oh, mistress, wouldn't that be lovely? And mayhap he do bring us some port, and silk and lace…oh, and fine Hyson tea!"

"Of course," she rejoined, succumbing to Primmie's enthusiasm as they began rolling up the carpet. "If we are going to have a fantasy, we may as well make it extravagant!"

Chapter 24

There was only a slivered moon to light the way when the *Peregrine* glided up Lerryn Creek. The hilly wooded banks on either side were black and eerily quiet except for an occasional call from a nightjar or owl. Because the night was still, the crew had put out the oars and were rowing up the creek. After a time, the boat swept around to the north, into the inlet toward a secret stone quay that was nearly hidden behind a curtain of low-hanging trees.

Everyone on board was wound tight with excitement.

"My lord, we must confess," Keswick said softly as he joined his captain on deck, "we rather feared that the Revenue men might be lying in wait for us when we entered the River Fowey. There is a perfect spot for them to hide their boat at Readymoney Beach, below St. Catherine's Castle."

"Keswick, I must say I am surprised," he replied drily. "You are as nervous as an old woman."

"We would have to be blind this past week not to have seen the Riding Officers on the cliffs, more than once."

"Have I not told you to trust me? They will not find us, and even if they did manage to do so—and board, they would find nothing." Sebastian turned his attention then to their landing. "Ah, there is Penrose with the torch to welcome us. Now, let us move quickly. There is a great deal to do."

The crew had already begun to bring up the cargo from the hiding places between the bulkheads. Barrels constructed with spaces filled with lace and tea went out quickly, followed by smaller casks called half-ankers, containing more than four gallons each of French brandy.

Sebastian joined Tristan in the clearing beside the quay. The younger man's naval uniform was now replaced by dark, plain clothing that helped camouflage him in the woods.

"Well done, my friend," Sebastian told him as they shook hands. "We have had a smooth operation thus far. And you?"

Tristan watched the crew bringing the cargo ashore. The men Jasper Polarven had recruited to act as tub-carriers emerged from the darkness to meet them, and the half-ankers were roped together in pairs on their backs for the climb up the steep path to the smuggler's hole.

"It's hard to believe that this is really happening," he said hoarsely. "It's as if we're characters in an adventure story!"

"This is quite real," Sebastian replied, his arched brow visible in the shadows thrown by Tristan's torch. "We've accomplished a great deal with just this cargo, and there will be more tomorrow night at Coombe Hawne. There will not only be a fine profit for all of us, but I've also brought a shipment of salt for the local fishermen. No more pilchard need rot on the fields for lack of salt to preserve them over the winter, especially after we've made a few more runs."

Tristan nodded slowly. "It all makes perfect sense when I am with you, but your wife makes quite a different argument, and she can be very persuasive."

"Why does that not surprise me?" Sebastian laughed softly. "As long as she does not suspect what we are doing, you can listen to all the arguments she wishes to make."

"Will you come up to the smuggler's hole with us? It isn't far." Turning, Tristan held the torch aloft and led the way for the tub-carriers and the carts that brought the bigger barrels. "Her ladyship has heard that there is a smuggling ship off-shore, but it would never occur to her that you might be the captain. On the contrary, she is quite vexed that you have gone to Hampshire."

"Ha! That's good." His gaze remained on the darkened path as they climbed a narrow path through the ancient woods. "Is she well otherwise?"

"Quite. Last I heard, she had rescued a baby hedgehog that appeared to have lost its mother. Henry, she calls it. She is going to release it tomorrow morning."

Sebastian felt a stinging in the region of his heart as a wave of longing for Julia came over him. However, except for a momentary grimace, he went on as calmly as before. "And what of that buffoon Lynton?"

"He and the others are madly combing the cliffs, but so far I have been able to distract them from the areas where they might find you. Also, Mixstowe has provided a couple of 'informants' to Lynton who have given him false clues."

"Excellent!" Sebastian approved in a mocking tone.

They had reached the nearly indistinguishable opening to the smuggler's hole that was carved into the hillside. Already the cargo was being unloaded and carried into the cave.

"We'll keep it safe here for the time being, until Mixstowe can arrange for the goods to gradually be transported inland," said Sebastian.

"No one will find it here. And, I found the tunnel that leads to Lanwyllow, so we may decide to make use of that."

"What would we do without you?" Sebastian put a dark hand on Tristan's arm, then drew back to meet his eyes in the darkness. "I'll see you again tomorrow night then. We'll watch for your sign from the cliffs before we bring in a long boat to land on the beach."

"Until tomorrow night. Good fortune to you, my friend."

"Good day, my lady," cried Robert Mixstowe as he helped Julia onto the ferry from Polruan to Fowey. "Are you well?"

"Yes, thank you, very well!" She certainly wouldn't tell him that ten entire days had passed since Sebastian went off to Hampshire, and she had no idea when he was coming back.

"'Tis a beautiful day for an outing. I'll own, though, that I'm surprised to see you on my ferry instead of rowing your smart little boat!"

"I felt like being a bit more sociable," she said, favoring him with a warm smile.

"Honored we be to have you, my lady."

It was a rather rough crossing. Pale gray clouds were scudding across the sun by the time they tied up at Fowey and Julia climbed the slate steps to the town quay. She wore a high-waisted gown of blue-and-white patterned cambric and carried a wicker basket over her arm. A fetching straw hat with a flat crown and some periwinkle ribbons down the back saved her hair from being blown into her face as she started up Lostwithiel Street.

Although she paused as usual to look in the shop windows, a part of Julia was feeling restless. It had been a mistake to leave her little boat back at Pont, she decided, for it would have been a perfect day to row off on an adventure. Perhaps she would have drifted into a hidden creek and come upon Primmie's Captain Rogue and his elusive smuggling ship!

"Well, if it isn't Lady Sebastian Trevarre!" exclaimed a familiar voice. "I wonder what brings that secret smile to your pretty lips?"

Julia forced herself to turn slowly, still smiling. "Oh, hello, Lieutenant Lynton. I was merely enjoying the sight of these rare books on display."

"No doubt they remind you of your unfortunate father."

"You describe Papa differently than I would, but it is true

that a fine book shop always reminds me of him. I was lucky to grow up in such a place."

"And now? Do you still feel so fortunate?"

"I am well pleased with my life, if that is what you mean."

He took a step closer so that Julia was forced to back into the sheltered doorway. "Do you never regret your impetuous behavior, marrying his lordship to save your sister Sarah from him?

"Sir, you overstep the bounds of propriety."

"But your own husband is famous for such behavior! I had assumed you must now find propriety to be quite dull." His voice took on a menacing tone.

Julia was beginning to feel a bit alarmed. He had boxed her in so that she was shielded from passersby. "You misjudge us both, sir."

"And where, may I ask, *is* your esteemed husband? His lordship is…*away*?"

"Yes, he has gone to Hampshire on a matter of business."

"Are you aware that a band of smugglers has been plying our coastline in recent days? It is rumored that the one they call Captain Rogue is particularly wicked and merciless, especially in his treatment of women, if you take my meaning! I would suggest that you lock your windows at night, my lady. Perhaps you should sleep with a dagger?"

Before she could reply, Tristan appeared behind Adolphus Lynton and looked curiously over the shorter man's shoulder, brows lifted. "Good day! I hope I'm not interrupting."

Julia laughed with relief. "Not at all, Lord Senwyck! It's lovely to see you." She saw that he was wearing his dashing uniform again, complete with a bicorne hat that he carried under one arm.

Lynton had no choice but to back away from Julia and let her step back into the cobbled lane. "You're quite tardy, Senwyck."

"Am I? We aren't such sticklers for punctuality here in

Cornwall as you Bathonians seem to be."

"I was born here in Cornwall, you know. Just up the road in Bodmin. That's what attracted me to a position as a Preventive Officer; I am determined to save my dear Cornwall from besmirchment by these nefarious smugglers."

"We are in complete agreement then, sir," Tristan replied with a polite smile.

Julia looked on, thinking that she had not known of Lynton's connection to Cornwall. It was rather a relief to learn this, since it meant that perhaps he had not come to Fowey on her account after all.

A sudden breeze, cool for a June afternoon, whipped around them, and Julia glanced up at the gathering clouds. "I see that we may have a shower. I hope you gentlemen will excuse me while I go inside to retrieve a book I've had mended." She nodded as they bowed and wished her good day. Inside the bookshop, she paid for her volume of Shakespeare's Sonnets, its spine now nicely repaired, and looked back outside to make certain that the two men had gone.

Emerging back onto Lostwithiel Street, Julia started up the hill only to hear Lynton's strident voice rising from another secluded doorway.

"I tell you, they've been sighted off Polridmouth Bay! As soon as the other officers arrive, we'll all ride out there together."

"But, sir, it would be far more strategic for me go ahead, alone on horseback, in case they are watching for us. Also, I may see something that will prove useful."

Julia crossed the street and hurried past them. The last thing she wanted to do was attract the attention of Adolphus Lynton twice in one day! As she climbed the steep hill, she could hear him ranting, "I mean to see that brigand swing from the gallows if it's the last thing I do!"

She was swept by a desire to keep walking, to stand on the cliffs and to turn her face to the damp breeze from the

English Channel. The thought that she might even sight Captain Rogue's ship was thrilling. She laughed at herself as she thought of Primmie's name for the newly infamous smuggler and even felt a little thrill of guilty pleasure to be entertaining a fantasy about a man who was not her husband.

Julia hugged her basket closer and continued up the narrow lane. She was about to turn west at the top of the hill when Tristan rode up behind her on his spirited roan.

"My lady!" he called. "I think that it is going to rain and you have a long journey back to Trevarre Hall. Since you came by the Polruan ferry—"

"How do you know that?"

Spots of color touched his handsome cheekbones. "I encountered Mixstowe and he mentioned it to me. However, that is not the issue. You may be caught in the rain, so I implore you to return to the Quay and request that Mixstowe take you across to Bodinnick, nearer Trevarre Hall. He will do it if you ask him."

"Whyever should he do such a thing? What would his other passengers think?"

"He would do it because all of us are watching out for you in the absence of your husband."

It came to her that he would not stop arguing unless she pretended to agree with him. "Although I sincerely doubt that everyone is as concerned for my welfare as you imagine, I shall do as you suggest, my lord. I thank you for your concern."

He looked slightly suspicious. "I would take you myself but I must ride in the other direction."

Turning a charming smile up at him, she replied, "I am quite capable of seeing myself home, but I do appreciate your concern, and of course I understand that you are on duty. Goodbye, Lord Senwyck."

Julia waved and began to descend Lostwithiel Street, heading obediently in the direction of the Town Quay.

When she stopped at the flower vendor to buy a bunch of blue and yellow irises, Mrs. Powell, the baker's wife, came out of her shop with a half-dozen warm scones studded with currants.

"Take these home for tea, my lady!"

Looking back up the hill, Julia was pleased to see that Tristan and his horse were gone. While Mrs. Powell was occupied chatting about her daughter with Garth, the unmarried flower vendor, Julia slipped away down a narrow alley between two half-timbered houses. Soon she was hurrying along a path that threaded the green hills, headed in a southwesterly direction toward the cliffs above the English Channel.

The wind was increasing. What had earlier been a sunny June day was turning gray and blustery, but wasn't that part and parcel of living in Cornwall? Afternoon showers were the reason for the lush green meadows, woods, and gardens, and Julia secretly enjoyed being caught in them. The sensation of soft raindrops on her face felt almost decadent.

Coming across the fields above Covington Woods, she saw that the English Channel was ruffled with whitecaps while the clouds overhead had gone lead-gray. A gust of wind nearly plucked away her flat-crowned straw bonnet, and she stopped for a moment to tie the ribbons tighter. Raindrops began to spit from the dark sky, but there was nothing soft and pleasurable about these; they stung when they struck her.

It came to Julia that perhaps Tristan had been right. It was later than she had realized; dusk was gathering. She should have returned to Trevarre Hall, where a fire had doubtless been lit in the parlor and Mrs. Snuggs would have a pot of good strong tea brewing.

How foolish she had been to strike out alone, imagining that the wicked smuggler's ship would be dancing about on the channel for her entertainment!

Rain had begun to fall in earnest by the time she came

over the brow of the hill on the path that would lead her down to the beach at Coombe Hawne. Her thin summer frock clung to her body and she found her footing threatened on the increasingly muddy path. As darkness gathered amidst the storm, it became harder to see. Lifting her skirts to climb over a stile, Julia paused to look out over clusters of gorse and hawthorn shrubs, searching for a glimpse of the tiny stone cottage set back from the beach.

The wind was blowing wildly as she clambered down the steep footpath. Waves were crashing against the rocks that jutted out from the sheltered cove. Then, in the midst of the gale, Coombe Cottage appeared like a beacon. When Julia reached it and opened the low door to its blessedly dry interior, Sebastian's warning flashed in her memory.

For God's sake, promise me that you will stay away from Coombe Hawne!

"But, what choice do I have?" she murmured aloud, pulling the door closed. "Isn't this storm more threatening to me than a supposed ghost?"

Julia stood in the tiny room and listened to the rattling of the raindrops against the loose windowpanes. As her breathing slowed, she became aware of the same pungent scent of tobacco she had noticed during her first visit to the cottage. Then she saw a corked bottle on the table where the books had been stacked before. They were gone now.

Setting down the basket of flowers, scones, and the volume of poetry, Julia peered through the tiny window, glimpsing what seemed to be the flash of white sails just off shore. And what was that dark shape pushed up on the stony beach? Could it be a longboat?

A cold chill skittered down her spine and her nipples stood out against the sodden fabric of her gown. She hurried to the door and laid the thick wooden bolt in place.

It was growing very dark in the little cottage and it suddenly came to her that she had no source of light. At least she had food, though, thanks to Mistress Powell. And, in the bedchamber there were blankets. The thought of wrapping herself in one was comforting.

Julia tried to calm herself as she turned the corner next to the bed. When had she ever let herself be frightened, especially by her own imagination?

However, in the next instant, something dark, thick, and voluminous covered first her face and head, then all her body, and it seemed that her heart might explode with terror. She screamed and screamed, but the sound was muffled even to her own ears. Powerful arms lifted her into the air as if she were a feather, tossed her over what felt like a broad shoulder, and pinned her easily in place in spite of her violent struggles to free herself.

Dear God, Julia thought wildly as raw fear coursed through her veins, *am I going to die?*

In the next moment, everything went black.

Chapter 25

Warm, soothing sunlight poured across Julia's face. It felt as if she were being rocked in a cradle and she let herself enjoy the gently rhythmic sensation, even though it made no sense. It was hard to remember the last time she had felt so blissfully relaxed.

Slowly, she let herself become aware that she lay snuggled into a feather mattress, covered by soft, fresh sheets. But, it wasn't her own bed at Trevarre Hall. Where could she be?

With an effort, she opened her eyes a fraction. Just a few feet above her head were low beams, and next to her was a paneled wall. The plush, comfortable bed was narrow and completely unfamiliar, and it was swaying as if rocked by the currents of the ocean…

Her heart leaped with fresh terror as she realized that she was on a *ship*!

How had she gotten here? Whose ship was it? Fully awake now, Julia started to sit up, but halted as the covers slipped away and she saw that she was *naked* except for the eye ring which dangled from a thin gold chain around her neck. Looking around nervously, Julia clutched the sheet over her breasts in case someone was hiding in the cabin.

Dear God, what had happened to her clothing? Perhaps she been taken by pirates—no, not pirates, *smugglers*! Of course! She had been kidnapped by the fiendish Captain

Rogue and he was probably sailing off to sell her to a sultan's harem!

She wanted to yell, to demand her clothing and to be returned to Trevarre Hall, but quickly realized that such a course of action would be not only unwise, but probably ridiculous.

As Julia threw herself back on the pillows, a new array of panicky thoughts chased through her mind. Who had undressed her? Perhaps she been drugged—and then raped in her unconscious state. She lifted the covers with a trembling hand and surveyed her own body. There were no bruises or scratches, and she had to admit that she felt fine.

Her anxious self-examination was interrupted by a knock on the cabin door. "My lady?" called a hesitant male voice.

Julia's urge to find a hiding place was quickly overcome by the realization that she couldn't go very far without clothing. Instead, striving for a calm tone, she called, "Y-yes? Who is it?"

The door opened and a slight, brown-haired young man peeked inside. His booted feet were spread wide to allow him to adjust to the motion of the ship without spilling the contents of the tray he held.

"Good morning, my lady! Colvithick be my name. I do have yer breakfast here."

"You'll pardon me if I don't curtsy," she said sharply.

Colvithick advanced toward her with the tray and set it on a low, braced table built in next to the bunk where she lay. Julia felt her stomach rumble as she stared at the poached egg, ham, two scones, clotted cream, and strawberry jam that filled a large plate.

"Are you trying to fatten me up for the sultan?" she demanded.

"The who?" Colvithick stepped backward, looking confused. "Do you be afraid, my lady? No need for fear. None of us do mean you any harm."

"Of course not. You just removed all my clothing."

A bright flush spread up the young man's face as he blinked nervously. "That be the captain's doing." Then he bowed and hurried out of the cabin.

As soon as he had closed the door, Julia wrapped the sheet around her torso, tucked the end between her breasts, and climbed out of the bunk. She wouldn't let herself think about the fact that the horrible, leering smuggling captain had stripped her naked. Instead, she turned her attention to a solution. There had to be some clothing or weapons stored somewhere in this cabin! Looking around, she saw a chest, but upon further investigation, found it securely locked. There were some cabinets built into the bulkhead, but those were also locked. Then her gaze fell on a wooden box that looked promising, but inside there was only a lot of navigational equipment. In the midst of tools like fancy sextants and an elaborate compass, the only thing that might have been useful to her was a brass instrument with two long, sharply pointed arms. Could she possibly frighten an attacker with this object?

"Blast," she muttered. The sight of the breakfast tray just increased her frustration. How dare these villains leave her in such a vulnerable position and then try to break down her defenses with delicious food?

Still, Julia reasoned, it would be wise to keep up her strength since terrible challenges must lie ahead. Climbing back onto the bunk, she hid the instrument with the two long points under her pillow. And then, feeling ravenous, she settled the tray onto her lap and poured milk and strong tea into a cup. She drank it down and filled it again. She spread buttery clotted cream onto a warm, currant-studded scone, added a dollop of jam, and bit into it with a sigh. Ambrosia! No doubt the smugglers had stolen this delectable food from an unsuspecting estate along the Cornish coast.

When she had finished the breakfast and returned the tray to the low table, Julia found a chair containing a chamber pot hidden discreetly around a corner. Thank God this crew wasn't completely barbaric! After using it, she crawled back into bed and was swept by another wave of fatigue. Vowing that she would only close her eyes for a moment, she curled up and immediately fell fast asleep, one hand under her pillow.

"A-hem!"

Julia felt as if she were rising through deep water. When she opened her eyes, everything was a blur. Dimly, she made out the form of a tall, broad-shouldered, dark-haired man, apparently the same one whose throat-clearing had awakened her. She blinked as he strode toward her, holding out a bundle of fabric tied with a ribbon.

"I understand you are looking for these?"

Julia rubbed her eyes in disbelief. "*Sebastian*? Is it really you?" He had changed. He wore a close-trimmed rakish beard and his black hair was caught back in a short queue, but there was no mistaking the familiar brow arched above compelling sage-gray eyes, the lines of his wide shoulders, and the faintly mocking tone of his voice. "Oh, thank God! You've come to rescue me!"

"Have I? From whom, may I ask?"

"From the smugglers, of course! Didn't you see them when you came on board? How did you find me?" She scrambled to a sitting position.

Sebastian sat down on the edge of the bunk. Never had he seemed more alive to her. When he reached for her and she went into his arms, the warmth of his skin through his linen shirt and the faint masculine scent of him made her giddy with longing.

"Devil take it, Julia, you are the most aggravating woman—yet I have never wanted to kiss you more." And he did just that, drawing her onto his hard lap as his mouth slanted over hers.

Julia heard herself moaning shamelessly. She kissed him back, opening her mouth to him, and twined her arms around his strong neck. At length, she was able to murmur, "Oh, how I have missed you! It's like a dream that you are here."

"Yes? And how are you feeling? I must say, you are looking better by the moment." His eyes were dancing as they wandered over her sheet-draped form. "Quite lovely, in fact."

Her relief and joy culminated in tears. "Oh, Sebastian, I think they were taking me to a h-harem!"

He laughed. "You've spent too much time in the minaret with Freddy, my darling."

"How can you jest at such a time? We must make haste and escape, before the smugglers return!" She tried to get out of bed to urge him along, but he easily pinned her down.

"Not so fast. How did this happen? Were you at Coombe Hawne—even though I warned you to stay away?"

"Oh, Sebastian, I am so, so sorry that I ignored your warnings—"

"You mean, you broke your promise to me," he said grimly.

"Well, yes, and I am contrite, truly, but it was raining—storming, in fact, and growing dark, and I had to find shelter!"

"And why were you near there in the first place? No, never mind, I don't want to know."

"Can we not talk of these matters later, after we are safely home at Trevarre Hall? We must not spend another moment chatting, or even kissing! I don't know how you found me, but now that you have we must *hurry*. There isn't a moment to lose. Those dastardly smugglers may burst in at any moment, particularly their leader, the one they call Captain Rogue."

His eyebrow had flown up again. "Is there really such a person?"

"It's what the fearful women of Cornwall call him. Now, please! Not only has he torn my clothes away after knocking me senseless, but I fear he would have no qualms about killing you outright." Julia couldn't understand how he could look so calm. She tried again to get off the bed, to no avail, and struggled in his arms.

"Gad, my lady, you make this captain out to be the blackest of villains."

"How can you laugh? Don't you understand what I said? There is an entire crew of despicable smugglers who would show us no mercy! We must steal their longboat. Why do you tarry?"

Sebastian caught her wrists and held her still. "Because, my darling, *we* are the smugglers."

Her struggles ceased; she could only stare in shock. "I—I don't believe you. You are in jest, again, at the worst possible moment!"

"Not a bit." Mischief glinted in his eyes as he leaned forward to kiss the soft curve of her shoulder, her neck, and the tender spot just below her ear. "It's true. Not only are we the smugglers, but you are in the arms of the dastardly captain."

"You mean—" She broke off as his warm lips teased her ear and she felt the sheet come loose from her breasts. It was exceedingly difficult to think when so much sensation was stirring mutinously between her naked thighs. "Are you saying that *you* are the notorious Captain Rogue, who slips into the bedchambers of fine Cornish women?"

"The only bed I have longed to slip into is yours, my love." Sebastian kissed her, lingeringly, before rising on his elbows to regard her with a sigh. He brought the sharp brass instrument out into the sunlight. "But first I must remove this lethal chart divider from under your pillow. Were you planning to use it on me?"

"Yes. I feared for my virtue! But that's before I knew the true identity of the dashing Captain Rogue."

He tossed the chart divider aside, shaking his head. "You do know that I have not been stealing into any houses along the coastline, don't you? I am your husband and those rumors are nonsense. Of course, the Cornish women doubtless *wish* that Captain—what do they call me?"

The corners of her lips twitched. "Captain Rogue. I assume it's because smugglers are also called 'roguers.'"

"Of course, and with a name like that, they naturally dream that he would steal into their beds." Then, in a more serious tone he continued, "But, more to the point, my crew and I are free-traders. I am making vast amounts of money by bringing in cargo from France, money that we desperately need. I've been able to provide the local fishermen with desperately-needed salt. The Pryces at Coombe Farm have a special underground room where we've stored most of our booty, and the beach cottage that you are so drawn to has more hiding places. It's been my safe haven, as well."

"This is absolutely outrageous!"

"Perhaps." He smiled into her shocked eyes. "There must be something powerful between us, darling Julia, because you returned to that cottage as if it were a magnet, despite my warnings."

Torn between horror and heightened, thrilling arousal, she had a sudden thought. "Was that *your* cheroot that I smelled in the cottage?"

"It was."

Dear God, how could it be? And yet, now everything made perfect sense and Julia wondered how she could have missed the signs. "But—what happened there last night? Was it you who took me?"

"Yes. We had just hidden the last bit of a new cargo and were getting ready to leave when you came in. When I realized that the intruder was you, I couldn't resist the temptation to have you with me. I have missed you."

"But—"

"Julia, I suggest that we stop talking for a while. There

are some conversations that don't need words.

Desire washed over her in a powerful wave, and yet she found that she couldn't stop thinking about his revelations. Memories returned of the completely powerless fears she had endured after realizing that her father was a compulsive gambler who could not stop even to save his own family. How could Sebastian be engaged in a practice that was even more dangerous and fraught with risks? As his mouth tasted the hollow at the base of her neck, Julia sank her fingers into his hair and tried to overcome the swelling sensations at the apex of her thighs.

"But wait," she gasped, "first you must promise me that you will stop this madness. Immediately!"

"You don't like to be kissed there?" came his husky rejoinder. "Fine; I know a few other places you'll soon be begging me to touch." His brown hand cupped her breast, massaging it in a way that made her wetter by the moment. When he bent to touch his tongue to her nipple, Julia pressed her fingers over his parted lips.

"That's not what I mean, and I think you know it! It's the smuggling that must stop. Before I can kiss you again, you must give me your word that it is over."

He reared back and stared at her, a beam of golden sunlight illuminating his chiseled features. "My darling, you are out of bounds. The smuggling will *not* stop, and you most certainly *will* kiss me again. This is not a situation that you can manage. On the contrary, you may as well relinquish all notions of controlling me, because this afternoon you are in my bed. I am your husband and I intend to make love to you until you beg me *never* to stop."

Never taking his eyes off her, Sebastian stripped off his clothing.

Julia felt as if she were on a runaway horse. All the old instincts, which had led her to take the reins when no one else seemed capable of doing so, came rushing to the forefront. She was breathing hard with a sort of panicky confusion borne of her inability to do what she had always done: manage the actions of other people.

"Please," she choked, "you must listen to me—"

"Julia, for once in your life, *let go*. You can trust me."

Tears pricked her eyes. She could see it in his face: the challenge to love him even if she couldn't control the outcome. Another wave of primitive fear swept over her. In the past, she had been let down so many times by loved ones who had asked for her trust—and then betrayed it. Only by finding solutions to their problems could she feel safe herself.

Yet, it came to her that this was different. She was a woman now, and if she was going to be a true partner in this marriage, she would have to at least *try* to trust Sebastian. He was asking her to risk all to have the love she'd always yearned for…but could she do it?

After a moment's hesitation, Julia inhaled, filling her lungs with air, and reached up for her husband.

Like a splendid jungle cat, he pulled the sheet out of the way and stretched out over her slim body, his own skin tanned, warm, and hard-muscled in the spill of sunlight. Julia was dazzled by his masculine beauty and power. All her nerves were taut with arousal tinged with trepidation. What did he expect from her? It was both frightening and exhilarating to leap into the unknown with him.

"You are beautiful," he whispered hoarsely. "So beautiful. You don't know how long I've wanted to hold you like this."

So that was why he had turned away from her so many times! He'd been holding his secret and couldn't let her in. Now, her heart pounded as Sebastian framed her face in his two hands and began to kiss her with deliberate slowness, tasting the inside of her mouth with his deft tongue. Julia wanted to weep. She could feel the flat, taut muscles of his chest against her swelling breasts and, when he moved just so, his engorged manhood nudging the wet, swollen bud of her sex, where every nerve in her body seemed to be concentrated.

She squirmed, arching her hips nearer until he almost entered her by mistake, but just that quickly, he drew back, laughing softly.

"Oh no, love. Not yet."

Now he was kissing her again, and she felt utterly drugged by passion. His mouth blazed a trail across her cheekbone to her ear, down her neck, and then slowly he circled one breast with tantalizing slowness. When at last his lips fastened on her engorged nipple, Julia gave a little cry of shock. But in the next moment, her hands were at his head, holding him there, praying that he wouldn't stop.

His tongue swirled round and round as he suckled until she thought she might die of arousal. Tingling streaks of fire traveled from her breasts to the aching bundle of nerves between her legs. Every bit of her wanted him inside her, releasing her from this torment. Her thighs opened to him, seeking, and her hand moved in search of his impressive erection.

But instead of entering her, he caught her wrist and pinned it to one side as he burned a new trail with his mouth down to her belly. Sensing her renewed panic as she realized what he meant to do, he found her other wrist and held it prisoner as well.

"You may as well surrender," he told her. "I mean to have all of you."

She began to whimper as he moved lower and blew softly on the soft tangle of reddish curls. And then he used his tongue to find the slick, congested bud. He knew that she longed for him to take it in his mouth and yet feared the precipice, for this time she would drop farther and faster than ever before.

Julia was writhing beneath him. A sheen of perspiration dampened her breasts. Methodically, his mouth worked its magic, gently sucking, licking, pausing, until at last she arched her back and released a cry that seemed to come from the depths of her soul. Sebastian could feel the contractions as the climax swept over her, and still he suckled, more gently now, until a second wave broke.

For so long, he had held a part of himself in reserve, even during their moments of intimacy, but now that was past. Julia was tugging at his hair and he went to her, kissing her ardently. Her face was glowing.

"My beautiful bride." Sebastian wanted to tell her how deeply he loved her, but even now he couldn't quite form the words. And weren't they somehow inadequate? Instead, he murmured tenderly, "My love."

Julia wondered if she were hearing things in her state of dazzled fulfillment. Had he really said that he loved her? It was sheer bliss to feel their bodies joined, to wrap her arms around his wide back, to kiss with abandon as they moved together in an eternal rhythm. And then, when he gave one last thrust and she felt the heat of him inside her, it came to her that she had never been happier.

"Yes," she whispered, echoing him. "My love."

Chapter 26

Sebastian slowly cut a plum into segments and fed them to Julia. They were sitting together in the narrow bunk, naked and completely comfortable together.

"Wine?" he offered, extending his cup of burgundy to her.

"I don't need wine when you are next to me," she replied. "Oh, Sebastian, why did it take us so long to abandon ourselves to—passion?" She decided it was safer not to use the word love, just in case.

He laughed in an ironic way that was familiar to her. "My darling, we both have had our share of reasons to stay at a distance, and I'll wager that we may find more in the future. As it was, I had to nearly take you by force."

"I only let you do that because I trusted you."

A few drops of plum juice drizzled from the corner of her mouth and he leaned closer to kiss them away. "I always knew that if you gave your passions free rein, you would be insatiable." He smiled at her suggestively.

"Truly? I honestly wouldn't have imagined it of myself. It's because of you, I suppose. I find you absolutely…addictive."

"Hmm. I like that." He set down the paring knife and cup of wine, turning his powerful body toward her in one fluid motion. "The feeling is mutual."

She boldly ran her hands over him, drinking in the sight of his naked body in the light of day. When she spied a narrow scar perhaps two inches long, low on his flat belly, she touched it with a fingertip and gave a little gasp of surprise.

"What is this? Why have I never noticed it?"

"It is a souvenir of a sword fight during a naval battle." Sebastian shrugged. "At the time, I nearly died, but now it's nothing. Perhaps you never noticed it because you hadn't examined me closely enough…" His voice trailed off wickedly.

"I am delighted to remedy that oversight," Julia laughed. Happily, she straddled his lap and moved her hips so that she was in intimate contact with his increasing erection. "I must say, I'm quite shocked at myself. Do I shock you?"

His laughter was husky with fresh arousal as he watched her brazenly kiss her way down his chest. "Only in the best sense of the word."

It was still dark when Julia awoke. She reached instinctively for Sebastian, longing to entwine her limbs with his again, but she quickly realized that she was alone in the bunk.

"I am here," came his husky voice.

Julia rose on an elbow and, peering into the shadows, saw him leaning back against the bulkhead as he drew on his boots. He was fully dressed and it came to her that the *Peregrine* was nearly still.

"Where are we?"

"We're at anchor off the coast of France, near Roscoff." As he spoke, Sebastian moved to perch on the edge of the bunk. "You are a temptress, you know. If you touch me, I'll succumb."

"Then come closer so that I may lure you back into bed," she replied, laughing softly, and reached up to touch his fresh-shaven jaw.

"I wish that I could, but the men are waiting. I have business to attend to and you must wait here for me. Here are your clothes—" He brought out the bundle tied neatly with a length of black ribbon. "Colvithick will bring you a hot breakfast."

"But, what are you going to do?"

Sebastian looked away, clearly trying to decide how much to say. "I am weary of keeping secrets from you, but if I tell you the truth, you must promise me that you won't have a fit of temper or—"

"I have heard that Roscoff is one of the places where smugglers come to obtain their illicit cargoes. Sebastian, you aren't here for that, are you?"

"Have you forgotten the conversation we had yesterday?"

"Of course not, but I didn't think that you meant to *continue*!"

He stared at her as if he couldn't believe his ears. "I thought you had agreed that it's unwise for you to try to direct my actions."

"Yes, but—"

"I'm listening." His tone had turned cold.

"Well, I thought that I was agreeing not to try to supervise your life, but that in return you would, I assumed…see the error of your ways and stop on your own." She paused, realizing how ridiculous her own words were. "Don't you know that it's simply mad for this to go on?"

"You no longer live in the refined world of Bath. It's time that you come to terms with the fact that smuggling is a way of life in Cornwall, a necessary evil due to tax rates that are so impossibly high your neighbors would starve without free-trading. Not only do I perform a service by paying my crew well and bringing in the goods that villagers need tax-free, I also include a shipment of salt in every cargo and I make a gift of it to the local fishermen."

"So you have mentioned. But Sebastian, the Revenue Officers have picked up your scent. I heard Adolphus Lynton and Tristan talking about 'Captain Rogue' just yesterday. If you are captured, you could hang—or at the very least, be transported!"

Slipping his arms into a well-cut coat of tan broadcloth, he shook his head. "I'm not afraid of that fool Lynton. As for Tristan—I can handle him."

Feeling vulnerable in her naked state, Julia opened the bundle of clothing and pulled the soft cotton shift over her head.

The sun was beginning to rise, bathing the cabin in jewel tones. She had to admit to herself that Sebastian had never looked more sinfully handsome and she had never loved him more.

"Can't you see, they are hunting you and this entire crew who you claim to be helping! Please, listen to me…"

He was removing a pistol from his binnacle. "At this moment, I cannot. Keswick is waiting for me. We have an appointment in Roscoff." Then, his expression softening, Sebastian came to the edge of the bunk. "Julia, I don't want to argue with you. This is one of the reasons why I didn't tell you the truth earlier. I knew that it would only create more conflict between us."

Unable to help herself, she scrambled to her knees and went into his embrace. "It's just that I worry so."

"It would mean a great deal to me if you could trust me enough to save your arguments for another day. Nothing you say will change what I mean to do now."

Sighing, she buried her face in his shirtfront. "All right."

Sebastian tipped her chin up and gave her a tantalizing grin. "Excellent. Will you give me a smile and a kiss to send me off?"

Tears misted her eyes as she complied, feeling that her heart might burst with love for him.

"Your agent is waiting for you, my lord," Keswick prompted as he followed Sebastian along the docks. "We sense that you are distracted. Is her ladyship well?"

"I'm not going to divulge any juicy tidbits to you, old meddler." Sebastian strode purposefully in the direction of an inn in the oldest section of Place Lacaze-Duthiers. "Although it wouldn't surprise me if you had been listening at the keyhole."

The manservant-turned-ship's master flushed. "You insult us, my lord."

"Let's talk about our meeting this morning instead. Do you know for a fact that St. Briac is here?"

"Eating eggs on the terrace. There is a place for you next to him."

"And Raveneau is nearby?"

"We saw him with our own eyes, my lord. He and his lady have rooms in that very inn."

"Excellent. After I speak to St. Briac, I'll pay Raveneau a short visit."

They had arrived at the medieval Auberge du Tocquer, its arched entrance of gray granite crowned by a carving of a ship in full sail. Roosters were crowing in the yard to herald the dawn while a boy stood nearby, holding the reins of a magnificent gray stallion.

"That steed belongs to Gabriel St. Briac," whispered Keswick. "We saw him ride up earlier. He cuts an impressive figure on horseback."

"No doubt," parried Sebastian. "He can afford to buy the best horseflesh with the enormous profits from people like me."

The innkeeper had appeared to greet them, a long white apron stretched taut over his belly. "*Bon matin, monsieugneur*! I am Tocquer. Welcome to our humble auberge."

He led the pair through the dark half-timbered public rooms of the inn and emerged onto a pretty stone terrace. Old-fashioned white roses meandered up the mossy walls, making a picturesque backdrop for one of the most arresting men Sebastian had ever seen.

"Ah, you must be Captain Trevarre," the Frenchman said, rising to his full height until they were eye to eye. He stretched out a strong hand. "Gabriel St. Briac, at your service. Please sit down. I know that Tocquer has prepared something special for you."

"It is my pleasure to meet you at last." They shook hands and Sebastian gestured toward St. Briac's plate. "Please, continue with your breakfast."

Oversized pottery cups of café au lait appeared as they both took their seats, and Sebastian tasted his appreciatively. "I must say, there is nothing like French coffee."

"Wait until you taste the buckwheat crépes. Madame Tocquer makes a filling with figs and yogurt that is utterly delicious." Gabriel St. Briac took another bite and lifted both brows expressively. "Ah! Be sure to drizzle a bit of the orange blossom honey on top. That is the magical ingredient."

Assessing St. Briac, Sebastian thought that he was an unexpected choice for a smuggling agent, whose task it was to deal with the local merchants and assemble the required cargo. The Frenchman had an air of easy, powerful grace, although he appeared to be several years younger than Sebastian. His dark chestnut hair was slightly curly, his blue eyes twinkled with ready wit, and a smile seemed always to hover at the corners of his mouth.

"I gather that everything is in order?" Sebastian inquired. His own breakfast had arrived and he found suddenly that he was famished, no doubt as a result of the passionate night with Julia.

"You will find that the cargo is perfect," St. Briac replied in perfect English. "My brother and I work together to make certain each item is not only present in the correct quantity, but also that it is of the very best quality."

"Yes, I have heard excellent reports of the St. Briac

brothers. You have acquired a fine reputation for men so young."

"Not so young. I am twenty-three, m'sieur, and my brother Justin is twenty-eight." The Frenchman pushed away his plate and took a leather-bound book from a satchel. Thumbing through it, he came to a page covered with neat script. "Ah yes, here is the list of your merchandise: the finest brandy, Congo tea, lace, and silk. In England, you can easily sell the brandy for five times the price you pay today." He ran his long finger down the columns and continued, "You will also find specific quantities of other items you requested: salt, cotton stockings, playing cards, and needles. As you may know, our Breton salt marshes are the very best, but due to the war, your English Navy is trying to prevent us from exporting it. We are grateful that other avenues exist to sell our salt."

"The fishermen of Cornwall thank you for that salt, which will preserve their fish for the winter ahead." Sebastian rubbed his jaw, smiling. "I am very impressed with your work, m'sieur. Will I not have the pleasure of meeting your brother? "

"Sadly, no. Justin is away on a voyage with our own ship, *Deux Frères*. We have clients who prefer to have their goods delivered rather than risk the crossing themselves, if you take my meaning." St. Briac winked almost imperceptibly. "I will tell my brother that you are pleased, Captain. We take pride in seeing that every detail is impeccable. Furthermore, we have packed your merchandise so that it is either in crates with secret compartments, or so that it is at least a size that may be efficiently concealed on board your ship." He paused to return the logbook to his satchel. "Your ship's master, Keswick, has delivered your payment and he has inspected the cargo, which waits in our family warehouse on the waterfront."

The two men stood and shook hands, smiling, and Sebastian said, "I hope this is the beginning of a relationship that will continue to be rewarding in the future."

Next to him, Keswick muttered, "Don't let her ladyship hear those plans…"

Standing outside the door of the suite of rooms rented by the Raveneau family, Sebastian was starting to wish he hadn't invited Keswick to accompany him.

"My lord, once again we urge you to confide in Captain Raveneau!" his erstwhile manservant was whispering.

"And I urge *you* to keep your own counsel." He raised his fist to knock, but paused just long enough to add, "You were there just now with St. Briac, our very competent agent. Your worries are groundless; everything is progressing very smoothly!"

"Perhaps too smoothly, my lord! May we suggest—"

He was interrupted when the door opened to reveal Devon Raveneau, looking especially lovely in an ivory and blue round gown. Her rose-gold curls were set off to advantage by a striped bandeau. She wore an exquisite collarette of sapphires, and her face shone as she gave an exclamation of pleasure.

"Lord Sebastian! I nearly didn't recognize you with that queue. How dashing you look. We did not know that you were in Roscoff. And Mr. Keswick, it's lovely to see you. Do come in, gentlemen!" Turning, she led the way into the large sitting room, where young Nathan and Mouette were seated at a game table engaged in a lively round of backgammon. "We have taken several rooms here, very nearly the entire floor, so it is quite comfortable. Our only issue is the very low beams. My husband has struck his head too many times to count and is rather cross."

Sebastian saw the impish sparkle in her eyes and had to laugh. "I'm delighted that our paths have crossed once again, madam. I was in need of a dose of your special charm."

"Surely that is nonsense, for I know your wife, and she is

every bit as charming as I." Laughing, Devon turned to Keswick. "Is that not so, Mr. Keswick?"

The little man raised his peaked eyebrows. "We can only say that both of you are exceptionally engaging women, Madame Raveneau."

"How very diplomatic!" Turning back to Sebastian, she continued, "What brings you to Brittany, my lord? Are you here, like André, to try to find a way to ship goods around the British blockades?"

"Something like that…" He broke off at the sound of André Raveneau's voice in the next room.

"Devon? I'm nearly late for an appointment, but I can't leave because I'm having a devil of a time with my cravat." He strode into the sitting room, coatless, an untied neckcloth dangling down the front of his shirt.

Little Lindsay Raveneau rushed across the threshold in her father's wake. They were followed by a rather plump, round-faced girl who appeared at first glance to be nearly Mouette's age. The bespectacled girl's pale blond curls were coming loose from their pins, and she wore a gown of white muslin trimmed with yellow ribbons.

Sebastian stared, but didn't believe his eyes. When he looked around at the others, he saw that they were all watching him. Even Raveneau had stopped, and instead of greeting his friend, he turned back to the fair-haired girl.

"Look who has come to visit us," Raveneau said. "Perhaps he sensed that you were here."

The young lady's eyes went wide behind her gold-rimmed spectacles, while joy and uncertainty mingled in her smile. "Sebastian? Can it truly be you?"

Chapter 27

In the next moment, the girl was hurrying toward him and Sebastian felt an uncomfortable rush of emotion. What could he do but open his arms to her?

"My dear, I had no idea—"

"The Raveneaus were so terribly kind to bring me with them, since, as you must know, I no longer have a home."

As she wept a bit against his shirtfront, Sebastian proffered a handkerchief with one hand and patted her back with the other. God's blood, what a time for his sister to turn up!

"Isabella had a holiday from school," Devon was explaining, "and so we traveled to Devon to collect her and bring her along with us to France. She and Mouette have become quite good friends."

Raveneau sent Sebastian a pointed look from across the room. "No doubt you were intending to contact her school."

"Of course," he lied. "If I had known, I would have come for you myself, Izzie."

Her eyes melted when she heard him say the pet name he'd given her as a child. "Oh, Sebastian! I knew that you had not forgotten me."

"I will own that I had forgotten how much you would have grown since the last time we met. It must have been five Christmases ago, just before I was commissioned and went to France."

Isabella laughed at that. "I was just a child then! Would you have known me today?"

"Truthfully? No." He patted her back, wondering what in the world he was going to do with her. "You have grown into a lovely young woman."

Devon came closer. "I think that we should plan to share a meal, all of us together, this evening. Sebastian, where have you hidden your bride? You did bring her, didn't you?"

"Can you imagine that Julia would tolerate being left behind?" Sebastian couldn't keep the edge of irony from his voice, and Keswick poked him in the back with an elbow. "However, she is on board my ship. Given the war, it seemed a safer course of action for her to remain with the crew."

"Nonsense! Roscoff is perfectly safe now. Napoleon has gone off to Egypt, you know, and the army is falling to pieces." She went to her husband's side and began to tie his cravat for him. "The two of you have business to discuss, do you not? But later, we shall all dine together. Perhaps M'sieur Tocquer will allow us to use one of his private rooms."

"M'sieur Tocquer has gone to great lengths to make this a memorable evening," remarked André Raveneau, looking around the large room with its low, dark-beamed ceiling. Serving maids were lighting dozens of candles and laying the silver, crystal, and china for a table of ten.

"The food smells delicious," said Sebastian. He ruffled the dark hair of young Nathan Raveneau, who stood between the two men. "Are you hungry, Nathan? I was constantly ravenous when I was your age."

The boy nodded. "Yes, I am! And I find that the sea air makes me even hungrier."

"How fortunate you are to have been born into this

family," Sebastian told him soberly. "Your life is filled with adventures like this journey to Brittany, but even better, you are surrounded by love."

Nathan looked up rather quizzically. "I shall have to ponder that, my lord, since I am accustomed to my family and have never known any other sort."

"Yes, son, go upstairs and consider your good fortune, and escort the women down to join us, will you please?" Raveneau was smiling at young Nathan, who was already starting toward the door.

"He is lucky indeed," Sebastian said pensively. "And so are we. It is kind of you and Devon to bring us all together, especially since our time here is short. We sail at dawn, but I know that Julia would have been very disappointed not to see your family…and meet Isabella, of course. I'm sure they're having a wonderful time already, while dressing for dinner."

Raveneau lifted one dark brow almost imperceptibly. "And did *you* desire to spend more time with your sister?"

"Of course." He hesitated, then decided to confide in the older man. "To be honest, I'm not certain what to do with her. Since returning to England, I have had to deal with my parents' deaths, my exiled brother's ambition to ruin not only himself but our family, a new and rather thorny marriage, and the realities of life in Cornwall." He paused, sipping his wine. "You know that I despise Cornwall."

"Do you—still?"

"I mean to live at Severn Park again."

"Knowing you, there is a daring plan in motion. I would caution you against risking your safety, or that of your lovely wife."

Sebastian glanced away. If Keswick were there, he knew he would have already poked him with an elbow, urging him to confide in the older man. "I am in the midst of executing such a plan, but I am not at liberty to discuss it."

"Of course not. I understand completely." Raveneau put

a hand on Sebastian's shoulder. "When I was younger, the last thing I wanted was advice from someone like me. And so, I will only repeat what I have said before: if you should ever desire assistance of any kind, you need only call on me."

Once again, Sebastian felt a tightening in his chest. His eyes stung, but he refused to let his emotions betray him. "I appreciate that, but everything is well in hand." He glanced toward the table, which was ready to receive guests. "I see that there are nine places, but I count only eight of us."

"Oh, your friend St. Briac made himself known to me in the courtyard this morning, and I invited him as well. He seems to be an engaging fellow."

"Gabriel St. Briac?" Sebastian forced himself to sound casual.

Just then, a handsome face appeared at the doorway. "*C'est moi*!"

"Is everyone ready?" Devon peeked into her daughter's tiny bedchamber where Mouette, Isabella, and Julia were clustered around the dressing table.

"Mama," asked Mouette, "do you think that this gown is too revealing? Isabella insists that I am making a spectacle of myself!"

Julia watched as Devon entered and brought a branch of candles closer to her daughter. "Hmm. Will you not wear a petticoat underneath? It is not that I disapprove, but I fear that your papa will be struck with apoplexy at the sight of you."

"Papa must realize that I am nearly a woman," Mouette asserted. "But, I shall do as you say, Mama."

She went off with Isabella and a lady's maid to add a petticoat under her nearly transparent gown, leaving Julia and Devon alone together.

"I have been longing for a chance to speak with you, my

dear," said Devon. "You will never know how many times I have thought of you, wondering if you were happy in Cornwall with Sebastian."

Julia beamed at her. "I am happy. I have made my own happiness, rather than depending on Sebastian and then being disappointed. However, that said, I will confide that my husband and I are finding our way toward happiness of our own. He isn't an easy man, but I love him madly."

"Ha! I know all about men like that, as I have told you. Our husbands are two of a kind, I suspect." In a spontaneous gesture of affection, Devon embraced her young friend. "How pretty you look in my gown."

"You were very kind to loan it to me. In my haste to sail with Sebastian, I left my traveling trunk behind." As she spoke, Julia noticed that Devon's gaze had come to rest on the delicate ring that she wore around her neck. It dangled from its thin gold chain, brushing against the first curves of her breasts.

"That is a very unusual piece of jewelry," Devon remarked. "May I?"

Julia nodded and watched as her friend examined the tiny miniature of a man's eye.

"How striking. Is this a gift from your husband?" queried Devon.

"Yes, it is a gift from him, and I like to think that it is a painting of his eye, but in truth we are not certain." She laughed a little. "It belonged to his mother, and she made a point of bequeathing it to him. It doesn't look a bit like his father. I must say, it is rather disquieting to think it could be a stranger's eye, watching me. That's why I wear it around my neck."

"Yet, it does look very much like Sebastian, doesn't it," Devon mused. "Are his eyes gray?"

"Rather, but I think of them as being more gray-green, like a stormy sea." Gently, she took it back and looked down at the compellingly handsome eye. "It means a great deal to me that Sebastian gave me this ring, especially since it was his mother's. I tell myself that it *is* his eye. Perhaps she had the ring made when he went away to university."

Slowly, Devon nodded. "Yes. No doubt that is what happened."

When Nathan came to announce that the women should come down for dinner, Julia and Isabella went into the corridor and waited at the top of the stairs for Devon and Mouette. Julia was happy for the moment alone with her sister-in-law and reached for her hands.

"I can't tell you how pleased I am that we have met at last," she told her sincerely.

"Truly?" Isabella blinked back tears behind her spectacles. "It is very gratifying to hear you say so. I had begun to fear that my brother might never send for me."

"I know that he has intended to do so," Julia said carefully, "but we were aware that you were occupied with your studies—"

"Ha!" the girl scoffed. "The academy where my parents sent me is not a place for serious study of any kind. I told Mama, and she tried many times to persuade Father to bring me back to London, but he would not believe what I said."

"But, what sort of place is it then?"

Isabella bit her lower lip. "Madame LaFlorence, the headmistress, is not even French! Just last week, I went through her papers while she was napping and discovered that her true name is Florence Jarrett. I believe that she is an *actress*."

"Well, that is disturbing news, but it does not mean that her school is without merit. What subjects do you study?"

"Needlework. Spelling." The girl's expression vacillated between indignation and despair. "We perform plays. And…we eat. I know that I am growing too plump from the bread and sweets they feed us. Sometimes I eat out of boredom, even though I am not hungry."

Julia's heart went out to her. Fourteen was such a difficult age, and how lonely Isabella must be without parents or a real home. "Is there nothing that you enjoy at school?"

"Well, there is one saving grace," Isabella admitted, brightening. "Last year, Madame brought an Italian artist to instruct us, and he has helped me learn to paint. That is my passion."

"Is it indeed?" Julia looked over as Devon and Mouette joined them and the quartet began to descend the broad staircase, escorted by young Nathan Raveneau. "I shall discuss all of this with Sebastian. I promise."

Isabella's green eyes misted over again. "It is a frightening thing to be an orphan. My parents weren't perfect, but at least they were there. Now, they are gone and our home is gone as well. If it weren't for the Raveneaus, I would be alone. They have been very good to me, but Julia, they are not my family."

She nodded, squeezing her hand. "I understand."

As they continued down the stairs, Julia caught sight of Sebastian, standing with André Raveneau and another man she had never seen before. The tall, well-built stranger had dark chestnut hair that curled slightly, sculpted cheekbones, and a merry smile that lit his eyes.

"Julia," said Sebastian, coming forward to take her gloved hand. "You look beautiful."

"Thank you. And doesn't your sister look lovely?"

"She does indeed." He turned to the younger girl, smiling, and kissed her cheek. "I still cannot believe how you have grown, Izzie."

As Isabella beamed in reply, the stranger came forward. He wore an impeccably cut coat of dark-gray superfine that outlined his broad shoulders, kerseymere breeches, and top boots of the finest leather.

"Madame, allow me to introduce myself," he said,

bending to kiss Julia's hand. "I am Gabriel St. Briac."

Sensing Sebastian's faint irritation with the Frenchman, she couldn't resist allowing her hand to linger a bit longer in his. "It is a pleasure to meet you, m'sieur. Are you a friend of my husband's?"

"You might say so," St. Briac replied, eyes twinkling. "We have not known each other very long, but we find that we have a great deal in common."

Sebastian gave him a quelling glance. "M'sieur, you must allow me to present my younger sister, Lady Isabella Trevarre. She is on holiday from boarding school and has traveled to France with our friends the Raveneaus."

St. Briac gallantly turned his attention to the young girl. Lifting her hand to his lips, he said in a low, husky voice, "My lady, it is my honor to know you."

Julia looked over at Isabella and saw the flush that crept into her round cheeks and the telling glow in her eyes. She appeared to be speechless for a moment, until St. Briac's kind smile finally allowed her to whisper, "The honor is mine, m'sieur."

Glancing past the Frenchman, Julia saw Sebastian rub his eyes with long fingers, as if he feared that it was going to be long evening.

In the end, the meal was a festive occasion. Madame Tocquer was an accomplished cook who prepared not only *cotriade,* a Breton fish soup, but also roasted partridges, and a fine leg of mutton with white beans. There were delicate fresh peas, and Julia declared that the strawberries with crème fraiche were the juiciest she had ever tasted. Even the sweet Muscadet wine was sublime.

Julia was happy to lose herself in the pleasure of the meal and the company. For that evening, she could almost pretend that her husband was not a lawless smuggler, but merely a dashing ship's captain like André Raveneau. When Sebastian looked at her, his eyes seemed to burn her gown away, and she found herself dreaming about the night to come, when she would be naked with him again, kissing and touching feverishly under the moonbeams that streamed in through the ship's transom windows.

Around them, the other dinner guests kept up a witty conversation. At the center of it all was Gabriel St. Briac, a man who had been unknown to her a few hours earlier. There was something so compelling about the Frenchman that both men and women were clearly drawn to him.

"M'sieur," Raveneau said, pausing to choose a piece of rustic peach tart from the platter of sweets and cheeses, "I have a friend who is the lord of Château du Soleil, in the Loire Valley. The nearby village is called St. Briac. Are you from there?"

Gabriel St. Briac's white teeth gleamed when he smiled. "You might say so, Captain Raveneau. Your friend is called Beauvisage, is he not? His family came to own Château du Soleil through marriage to one of my female St. Briac ancestors."

Isabella, who sat beside him looking bewitched, protested, "But, m'sieur, why would it pass to her if there were St. Briac males?"

Sampling a piece of cheese, he replied, "Because, my lady, my great-grandfather was…misbegotten. How do you say it? Born on the wrong side of the blanket? His father was the son of Paul Mardouet, seigneur de St. Briac, but his mother was a nun."

"How is that possible?"

"You are very young," he conceded. "Perhaps this is the sort of thing that should wait until you are older?"

"No! I have more knowledge of the world than you imagine, m'sieur. I insist that you tell me."

St. Briac looked across the table to Sebastian, who sighed and lifted both eyebrows in assent.

"*D'accord.* Suffice it to say that Philippe Mardouet, the only son of the lord of St. Briac, had a love affair with a young woman in the village, and shortly thereafter, Philippe was killed in a hunting accident. When his father died the next year, the property passed to Philippe's sister, Marie, and her Beauvisage husband." St. Briac paused and the room was utterly silent as the guests waited to hear more. "Meanwhile, Philippe's broken-hearted lover entered a convent when he was killed. After she had taken vows, she found that she was with child. That baby was my great-grandfather. He was raised by his Tante Marie, in the family château, and they christened him Philippe, after his father, and gave him the surname of the village of St. Briac. Of course, there was never any question of him being the rightful heir to the title or lands, because he was a..."

"A bastard," Isabella supplied, her eyes round behind her spectacles.

"Exactly so, my lady." A wry smile touched St. Briac's mouth. "Philippe went out into the world and made his own fortune and built his own manor house, here in Bretagne. But our family has carried the name of St. Briac to remind us of our origins."

"That is the most romantic story I have ever heard," the girl murmured, seemingly unable to tear her gaze from the handsome face of Gabriel St. Briac.

Watching them, Julia couldn't help worrying a bit about Isabella, and when Sebastian turned toward her, she saw by his expression that he shared her concern.

"God's blood, what are we going to do with that child?" he muttered.

"Child? She is on the verge of womanhood."

Devon Raveneau took charge of the situation from her chair at the head of the table. "I have eaten far too much of Madame Tocquer's cherry tart! I fear I am in danger of nodding off in my chair."

"It's late," said her husband, rising.

Surveying the remains of their meal amidst the guttering candle flames, Julia found that she was suddenly very tired. As they all moved slowly toward the door, she and Sebastian made their farewells to the Raveneau family.

"Now that I've been reunited with Isabella, I don't feel right about leaving her with you," Sebastian told them in a low voice.

Raveneau laughed. "You forget that we already have a daughter and she is just two years older than Isabella."

"I have loved having Isabella with us," exclaimed Mouette, linking arms with the younger girl.

"We will bring you to Cornwall very soon," Julia told her sister-in-law. They embraced and she smiled into her eyes. "You are not alone, my dear. You have a home with us and you shall see it before the summer wanes."

Farewells were exchanged and Gabriel St. Briac kissed the hands of all the women except Julia. "I bid you all adieu, for I shall walk with Lord Sebastian and his lady. One can never have too much protection on the waterfront at this hour."

When the Frenchman had disappeared with Sebastian and Julia through the arched granite doorway of the inn, Mouette turned to her young friend and shook her head.

"I have never seen you behave that way before! Don't you know that he is a fully-grown man and you are just a schoolgirl?"

Isabella pretended to swoon, and her spectacles slipped down her nose as she exclaimed, "Oh, Mouette, can't you see? That is the man I intend one day to marry."

Chapter 28

It was nearly midnight by the time André Raveneau slipped into the carved tester bed beside his wife.

"I can't remember the last time I felt this tired," he complained, shifting uncomfortably on the rather lumpy feather mattress. "Being a host has never been my strong suit."

Devon made no reply.

"Are you sleeping, *petite chatte*?" He rolled toward her and reached for her, but she managed to elude his embrace. "What's wrong? Has that cherry tart upset your stomach?" Shaking his head against the meager pillow, he added, "The food was good enough, but too rich for my taste. When can we go home to Connecticut?"

That was too much for Devon. She sat up in the bed and looked down at him. "I want to talk to you."

His dark hand reached out to touch the bed gown she wore, only to find it was fastened up to her neck. "What the devil is this?"

"Never mind. Sit up and talk to me."

"Why can't we lie down and talk? Take off that ridiculous piece of clothing, *cherie*, and come into my arms where you belong."

"André, I am very serious." She narrowed her eyes at him for emphasis. "Heed me."

He stared at her, clearly thinking. Devon thought it was terribly unfair that just the sight of him continued to stir her as no other man could. "*Eh bien.*" Slowly, he pushed himself up until they were sitting side by side. "For you, I will do it. Do you want to talk about one of the children?"

"You might say that."

"*Morbleu*! Stop looking at me as if you would like to feed me poison and speak your mind!"

"All right, I will." She then found herself speechless and waved a fist at him. "Ooh! Why is that, even after so many years, you can make me feel so angry, so helpless, so—so—"

"Are you mad? I haven't done anything wrong!"

"André, I know about Sebastian." Devon waited, rather enjoying the sight of his suddenly stunned expression. After a moment, she turned the knife. "I know about you and *Charlotte*."

"Of course you do. I told you that I knew her many years ago," he said carefully.

"No. That's not what I'm talking about."

Raveneau threw back the covers and got out of bed, stalking naked across the room. Moonlight lent a faint silvery glow to his movements and the contours of his lean-muscled body. Devon watched as he poured a small amount of brandy and drank it.

"Am I to be condemned for having known other women before our marriage?" he demanded.

Devon gave a mirthless laugh. "You can't be serious! You? I know that about you better than anyone. I had to accept you with your flaws—"

"*Flaws*? Is that what you call them?"

She pretended not to hear him. "The fact that you were a libertine before we met is not the issue tonight, and I'll thank you not to attempt to distract me. I want to talk to you about Charlotte Trevarre, the Marchioness of Caverleigh."

His eyes narrowed. "You needn't describe her further." He found his breeches on the back of a chair and began to pull them on, followed by a fine linen shirt.

"What are you doing?"

"Is a man not allowed to have even a small corner of privacy in his life? Must I share all of my past with you, even matters that do not concern you or our marriage in the least?" Raveneau fumbled around in the shadows for his boots. "I am going out, where I will not be forced to divulge every last secret to my *wife*!"

"I have always respected your privacy. You were an adult for a dozen years before we met and I have always realized that there would be parts of your life that would remain hidden to me. However, sir, one person from your past has caught up to us and demands to be shared."

"What the *devil* do you mean?"

"Kindly lower your voice before Lindsay awakens and starts to cry!"

"Another reason to take my leave! A man ought to be able to raise his voice when justifiably angry without being told to hush as if he were an errant child!"

"Do you mean to go outdoors and shout, then?"

"*Mon Dieu*," he growled, "you try my last bit of patience, Devon!"

She scrambled out of bed and rushed to the door, pressing her back against it and spreading her arms wide on either side of her petite, nightgown-clad form. Rose-gold curls fell across her brow as she faced him defiantly.

"You are too fine a man to run away from me, André. Sit down!"

Their eyes met and, after nearly two decades, she could almost read his thoughts. Raking a hand through his hair, Raveneau pivoted and walked back to bed.

"I am at your command, madam. Do you see? I sit."

"Don't you dare mock me." She marched after him and perched beside him on the edge of the heavy bed.

"Clearly you believe that you know something quite shocking. I would have you share it with me."

Devon pursed her lips, wondering how her husband had

managed to turn the situation around so that he was the inquisitor. "This is not a game. If you imagine that I want to delve into your secrets, you are mistaken." Her eyes softened. "In truth, I have always found it appealing that there were parts of you I would never know, and that will continue to be the case after tonight. But André, we must talk about Charlotte—and Sebastian."

Raveneau leaned against the dark, carved bedpost and gave a harsh sigh. "You know me too well, *cherie*, perhaps better than I know myself."

"Yes. And I am aware that you would rather not revisit your past." Moving closer, she reached for his dark, strong hand, and felt the tension in it. "We can face this together, you know."

After a long minute of silence, he said, "I was only nineteen when I met Charlotte here on the Breton coast, where she had come to paint. She was already married, unhappily, and had a son, George." Raveneau arched a cynical brow. "The same son who is now hell-bent on squandering his family fortune."

"Nineteen." Devon considered this. "Did she…school you in the ways of love?"

"*Ma petite*, I am shocked that you would ask me such a thing!" Relaxing a bit, he laughed softly and drew her against him. "Charlotte was older, it's true, but perhaps not more experienced. It was a passionate romance, but it ended when she returned to England and I went to sea. I didn't see her again for many years, until you and I married and traveled to London."

"And, did Charlotte tell you then that you were the father of her younger son, Sebastian?"

He didn't flinch, but Devon saw the scar that marked his jawline whiten. "She did not. Why do you say such a thing?"

"Well, first of all, his parentage is quite obvious now that he is a grown man. I knew it in my heart the day that he and

Julia arrived in London and I saw him standing in our doorway." She turned against him and searched his face. "Surely you saw it, too?"

"I will be frank with you and admit that the thought did cross my mind, but physical resemblance is not proof, Devon. It could be purely coincidence."

"You and I both know differently. It is there in so many ways: the set of his shoulders when I see him from behind. The certain way he arches his eyebrow. The shape of his hands. Even the sardonic tone of his voice and laughter. He is so eerily similar to you at the same age—but perhaps I can see it more clearly than you."

Raveneau shook his head. "Your imagination is very powerful."

"I have tried to tell myself the same thing. After all, why would I want to believe that you created a child with another woman? But then, tonight, I saw the eye ring."

The look on his face told her that he knew exactly what she was talking about. "I despise that...*objet*." He said it in the French way. "It is *disturbing*, a disembodied eye staring out from a piece of jewelry!"

"You have seen it yourself then? Before tonight?"

"Twice. The first time was perhaps six years ago, when we brought Lisette Beauvisage to London and we were staying in our former, smaller home in Grosvenor Square. I encountered Charlotte outside one day; I recall that she had little Isabella with her. We chatted and then she made a point of removing her glove so that I couldn't help seeing that damned ring."

"She said nothing?" Devon was grateful that, now that this subject was in the open, she could depend on her husband to be honest.

"No. But she watched me. And I confess that a chill ran down my spine when I saw it."

"You recognized your own eye?"

He shrugged. "Not exactly, but I had the thought. I

remembered that she had painted a miniature of me that summer in Bretagne. It occurred to me that she might have used that likeness as her model for the eye ring."

"But why would she make such a thing so many years later? Do you think that she continued to love you?"

"I couldn't say. Perhaps she made it as a lark, after eye jewelry came into vogue. On the other hand…"

"Yes?"

"Ah, well, the second time I saw that ring was when Sebastian brought it to our home after his meeting with Miles Bartholomew. He said that his mother had left it with the solicitor, with explicit instructions that Sebastian should receive it if she died."

"Of course; a message!"

"Perhaps. There was a second ring, set with sapphires, which she bequeathed to him. My suspicions were strengthened with I saw them together."

Devon waited. She could hear the rapid beating of her own heart.

"You see, the second ring was one that I gave Charlotte during that long-ago summer on the coast of Bretagne. It had belonged to my own deceased mother, and I was foolish enough in my love-struck youth to part with it." Raveneau rubbed his brow with long fingers, then looked directly into his wife's eyes. "Ah, *cherie*, no doubt that our thoughts are the same at this moment. Charlotte left the two rings to Sebastian to supply clues that might never have been deciphered if our paths had not crossed this summer."

"You have known, then, but did not intend to act?"

"I saw no reason to go that far. We are all perfectly happy in our lives. Until you insisted on this discussion tonight, I had every reason to continue to keep my own counsel." He gave Devon a faintly defiant look. "It is not as though I have turned my back on Sebastian. On the contrary, I have offered him my friendship in the strongest possible terms, but he is a grown man and perfectly able to manage his own affairs. He is past the age of needing a father, especially one who has been absent his entire life."

She went into his arms and held him close. "My darling, is it possible that you might be wrong?"

"It is highly unlikely, but I shall consider the matter. Later." Raveneau kissed the tender spots on her neck, drawing a throb of surrender from Devon's traitorous body. "At the moment, I am very weary of talking and thinking. Kindly remove that ridiculous garment and come to bed with me, where you belong."

"But André—"

He arched a brow in a gesture she found irresistible. "I perceive that I must attempt to reassure you that you are the *only* woman I have truly loved. Will you let me try, *petite chatte*?"

Chapter 29

As the wind blew black clouds across the moon, raindrops began to spatter the transom windows outside the captain's cabin. Sebastian, fully dressed, had just pulled on his boots and drawn his hair back into a queue when Julia stirred in the cozy bunk. She had slept soundly through the night, rocked by the motion of the *Peregrine* sailing through the currents of the English Channel, but now the ship began to surge erratically. A storm was brewing.

Julia's beautiful eyes opened and his heart turned over. Whenever he thought back to the way she had looked when they'd first met in Bath's Royal Crescent, he wanted to laugh. She'd been so crisply discerning then, her rich sable hair neatly twisted into a knot atop her head, her dark-blue eyes clear and direct. Now, when they were alone together, his wife was like a tiger cub. She purred in his arms and regarded him through eyes that were half-closed with passion. The transformation she had undergone made him love her and yearn for her even more ardently.

"Are you going away without even coming to bed?" she mumbled now, frowning.

"You're not making sense, love." Sebastian sat down on the edge of the bunk. "I've just been in bed, but you were sleeping. I can assure you it drove me mad, having you nestle up against me, but I didn't have the heart to wake you." He didn't add that he'd resisted because every minute of stolen sleep was precious on a night like this. There wasn't time for love play just yet.

"All I remember is falling asleep waiting for you to come back from talking to Gabriel St. Briac." Julia paused, pushing the mass of her hair back. "M'sieur St. Briac is your agent, isn't he? That's why we've been consorting with him, isn't it?"

"Yes. Of course, if he'd been an uncivilized brute as I half-expected, you would never have met him and Raveneau wouldn't have invited him to join us last night." Sebastian searched his chest for his heaviest tricorne hat, then drew it on firmly. The wind had begun to howl and the timbers of the *Peregrine* groaned in response. "I wasn't lingering on the dock until nearly midnight just to be sociable, you know. Our cargo had to be loaded."

What he couldn't share with Julia was the new plan he and St. Briac had made while standing on the docks. Sebastian and his crew would soon return to Roscoff, to load an especially valuable cargo of the very finest French brandy and Breton salt. The brandy would fetch so high a price that Sebastian's share should enable him to achieve financial solvency at last.

Julia stretched out a hand to him. "Must you go now? Can't Keswick or one of the others sail the ship?"

"They have been, for nigh on two hours, while I've slumbered in your arms. It's time for the captain to take a turn at the wheel. Go back to sleep, Julia; it's not yet dawn, and you'll need your rest when we make landfall."

"Hmm. I suppose it's the price I must pay…for being married to a wicked smuggler."

"Shh." He was gratified to see his wife's smile when he tucked the quilts snugly around her and grazed her lips with a tender kiss. With luck, Julia would be sleeping soundly before she realized that they were headed into a ferocious summer gale.

Sheets of black rain drove against the decks when Sebastian emerged through the hatch.

"We're only two dozen miles from shore," Keswick told him as he came up beside him at the wheel. "The wind has hastened us across the channel, but the weather—"

Before Sebastian could reply, one of the crew who was manning the lines gave a sudden cry and pointed abaft, over the stern rail, toward a flash of white in the night sky.

"By God," shouted Sebastian into the wind, "I believe it is another ship, brazen enough to give chase! Bring the spyglass, Keswick."

As the waves swelled beneath the *Peregrine*'s hull and sea-spray mixed with the rain to cascade across the decks, Sebastian was thankful for the fore-and-aft rigging that allowed the compact ship to shift course and maneuver more efficiently, using the wind to her advantage.

"She's a big, hulking thing," he told Keswick, holding the brass telescope securely against the storm. "She may be a powerful foe, but if we set extra sails and change course, she'll be hard-pressed to follow."

Keswick peered into the night, shaking his head at the sight of the bigger craft speeding closer, her great sails swollen by the storm winds. "We wonder at times why we are here, my lord," he muttered under his breath.

"I heard that! But you can't fool me, old fellow. You wouldn't trade this adventure for a warm bed on land, would you?" Before Keswick could speak, Sebastian answered his own question. "Not bloody likely! And you and I have been through worse, have we not?"

"Perhaps," the little man allowed. "But then we were sailing for His Majesty's Navy, on the right side of the law. Tonight, if we are caught, we all may very well hang."

Sebastian shook his head, laughing. "That will never happen. However," he conceded, lifting the spyglass to his eye once more, "the danger is real. That ship is flying a Customs pennant. Mr. Keswick, give the order for additional sails. We'll then tack to starboard and those eager lads will soon see the last of us."

No sooner had the order gone out than a cluster of crewmen rushed across to the captain, protesting, "It be folly to set more sails, sir! The storm'll tear the rigging to shreds and snap the yards like matchwood!"

Sebastian only gave them a grim stare. "Obey my orders."

They exchanged panicky looks before reluctantly staggering off in the raging storm to hoist new sails. Finally, when the sheets of canvas were set, the men dropped to the deck, loudly praying to St. Elmo for deliverance.

A moment later, Sebastian saw Colvithick scrambling across the deck, rain streaming from his terrified face. "It be a King's ship, Captain!" he cried. "We'll all die!"

It was Keswick who pulled the young man aside and gave him a shake. "See here, lad, you've forgotten who your captain is. Already we're beginning to outrun them. Now calm down and return to your station before you're sent below."

Just then, across the churning sea, there was a flash of light from the other ship and Sebastian realized that they had been fired upon. The shot had fallen short, but as the *Peregrine* tacked up-wind, Sebastian had a better look at the Revenue cutter and saw at least twelve gun ports yawning open on her larboard side.

His adversary was an imposing vessel of perhaps two hundred tons, with a crew that appeared to be twice that of the *Peregrine*. Yet, even though it had more men, firepower, and brawn, the ship was hampered by its size. It was surging ahead, but now that the *Peregrine* had set more sails, it could not keep up the chase and it dared not spread the same amount of canvas to the wind.

"Shall we fire back, Captain?"

Sebastian turned to find a lanky young man named Martin, a relative of Primmie's, standing close behind him. He was white as a ghost against the stormy night sky.

"I'll give that order, Plyn. You may wait for it."

"But, Captain—"

Before Sebastian could lose his temper, he was further distracted by the sight of the hatch opening in the deck a dozen feet away. A moment later, a head peeked out. Although she had drawn a dark shawl around her head and shoulders, he quickly recognized his wife.

"Julia, get *down*!"

She did the opposite, clambering up out of the hatch. Almost immediately, a gust of wind caught her and tossed her down on the rain-washed deck, but Julia looked up with an expression that said she was too angry to care.

Sebastian reached her side in an instant, lifting her into his arms. A crazed mixture of fear and passion swept over him. "What the devil are you about? Are you trying to kill yourself? Get back down to my cabin and wait for me there."

"This is madness!" she shouted. "We are in a horrendous storm and that ship is *firing* at us! Sebastian, nothing is worth the loss of life!"

"Can you not trust me?" He could feel the angry fire in his own gaze as it met hers.

"That has nothing to do with this!"

"It has everything to do with it. What are you suggesting? Would you have us surrender now and be hanged?" Grasping her arm, he pulled her to her feet and shouted to Colvithick. "I want you to take her ladyship below to my cabin and see that she does not leave until I give the order."

When they had disappeared into the hatch, Sebastian looked around to see that the storm had eased a bit. The frightened crewmen were on their feet and *Peregrine* was tacking once more into the shifting wind, this time to larboard, charting a zigzagging course that the Revenue cutter was unable to match.

Watching the larger ship drop back farther and farther into the pitching seas until it no longer attempted to fire across the gap to the *Peregrine*, Sebastian leaned back against the mizzenmast and took a deep, harsh breath. Rain blew at his face, and he wiped it away with both hands, pausing to close his eyes for one blessed moment. Although threats lay all around them, he knew that the real danger of that night had passed.

Of course, Sebastian thought, there was still Julia to deal with, and he would need all his wits for that challenge.

"I insist that you leave me," Julia told young Drew Colvithick. "It is ridiculous for you to remain in this tiny cabin, watching me as if I were some sort of criminal who needs guarding!"

"I be doing as the captain ordered," the boy repeated. His brown hair had dried now and stuck up in spikes, and his face was streaked with grime.

Julia could smell him from where she sat on the bunk and fought an urge to wrinkle her nose. "Won't you at least look to see if we are out of danger?"

Dawn was breaking and a soft, rosy light bathed the cabin. She could sense that the seas had calmed, although they still plunged and pitched as the *Peregrine* charted a southeasterly course toward Cornwall.

"I did fear we all be going to die," Colvithick exclaimed, suddenly animated.

"I know. I shared your anxiety," she murmured. "Kindly peek out the hatch and tell me if that horrid ship is still upon us."

The boy stood to do her bidding, but before he could exit the cabin, Sebastian appeared. He bent his head to come through the low doorway, his face stern yet weary. "Where do you think you're going?"

"Her ladyship be askin' if the King's ship do chase us still!"

He looked as if he wanted to shout at the boy, but only waved a hand instead. "Go on then, but don't return. I'll make that report to my lady."

When they were alone, Julia looked at Sebastian and was overtaken by a surge of emotion that brought tears to her eyes. "Tell me then, what is happening?"

"It is just as I said to you earlier. We led the Revenue cutter on a merry chase across the channel, but that great hulking ship was no match for our quick and agile *Peregrine*." A smile touched his mouth. "Of course, it doesn't hurt that our crew is highly skilled, and I might be so bold as to add that your captain had the situation well in hand."

Waves of anxiety made her breathless. She wanted to beseech him to listen, to swear he'd never put himself in jeopardy that way again, but the expression on his darkly handsome face told her to save her words.

"I must ask you to stay here," Sebastian was saying with a bit more tenderness than before. "The seas are still rough, and there are challenges ahead this morning."

"What do you mean?"

"The landing must be effected. We are far off the time we'd planned to come ashore with the cargo, so no one will be there to meet us. There will have to be an alternate plan. Sowing the crop, perhaps."

She watched him think, intoxicated by his nearness. "What on earth does that mean?"

"Oh, it's a means by which the smaller kegs may be strung together, sunk with weights close to shore, and then retrieved at a more convenient time. The men know all about it."

"Can you not hear yourself? You sound like—like one of them!"

Sebastian was peeling off his sodden garments and replacing them with dry clothes. "Them?"

"Yes, you know—a real smuggler!"

"Shocking! Perhaps that's because I am one." He took up his sword and pistol, pausing beside the bunk where she perched. "Will you kiss me, my lady?"

Powerless to resist, Julia came into his embrace, twining her own arms around his neck where his hair was caught back in a rough queue. It seemed impossible that the rake she had met in Bath's Royal Crescent could have become this dangerous smuggler, but it was true. And when he took her face between his two sun-darkened hands and kissed her with an intensity that defied words, Julia surrendered, losing herself in the moment.

Chapter 30

Just offshore from Coombe Hawne's pebbled beach, dawn was streaking the eastern sky in shades of magenta and gold. Nearby, the *Peregrine* rested at anchor as barrels of brandy were carried up from their hiding places below decks. The casks were then linked together with ropes, weighted with rocks, and dropped into the shallows.

"Everything will happen tonight according to our original plan," Sebastian told Keswick as they stood at the forward rail, watching the operation. "The only missing element will be our ship and crew. Jasper's men will arrive with their carts and ponies to retrieve these barrels and move them inland."

"We must admit, it seems to be a wise strategy, particularly because the crew will be elsewhere when the night-time landing occurs, and it will be harder to connect any of us to it, should suspicion be aroused."

"Exactly so." He looked around. "I am impatient to weigh anchor and be on our way. Are we ready?"

"Yes, sir. We'll give the order."

Sebastian stood alone, thinking, as the *Peregrine* sailed eastward along the rugged coastline, toward Fowey. When he had explained to Julia the reasons why they were not landing at Coombe Hawne, he neglected to mention his worry that the vessel had been identified by the Revenue cutter. He wanted to sail up the Fowey estuary as soon as possible, since the changing winds would prevent the King's ship from following them if it happened to reach the coast at the same time. The sooner that the *Peregrine* was safely tucked away in Tristan's secret quay off Lerryn Creek, the better Sebastian would feel.

The Fowey estuary was bathed in a soft morning glow as the *Peregrine* sailed under the picturesque cliff-top ruin of St. Catherine's Castle and into the harbor mouth.

As soon as they started into Pont Creek and were clear of Polruan's jumble of whitewashed cottages, Julia was summoned by Colvithick to join her husband on deck. She was clad in the same blue-and-white patterned cambric gown and flat-crowned straw bonnet that she'd worn the day of the storm, when she'd taken shelter at Coombe Cottage.

It seemed almost like another lifetime.

Now, as the *Peregrine* glided up the creek, its sails spread like one of the water birds that watched from shore, Julia sighed. Deep green, magical woods covered the hills right to the water's edge, woods that she knew by heart, and she inhaled the rich scents of rain and moss.

She felt Sebastian come up behind her, but he didn't touch her. "I'm going to take you home now," he said.

"And what then?"

"I'll return here to the ship and then sail her north, to a hiding place off Lerryn Creek."

"But, that's where Tristan lives! Isn't that dangerous? He is a Revenue Officer!"

"Kindly allow me to manage this situation, my lady," he said coolly. "I assure you that I am fully capable of doing so."

As the *Peregrine* came alongside the quay near the lime kiln, Julia was distracted by the sight of her swans approaching on the quiet water. The cygnets clearly recognized her and a few tried to fly in their haste to reach her.

"This is your world, isn't it?" asked Sebastian.

"Yes." Tears pricked her eyes. "I love it more than you'll ever know. It's the home I have searched for all my life."

Julia felt him watching her intently, but he said nothing. Instead, he leaped to the quay and reached up with both hands to lift her down beside him.

The men were ranged along the starboard rail, and they took off their caps to bid her farewell. Keswick winked, and Julia smiled and waved to him.

"Thank you all for allowing me to join you," she called to them. "I can assure you that your secrets are safe with me."

Sebastian took her arm and they started across the little footbridge and up the path that led into the beautiful woods below the Trevarre Hall estate.

"That was quite an adventure," Julia remarked with a note of finality. "Perhaps it's something we'll tell our grandchildren one day."

"That's an odd thing to say. What's really on your mind?"

All the feelings and thoughts that had simmered inside her, unspoken, suddenly came bubbling to the surface. "You aren't going to continue with this madness, are you?"

"Am I not?"

Furious and heartsick with love, Julia turned to him on the path and caught his arm. The trees, with their leaves in myriad shades of greens, made a magnificent canopy above their heads.

"Sebastian, I know that you will not want me to say these things to you, but I simply cannot help myself. After the brush with death we experienced at sea last night, I assumed that you would realize that this cannot continue. Were your eyes not opened by the fact that we all nearly lost our lives, or at least were almost captured by that Customs ship?"

"If I had spent my adult life running away after every brush with death, I would be a very sad excuse for a man." His eyes were as stormy as the night seas had been. "You and I have had this conversation already. And the smuggling will stop when I have made enough money to re-purchase Severn Park."

She gasped, shocked that he could still be talking of living anywhere but Cornwall. "Severn Park! How can our minds and hearts be so far apart? And as for the conversation you refer to, that happened before last night's battle at sea, when a warship was firing upon us. Your own men were frightened out of their wits!"

"Julia, calm down. Do you imagine that I have no regard at all for your feelings?"

"In truth, I wonder. I know that I have been guilty in the past of trying to manage other people's lives, but can I not at least voice my opinion?" Blinking back tears, she paused to breathe, hoping to ease the pain in her heart. "I am afraid for your safety, Sebastian. I—I—care for you so very much." Somehow, in the light of day, with so much at stake, she didn't have the courage to tell him that she loved him with every fiber of her being. It came to her that he had never actually said it, either, except to call her his love.

His face was dark with consternation. "Devil take it, Julia, this is the very reason why I didn't want you to know that—I mean to say, what we were doing."

"Don't you want to speak the word? I will say it for you then: smuggling! I thought you were proud of your new calling."

She could see in his face that he was at war. Part of him wanted to turn his back on her, she knew it.

"You are the most provoking female I have ever known!"

"I am your *wife*." She waited for him to throw back in her face the fact that he had not chosen her at all, that their very marriage was based on a charade fueled by her misguided need to manage the lives of people around her.

Instead, Sebastian turned away on the muddy path and raked a hand through his windblown hair. "You will drive me mad." After a long moment, he unclenched his fists, turned back, and opened his arms. Julia went into them with a little sob of relief.

"Thank God," she whispered, pressing her face to his shirtfront.

"I will consider stopping." He paused and she could feel the thump of his heart. "We have one more important run to make, and when it is over, I hope to have enough capital to reclaim Severn Park. We'll talk about it then."

She blinked, trying to take it in, and a cold chill spread over her. "One more run?"

"Yes, a crucial one."

"Do you have any notion how many times Papa told me that he would be done with gambling after just one more game? That recklessness cost him his life. Your own brother played with fire in exactly the same way, losing every material thing your family owned, yet you cannot see the parallels."

"No, I cannot. I am *getting* money for us, to rebuild those fortunes they gambled away. It is not the same thing at all."

"You're quite right." Hopelessly, Julia pulled free of his embrace and started back up the path. Tears blurred her vision. Thick tree roots coiled out of the dirt, catching her worn slippers, and she nearly lost her footing. "It's not the same thing, it's *worse*. You are not gambling with money, but with your very life!"

Sebastian reached for her arm. "Let me help you at least."

"You'll help me, but you won't listen, will you?"

A muscle ticked in his jaw as they started forward together. "No. And I'll ask you to stop talking about it."

Sebastian did not choose the beautiful Hall Walk as their route. Instead, he led Julia out of the woods to follow a cart track that crossed the meadows of their farm. The hay fields were lush and wet after the storm, brushing their clothing as they walked silently together past the cows and sheep and the medieval chapel built by Charlotte Trevarre's ancestors.

He knew that his wife felt a connection with his home. From the moment they first arrived, to the sight of a neglected manor house that anyone else would have shunned, Julia had embraced the echoes of the past that were everywhere.

"Hello Mabel," she greeted a spotted cow who stood with her calf on the other side of an old hedgerow, watching them with soft eyes.

It amazed him that she cared for all the animals and they seemed to return her affection. He knew that soon they would reach the house and the doors would burst open and the occupants of the Hall would rush out to greet their mistress. A part of Sebastian longed, even ached, to feel at home here as Julia did, but a different, dark feeling always closed around his heart and eclipsed that longing.

"Mrs. Snuggs and Primmie have doubtless been very worried about me," Julia was saying, seemingly to herself more than to him. "I'm not certain that Mr. Snuggs cares for anything but his cider."

And just then, as they came down into the courtyard, the door did open and Primmie and Mrs. Snuggs emerged, beaming.

"Ah, my lady, you be well!" cried Primmie, wiping her hands on her apron as she and the old woman approached. "We've missed you."

"You must have worried that a terrible fate had befallen me," said Julia.

"Oh, no, yer ladyship," cried Mrs. Snuggs. "Lord Senwyck do come and tell us that you be away with his lordship."

"He told you that?" She turned a quizzical look up to Sebastian, who schooled his own features to betray no reaction. "I saw Tristan in Fowey, and he warned me to go home because a storm was brewing. How could he possibly know—?"

Before Sebastian could suggest that they discuss it later, Dick the tiger cat came racing out the open door, closely followed by a barking liver-colored spaniel. As they ran right through the kitchen garden, trampling the tender lettuces, Mrs. Snuggs pursued them armed with a broom.

"Where the devil did that dog come from?" Sebastian demanded. It seemed that he inevitably felt like a stranger in his own house.

"Why, Sylvester is *our* dog!" cried a voice that was unnervingly familiar. "That cat delights in provoking him, I fear."

He and Julia turned at once to behold Polly Faircloth standing in the doorway and wringing her plump white hands. Clad in a lilac gown fashionable enough to grace the Bath Assembly Rooms, she looked alarmingly out of place on the crumbling doorstep of Trevarre Hall.

"Mama?" Julia was looking at her as if she didn't believe her eyes.

"We thought you would never return," Polly said in stricken tones, "and we would be stranded forever in this ruin at the end of the world!"

"But, why are you here?" Sebastian tried to keep the note of annoyance out of his voice. "We had no knowledge that you planned a journey to Cornwall."

"Indeed, my lord, but I think that when you learn the reason for our visit, you will understand." As Polly spoke, Sarah and Freddy came up behind her, accompanied by a portly gentleman who wore an old-fashioned white wig and a broad smile. "Lord Sebastian, I would like to present to my daughter and you the Honorable Clarence Pippet. Dear Pip and I are…betrothed!"

Julia and her sister, clad in batiste nightgowns, sat close together in Sarah's bed. The window was open to let in the summer breeze, and on the bedside table, a candle flame danced and flickered.

"How I have missed you!" cried Sarah as she lovingly plaited Julia's hair into a long braid down her back. "Aren't we fortunate that we can pick up like this, even after a separation. I can almost imagine that we are back in your bed at Turbans."

Julia tried to imagine it also, but far too much had happened to her since their last late-night tête-à-tête in her bed. On that occasion, she had informed Sarah that she meant to marry Sebastian in her stead.

It seemed almost as if she had been another person, living a different life, so changed did she feel.

"I'm exceedingly glad to see you, darling," she told her sister. "I have missed you, too! But you must tell me now about Mama and that Pip person. I had no inkling—"

"They met at the Pump Room. Mr. Pippet had come to Bath from London to take the waters, soon after the death of his wife from a wasting disease."

"I see. Well, he does seem to be a nice enough man."

Sarah widened her eyes tellingly. "Yes, and he has means. Considerable means."

"I'll own that I am shocked by this. Papa has only been gone for a few months…"

"I know. But Mama insists that love has no regard for time." In the candlelight, her face took on an impish glow. "She also says that this is an opportunity we all must seize."

"Indeed? But Mama should still be in mourning. I noticed that her gown was vivid lilac, with not even a black accessory. It is behavior that would horrify her if anyone else engaged in it."

"Yes. Perhaps it may help you to understand if I reveal that Mr. Pippet lives in London, in a large home in Russell Square. It may not be Mayfair, but you will appreciate that it is a more impressive address than we claimed. He has ten servants and two carriages. He insists that Mama deserves only the best, and that he means to provide her with it."

Julia held up her hand. "You needn't go on. I understand completely that all of this has turned her head. No wonder she is calling him 'Pip'."

Overcome by mirth, Sarah threw herself back on the pillows and giggled for long moments. "Oh, Julia, I have missed you so! Only you could know what is really happening, and how Freddy and I feel. You know, Mama insisted that we all travel to Cornwall, not only to get away from the gossiping dowagers in Bath, but also because she thought you might be unhappy, and would want to join us in our new life in London."

Julia ignored the sentiments directed at her and asked, "Are you pleased to be going to London? What about Mr. Whimple?"

"Oh, Charles and I are finished!" Sarah exclaimed dramatically. "I don't know how I could have ever entertained such tender feelings for him."

"Really! This is quite unexpected."

"I think that, when he learned the Faircloth family no longer possessed a fortune of any size, he stopped caring for me."

Julia saw tears sparkle in her sister's eyes. "How odious. I am grateful, then, that we had a change in circumstances, if only because it brought out Mr. Whimple's true colors. He did not deserve you, my dear."

"No, I realize that, too. Do you suppose I shall ever meet a man who worships me and longs to take care of me?"

"I have no doubt of it." Although she was smiling at her sister, Julia thought how terribly different they were, for their dreams of a man to love were very far apart.

"I must confess that, even before he proved himself unworthy, Charles was growing tedious. I even grew tired of his poems. Do you think that I am terribly inconstant?"

As they talked, Julia remembered why she had been so unsatisfied by society and the effervescent quality of life in

Bath and London. There was no substance to any of it, at least as far as she was concerned. She needed more, and she had discovered it here in Cornwall…with Sebastian.

"I don't think you are inconstant, Sarah. I think you are merely growing up, as I have been doing since I married."

Her sister's voice dropped to a whisper. "Is it *thrilling*?"

Julia didn't have to ask what she meant. "I suppose it depends on the man," she replied vaguely, all the while feeling a traitorous heat rise in her cheeks. "Darling, it's late. I am very tired. Do you mind if I leave you now?"

"Are you happy then?"

"Happy? It's more complicated than that, I'm afraid."

"Yes, I can only imagine! Lord Satan, if I may still dare to call him that, remains quite terrifying. You can come away with us, you know. Freddy and I would adore it if you did, and no one would know about your past." Realizing that she might have gone too far, Sarah amended, "Or you could simply visit us in London for long periods of time…"

"We'll talk more tomorrow." Julia embraced her sister, then slipped out of the bed and went across the corridor to her own bedchamber.

Beyond the white muslin bed hangings she had put up for summer, she saw Sebastian, lying in his customary sleeping position, on his back. He was brown in the moonlight, his black hair ruffled, his chiseled features proud even in sleep. Nearby, Clover lay curled, purring, her plush gray face resting in the palm of his hand.

After a moment's hesitation, Julia threw caution to the wind. She unplaited her hair and let it fall free, slipped the bed gown over her head, and went naked to join her husband under the soft sheet.

It felt like heaven to be home at last, nestled into the crook of his strong shoulder. A moment later, sleep carried her off..

Chapter 31

"There's nothing like good clotted cream from Cornwall," Mr. Pippet pronounced as he helped himself to a large dollop. "And this jam is nectar from the gods."

Julia smiled at him from across the garden table. "Thank you. It's made with hedgerow berries from our farm."

"Never heard of 'em before, but now I will see to it that we obtain a plant for my garden in Russell Square." He leaned closer to Polly Faircloth, who wore a giddy expression. "Would you like that, Mrs. Faircloth?"

"I'm afraid that that's impossible," interjected Sebastian. "These berries grow wild on old Cornish hedgerows and in no other place in England."

"I am finding Cornwall to be a magnificent place!" Freddy chimed in as he started on a second plate of eggs and scones. "It is filled with legends, you know. One can almost imagine Tristan and Isolde in those woods by the river."

"We shall explore the Hall Walk later today, Freddy, and I'll show you the place where King Charles the First was shot at during the Civil War!" said Julia. She was beginning to enjoy the novelty of having her family at Trevarre Hall, all eating breakfast together in the sunlit garden. The hydrangeas and roses she had been tending were in full bloom, Clover and Dick were actually lying together on the flagstones, the kitchen garden looked prosperous, and warblers were singing in the hedges.

Sebastian pushed back from the table. "How ironic that Freddy should mention the legendary Tristan, for I see our own Lord Senwyck making his way toward us."

The wide-shouldered, slim-hipped young man walked down the gentle hill from the stables, again wearing the naval uniform that served a new purpose now that he was a Riding Officer. The sun shone on his russet hair that appealingly stuck out a bit, as if he'd just lifted a hand to absently ruffle it.

"Good morning," said Tristan as he drew near. "I hope I'm not interrupting."

"Not at all." Sebastian rose and introduced their guests, finishing with, "I would like you all to know our friend and neighbor, Tristan Penrose, Viscount Senwyck."

Julia watched as her family and Mr. Pippet exchanged greetings with Tristan. However, when her gaze fell on her sister, it appeared that Sarah had fallen under a spell. Her cheeks were pink, her eyes sparkled, and she tilted her head shyly to one side.

"Lord Senwyck," she murmured prettily. "It is a great honor to meet you."

"Are you named for the sixth century Tristan who was King Mark's nephew?" Freddy interrupted excitedly.

"Well, it is a Celtic name, and fairly common in Cornwall, but my mother did confide that she had that knight in mind when she chose my name," Tristan told the boy with a grin. "Are you a student of history?"

"Most emphatically yes, my lord! I am currently deep into a study of ancient Greece!"

Before he could continue, Sarah gave her brother a glance that immediately stopped his chatter. Then, turning her lovely face up to Tristan, she said, "My lord, may I say how fine you look in your uniform? Are you in the service of the King?"

"I am indeed, Miss Faircloth." He bowed to her and the sun flashed on his gilded sword scabbard. "I have served in the Royal Navy and am currently a Customs Riding Officer."

Julia felt her face growing warmer when she heard him say those words. She glanced at Sebastian, but he seemed perfectly at ease. Now that she knew the truth, his association with Tristan took on new meaning. As she wondered how Sebastian could be so cool in the company of a trusted friend who was also unwittingly dedicated to his capture, it occurred to Julia that there might be more to the situation than met the eye.

"A Riding Officer? Whatever might that be?" Sarah asked. Julia had never seen her sister appear more fascinated by another person.

"We are endeavoring to apprehend the smugglers who would take the law into their own hands and deprive His Majesty of much-needed tax revenue," Tristan replied soberly.

"Lord Senwyck," Julia said, wishing to change the subject, "may we offer you breakfast? Mrs. Snuggs has baked her famous currant scones, and we have fresh clotted cream."

"Thank you, my lady, but I have already eaten. I have come to beg your husband to accompany me to Bodinnick. A friend wishes to meet with him."

"Ah yes. You must mean Polarven," Sebastian said, looking rather relieved to have an excuse to escape from the Faircloth family. To Julia, he added, "Jasper was the factor here at Trevarre Hall for many years. He lives in Bodinnick now."

"How interesting. Perhaps he can be persuaded to return?" Julia wondered why was it so difficult for Sebastian to focus on *this* estate and forget about Severn Park in Hampshire. He didn't seem to want to discuss the matter, though, for he and Tristan had begun their goodbyes to the Faircloth family and Mr. Pippet.

"My lord," said Sarah, attempting to gaze into Lord Senwyck's blue eyes, "I hope that we may meet again before I leave Cornwall."

He surprised Julia by blushing slightly and nodding. "Miss Faircloth, I think that we may."

The Ferry Inn in Bodinnick, which was only a few dozen yards up the steep hill from the river, looked out on a charming view of Fowey on the opposite bank. The ferry had been in constant operation since the thirteenth century and the inn was just as busy, providing refreshment and a resting place for tired travelers.

Behind the inn's public room there were two steps leading down to a low-beamed, damp-smelling chamber used for storage and, occasionally, private meetings like the one Sebastian had convened that day.

"Where's Keswick to?" asked Jasper, sipping his cider in the gloom. "How can we hold a proper meetin' if he not be here?"

"He may turn up yet," Sebastian said in ironic tones. "He received a message from an unidentified person and has gone out for a few hours. You might imagine that he would confide in me, but in fact, Keswick can be vexingly inscrutable."

"Let's get on with it, then," said Tristan. "Lynton has become very edgy and he isn't talking much, either. It wouldn't do for me to turn up late for our afternoon patrols."

"Has he mentioned anything about a Revenue Cutter giving chase to a smuggling ship at sea two nights ago?"

"God, no. I take it that was you?"

"Yes. Quite exciting, but I do worry a bit that the *Peregrine* could be identified if we take her on another run. I've been pondering a solution. Do either of you have any thoughts?"

"We might paint the *Peregrine*," Jasper mused.

Tristan looked slightly alarmed. "We can't just wait for things to die down a bit? Lynton was already foaming at the mouth before the last run, when Julia had to be abducted and taken along. He insisted that I and the other Riding Officers cover every inch of the coastline near Polridmouth Bay because the smugglers had been spotted offshore there. If indeed he knows about the Admiralty ship pursuing you at sea, and he's decided to keep it to himself, I can only imagine what thoughts he's having…"

"We can't put off this run, if that's what you're suggesting." Sebastian said flatly. "A very special cargo is being assembled in the Roscoff warehouse. St. Briac is waiting. And perhaps most importantly, a smuggler's moon is in store two days hence."

Jasper's eyes went round and then he repeated with relish, "A smuggler's moon!"

"What the devil is that?" demanded Tristan.

"It means no moon at all." Sebastian calmly leaned back in his chair. "It's ideal for a landing, and if we wait, it will be a missed opportunity. Perhaps we might throw Lynton off balance by choosing a different beach, on the east side of the Fowey estuary?"

"Lansallos," murmured Jasper. "It be a long walk t' the cove, down a path hacked through the stone cliff. The Revenue men do never think of it."

"Fine then. You and Mixstowe work out the details. All that's left is the matter of the ship—"

Just then, Keswick called out from the steps leading to the public room. "We have come just in time to provide a solution!" He was bent over in the doorway, smiling, a mug of ale in his hand, and he raised it to Sebastian. "You'll thank us, my lord, when you hear the plan we have arranged."

Perceiving that Keswick intended to convey this information privately, Sebastian stood up. "All right then, Senwyck is off to play at being a Riding Officer, Polarven is going to make the arrangements for the landing and distribution with Mixstowe, and I'm going to see what Keswick has in mind."

As the other men rose and stood together, Sebastian shook their hands. "You know, I've half-promised my wife that this will be my last run, so we must make doubly certain that it is magnificent."

Jasper gaped at him. "Why'd ye do *that*?"

"I am a married man. I've been thinking that perhaps I should behave like one."

As they filed out into the public room, Sebastian was too preoccupied to notice the sallow-faced Colvithick sitting in the nearest corner, drinking ale as he waited for his uncle Jasper.

"Devil take it, Keswick, why must you be so mysterious? I really didn't have time to ride to Polruan this afternoon, you know. There is so much that must be done before we sail."

Sebastian and Keswick were leading their horses down one of Polruan's steepest lanes.

"We can assure your lordship that this meeting will be worth your time. You will thank us."

"Yes, yes. Has anyone ever told you that you have an inflated opinion of your own worth?"

"Yes, my lord. *You* have." As they laughed together, Keswick stopped walking. "Here we are."

When Sebastian abruptly halted behind Keswick, Lucifer nearly bumped into both of them. They stood before a plainly dignified two-story house built of rubble stone, the sort of house that Polruan sea captains had been occupying for centuries.

"We will stay with the horses while you go inside," Keswick said.

Before Sebastian could question him further, the door opened and André Raveneau stepped into the summer sunlight.

"Greetings, my lord," he said with an enigmatic smile. "We meet again."

Inside the cramped, modestly-furnished parlor at the front of the house, Raveneau brought a pot of tea and poured two cups.

"I am surprised to see you here, sir," Sebastian told him, stirring milk into his hot, strong tea. "Is your family still in France?"

"No, they sailed home on *La Mouette*, but Keswick found me this house to let so that I might visit you."

"May I ask why?"

"I had an idea that you might like to use another ship for your next crossing and so I have brought you my new sloop, the *Raven*, if you would like her. She is moored nearby, down Fore Street at the village quay."

"That's very kind of you. And frankly, it's an answer to a prayer. There is something you should know, however—"

"I already know." Raveneau's flinty gaze met Sebastian's. "You have been smuggling. I guessed that you would the day you came from seeing your solicitor in London."

Sebastian felt a thump inside his chest. "Indeed, sir?"

"Yes, but it does not shock me. Long ago, I had my own smuggling adventures, but that's a subject for another time. In fact, although I want you to have the sloop, I really came to speak to you about a matter of greater importance." He set down his cup and rubbed his eyes with long fingers, then sighed. "*Mon Dieu*, there is no easy way to tell you this, so I will be direct. Are you prepared for a disclosure that will change your life?"

Somehow, Sebastian knew then, before Raveneau said another word. He nodded.

Leaning forward, the older man said, "It seems that I am your father. Of course, I have no proof, but the evidence is overwhelming."

Sebastian closed his eyes against a tide of emotion. Tears bit at his eyes; his throat swelled. His heart hurt with a sort of burning relief. At length, when he could speak, he looked at Raveneau and said, "Of course. Why did I not see it myself? That's your eye on that ring. That's why my mother wanted me to have it, why she gave it to Miles for safekeeping, she didn't want to take a chance that Father would see it and—" He broke off. "It all makes sense now. No wonder he couldn't bear to be near me."

"I cannot imagine that he knew. If he did, I think that Charlotte would have come to me and told me."

Sebastian sat still again, mentally scrolling back through countless memories, searching them for new truths. "Yes, you're probably right. Father was such a bastard, he would have probably murdered her. But I do think that on some level, he sensed that we were not…connected. He always went out of his way, with cruel subtlety, to let me know that I meant nothing to him."

Sebastian saw the scar on Raveneau's jaw tighten. "I am so sorry. If I had known, I would have acted."

"At the expense of your own marriage—and my mother's? No, clearly she didn't want that." He sat back in his chair, still in the grip of a thousand emotions. "God's blood, what a coil."

"But now your parents are both gone, and you and I are left. It doesn't have to be a coil if we choose otherwise." Raveneau walked across the room and returned with a bottle of French brandy. Pouring a small portion for each of them, he said ironically, "I perceive that tea will not suffice for this occasion, *n'est-ce pas*?"

Sebastian laughed. "I fully agree." After a drink, he said, "Will you tell me more one day, about you and my mother?"

"Yes, one day I will answer all your questions."

"I have always felt a warm regard for you, sir, especially since we met again in London this year. I confess—" He stopped, knowing what he wanted to say, but held back by old fears.

"Yes?" Raveneau prompted softly. A moment later, he added, "It's all right, you know. I understand you because we're alike. You've spent a lifetime holding your own feelings at a distance out of self-protection, but it's all right now. You can say these things to me."

Sebastian's eyes and throat filled with hot tears. "Yes," he replied, his voice catching. "Thank you. I was going to say that your friendship, which you have freely given without asking anything in return, has been a balm to me. During solitary moments, I have reflected that you were the sort of man I would have chosen for a father."

Raveneau nodded, and his own eyes gleamed with emotion. "I am very proud that you are my son, Sebastian." He reached across the space between them and put a hand on Sebastian's shoulder. "I realize that you are a grown man and you don't need the guidance of a parent, but perhaps you will be grateful to know that now you have a father who loves you. And, you may call on me at any time, for any reason."

"But what of Devon? I would never want to be the cause of any pain for her."

"On the contrary," Raveneau said drily, "it was Devon who forced me to face the truth and come to terms with this. Like most men, I am rather a coward when it comes to confronting emotional matters, especially when they might have an impact on the lives of those around me."

Sebastian rose then and paced across the modestly-furnished room. When he returned to stand before Raveneau, he said, "You already have a family. You have a son who has enjoyed your love since the moment of his birth. Nathan is your heir. Nothing must change that."

"I know that my other children would love you as the

brother that you are, and of course Devon is already very fond of you and of Julia."

"That's all very well, but I insist that this must not change their lives. Let your children care for me as a family friend. The rest shall remain between us and our wives."

When Raveneau rose and stood before him, Sebastian looked directly into eyes that mirrored his own. It was both unsettling and exhilarating to realize that this was his father, and that they shared much of the same emotional underpinnings.

"I know that you sail with the tide," said Raveneau, "and your time is short. Will you allow me to ride home with you and be there when you tell Julia?"

"I was just about to ask if you would do that very thing," Sebastian replied, amazed. He then thought for a moment of all the times he had stood before the Marquess of Caverleigh during his childhood, longing to be held by his father yet terrified by the thought of touching him.

Raveneau seemed to read his mind. When he opened his arms and they embraced, Sebastian felt his heart clutch again, but then it grew calm. A warm sense of completion spread over him as he heard his father murmur, "My son."

Chapter 32

Dusk had gathered over the village of Polruan as Sebastian, accompanied by Raveneau and Keswick, left the Stag Inn after a hearty meal. The trio mounted their horses and set off up the steep lane, bound for Trevarre Hall, less than four miles away.

At the same time, across the river in Fowey, Adolphus Lynton and Tristan Penrose were entering the Ship Inn. It had once been the home of the Rashleighs, the town's foremost family, but Philip Rashleigh had moved to Menabilly, to the west near Coombe Farm, and now the stone house with its view of the quay was an inn.

"I have a prodigious thirst!" cried Lynton. "I'm not certain there is enough ale in Cornwall to quench it."

"It has been a rather exhausting afternoon," Tristan agreed.

Seating themselves in the shadowy, dark-beamed public room, they ordered from the serving girl.

"What I want to know is, where does that villain hide?" Lynton complained in ringing tones. "How can he make his ship simply vanish? I've just received a full description from the Revenue Cutter that nearly captured them just two nights back, and we know those thieving smugglers had to have made landfall, but *where?*"""

"I wish I knew, Lieutenant," Tristan replied calmly. "I

am as tired of riding up and down the coast as you are."

The girl brought them their ale and Lynton drank deeply, his eyes narrowing as he cried, "I find it very curious that Lord Sebastian Trevarre happened to be away in Hampshire at the same time our 'Captain Rogue' was conducting a smuggling mission. Do you not find that curious, my lord?"

Tristan looked uncomfortable. "I'm not sure I know what you mean, sir. Are you implying that Lord Sebastian and the smuggling captain could be the same person?"

"Perhaps, though it's doubtless an idle wish on my part. I confess that nothing would please me more than to do away with him, releasing her ladyship from a marriage she entered into only to save her sister from the same fate."

"I beg your pardon?"

"That's right. Lord Sebastian wanted *Sarah* Faircloth for his bride, but Julia sacrificed herself because she knew that her sister was too sensitive and refined to survive marriage to such a libertine." He held his glass up for another ale. "Perhaps you have forgotten that I lived in Bath. I was very well acquainted with the Faircloth family."

Tristan's brow furrowed. "I'm not certain I understand what you're getting at about Sebastian, but does it really matter now? I believe that my friends are quite happy together."

"He took her father's estate, did you know that? Won it from him during a weak moment at the gaming tables, and it drove Mr. Faircloth to his death! I believe Julia gave up her own future so that her family might remain at Turbans, their home in Bath. It's a palace compared to that ruin she is forced to live in now!"

"I can only repeat that I believe them to enjoy a satisfying marriage."

"No! How can someone with the refined sensibilities of Julia Faircloth be happy with a rake like that, in so primitive a place as this? I cannot describe to you the joy she took from listening to me play the cello. Do you imagine that Trevarre has any artistic sensibilities?" Lynton laughed scornfully. What a relief it was to finally speak about this to someone! "Why do you think I came here? Of course, I was attracted by the Customs position offered to me, but secretly I have been fueled by dreams of rescuing my Julia from that devil."

"I see." While nodding politely, Tristan consulted his watch. "It's dark and I should be getting home to Lanwyllow. I hope you'll excuse me, sir."

"Fine, fine, go on. I'll just have another drink." Lynton raised his glass again and the girl came to fill it as Tristan rose and took his leave, making his way between the tables filled with sweaty men all enjoying a pint after a long day's labor.

"You do hear me right," a young man was exclaiming from a nearby table. "There were a real *lady* on board. Sailed with us all the way to France and back. But I must not say more! Cease your questions, Isaac!"

Adolphus Lynton nudged his chair back so that he could discreetly turn one ear toward the speaker, just in time to hear him shout, "Mayhap it be someone you know, but that be all I'm goin' to say!"

Lynton signaled to the serving girl to bring the pallid youth another drink. When it arrived, the lad looked around in surprise and met the calculating gaze of Adolphus Lynton.

"Drink up, son. I would have a word with you," he yelled over the din. Lynton bided his time, watching from a distance, until he sensed that his prey's companions were growing bored. Finally, he left his chair and went up behind the boy. "Care to step outside for a bit of air? I will make it worth your while, Mr.—"

"My name be Colvithick, sir. Drew Colvithick."

High above Trevarre Hall, a thin sliver of moon hung in the night sky, barely illuminating the estate grounds. When

Sylvester the spaniel began to bark insistently, Julia looked up from the library settee where she had been sitting with her brother.

"I'd better see what that's about," she said, rising. "You stay here and enjoy that book, Freddy."

"I shall be pleased to do so, for his lordship has a most impressive library!"

Julia went out through the courtyard door to see a pair of shadowy figures making their way down from the stables. One of them carried a glowing lantern.

"Sebastian? Is that you?" she called.

"Yes, love." He went ahead of the others and embraced her. "I'm sorry to be late."

"We had to eat dinner without you." Searching his face, she added, "I told Mama that you were looking after estate business. They've moved on to a game of whist and Freddy is reading a book from your library."

"Excellent." When he motioned back into the darkness, André Raveneau came forward. "We have a guest."

Julia blinked. "Why, Captain, what a surprise! I thought you and your family were still in France."

"They are en route to London, but I had business here with Sebastian—and you, my dear."

She felt Sebastian take her hand, his own fingers reassuringly warm and strong. "André has brought us a sloop to sail on this last run, in case the *Peregrine* could be identified. And there is more that you need to hear. It's such a nice evening; perhaps we can sit outdoors."

He led her to the table on the garden terrace, set the lantern on the low stone wall, and the trio sat down together. Moments later, Clover appeared and, to Julia's surprise, jumped onto Sebastian's lap. As he absently stroked her soot-gray head, she began to purr.

"I know that both of you have things to attend to tonight, and your family is here, Julia, so I will be brief," said Raveneau. "Devon asked me to speak to you personally, though."

"I hope that nothing is wrong?"

"Not at all."

She listened in growing amazement to his tale, and as the pieces of the puzzle came together, Julia felt a sense of warm elation come over her.

"This is simply wonderful." Looking from Raveneau to Sebastian and back again, she added, "It's really a dream come true. You both are happy, aren't you?"

Nodding, father and son smiled at each other, and it was as if each of them were looking in a mirror.

"I am beyond happy, as you may imagine," Sebastian said with feeling. "You know what my feelings have been for the marquess."

"Wouldn't it be splendid if you could cut all those awful memories loose and let them drift away to another place, far away from here?" she mused.

"Splendid indeed." His hand tightened over hers. "And in the meantime, this man, whose honest friendship I have come to value, has become the loving father I thought I could never have. It is a gift beyond price."

"A gift for both of us," said Raveneau. "I wanted to tell you, Julia, that you may depend upon me, and all of my family, to care for you as well."

"Thank you," she whispered. "That means a great deal."

The sound of an approaching horse came from the darkened lane, followed by voices.

"It's Tristan," said Sebastian. Setting the cat down on the flagstones, he got to his feet. "No doubt he has a report for me."

Julia stared. "What are you talking about? Wait—am I to infer that Lord Senwyck is in *your* service, rather than that of the King?"

His smile flashed in the darkness. "I forgot that you didn't already know. Yes, of course. You didn't really imagine that he supported the views of that fool Lynton, did you?"

Watching him go off, Julia sighed helplessly and looked at

Raveneau. "It is the most frightening coil and I am sick with worry, particularly regarding this next planned smuggling run. Can *you* not persuade him to stop this madness?"

"Ah, *cherie*, if either of us had the power to change his mind, he would not be the man you love." His eyes gleamed. "Perhaps you were drawn to Sebastian because you sensed his love for danger…and you hoped to reform him?"

"I don't know if I ever quite thought about it, but perhaps there is truth in what you are saying." Julia thought for an instant of her efforts to reform her own father. "Now that you put it into words, I can see that I've been foolish."

"Not foolish." He reached out and touched her cheek. "I wanted to see you tonight because I have a piece of advice for you, which you are quite free to disregard."

"Oh, yes, please! I am longing to hear it."

"I understand Sebastian because he is my son; we share the same blood. The very best way you can help him now is simply to give him your unqualified love. If you release your hold on the reins, he will come to you of his own volition."

Julia stared at Raveneau, pondering his words. She thought again of how miserably her efforts to change her own father had turned out.

"As my own methods do not seem to be working, perhaps I would do well to follow your advice."

"It is not really my advice," Raveneau told her with an irresistible smile. "Devon would tell you that this is her secret formula for a happy marriage."

"Are you not going to ask me about Tristan's visit?"

Julia stopped in the midst of turning down the bed and looked back toward the newly acquired copper bathtub where Sebastian was enjoying a leisurely soak. Of course, she was longing to ask lots of questions, and give lots of advice, but Raveneau's wisdom intruded.

"I will listen if you want to tell me about it," she said sweetly.

He arched a brow. "Why don't you join me, then, and we'll—talk."

The suggestive tone of Sebastian's voice and the sight of him, brown and gleaming wet in the candlelight, made her weak with desire. Yet, she was also heartsick about the dangerous smuggling run that lay ahead. It was difficult to allow herself to surrender to the deep yearning to be close to him.

"There is a spot on my back I can't reach," he said, and pointed under the water.

Without another word, Julia shed her clothes. It was such a warm night that the lukewarm water in the tub felt refreshing to her as she stepped in. As she settled down in the small space in front of him, her breasts began to tingle under his smoldering gaze.

"So much has happened," she said softly. "But…do you really want to talk?"

"Not a bit." He reached for her then. "Ah, my darling, how beautiful you are. I should go very slowly, I know. Kissing you, like this…"

Julia groaned when his mouth covered hers and his tongue began to work its magic.

"And I should touch you," he muttered, "like this…"

She found herself climbing onto his wet lap, straddling him shamelessly as his fingers strayed under the water to find the swelling core of her. The slick water heightened each sensation as he touched her, lightly pinching and stroking, until she began to move against his hand in a timeless rhythm.

"I also know," he was whispering, "that you would love it if I would do this…"

And then his dark head dipped and his mouth fastened on her tender nipple, suckling with just the right amount of pressure. Somehow, he knew exactly what she needed and wanted. Currents of arousal traveled down from her breasts, heightening the sensations that were building to a crescendo between her legs. When Julia felt his fingers slide inside her, probing, it was as if a dam burst. She was trembling as she climaxed, her head thrown back, her breasts pushing against his muscled chest.

"I should take more time for you," he was murmuring again, "but all I want to do is be inside you, just like—" And then he lifted her hips with his strong hands and brought her in contact with his erection, "—*this.* Yes. Oh, God, Julia, yes."

The shock of him filling her as she was climaxing brought another, even stronger wave of contractions. She could feel herself gripping him as she pushed up on her knees and then came back down. Both of them were heedless of the water that splashed from the copper tub, heedless of Dick the cat who scuttled under the bed in alarm, heedless of their muffled cries as they clung together, thrusting, until almost in unison they found a fulfillment that defied words.

Julia sank her fingers into his thick, wet hair and kissed him, pushing her tongue past his teeth and into his mouth as he had taught her to do. Sebastian cupped her buttocks and angled himself so that he was as deep inside her as it was possible to go, and then she felt the throb of his lips disengaging from hers.

"Julia," he said in a harsh whisper, "look at me."

Their eyes were just inches apart and what she saw made her heart soar. She tried to speak, but the only sound she could make was a little sob.

"I love you," said Sebastian. "Do you believe me?"

She was nodding, weeping now. "Yes! I love you, too."

"My darling." He moved slightly inside her and groaned. "More."

"Let's go to bed," Julia agreed, laughing a little through her tears.

Sebastian reached for a towel and lifted her, dripping, to

her feet. "For God's sake, hurry. I want you again."

"This time, my lord, I am going to make you wait for it," she promised, and boldly put her hand on him. "I have been taking lessons from the master..."

Chapter 33

Julia opened her eyes to sunlight and a pleasurable aching between her legs. Her nostrils twitched; she caught the faint scent of their coupling in the sheets, and it had an aphrodisiac effect on her. As impressions and sensations coursed through her memory, she was wet again, lusting for her husband.

Turning on the pillow, seeking his warm, protective body, she found that she was alone. The spell was broken.

"My lady?" came Primmie's voice from the corridor. "Be you awake yet?"

Hastily, Julia scrambled to snatch her nightgown from the floor near the cold bathtub. Pulling it over her head, she called, "Of course. What is it, Primmie?"

"A boy do come here, at dawn, saying that you would know him. I think he be sick, my lady."

"What time is it now?"

"Mid-morning, my lady. We do begin to worry about you."

Julia dressed as quickly as she could, twisted her sable hair into a knot atop her head, and rushed downstairs. How could she have slept so late? Of course, she and Sebastian had been up what seemed like most of the night, but the notion that she'd slumbered past ten o'clock was outrageous!

Coming into the kitchen, Julia discovered a thin, pale

young man with lank brown hair sitting in a chair near the hearth. Mrs. Snuggs was offering him something in a bowl, and when Julia entered, the old woman looked up.

"Mayhap you be wantin' to see to this sad fellow, my lady!"

"My goodness, it's Mr. Colvithick, isn't it?" Julia exclaimed as she drew near.

"Yes, my lady," he said miserably.

"I am so surprised to see you here!" Feeling Mrs. Snuggs's curious glance, she broke off. "Mrs. Snuggs, where is my family?"

"Mayhap ye know that his lordship goes off again, with Keswick, afore sun-up. Yer mum and the others went to Truro, to visit Mr. Pippet's cousins. Mrs. Faircloth says you do know of their plans."

"Oh yes. I remember now." She tried to think of a reason to send the old woman out of the room so she could speak freely to Colvithick. "Will you kindly see to the bath that is still in our bedchamber? Perhaps Mr. Snuggs can help you."

"Hmph!" was the old woman's reply, but she obeyed.

Realizing suddenly that she was very hungry, Julia took two ripe figs from a blue bowl and sat down near the hearth. "Why are you here, Mr. Colvithick? Is something amiss?"

"I be ailing, my lady. Keswick do send me here. He says you'll look after me until they return."

"And what exactly is wrong with you?"

"Food won't stay down. I be feverish as well."

She touched his brow and found it cold and clammy. Perhaps the fever had broken. "I'll have Primmie make a cot for you in one of the spare rooms. My brother has been sleeping there, but he is away in Truro."

Just then, Primmie appeared in the doorway. "My lady! You'll never believe it! Clover's just birthed a litter of kittens in your dressing room, and that rogue Dick be struttin' about looking mighty proud. Come and see!"

Julia was grateful to Clover for the diversion her kittens provided over the next thirty-six hours, for she had little chance to worry about Sebastian. There were six adorable balls of fluff, three gray and three orange tiger-striped, and one of the little orange males wouldn't nurse or even lie close to his mother.

Julia kept the kitten warm and tried feeding him warm milk squeezed from a soft cloth. She dipped the cloth in milk and twisted it, hoping the kitten would nurse from it. Finally, a full day later, when she feared he might die, they tried taking the other kittens away and bringing the outlier to his mother by himself. At last, as he snuggled up to Clover began to nurse, there was general celebration among Julia, Primmie, and Mrs. Snuggs.

It was past six o'clock in the evening when she went to find some dinner. On her way down the corridor, she peeked into Freddy's room and saw Colvithick sitting on the side of his narrow bed, apparently examining something that he held in his hands.

"Ah, you must be feeling better!" she exclaimed. "I'm pleased. I know I haven't been much of a nurse; our cat has unexpectedly had kittens and one has struggled to survive."

The face he turned up to her was wretched. "No matter, my lady."

"Can I get you a plate of food?"

"Oh, no, my lady." As he spoke, he fumbled with something that jangled, stuffing it under his pillow. "I be fair tired. Goin' to sleep now."

It wasn't long before Julia went to bed herself, but alone in the gathering darkness, all she could think of was Sebastian and the rest of the crew. At least they were sailing Raveneau's fast sloop. With a good wind, they would land in a few hours.

"My lady!"

She sat up in alarm. "Mrs. Snuggs? Is that you?"

"Aye, my lady!" She held a candlestick up, the wavering flame illuminating her craggy face. "That boy, the one who says he be sick—something's not right. No sooner do Mr. Snuggs and me go to bed than I hear him rummagin' in the kitchen! When I do peek in, I seen him carry a cold chicken from the larder! "

Julia got out of bed, all her instincts on alert. She put on a cotton wrapper over her nightgown, took a candlestick from the bedside table, and followed Mrs. Snuggs downstairs. Recalling the image of Colvithick pushing something under his pillow, she turned to the housekeeper.

"I will ask you to go to the kitchen and try to keep our guest occupied. Offer to feed him or find some other distraction. Perhaps he'd like a drink!"

When Mrs. Snuggs had hurried off on her mission, Julia entered Freddy's room and went straight to Colvithick's bed. Reaching under the pillow, she discovered a leather drawstring bag filled with coins, some of them guineas. Her heart began to pound. What could it mean?

She looked around and saw his soiled coat draped across the arm of a chair. When she searched through the pockets, she found a folded piece of paper, quickly plucked it out, and began to read.

"Do not sail with Trevarre's ship. Plead illness and stay behind. Hide the money. Wait for word from me after it is over." The cryptic note was signed with a large, flowing L.

Waves of terrified panic swept over Julia and for a moment, she thought she might be ill right there on the threadbare tapestry carpet. Instead, however, she straightened her shoulders, took several deep breaths, and went in search of Drew Colvithick.

Mrs. Snuggs had apparently taken him prisoner in the kitchen. She stood over him at the table while he lifted a spoonful of gruel to his mouth and grimaced at it.

"I would have a word with you, young man." Holding up

the bag of coins, Julia continued, "Explain yourself. Quickly!"

"Ohh…my lady! Thank the good Lord you've found me out. I do be guiltier than Judas this past day!"

"Tell me, then. Hurry!"

He covered his face with his hands and began to sob. "It were that Lieutenant Lynton. He do hear me say things that made him suspicious, and he says that he be giving me enough gold to feed my family for years." Shaking his head, he added, "I confess that I were drinking, my lady."

Julia stood listening, a cold chill spreading over her body. "What exactly did he pay you to do?"

"When the plan were made for this run, I be in the Ferry Inn, near enough t' hear the captain talk to Keswick, Jasper, and Lord Senwyck."

"And you told Mr. Lynton where they would land? And when?"

Colvithick hung his head and nodded. "Aye, my lady. God save me, it be true. I do try to back out, but he says if I refuse, he'll send the press-gang for me!"

"And what of Lord Senwyck? Please say that you did not betray him to Mr. Lynton!"

He cowered before her and began to sob again. "Lord Senwyck were to signal with the spout lantern from the cliffs, that it be safe for the longboat to come ashore."

Mrs. Snuggs looked over the boy's head at Julia and rolled her eyes in disgust.

"I want you to get dressed, Mr. Colvithick," said Julia in crisp tones. "Put on your boots. You are going to take me to the beach where the landing will occur tonight. It is up to us to save his lordship and the crew from the Revenue men!"

Julia put on her brother's breeches, shoes, and coat, and was grateful to discover that they all fit her quite well. She rode Sally, her favorite mare, and Colvithick was astride his own horse, which appeared rather undernourished.

"Are you sure they aren't going to Coombe Hawne?" Julia shouted to him as he led the way down a wooded lane toward the shore.

"No, my lady, his lordship do plainly say Lansallos Cove."

"And you're certain you know the way?"

"Aye, my lady."

She'd never been to Lansallos before. It was so very dark, with virtually no moon, and the wooded lanes they traveled were unfamiliar to her, even by daylight. And when she realized that she had foolishly forgotten to bring a weapon, it was far too late to go back.

Up and down hills they rode, through openings in hedgerows, past stone farmhouses, stiles, and signposts that were impossible to read in the darkness. At length, they reached more level meadows, and Julia could tell by the shape of the horizon that they were nearing the coast.

Colvithick slowed when an ancient church came in sight to the west. It sat up on a high bank, its square granite tower silhouetted against the dark sky.

"That be Lansallos Church, my lady. We must leave the horses here and go on by foot."

It occurred to Julia, as they tethered their horses and entered a pathway surrounded by dense foliage, that the boy could be leading her to her death. Although she normally would have wanted to take control, she had no choice but to trust Colvithick, and she cared for nothing except getting to Sebastian. Nothing else mattered. For the first time, she understood why people prayed and evoked the fates. That was all she could do. Her heart raced, but then she took more deep breaths and scrambled on after Colvithick.

This was the only chance she had to save her husband, and it came to her that she would die for him, just as she knew he would die for her. She'd felt it the last time they had made love, the forging of a deeper, more intimate bond than either of them had experienced before.

A narrow stream went rushing past near the slippery, downhill slope of the path. It was almost impossibly dark. Julia stayed close to Colvithick, who did his share of stumbling, but at least he was a shape that she could see ahead in the blackness. On and on the path went, crossing back and forth over the stream.

"Good God, does it never end?" Julia cried at one point.

"It be a mile or more," he replied. "They do choose it because they think Excise Men never want to work this hard to look for smugglers."

Just then, as they approached a fork in the path, Julia heard a groaning sound.

"What was that?" Part of her wanted to keep going, even to run away, for it might very well be a Customs Officer or some other enemy. Yet, her instincts said otherwise. "Who is it?"

The sound came again and she felt a chill of recognition.

"It be over here, my lady," said Colvithick. He crossed the stream and rustled around in some hawthorn shrubs. "Saints be praised, it's Lord Senwyck!"

Julia clambered over a jumble of tree roots to join him. There on the ground, bound and gagged, lay Tristan. He appeared to be unconscious, but still moaned softly.

"Oh, Tristan, what have they done to you? Drew, help me to untie him!"

Working together, they managed to free Tristan, but his eyes remained closed.

"Mayhap he be drugged, my lady," said Colvithick.

"We'll have to leave him here for now, but we'll be back." She knelt down, cradling Tristan's head in her lap. "We'll return, dear friend. Don't worry; just rest."

With that, they positioned him on his side closer to the shrubs and started off again toward the beach. They soon came out of the wooded path and onto the cliffs overlooking the English Channel.

Instinctively, because there was no moon to light the view, Julia stepped behind a nearby shrub and brought Colvithick with her.

"I can scarcely see a thing," she whispered.

"Aye, my lady. It be a smuggler's moon."

A now-familiar chill swept over her at his words, and she realized that the lack of moonlight, clearly desired by Sebastian and his crew, could have more than one consequence. True, it would keep unsuspecting Customs men from noticing a landing, but if they did indeed suspect and then plan an ambush, the smugglers would become the victims.

Just then, she noticed something on the ground. It was a strange metal object with a long, hollow projection extending off one side.

"It be Lord Senwyck's spout lantern," fretted Colvithick, kicking it with his shoe. "As soon as he lit it and uncovered the spout to signal to the ship the coast be clear, the Riding Officers doubtless knocked him down and did carry him off."

She was so angry that she could barely speak. "What have you done, you foolish boy?"

Taking a deep breath, Julia turned her attention to the rocky cove below them. Dimly, she saw a mist-draped beach punctuated by a piece of cliff that made a high wall, extending into the sand toward the sea and separating the beach into two parts. In the distance, a lean, graceful sloop lay at anchor on the glimmering water. A longboat filled with dark objects could be seen rowing toward the beach.

"Look there," breathed Colvithick, and pointed down to the high rocky spine that bisected the beach.

Julia thought that her heart might leap out of her chest when she saw them. Behind the protruding cliff, there were at least a dozen uniformed Riding Officers, muskets at the ready, crouching in wait for their unsuspecting prey.

Chapter 34

There were no horses in sight.

With the intelligence provided by Colvithick, Julia realized, Lynton had been able to bring his men down the long path on foot so that they could be in place before Sebastian's ship appeared on the horizon. Lynton must have decided that the King's men stood a better chance of converging on the smugglers on land, rather than trying again to chase them down at sea.

The longboat had landed on the shingle. Some of its men were carrying barrels and crates up to the sandy crescent, while others moved the smuggled goods into a cave nearly concealed behind distant rocks.

Still the Riding Officers huddled behind the cliff, weapons drawn.

"They be waiting for the captain to come," Colvithick whispered. "He do come on the last boat, when all the goods be on the beach."

Julia saw that the longboat had returned to the ship. "We can't stay up here and just watch!"

"That be the only way to the beach," he replied, pointing to a path that led precipitously downward through a tunnel of granite. "Smugglers do carve it in ages past. The stone be worn with the marks of cart wheels bein' rolled up from the beach."

Julia went closer and saw that he was right. The granite surface of the path was worn down in ridges, curving in toward the middle like the shape of a barrel.

A movement on the beach drew her attention and she caught a glimpse of Sebastian in the darkness, recognizing him by the shape of his shoulders as he emerged from the longboat onto the shingle. Tears sprang to her eyes.

"I must warn him—before they can strike!"

"My lady, no! Let me go—"

Julia felt Colvithick try to grab for her, but she was too quick. Her buckled shoes slipped on the stone pathway as she hurried along, oblivious to everything except her desire to save Sebastian. Emerging from the tunnel onto the beach, she collided headlong with a soldier who had apparently been standing guard.

Before Colvithick could intervene, the Riding Officer lifted his musket and struck him over the head with the butt, sending him down flat on his back.

"Sebastian!" Julia cried blindly. "Watch out!"

At the same moment, Lynton began to shout hysterically, "Fire men, fire on these criminals!"

Julia kept running as shots rang out, but she could hear the panting of the big man close behind. As he came alongside, his leg shot out in front of her, tripping her, and she sprawled facedown in the sand. He fell on top of her and for an instant she thought that he had crushed her, for she couldn't get her breath and there was a pain in her arm.

"Good work, Brewster!" crowed another officer as he ran by.

As shots were fired from both sides, orange blasts of musket fire illuminated the misty night air. Julia struggled mightily to be free of her captor, trying to call, "Sebastian!" but her warnings were muffled.

"Hold still, boy!" Brewster growled. "God's eyes but you're a feisty one!"

Just then, Adolphus Lynton loomed up over them, his

shadow blocking the sliver of moon that faintly illuminated the cove. "That's no boy, you fool! It's a woman. Get up, both of you. Now!"

Julia was frantic as the officer hauled her roughly to her feet. Her hat had come off, her hair was spilling down around her shoulders, and her arm throbbed in Brewster's grasp. In the distance, near the narrow opening of the cave, she could see Sebastian, Keswick, and the others crouching behind barrels and large jagged rocks. Every time she saw her husband stand to fire at the Revenue Men, her heart leaped with fear as she realized that his life could end in an instant.

The battle intensified as Lynton's men charged forward and some of Sebastian's crew, brandishing pistols and daggers, emerged to rush toward the hated Excise men. One of the officers fell on the sand just a few feet away from Julia, groaning as blood oozed from his side. Lynton was apoplectic with rage. His thin, pale visage suddenly loomed up inches from hers and she smelled his foul breath.

"Brewster, bring this wench behind the cliff and bind her wrists. Hurry! And tie up that traitor Colvithick as well!"

Julia continued to struggle as she was dragged back behind the rocky outcropping. Lynton brought a length of rope and watched as the bigger man roughly tied her hands together in front of her waist.

"You have always been so *proud*, so quick to reject me, my lady." He brought his face back to hers while Brewster dealt with the unconscious Colvithick. "How does it feel to be completely in *my* power? You may watch as we shoot your husband—that is, unless he surrenders to me, in which case you shall see him swing from the gallows. I would almost prefer the latter fate, since his suffering would be prolonged."

"In your power? Hardly." In spite of her terror, she spat at Adolphus. His expression of shock and humiliation gave her a moment of satisfaction. "My spirit will never bow to you, and neither will my husband's."

The battle between the Revenue Men and the smugglers continued on the beach. A man from Sebastian's crew lay near the front of the cave, his blood staining the sand.

"For God's sake," she cried to Lynton over the combatants' shouts and the din of musket fire, "stop this madness!"

"No, my lady, *you* shall stop it for us." Turning back to Brewster, who grasped her around her waist with one arm and held a dagger to her neck with the other, Lynton ordered, "Come along, but keep her behind me!"

The night air smelled eerily of sea mist and gunpowder. Julia went willingly with her captor, not just because of the pressure of the blade at her throat, but also because he was taking her closer to Sebastian. Her heart hurt with fear for him and remorse that her own plan had gone so far awry. Instead of warning Sebastian and *saving* him and his men from peril, she had added to their danger by providing Lynton with a hostage!

"Hold your fire!" Lynton shouted to his Riding Officers. Then, staring toward the men who stood or crouched near the cave, he added loudly, "Lord Sebastian will not wish to shoot his own wife, I'll wager!"

With a flourish, Lynton gestured to Brewster to bring Julia into the open. As they emerged, she saw Sebastian standing in the mist, one hand raised to stop his own men from firing. He was tall against the background of the longboat and the silvery sea, his black hair wind-blown, his loose white shirt partially unbuttoned. Even at a distance, Julia could see his stricken eyes, although his expression remained impassive.

"Throw down your weapons and step away!" Lynton ordered. "All of you!"

Sebastian signaled compliance to his men and one by one they laid their muskets, pistols, and swords on the beach. When the entire crew had disarmed, their captain stood with hands on his lean hips and stared hard at Lynton. It was almost as if Julia were not there.

"Lieutenant, I have always thought you were a fool," he called in a cold, angry voice, "but I didn't guess that you were also a coward who would hide behind a woman to avoid a fair fight."

"A fool? A coward?" Adolphus cried indignantly. "You have sadly misjudged your enemy, sir! I'll show you who is the fool. Open those barrels. Let us display the evidence before I arrest you, your crew of criminals, and perhaps your conspiring wife as well!"

"We have laid down our arms, sir, and are defenseless. Now tell your man to remove the blade of his knife from her ladyship's throat."

"You have no right to make demands of any sort, *my lord*," he sneered. For good measure Adolphus pointed his own pistol at Sebastian's broad chest. "You have been laboring under the illusion that you have power, but in truth you are nothing but a traitor to the King and I am going to see to it that you pay the ultimate price for your crimes! Open the barrels!"

"I am not doing anything until you tell your lackey to put that cursed knife down," Sebastian ground out.

Julia could feel the raw tension in the air and she knew Adolphus felt it too. He waved a hand nervously at Brewster and tried to sound casual as he said, "Oh, confound it, take the knife from her neck. It doesn't matter and I'm weary of hearing this villain going on about it."

Sebastian gave a grim smile and then gazed into her eyes. "Julia, my darling, tell me that you are all right."

"Yes," she managed to say, trying to ignore the burning pain in her arm. "I am fine. But I came to—"

"You shut *up*!" Lynton railed, turning on her. "Both of you! You are my prisoners and only I can give you permission to speak!"

It came to Julia that she should be terrified, but Sebastian's demeanor was infinitely reassuring. Was it pure bravado that allowed him to look so cool and unafraid? She tried not to think of what was in store for him: arrest, long weeks spent languishing in a foul prison, and then…quite possibly, execution.

Adolphus swaggered toward Sebastian, gesturing for Brewster to bring Julia as well. In the distance was the cave, a long slit in the cliff, only a half dozen feet wide at its base, where an assortment of barrels and wooden crates had been stacked by the smugglers. The tide was beginning to come in, bringing the sea nearer to the cave's entrance.

"Open the barrels!" Lynton shouted again, clearly enjoying the sound of his own orders.

They went nearer. Julia saw Sebastian's eyes drop to her bound wrists and for a moment she feared he might physically attack Lynton and Brewster. But then his expression hardened again and he even gave a faintly contemptuous smile.

"I am at your command, Lieutenant," he murmured. "Perhaps, since we have no weapons, you would care to do the honors and pry them open?"

"Yes, yes." Lynton glanced over at Brewster. "Put her over there and bring your dagger."

Julia was feeling rather faint and she gladly sank down on a wooden crate near Sebastian. She wanted nothing so much as to reach toward him, to feel him lift her into his strong arms, but instead he was staring into the barrel of Lynton's pistol.

"Hurry up, man," Adolphus was urging as Brewster worked to pry open the nearest half-anker-sized cask. "No doubt it is French brandy, which warrants a fine tax for the King!"

When the lid came free, the two Riding Officers peered expectantly inside. They both put their hands in, brought them up wet, and tasted expectantly.

"It's—it's only water, Lieutenant!" Brewster stammered in surprise. "Plain water!"

Lynton gave a cry of frustration and pushed the barrel

over, sending a spill of water across the sand. "Another! Open another, you fool!"

The bigger man complied while Sebastian looked on with both brows lifted in mock surprise. Soon there were five barrels and casks of various sizes open and lying on their sides on the beach. All had been filled with water, except for one that held several coils of rope.

Finally, Lynton turned on Sebastian in a rage. "Where *is* it? What have you done with it?"

"It?" he echoed innocently. "I'm afraid I don't know what you're referring to. You have attacked my law-abiding crew when we were in the midst of storing some barrels of surplus drinking water, in addition to a few extra supplies from our ship."

"Law-abiding? Ha! You are a *smuggler*!" Lynton was screaming now and all the men assembled on the beach stared at him. "You're all smugglers! Criminals who mock the Crown by bringing in goods and evading the tax laws!"

"I'm afraid you've got that all wrong," came Sebastian's cool, taunting reply. "And as you can see, there is no proof. You've made a big mistake."

"Mistake? Hardly! Your own crew member, Colvithick, told me that you are all smugglers—"

"That boy would do anything for the kind of money you offered as a bribe. His family is destitute; they can't continue fishing since the tax on salt has risen so high." With that, Sebastian boldly walked past Lynton and reached for his wife. "Now then, if you are quite finished, I will tend to my wounded crewmember and return my wife to the safety of our home."

Julia looked up at him, awash with love, relief, and a strange, burning pain near her shoulder. When he lifted her into his arms, she thought she might faint.

"Sebastian—"

Above her, his eyes darkened with concern, and then he withdrew his hand from her side and she saw that it was covered with her own blood.

"Good God," he said hoarsely, glancing toward Lynton. "You've shot her!"

As Julia tried to speak, Sebastian's face swam dizzily before her. She attempted to reach toward him, but was beset by an overpowering wave of weakness.

From a distance, she heard him say in agonized tones, "My darling, I cannot lose you," just before a hazy white tide carried her away into a sea of blackness.

Chapter 35

Sebastian stood in a pool of warm sunlight near the four-poster bed where he had lain naked with Julia just five nights ago, before the last smuggling run. The gauzy batiste curtains she had hung for summer were tied against the carved posts and they fluttered slightly in the breeze.

His mind returned to that night when he had taken her in the copper bathtub, then had gone on to make love to her for most of the night in that very bed. How vital and alive she had been, wrapping herself around him, playfully pushing him back against the pillows and laughing as she had kissed her way down his chest and tasted all of him. They had both been starved for one another and it had been so much more than lust. When he was inside her, Sebastian had felt as if their hearts were fitted together as well.

Now, however, when he thought of everything that had happened since that night, his heart clenched with pain. Not for the first time, he asked himself what he could have done differently to keep Julia out of harm's way. If only he had known sooner that she was injured, he would never have continued to verbally spar with Adolphus Lynton, wasting precious time opening those cursed barrels…

"You mustn't blame yourself," a familiar voice said from the doorway.

He turned to see Tristan leaning against the doorframe.

His face was pale, there was a large purple bruise on his left cheek, and he looked very tired, but today he was dressed and moving about, which was an excellent sign.

"How can I not blame myself? I was more focused on toying with that rodent Lynton than on quickly freeing Julia. I think I was even performing for her benefit, showing her that I had the situation in hand all along by disposing of the cargo off-shore and then making a fool of Lynton."

Tristan crossed the room and touched his sleeve. "You did have matters in hand, brilliantly so. Without your quick thinking, all would have been lost."

Sebastian was still for a moment as he reflected on the sequence of events that night on the beach. When Tristan had not completed their agreed-upon two-part signal with the spout lantern, he'd realized something was amiss. Quickly then, he and the crew had "sowed the crop" with their valuable cargo by putting it all over the larboard rail, out of sight of the Riding Officers. If instead he had brought that cargo ashore, as Lynton expected, no doubt they would all be in prison right now.

Turning to Tristan with a rueful smile, Sebastian said, "I appreciate your kind words, but I didn't outwit Lynton alone. Thank God you came to me after your exchange with him at the Ship Inn. Your suspicions allowed us to construct a back-up plan." He paused to shake his dark head. "But still, you could have died from your own injuries, and Julia—"

"You could not have known she had been shot; even she didn't realize it until you saw the blood!"

"When I was carrying her up that endless path, all I could do was pray that she would open her eyes and look at me again. I would have gladly laid down my own life just to hear her scold me not to be a 'wicked, lawless smuggler'..." His voice broke as memories cascaded back of that terrible night.

"Sebastian, you must stop this. Look here." Tristan took his arm and led him to the window, pointing down to the garden terrace. "What do you see?"

He inhaled harshly at the sight of the slim, dark-haired figure resting on the wood-and-cane daybed that he had carried outdoors himself. He had even arranged the cushions on it with painstaking care.

"I see my once-vibrant, provoking wife now lying with a bandaged shoulder, weakened and in constant pain. She nearly died from the loss of blood." Turning, Sebastian added, "If I had lost her, I don't know what I would have done."

"But you did *not* lose her, and she is going to be perfectly fine. Dr. Carter has told you so repeatedly. It's patience that you need." Tristan started to shake a finger at him, but stopped. "Clearly, I'm not succeeding in cheering you up. What did you come upstairs for?"

"Julia asked for her book." Glancing around, Sebastian saw a leather-bound volume stamped *Robinson Crusoe by Daniel Defoe* on the chest beside their bed. He picked it up and saw a dried yellow primrose peeking out to mark her page. "This has been a favorite of mine since I was a boy. How could I not have known that Julia was reading it? We should be talking about such things."

"No doubt you will, from this day forward," Tristan reassured him. "Why not stop berating yourself over the past and start living in the moment? Your wife is alive! Let's go down and see her, shall we? I believe I glimpsed the lovely Sarah Faircloth bringing tea into the garden…"

A profusion of foxgloves lined the courtyard of Trevarre Hall, their speckled pink bells quivering in the July breeze. Nearby on the sun-splashed flagstones, a willow basket lined with a soft blanket held Clover and her six napping kittens while Dick, the proud father, stood guard.

"Who would have ever imagined that Dick could win Clover's heart," murmured Julia drowsily.

Sarah, who was arranging the tea service on a low table beside Julia, blushed. "Love can be quite surprising, I have found."

"You're very cryptic, my dear!"

Before she could continue, voices came to them from the house. Shading her eyes against the sun, Julia looked up to see Sebastian and Tristan walking toward them. Her heart turned over at the sight of her husband. Since she had regained consciousness the day after the smuggling adventure on the beach, every time she saw him he appeared more handsome and heroic.

"You're awake," Sebastian was saying as he drew a stool near to her and sat down. In his masculine hands he held her copy of *Robinson Crusoe.*

Smiling dreamily, she reached out for him with her uninjured arm. It was a luxury to see Sebastian relaxed and warm-eyed, to be able to touch him without someone yanking her out of reach and threatening to kill them both. Never again would she take a moment of life for granted, especially the life they were making together.

"Sarah has brought tea," she said. "Would you like some?"

"Please." He watched as Tristan went to help Sarah, then leaned down close enough so that his warm breath caressed his wife's ear when he spoke. "How can it be that you look so beautiful when you've just had a near brush with death? There is something very nearly erotic in your expression."

"That's because I'm looking at you, my lord," she whispered back.

Tristan was watching them. "Why do I suddenly feel as if I'm in the way?"

Looking like an angel, Sarah brought their tea and turned to Tristan. "My lord, I would be pleased to fetch tea for you. Do you take milk and sugar? And what about scones? I believe that Mrs. Snuggs has just taken a tray from the oven."

Sebastian wore a look of mock indignation. "No one's offered *me* any scones."

"Why, Lord Senwyck is a hero, is he not? When I think what he suffered—nearly dying on the cliffs—" Breaking off, Sarah gave a little sob.

Tristan wore an expression of enchanted surprise. "Miss Faircloth, you are too kind."

"Why don't you two go and see about those scones? Take the long, leisurely way around the garden," Sebastian suggested drily. "Dr. Carter left instructions that Tristan should take as much exercise and sunlight as possible."

Julia closed her eyes for a moment, resting and listening to the sounds of her sister and Tristan setting off. It made her happy to think of them together. If anything, Tristan's injury had only made him more attractive to Sarah, and she had taken to blushing prettily whenever his name was mentioned. It was far too soon to hope, she knew, but she couldn't help feeling elated by the sight of them together. Viscount Senwyck seemed to be the perfect man for her sister: handsome, witty, wealthy, rather roguish, and most of all, kind.

"What makes you smile?" Sebastian asked. He threaded his fingers into the curls on her brow and brushed them back so gently that a shiver of arousal chased down her spine.

She looked at him. "Sarah and Tristan. And you. Always you."

"Do you have any idea how badly I want to lie down next to you, hold you in my arms, and kiss you?" His eyes smoldered so that she could feel his desire. "But instead, I can't touch you, and it's worse torture knowing that I'm the reason for your injury."

"You are no such thing," Julia told him emphatically. "No one is responsible for that but me. In fact, it is a lesson to me once and for all to stop meddling in the affairs of others. You told me often enough to trust you, and I should have. You knew exactly what to do that night, and if I had stayed away, no one would have been hurt."

He blinked in surprise, and then his eyes darkened.

"Gammon. You thought you were saving my life! Do you have any idea what that means to me?"

"But Sebastian, you didn't *need* saving by me!" She laughed at the thought, and then her shoulder hurt and she winced. "You're the one who does the rescuing around here, and I am finally quite happy to let that be the case."

"I'm not certain I want you to change." A faintly sardonic smile touched his mouth. "Nor am I certain that it's possible. But I appreciate the sentiment."

Just then, the door from the courtyard into the library flew open and Freddy emerged, carrying his fez in one hand. He grinned at the sight of Julia and Sebastian and walked over to stand before them.

"I'm on my way to that old chapel you have," he told Sebastian. "There's that old Rood loft that no one ever bothered to take down after the Reformation, and it would serve as a bang-up minaret, don't you think so? At least for the time being, until I am back at Turbans."

Sebastian's brows went up. "You do have quite an imagination…"

"Does it offend you, my lord?" Freddy broke in anxiously. "It's just that your chapel ain't really a chapel now, is it? It's filled with a lot of farm equipment as far as I can tell."

"I don't think that even God would be offended to see you make good use of our chapel. Go on then, and leave me alone with your sister."

As the boy cheerfully departed, Sebastian was surprised to realize that he was enjoying the presence of Julia's family, even her eccentric mother, the whimsical Mr. Pippet, and Sylvester the spaniel who barked a bit too frequently.

"Your mother and Pip aren't going to burst onto the terrace next, are they?" he asked Julia.

"They've gone off to stroll the Hall Walk with Sylvester," she said in reassuring tones. "I confess that I am more concerned that Adolphus Lynton could burst in. My mind has been so muddled with laudanum these past three days that I am not certain what's become of him. I had a dream that he came back to arrest us both."

Sebastian stirred milk and sugar into her hot tea and held the cup to her lips. "It might not have been a dream, for he did come that next morning. Your condition was still very grave and I was so enraged at the sight of him that I nearly killed the little stoat."

"You shouldn't call him a stoat. Stoats are better than he is."

He gave a derisory laugh. "Lynton won't be making any more trouble for us. Keswick reminded him that we are local heroes, particularly because we've provided the local fisherman with shipments of salt. The fact is, it's nearly impossible to get a Cornish jury to convict smugglers, especially those they know."

"Furthermore, he found no cargo to produce as proof of smuggling, thanks to your resourceful and courageous plan."

"You are shamelessly biased," Sebastian chided, then he continued, "The final blow to Lynton's grandiosity came when Mr. Pippet entered the room, recognized him, and announced that there is a rumor circulating in Bath that Lynton only left town because he'd tried to seduce a fourteen-year-old girl who was his cello student. Fortunately, the girl was not intimidated. After she hit him with the bow of her cello and told her mother, the good woman set about ruining his reputation in Bath."

Julia put her hand over her mouth in dismay. "Oh my, could he be a worse person?"

"It's tempting to think of him as a ridiculous worm, but men like that can turn vicious, as we saw on Lansallos Beach. However, I do feel confident that he's gone for good now."

"That's a great relief." She closed her eyes again.

"Are you in pain?"

"Perhaps a little, but I don't want any more of that awful laudanum, at least not yet." A moment later, she opened her eyes to find him wrapping a soft woven blanket around her legs. "It is one of the warmest days of the summer, my darling. I don't need any blankets."

"Devil take it, Julia, I'd knit a dozen cursed blankets myself if it would take away your pain."

"That is so amusing an image, my lord, that I am tempted to ask for needles and yarn."

He arched a brow to acknowledge her wit, then remarked, "What about new furniture? Wouldn't you like that? I'm fed up with that hard wooden settle in the parlor. Keswick and Jasper brought up the brandy from Lansallos Cove last night and there will be a fine profit from it, enough to make the repairs to the roof before the rains begin and order new furniture as well."

The love that showed on his handsome face made her heart turn over. "But, I thought you intended to leave Trevarre Hall behind forever after that last smuggling run. You said that you could only be happy at Severn Park, in Hampshire, breeding horses."

"I've said a lot of very stupid things, haven't I," he said ruefully. "I was a fool to think of leaving Cornwall, especially knowing how happy you've been here."

"But I would never want you to make a choice like that simply to please me," she insisted. "We are building the foundation for the rest of our lives. I'm sure we could compromise. "

"No. It's what I want. The man I thought was my father ruined this place for me, but you've helped me see it in a new light." He tenderly traced the line of her cheek with his fingertip. "And, in case there is any doubt in your mind, I am finished with smuggling. Not only because of you, or because that fool Lynton knows, but because it's over. I am ready for a new phase of life."

"No horse breeding *or* smuggling?" She teased gently. "How then will you pass the time, my lord?"

"I intend to restore the fortunes of Trevarre Hall. Keswick has been telling me that when he was a lad and

Mother's parents were still alive and in residence here, this estate was the finest in the Fowey River Valley. The farm did handsomely, as did the lime kiln. Even the chapel was still in use." There was an edge of real excitement in his voice. "It will be that way again, and we'll make it happen together."

"We'll have lots of animals and they'll live with dignity," Julia exclaimed, already imagining the possibilities. "There will be flocks of sheep to provide wool that we can sell!"

"Yes. I have already secured a promise from Jasper Polarven that he will return as factor, and Keswick will work right beside us. I also hope to provide work for any members of my crew who need it." Sebastian took a deep breath. "I want to do this not only for us and for our children, but also for my mother. I believe she had dreams for me when she left that bequest with Miles…"

"Yes, and your mother would also want you to take an active part in Isabella's life."

"I know. I've already written to Raveneau—that is, to my father, about that. We'll bring Izzie here for the month of August and then discuss the future. Perhaps we can help her to study painting, since that is her dream."

Julia settled back against the cushions, beaming, and her eyes brimmed with tears. "I am so very happy."

"So am I, but there are moments when I can hardly trust such happiness." Their eyes met and she saw his expression slowly relax under the radiance of her gaze. "There is something I have been waiting to give you. A few nights ago, I feared I had waited too long."

Reaching into his coat pocket, he withdrew a blue velvet pouch, and from that he took a delicate gold ring set with two round sapphires. Julia instantly realized that it was something special.

"Sebastian," she said reverently. "It's exquisite."

"I know now that Raveneau gave this ring to my mother, many years ago in France. It will mean so much more to me to see it on your hand." Slipping it into place on her left hand, he added, "I thought that we might be married again. Would you like that? We'll clean the chapel and have a small, honest wedding there before your family goes off to London."

Julia had begun to weep as Sebastian fit his dark hand to the fragile curve of her jaw.

"It's my fault that our first wedding was dishonest," she managed to say at last.

Wiping her tears with a fresh handkerchief, he leaned closer to gently kiss her lips. "The past can't be changed. Neither one of us was fit for an honest wedding that rainy night in Bath."

"But now we are," Julia affirmed.

"That's right, love. And after we say our vows properly, I mean to give you a wedding night that you will never forget..."

Author's Note

I hope so much that you enjoyed *Smuggler's Moon* and the story of Sebastian and Julia! There is quite a story behind the creation of this book and I'd love to share just a bit of it with you here.

In 1994, my dear friend Ciji Ware invited me to come with her to England while she researched a novel she was writing (that became the fabulous "time-slip" *A Cottage by the Sea*). We stayed in a little National Trust cottage next to a secluded creek near Fowey, Cornwall.

I felt much like Julia when I saw the River Fowey and the charming towns that frame its harbor: I was absolutely enchanted. Our cottage was set on Pont Pill, next to Sebastian's lime kiln. Julia's swans are still there, the little footbridge survives, and the Hall Walk is very real.

I knew immediately that I wanted to write a book set there. Over the years, various things delayed that project, but I returned many times to that magical spot in Cornwall.

Nearly every location in the book is real, including Lerryn Creek, Tristan's little stone quay and smuggler's hole, Lansallos Cove with its stone path, and the hidden beach at Coombe Hawne. Trevarre Hall is based on the still-operating Hall Farm, and the ruined medieval chapel is real. Bodinnick's Ferry Inn and Fowey's Ship Inn still receive guests.

I hope you enjoyed reuniting with André and Devon Raveneau as much as I did! I'm back at work already, writing Book 2 in the Raveneaus in Cornwall series. This is Isabella and Gabriel's story, set in 1808, and it's already a huge favorite for me! I also have to tantalize you with the news that Book 3 will be a rousing adventure about a Raveneau who we all have thought would not get a happy ending…

If you'd like to see photos of the real settings in *Smuggler's Moon*, I hope you'll explore the Pinterest Board I made. (And there are boards there for many of my other books!) http://www.pinterest.com/cynthiawright77/smugglers-moon/

I am so grateful to you for reading my books and staying in touch with me. I would love to hear from you at Cynthia@CynthiaWrightAuthor.com and I promise to write back.

Until next time—warmest wishes and happy reading!

Cynthia Wright

Meet Cynthia Wright

My career as a novelist began when I was twenty-three, with a phone call from New York announcing that CAROLINE would be published by Ballantine Books. Can you imagine my excitement? I went on to write 12 more bestselling historical romances set in Colonial America, Regency England & America, Medieval England & France, and the American West.

My novels have won many awards over the years, but what means most are readers' messages like this one: "*When I read your books, I can't wait to turn the page, but never want the story to end.*" It's been a thrill to have all my novels published as e-books (newly edited, with gorgeous new covers!). Plus, I released a new Raveneau novel, TEMPEST, in December, 2012.

Today I live in northern California with my husband, Alvaro, in a 1930's Spanish cottage. When we aren't riding our tandem road bike or traveling in our vintage airstream, I love spending time with family, especially my two young grandsons. I also recently received a degree as a Physical Therapist Assistant and feel blessed to have two rewarding careers!

I'd love to have you join me at my website:
http://cynthiawrightauthor.com/

And on Facebook :
http://www.facebook.com/cynthiawrightauthor

And on Pinterest:
http://pinterest.com/cynthiawright77/

P.S. So many of you have asked, "In what order should I read the Beauvisage & Raveneau books?"

Although the titles stand alone, these two series intertwine with some characters crossing over, and many readers enjoy them in chronological order:
1781 - SILVER STORM
1783 - CAROLINE
1789 - TOUCH THE SUN
1793 - SPRING FIRES (A Beauvisage/Raveneau Novel)
1798 - SMUGGLER'S MOON
1814 - SURRENDER THE STARS
1814 - NATALYA
1818 - SILVER SEA (A Raveneau/Beauvisage Novel)
1903 - TEMPEST

Novels by Cynthia Wright

CAROLINE
The Beauvisage Novels, Book 1
~
TOUCH THE SUN
The Beauvisage Novels, Book 2
~
SPRING FIRES
The Beauvisage Novels, Book 3
(A Beauvisage/Raveneau Novel)
~
NATALYA
The Beauvisage Novels, Book 4
~
SILVER STORM
The Raveneau Novels, Book 1
~
SURRENDER THE STARS
The Raveneau Novels, Book 2
~
SILVER SEA
(previously published as BARBADOS)
The Raveneau Novels, Book 3
(A Raveneau/Beauvisage Novel)
~
TEMPEST
The Raveneau Novels, Book 4
~
SMUGGLER'S MOON
The Raveneaus in Cornwall, Book 1
~

~

YOU AND NO OTHER
The St. Briac Novels, Book 1

~

OF ONE HEART
(previously published as A BATTLE FOR LOVE)
The St. Briac Novels, Book 2

~

BRIGHTER THAN GOLD
The Western Novels, Book 1

~

FIREBLOSSOM
The Western Novels, Book 2

~

WILDBLOSSOM
The Western Novels, Book 3

~

CRIMSON INTRIGUE
(Not yet released)

View all of Cynthia Wright's unforgettable novels here:
http://cynthiawrightauthor.com/books.html

CPSIA information can be obtained
at www.ICGtesting.com
Printed in the USA
LVHW011658080119
603165LV00019B/1111/P